He wanted to thank her for being pregnant with their child

He wanted to thank her for loving that child so unconditionally. "I love you," he said.

Dru watched his lips. Her legs shivered, her heart pounded. A prickling warmth needled her face and scalp. She hugged herself.

Ben stood closer, touched her cheeks.

"I love you," he repeated, his body almost brushing hers, ready to catch her if she fell into another fearful trance—a memory of their past, in the desert. Ready to catch her whenever she fell, or at least help her up. "Will you marry me?" he asked.

Dru saw the man across from her, and on the thought that she'd never love another, her eyes filled.

She'd believed that about Omar, too. Her husband. Now dead.

But Ben Hall was this baby's father—and would be her husband. Soon.

Award-winning author Margot Early is in the forefront of romance writing today. With her dramatic, emotional and innovative stories, she's a writer to remember!

Dear Reader,

I'm happy to introduce the fourth book in my continuing Harlequin Superromance series, THE MIDWIVES. While the characters from *You Were on My Mind, Talking About My Baby* and *There Is a Season* enjoy the love they've found, we meet two new midwives, best friends Dru and Keziah.

Keziah attends home births on the island of Nantucket. But Dru, a certified nurse midwife, was torn from her vocation years ago by family notoriety and her marriage to a renowned financier. Just as it seems all her dreams will be lost, her husband's death brings her a chance at love with childhood friend Ben Hall, and much more. Finally Dru has the chance to regain herself—and to bear a child of her own.

I hope you enjoy this story and that you'll be eager to learn what happens between Keziah and Dru's twin, Tristan, in *The Story Father*. And what happened between them in the past.

Thank you so much for reading my books.

Sincerely,

Margot Early

Books by Margot Early

HARLEQUIN SUPERROMANCE

FOREVER
AND A BABY
Margot
Early

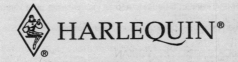

TORONTO • NEW YORK • LONDON
AMSTERDAM • PARIS • SYDNEY • HAMBURG
STOCKHOLM • ATHENS • TOKYO • MILAN • MADRID
PRAGUE • WARSAW • BUDAPEST • AUCKLAND

ISBN 0-373-70912-9

FOREVER AND A BABY

Copyright © 2000 by Margot Early.

ACKNOWLEDGMENTS

The nature of this book, its landscapes and seascapes, its peoples and their backgrounds, dictated two things. One is that I would do extensive research; the second is that I would both take artistic license and make some mistakes (which are two different things, though they can look the same). The following people generously gave of their time:

Marina Alzugaray, MS, ARNP, CNM, Cathy Hartt, CNM, and Bill Dwelley, MS, LM, WEMT-I, thoroughly answered extensive questions about the art, science and business of midwifery.

David M. Good, M.D., P.C., thoughtfully addressed the mental health questions I asked. Without his help, this book would not have been written.

My sister Joan Early Farrell, Matt Hunder and James M. Early, my father, answered questions about fishing, boating and sailing. My family has always speedily assisted when I've needed help with my books.

Deb Kidwell, owner and breeder of the Azawakh of Kel Simoon, told me about these noble sighthounds and helped me name both of the heroine's dogs, always increasing my appreciation for this beautiful and unusual breed.

Julie Elliott allowed me to use invaluable information for sections of the book having to do with belly dancing. Nearly all of my information on belly-dancing, including song translations, came from her rich and fascinating Web site, The Art of Middle Eastern Dance.

Finally, this book required the use of numerous reference texts. They include: *Serpent of the Nile* by Wendy Buonaventura, *Return of the Tribal* by Rufus C. Camphausen, *The Hungry Ocean* by Linda Greenlaw, *Nantucket: Seasons on the Island* by Cary Hazlegrove, *The Ocean Almanac* by Robert Hendrickson, *The Perfect Storm* by Sebastian Junger, *Ethnic Dress* by Frances Kennet, *Sahara Unveiled* by William Langewiesche, *Veiled Sentiment* and *Writing Women's Worlds* by Lila Abu-Lughod, *Nantucket Gardens* and *Houses* by Taylor Lewis and Virginia Scott Heard, *Lonely Planet Travel Guides*, the mystery novels of Francine Mathews, *Black Tents of Arabia* by Carl R. Rasway, *Dangerous Places* and *Come Back Alive* by Robert Young Pelton, *Arabian Sands* by Wilfred Thesiger. Internet resources were too numerous to mention.

PROLOGUE

"WE NEVER KNOW OUR ANCESTORS because it's their prerogative to lie to us." Dru said this to me while standing beneath the oldest portraits her family owns, full-size likenesses of a thirty-nine-year-old whaling captain and the fourteen-year-old girl he brought back from Morocco. The girl wore long gossamer pants and a floor-length gown, with a belt of silver coins at her waist, coins everywhere but at her throat. There, an elaborate necklace of hammered silver. Cuffs of silver covered her wrists, and bangles of silver and dyed leather interrupted her forearms, while a crown dripping with more coins swirled round her head. From the crown fell hair as thick as Dru's but hennaed red. Henna stained her skin, as well, in the intricate designs Dru called mehndi. The shade beneath, her own, was luminescent. The artist had not altered it. It was the color sand takes on in the shade. Weak coffee with a spoon of skim milk. Slavery had left Nantucket long before 1842. Nudar was Captain Haverford's wife. I found her exquisite. They were my ancestors, too.

"Imagine it, Ben," Dru said. "Imagine being forced into marriage with a man of a different color, a different culture, a different country, twenty-five years older than you—"

She stopped.

Her eyes fell. Her back to me, her thick black hair caught

on the hood of her sweatshirt, she lifted a *riqq,* a small tambourine, from the seat of the grand piano. Like mehndi, this instrument had different names in different places. She played, and I heard the desert sing and smelled indigo on skin. The music stopped. "But perhaps she loved him."

Perhaps she did.

Ancestors, as she said, can and do lie. Which alters things. Dru has said it this way. "Our family is large and interconnected. We have married cousins and stayed on this island. We like each other."

Like the Bedouin, I thought when she said it. The Bedouin would say that it is good to marry cousins, just as one must know one's lineage, or how can one have a name, the kind of name that comes from Allah? A name that names the person by naming the loved ones. There is a debt and a weight on this name, and there is a duty to it, a duty to one's line.

I know this because I hadn't stayed on Nantucket, nor had my father, Robert Hall. The desert is in my blood.

One must know one's lineage.

Ancestors can and do lie. And they may omit…falls.

A fall can change the course of history. Not just the fall of Rome or a fall in the Dow Jones, but a human being falling down.

For instance, my grandmother's fall, as told to me by the father who raised me, Robert Hall. Not an omission. Something he chose to tell.

In the year of her accident, 1947, Faith Hall was Nantucket's only midwife. Dad was thirteen that year. His father, Ben, for whom I'm named, was a veteran of the recent war and a Nantucket scalloper. The family lived in a fishing shack in 'Sconset, the cottage my father never sold and where I sometimes came from Africa to hammer and saw and keep the building from the sea, while the Atlantic steals prime real estate by inches. On the day of my grandmother's fall, it had rained, and my father came inside with muddy feet, and his mother scolded him to clean the floor, and he did. She went outside to empty dishwater in her garden, and mud from his feet had tracked the steps, as well. My father heard her body strike the shack's flimsy siding. She had fallen head-first four feet and broken her neck. Even before the funeral, her mother came for the year-old baby, Dad's little sister, to raise her in her dark home on India Street in town. The men—Dad and his adopted brother and their father—harvested scallops.

Dad told me of another fall, one that happened earlier, a plane falling from the sky over the desert and one crew member escaping, floating to the ground with his precious silk. The soldier had hiked, lost until he met a Bedouin boy paused in the shade of a camel. The camp of twelve families had been slaughtered by tanks. Bloating camel carcasses and dead salukis lay near the collapsed tents. The soldier covered his nose and mouth with his bomber jacket to keep from vomiting at the stench.

Nonetheless, the boy greeted my grandfather in a tribal dialect and rushed to a demolished tent. He made coffee, insisted that my grandfather sit against a camel saddle, and behaved as though the carnage did not exist. When his guest would drink no more, the child showed him his father's body, and it was the body of the sheikh. Working till dusk, they buried each person, seventy-one bodies, in a shallow grave in the sand, placing stones at the head and feet, leaving any intact garments on the graves for the less fortunate. Next morning at dawn, they saddled the camel. The boy knew what they would need and took the little he could of his family's wealth. Before he left the graves of his loved ones, he bowed against the sand and prayed.

He and the American soldier crossed the desert, walking northwest to the coast, milking the camel to quench their thirst. Many times, the boy spoke his name and the name of his father

and grandfather and his great-grandfather and his tribe. It was
his entire name, a proud name. My grandfather agreed to call
him Omar and sent the eight-year-old Bedouin ahead of him
to Nantucket Island to become his second son, although the
name Omar means "first son." When my grandfather came
home from the war, it was the dark boy he lifted in his arms
and held as he embraced the others. They became a family of
five. My fisherman grandfather, my midwife grandmother,
Robert, Omar, and, briefly, baby Mary Hall. Then, my grandmother fell.

When my father first told me these stories, I had played
with dominoes but still didn't understand the nature of falls.
I'd learned that midwives helped women have babies, which
meant they were like doctors or nurses—not partially your
wife and partially mine, as the name implied. I never guessed
the part these falls—a soldier falling from the sky, his wife
falling on her head—had played in my existence. Or that other
falls in my life would so shape my destiny.

That I could be one of the fallen.

There are many ways to fall.

WHEN I MET with my father's brother, Omar Hall, in Nantucket in early March of the year of his death, I had not seen
his wife, Dru, for two decades. At that time, I had not heard
her remark about the lies ancestors tell. My father lay dead
nine weeks and three days.

Omar—he never encouraged "uncle"—and I spoke in the
garden behind his home, the Federal-Greek Revival on Orange
Street. Spruce and pine, the ivy-draped fence, the waterfall of
unawakened climbing roses, all edged the long garden with its
terraces, its beds with the green tips of bulb leaves emerging,
other blooms dormant around the wintered lawn. We had privacy, the kind you can buy. Or he could.

His man, Sergio, had led me through the house to the garden, where Omar himself had held back the two long-legged dogs, gazelle-chasing desert sighthounds, one sand-colored with white stockings and chest, the other blue brindle. I knew both. I'd brought them from Mali, for Omar's wedding gift to Dru.

While the hounds galloped down the long, deep yard, leaping and floating in mesmerizing fairy bounds, Omar brought me a beer and glass, offered me food. I've accepted coffee from faces like his in desert tents and in mud and stone houses of powder-puff colors. In him, the Bedouins' sacred respect for a guest was warmth, a face that lit up as though this was the Libyan Sahara. Instead of an island soggy as a whaler's death.

This was his hospitality. Years earlier, Omar had bought a mansion on the shore near Broad Point, hoping all his family and extended family, distant cousins included, would come to live with him. When he asked one of those distant cousins to marry him, when he asked Dru, she came—the only one. He and Dru sold the mansion and bought this house, two doors from her childhood home, with a yard for their dogs.

Omar and I stretched out our legs, half-turned from his round iron table, mismatched with plastic chairs. I wore my grandfather's World War II bomber jacket, which Omar had presented to me on a visit to Cambridge when I was a teenager and old enough to notice my own father's lip curling over the gift. But then, Robert Hall had relaxed and said, *Looks good on you, Ben. And you're named for my father. It should be yours.* So it was always his and mine, never Omar's, never the Bedouin boy's.

In his herringbone overcoat, Omar scooted his chair closer to the table. He blushed. His smile showed embarrassment and pleasure. ''My wife has a mission this summer, Ben. She is to search for a man whose child she would like to bear and arrange a tryst with him, for the purpose of conceiving a child who will be ours.''

The paler dog, Femi, circled the brickwork haughtily, stepping like a cat.

Arrange a tryst... Purpose of conceiving... His words caused a wound. No, something more complex.

The financier's eyes curved, wrinkles kind. ''Good. You're not surprised.''

''I'm a journalist. I'm surprised.''

He laughed.

I didn't.

The encapsulated Omar Hall: Son of a Bedouin sheikh, brought to America after the death of his family, adopted by my grandparents, their own deaths five years apart. Establishment in investments, speculation in hedge funds, marriage to distant cousin Dru Haverford, not of *the* Haverfords, also cousins, but of quiet poverty, they said, and young and beautiful. A midwife. A serious mountain-biking accident—his—on their honeymoon. During his marriage, Omar had become a global philanthropist, dropping a hundred million here, a hundred million there, every year.

Dark olive skin like a fine grade of sandpaper folded over the rigid white collar of his shirt. His eyes were black as mine, eyes like my ancestor Nudar's. ''Tell me why you're surprised,'' he said. ''Let's talk.''

Talk? ''You can start.''

''Do you know my age, Ben?''

''Sixty-six.'' According to *Fortune*. I reached for my glass. Talk.

''Dru is thirty-one. What do you suppose our marriage is like?''

The beer went down. A breeze brought a taste of scallops and salt water and brine. Everything wet, the gray air soaked in the sea. The damp suffocated me. So much water. The dogs collapsed at a distance. I still saw an eleven-year-old Dru at a Nubian oasis, water slipping through her hands beneath her ghost eyes. She was the one who'd been seized by the *jinn,* and the women danced to placate the demon. The rest of us went on, in our own ways. I found a scorpion. Tristan found a tribe. Skye found an Australian backpacker.

"Every marriage is different," I said. Even in the desert. The nomadic Bedouin, occasionally with an extra wife. The Tuareg and their brides. An anthropologist and a minister's daughter. A lone American journalist in a hundred-and-thirty-degree sun...

Omar smiled. "You're diplomatic and wise. Dru and I are happy." A pause—because of dissembling or curiosity? A pause that made me wonder which. "How are you?"

"Well."

Omar's forehead formed crevasses. He looked the same on the cover of *Money.* Then the lines smoothed. "Death is hard." Difficult silence. "I still remember your grandfather's death. We should all have died that day. Mixed seas. Bob and I couldn't find him. Can you imagine making the decision to bring in the catch and the boat? And on another day, to go out again?"

He and Dru shared this; her father had also died at sea. But I already knew what Omar told me. My grandfather's assets were divided equally between his two sons, the absent Mary ignored. Omar sold the boat. My father kept the house. They both went to college. Omar studied finance, philosophy and religion, went into investments. Robert—Bob—became an anthropologist and left for the Sahara, later traveling with his wife and baby, looking always, I think, for the father he'd lost. The father who'd fallen from the sky into the desert and was never seen again. Not the veteran who adopted a Bedouin boy and gave him to his family. I wanted to know about Omar's other father, the sheikh. More than his name, which had been enough for my father to find some of Omar's relatives who had survived the war, for Omar to meet them. "You lost two fathers." The words hollowed the air, like a prophecy.

"Yes." Omar closed his eyes. "My father." *My only father,* his voice said.

I forgave him. Almost. For things of which we'd never spoken. And that I fantasized we would.

"I remember very little. I dug myself into the sand. A tank passed over me." He shook his head. "The next thing I knew, your grandfather and I were in Tripoli, with the possessions I'd salvaged. He was good to me. And your father was a good brother. Bob asked me things. He wanted to know everything. About the desert."

The blue brindle, Ehder, brushed my leg. Did he know my scent or remember the border post where no one loved the Tuareg or their puppies? I petted him, dreaming Niger and the last days of my father, Robert Hall. He'd said, *I'm dying. It won't be long. Inshallah.* White filled the crevices in his sun-beaten skin. His cataract-ridden eyes, blue, red-lined, had sunk deep. He lay in the hot shade of his tent. He'd rejected the mud walls of the house where he kept his research materials. Sand had begun to blow. Heaping outside. It could bury a tent or a village. He was bleeding from the rectum again. Diarrhea. Vomiting. He wouldn't leave this place, and he told me he had cancer, had known for seventeen months. *I was a sorry parent,* he'd said. I'd said, *You're a great man. I love you.* He'd said, *Does a good son always lie? Is it the job of a child to make the parent great?* I recited the Koran to him in the language in which I'd learned it. The men came to talk with him. Magicians came. I had brought morphine, and an American trekker had more. I sat with him five days, reciting the Koran until dehydration won and he lay with his lips gaping and eyes already shut.

I considered the nature of fraud. I had lived among the

devout and among the Tuareg—refugees, caravan traders, pastoralists, the descendants of nomadic bandits, a people whose Arab name means "abandoned by God." My father had chosen them, the traditional enemies of the Bedouin, had finally chosen their independent faith and untouchable spirit. He had fought the painful war for their mountain territory. Omar called himself an atheist. But the rest of my family played hard at their connection to the desert world. The women and their singing and dancing. My father in his pain had said, *Inshallah.* Allah willing. He had believed that our days are numbered by God, and that nothing can change that plan. He had worn an ancient silver cross, a bowed and beautiful thing. The proof missionaries gave that the Tuareg in their indigo robes had been Christian once. I'd asked Tanelher about it. She'd laughed, and I'd smiled, wishing I were of her tribe, a masked blue man of the desert. Instead of seen and vulnerable—to spirits and the scrutiny of a beautiful woman.

Who are these people, the Tuareg? *A photographic negative of the Bedouin?* another journalist once asked me. The Tuareg men mask themselves, while the women veil only against the elements. Descent is matrilineal, traditionally. They and the Bedouin have settled on opposite edges of the vast Sahara. But the analogy of a photographic negative fails, limited by its two dimensions. I know because I grew up wandering in the shadow of an anthropologist, and as a man I've tried to know—and rescue, in arrogance—the Tuareg and Bedouin and others.

Maybe I, too, seek the father I lost.

"Ben." Omar leaned closer over the cold wrought-iron tabletop. Perhaps to take my mind off Dad. He blushed again, another blushing smile. "I want you to follow Dru. She's…indifferent to her safety. And has some unwise notions of where to look for—our man. I want you to protect her. But don't let her know."

Dru. I'd forgotten this. Omar's plan for a baby.

This Tribe

LONG AGO, a New Bedford whaling captain named Haverford left his town and settled on the island of Nantucket, where he married and had children who had children. From Nantucket's harbor, he sailed his ship, and his descendants sailed their ships. One of these men was **Tobias Haverford**.

In the winter of 1840, a storm blew Tobias's ship to the shores of Morocco, where he took on a passenger, a girl named **Nudar**. He brought her home to Nantucket and married her.

Nudar was a Muslim. That much is known. Her husband allowed her to practice her faith, and she kept many customs of her culture, as well. She passed these traditions to her daughter, who passed them to her daughter, and so on. Her son's life was the sea. His descendants were Haverfords. His daughters, too, learned the ways of Nudar. In the privacy of their rooms, they sang and danced in a manner alien to Puritan New England. Their tambourines and single-string boxes and ululating *zaghareets* could be heard on the street. This eccentricity they passed to their daughters as well.

Being Americans, these women became dissatisfied with what was passed down and added to it with the dancing and singing of other cultures. By the year 2000, no one was certain where Nudar had really come from or who her people were.

But these are members of her tribe, by birth or marriage:

My grandmother, **Faith Hall,** who fell from the stoop, and her husband, **Ben Hall,** who fell from a plane.
Their son, my father, **Robert Hall,** who died in the desert.
Their adopted son, **Omar Hall,** who fell. Who fell.
Their daughter, **Mary Hall,** who embraced the traditions

of Nudar and other women who sing and dance in the ways called *raqs sharqi, danse du ventre,* Middle Eastern dance, Oriental dance. Belly dance.

Mary's husband, **Daniel Mayhew,** her brother Omar's attorney and an Islander.

Their daughter, **Keziah Mayhew,** a midwife who teaches Nudar's dances to pregnant women. I always see Keziah not in the ethnic dresses she favors but in a Puritan bonnet and dress, the costume of a pilgrim, because she has the stare of a New England winter. People say our eyes are alike—and came from Nudar.

Keziah has a daughter, and *her* name is **Nudar.** She is eleven and blond for a Hall or a Mayhew. Like my grandfather and Dru's father, Keziah's man died at sea. Only Keziah knows his story.

There are Haverfords, too.

Wealthy Haverford descendants in California, in publishing. Many cousins. Their own papers carried the story, eight or nine years ago, of the death of heiress **Skye Haverford Blade.** Skye had married world-renowned marine explorer, **David Blade,** and borne his child, **Christian.** She died after falling from the bow of his ship. He remarried, and his wife **Jean** bore two children at sea. They are of our tribe.

Joanna Oliver left her Charleston home at eighteen and traveled to New York to become an actress. She was discovered, first by Andy Warhol, then, while dancing with the Velvet Underground at the Boston Tea Party, by Nantucket scalloper **Turk Haverford.** Joanna was the family's most exotic bride since Nudar, even to her hair that was the color of bleached shells. She thawed even the frozen hearts of the Nantucket Lightship Basket Historical Association. Turk Haverford lost his ship on Georges Bank seventeen years ago. Four men died with him. I imagined the ways a ship can sink, how the keel or bow can rise. It's possible he fell.

He left fourteen-year-old twins.

One, named **Tristan,** had once fallen into the wrong hands. He grew into a fisherman like his father, and his fisherman wife died at sea, falling on a line, impaled by a hook. Their daughter, **Keri,** survives.

Tristan's twin is a woman named **Dru,** who once—or twice—fell in love. She can fall no farther.

She carries the egg and the sperm of this line.

Of the tribe of Haverford and the tribe of Nudar.

CHAPTER ONE

When our cousin Skye was fifteen, she told her father she would like to see the desert, and he paid for her and for the twins from Nantucket to come to the Sudan. Skye's father had escorted them, to leave them in our care while he went elsewhere. It was in August, during the rains and also a several-year lull in the civil war, and my father and I met them in Khartoum with our Land Cruiser. In the air terminal, spotting me for the first time, Skye clasped her fingers around each side of my head and said, "Are you an urchin or a sheikh?" and kissed me, which women rarely did to me at my age, especially in the Sudan. I was twelve, and she was beautiful. I always remember her that way. And, often, myself as well.

—Ben, recollections of a fall

Nantucket Island
October 21

TRISTAN BROUGHT a pregnant woman to Omar Hall's funeral.

The woman. That woman.

He had come from Gloucester, off a longliner, a swordboat, blond hair lighter, blue-green eyes bloodshot, the scent of the fish and diesel still about him, the carved-away symmetrical marks on each cheek disconcerting to anyone unused to disfigurement. But Dru was used to her twin. Fishermen were, by definition, often gone. They returned unannounced.

In the church vestibule, protected by security from the media and the condemnation of the world, Dru embraced him. Then she saw the woman. The blond dreadlocks and ring through her nose. Come from Gloucester. And pregnant.

Dru's reaction wasn't a midwife's, perhaps because it was so long since she'd felt like a midwife. It wasn't even that of a woman who wished she was carrying or had carried her dead husband's child, anyone's child. She thought, *It's her. It's the woman I saw with that man in Gloucester.*

Dru dismissed it. All imagination. All hope.

And the baby would not be Tristan's. Not a chance. After his wife had died, he'd married the sea. Some of his time ashore belonged to his boat. But the rest he gave to his daughter, to Keri.

Dru kept his betrayal to herself, walked to her oak pew. From there, the casket accused her of her own crime. Not the crime the media proclaimed and nobody seemed able to forget. There had been no adultery. But would her guilt be greater if there had? She could no longer judge her brother or anyone else.

A minister spoke over the body of an irreligious man. This was Omar's choice. She wanted to cremate him and scatter his ashes to the wind. No, she wanted *him,* wanted the charming protector who'd brought her such a lovely gift after graduation from Georgetown with her Master of Science in Nurse-Midwifery. Now so dusty. Omar had appeared more frequently in her life over the next two years. On one of her visits home from New Bedford, where she'd worked in the hospital and provided maternity services for low-income families, he'd hinted at his feelings. Afterward, he'd come to New Bedford often, flying her to Manhattan for dinner or theater. Comfortingly old-fashioned in his expectations but truly in love with her, desirous of her. So safe. *Omar, I want you back.*

He'd bought a plot in the cemetery. One. Expecting her to remarry. She cried. Other losses. Other deaths. Her father's boat sunk. *That woman Tristan brought...the man she was with...* Wishful thinking. Omar would go to the earth, all of them taken by the water or the earth. Water deaths, for all who loved fishermen, were the worst.

After the funeral, the few family members she'd invited gathered at the cemetery for the graveside service. No children. No strangers. Outside the gate, Tristan said, "She can come, right? I need to stay with her."

The dreadlock woman.

Pregnant...

Tristan's ponytail blew in the October wind.

Dru resented the woman again. She wanted her twin to herself, wanted to walk alone with him on the beach, wanted to explain the truth. Explain those tabloid photos, the photos from Gloucester. Why a man, a cousin much too distant to be accorded the trust of a brother, had been touching her hair and her skin so that the aching of man and woman translated through newsprint. Tristan would have heard gossip, too; Gloucester was his world.

That vision from the Gloucester Marine Railways needled her. Again, she saw the gray-haired man—a ghost—and this woman, hugging, like a father wishing farewell to his daughter. *Like my father.* So much like her father and Tristan's, who had never come home.

"She's not welcome. This is private."

A pause. His blue eyes said she'd changed. "I brought her for you. You can help with her birth."

Presenting his companion like a gift. A birth to attend.

"I'm not a practicing midwife, I don't do home births—" she didn't do any births, now "—and I know nothing about her.'' Except that no one in pregnancy should be exposed to unpleasantness. A burial.

Tristan's eyes had slanted, his slim jaw set.

A stalemate with this tall twin who had never looked anything like her. He'd never looked like a Haverford, with the white-sand hair he tied in a knot for fishing, with his gaunt cheeks and sensuous mouth, and the vertical scars where flesh had been gouged away from the base of his lower eyelids to his jaw, three on each side, discolored shades of black and purple and blue. A face that seduced by hypnosis—you couldn't look away.

Years ago, Omar had said, with resignation, *You love Tristan best.*

Dru couldn't explain that she and Tristan were each other. She knew no words that meant twin, no words that explained.

But that pregnant woman—girl, college girl—was not coming to Omar's graveside.

Tristan said, ''I'll have to miss it, too.''

''You're excused.'' She walked away, Louis Vuitton shoes sinking in the dry, pale-yellow grass. The fifth richest woman in the world. Wishing *she* was pregnant. By some reversal of fortune, with Omar's child.

Outside the cemetery gate, photographers rustled dry leaves, cameras clicking and whirring, capturing the widow, framing the ebony casket hovering over the hole in the earth. Men in tailored suits, ambassadors from countries Omar had assisted, fund managers and financial gurus and the media had flocked to Nantucket. Inexplicably, the cameras made her feel lonely.

Those assembled at the grave were Islanders. Tristan wasn't the only one missing, the only relative who should have been there. Omar wasn't the only one Dru missed. She wanted another. And couldn't help it.

Dru caught the gagging in her throat, swallowed it. Earlier, she'd noticed the conspiratorial look of a cousin from California who'd pretended consternation. But wouldn't say aloud, *Where's Ben, for goodness' sake? He's as close to Omar as any of us.* Other relatives murmuring to each other.

The wind blew October through her hair. The season of ghosts and regrets. She sent wordless messages to her twin, images of Gloucester. She pictured, carefully, another face, with black-brown eyes. Two Land Cruisers meeting in dust without horizon, a twenty-year-old image. *Remember, Tristan?*

How could he forget? As she'd said to Ben, how could any of them?

When the time came for her words, Dru unfolded the piece of paper she'd brought. Here, she could read with no press listening. She trusted the few at the grave.

There was Sergio, Omar's personal assistant, who had served the Hall family for thirty-eight years.

And Keziah Mayhew, Dru's dear friend since childhood, a fourth cousin twice removed, the midwife of Nantucket, fighting for her share of the island's two hundred and thirty births a year. She and Dru had planned to practice together someday. They never had and never would.

And over Omar's grave stood his sister, Keziah's mother— Mary Hall Mayhew.

And Dru's mother, Joanna.

That was all.

"I just wanted—" was that her voice? "—to say some things about Omar. I agreed with every word of Roger's eulogy at the church." The manager of The Caravan Fund had spoken about Omar. "But this is for family." Pressing her lips tight, she ignored the glimpse of Tristan's blond head somewhere on the perimeter, outside the gate. "I guess it's for me." She read, "Omar was a good man. I loved him—because he was good. We had no secrets. I did nothing against his wishes. He did nothing against mine. This is the truth. We loved each other deeply till the day he died." *A lie, a lie, isn't it, Dru?*

*Aren't you lying? Your voice is shaking. Your face is so warm
you feel it through the cold wind, that wind blowing Keziah's
long auburn hair.*

They waited to see if she was done.

All she'd given was self-defense.

Security apprehended a photographer inside the fence. Dru
looked toward the casket where Omar wasn't, with the winds
of Nantucket. Spontaneously she crumpled the paper. You all
know who he was. *As well as I did.*

She would have liked to sing a Bedouin love song, to mourn
him her own way. Mary would sing, too, for the death of her
adopted brother, her last surviving brother. But Omar had dis-
liked their singing and dancing, just as he'd been ambivalent
toward Dru's midwifery. This staid burial was what he'd re-
quested.

Only one thing Dru had done differently. She had gone to
the funeral home and dressed him. She'd needed to touch and
know his cold, thick, unmoving limbs, the stone feel of his
body. To kiss his face in death. So that it would not be the
way it had been with her father, whose boat had never returned; she saw his ghost, his double, everywhere.

As in Gloucester. With Tristan's pregnant friend.

When they'd all crossed the dry grass, left the grave site
and the casket, exited the cemetery enfolded by security, Tristan and the young woman merged with them. Dru stopped,
handed him the crumpled piece of paper. "I read that." Cameras, their ceaseless motors winding, advancing shutters falling
on her sorrow.

Tristan circled her shoulders with his arm, his free hand
touching the pregnant woman, assuring her presence. Or assuring her of his. "Look, I'm sorry, Dru. She was in Conway's
Tavern. She needed help. Her name's Oceania. She's deaf. She
reads lips some. I brought her here so you could help her with

her birth. You *are* a midwife. You didn't go to school for six years to pretend you're not.''

She'd also attended workshops, earned continuing education units. She'd done everything to keep her certification current. Even attended two births.

Oceania. She must have renamed herself.

''She should go to a hospital. Or to Keziah.''

Tristan shook his head. ''She's afraid of hospitals. And she doesn't want Keziah. I told her I was sure you'd do it. That you're my twin and I know your heart like my own.''

He could be so manipulative. But precious to her.

Joanna, their mother, intervened. She winced over the girl— just college age—with her yellow dreadlocks and heavy belly. ''Dru's husband just died, Tristan. Not to mention...''

No one did mention The Scandal.

Except, of course, the press.

Tristan said, ''A birth is just what you need.'' Watching Dru. ''It's about time.''

Omar never stopped me from practicing.

His money, his position, their celebrity, had. No woman wanted a media circus at her birth.

Two girls braked their bicycles in the road. Security parted for family. Tristan's ten-year-old daughter and Keziah's eleven-year-old. Best friends, longing for horses of their own, collecting Breyer horses, reading horse books and L.M. Montgomery.

''Dad. Dad.'' Keri's bike crashed against the curb and she jumped into his arms, wrapping her legs against him, just as Dru and Tristan used to spring into the arms of their father, fighting for the first embrace of the scalloper captain ashore and losing to their mother.

He had been so decent.

Dru studied the dreadlock girl. Deaf. Going to have a baby. Dru tried to guess gestational age. The baby had dropped.

Oceania's face had that ripe, full-moon look. It comforted her to think like a midwife again.

Instead of the woman she had become.

Dru glanced to Keziah, a midwife unafraid of home births—*or ship births,* Dru reflected ruefully. Keziah was committed to doing things in whatever environment the mother chose. She strode behind Dru to one side, long hair, dark fire, whipping in October's gray wind, disdain flaring her nostrils over Tristan's bringing a stranger. Not seeing, yet, a pregnant woman in need. Keziah's brown, almost black, witch-eyes drilled Tristan's back, as though delivering a curse.

Dru asked Oceania, "How old are you?" She flashed up her own fingers, demonstrating.

Barely concealed annoyance. Ten fingers. Twice.

Tristan smiled for the stranger he'd brought. His straight teeth were discolored internally from rheumatic fever when he and Dru were eleven and in the Sudan, that awful time. Dru felt the heat and sand that was really dust, saw the wounds left where strips of flesh had been gouged in such deliberate pattern from his adolescent face. She saw him slipping in and out of consciousness with fever, fever from a strep infection, probably from his wounds. He hadn't let her hold his hand, because now he was a man; the dark and festering scars said so, as did the private male wound for which Robert Hall surreptitiously took him to the blacksmith healer from a neighboring tribe. The blacksmiths, born in fire, keepers of fire, were magicians everywhere in the Sahara. The Rashaida, the Bedouin with whom they'd stayed, the group Robert Hall was studying, avoided blacksmiths, but Tristan had needed magic.

For months, Dru had lived with the women and children, in their section of the tent, by the hearth, and learned to spin goat's hair and cotton. But when Tristan returned, she'd refused to leave him, had slept beside his cot in the tent Robert Hall had pitched for him. And when Tristan was lucid, she'd asked, *Why didn't you take me with you? Whatever you do to you, you do to me.*

I'm a man. You're a girl.

They were twelve. Just.

The Rashaida, Bedouin devout in their faith, had taught her to pray, differently than the Sunday-school teacher in Nantucket had. She forgot the "Our Father" and memorized the words and syllables of *salaat,* Muslim prayer. The Rashaida children learned no formal prayer until they were fifteen, but Dru had heard the moment-to-moment acknowledgment of the constant presence and power and greater plan of Allah. Their prayers made great sense in the desert. Where, sometimes, nothing else did.

Keziah made some sound, and Dru glanced behind her. Her friend raced to her on the brick sidewalk. Sandalwood and jasmine from her auburn hair filled Dru's nostrils. Her look said, again, why she'd never asked about the photos in the tabloids, never said, *My cousin Ben?* for he was the son of Keziah's uncle, her mother's brother Robert Hall. Her look explained why she'd never said, *The two of you are lovers?* Or asked why Ben was missing from the funeral. Their friendship trusted without asking. Each trusted that the other was essentially good. Keziah rested her head against Dru's.

"Thank you," said Dru. There was no appropriate word for the situation. Guilt whispered in one ear; sin stank in one nostril. The other ear heard the white wing-beat of innocence, while the memory of chaste and tender blushes filled her senses. Every awkwardness had aroused her. And him, as well.

The truth lay hidden under cloak and veil and downcast lids, under his clothing and hers, in the deepest recesses of their beings, and it twisted through the ambiguity of her mourning like a thread of the wrong color.

She was relieved and sorry when Keziah turned to Oceania. "We'll help you. You can teach us sign language."

Tristan turned, tall and cold, like a judge at a witch trial. "I didn't ask you."

Hatred poured between them.

Dru ignored it, had never wanted to understand it. Instead, she replayed the last of the two births she'd attended during her marriage. Crammed in the tiny head of the converted minesweeper, her friends' research vessel. Ship birth, home birth. The shower steaming into the room. She'd sat on the toilet seat, the newborn lying face-down on her legs and trying to cough, trying so hard, dear baby. Darling precious baby. Dru had felt no elation in victory, no faith inspired by the happy outcome, the only bearable outcome. Rather, a ball of sickness had formed in her stomach and transformed to anger—at herself, for agreeing to a birth in those conditions. Yes, there had been a third birth, one more birth since then, in Mali, with no hospital nearby. Again. But Dru had only observed, as a woman and honored guest, studying the technique of the traditional midwife, the important role of the mother's mother and kin. During transition, she'd walked away, to return as the head emerged. She'd crouched nearby while the *marabout,* a holy woman, thrust a knife deep in the sand near the newborn's head to protect her from evil spirits. Later, when mother and child were secluded, the *marabout* had given Dru an amulet made for her. Cowrie shells on leather. That was months ago.... When the baby project with Omar—without Omar—had begun.

Now, there was Oceania, and it was Tristan who'd asked Dru to attend the birth. *I can't.*

I won't.

But Keziah would be there. The hospital was close. And Oceania was the woman Dru had seen in Gloucester. With the man who could be... *She will tell me. She can write the answer. She can tell me who he was, who was that man.*

Her father's ghost.

His double.

He's alive. He can come home.

The daydream took her mind to a gentler place. Far from what she'd done with Ben, from the warmth in her heart made repulsive by grief. To a miracle that might be, a reunion with her father—instead of everything that was.

THE RECEPTION WAS AT OMAR'S—Dru's—house on Orange Street, two doors from a more ornate Greek Revival where Dru's mother, Joanna, lived with Tristan's daughter, and sometimes Tristan. That home, the Tobias Haverford House, was number six on the Orange Street tour led by the historical society. Omar's and Dru's house was never toured, though for *W* and *Town & Country,* they had been photographed in the garden, the sighthounds at their feet.

The Azawakhs, Femi and Ehder, greeted the funeral guests. Mitch, Dru's driver, kept the sand-colored bitch from lunging at strangers and the blue brindle from putting his forepaws on the shoulders of friends, Keziah in particular and Omar's fund manager, Roger. Mitch introduced the brindle, putting the accent on the last syllable. "His name is Ehder. It's a Tuareg word. It means Eagle." And—less patient—"Femi."

More people entered the Federal-Greek Revival than had the cemetery. A few more friends, family and servants. They stood on the original wide pine floor planks. The boards were washed to a light tan, flooding the rooms with their bareness, celebrating the modern Danish furniture that had been Omar's passion. Previous owners had sold off the antiques, a story Dru had lived herself, after her father's boat went down, as her mother struggled to keep their home. An oriental end table for groceries and electricity. Within two years, Joanna had been forced to sell the Tobias Haverford House. Dru had ransomed it back after her marriage, returning it to her mother.

Omar had been generous.

In their own house, he'd given her a spacious second-floor bedroom to use as she wished. Despite his unspoken censure, she'd created a studio. A Bose stereo system, a view of the harbor, luxurious Indian pillows, a Berber rug from Morocco and room to dance. In a sea chest, she collected instruments. The *'ud*, the *qanun*, like a zither, a *nay*—a reed flute—the *darbukkah*, the hand drum shaped like a vase, the *rababah*, played with a horsehair bow. The double *naqqarat*, kettle-drums, in one corner. Silk and cotton wall-hangings, harem images. A precious miniature of her ancestor, Nudar, in a dark, possibly indigo, headdress and silver necklace.

You're playing at things you know nothing about, Omar had said of her singing and dancing.

Tell me.

He'd become silent. And she'd imagined a little boy helping to bury the bodies of his loved ones, who'd been killed by tanks. There might have been limbs detached—her imagination saw the blood and the wounds. The trauma.

After that conversation, she had never once sung or danced while Omar was home, nor painted her skin with henna. But she had danced when he was gone, and she read even more assiduously of desert peoples and their traditions. She did this for two reasons. It was part of being a Haverford, this studying and collecting. The Nantucket museum held scores of treasures gathered from abroad by her seafaring ancestors. Tobias Haverford had brought home the dearest prize—his wife. But also, in the books she read, the academic domentaries she watched, Dru searched for Omar, for some key inside him she couldn't reach, something to explain the contradictions. Something more fathomable than the indelible scars of war.

She had not found it. Now she was left with the freedom to dance whenever she liked, to spend her life dancing and singing.

She did not feel like dancing.

But at Omar's wake, women gathered in her studio. Dru and her mother and Keziah and hers. The two little girls. The pregnant woman, Oceania, whom Dru had coaxed from her brother's side, to gain her trust and learn her secrets. Two of *the* Haverfords, the wealthy branch of the family, from California, speaking ever so often of their—and her—dead cousin, Skye.

Someone hummed softly. Keziah picked up the *mizwid,* the smaller Algerian equivalent of bagpipes.

The deepest rituals of song and dance, to honor the stages of life.

Joanna took Oceania's hand. "Come with me, darling." Removing the pregnant woman from the grieving place.

Keziah's mother, Mary Mayhew, followed them with her eyes. The door shut. "What's she going to do? Where's the father? It's so hard to give up a baby."

Or to raise one alone, Dru thought. As Keziah was doing. But she would choose Keziah's path herself. In any circumstance she could imagine.

Mary shook her head heavily. "So hard to part with one's child." Shivering back tears, she embraced Dru. "Oh, darling, I shouldn't be talking about babies."

Mary had taught all of them, all the women, to sing and dance and paint their skin with henna. She had taught the spiritual traditions and beliefs behind these customs. Mary had learned from her grandmother, who had learned from her mother. In the 1920s, two Haverford women had traveled to North Africa, seeking their heritage; they were photographed in long skirts on camels in Egypt. The Haverfords clung to a strange past. Their tradition said women's dance was for women, a ritual between them, part of their power. They hoarded long cotton or silk dresses from Egypt and Palestine with brilliantly embroidered bodices and elegant pleats falling from beneath the yoke, with lace collars. There were dances for all the seasons of life.

Dru caught Keziah's tune. She knew the Arabic words, because Mary had taught her and Dru had studied the language as an undergraduate. Too, she still remembered bits of Rashaida dialect she'd picked up as a child during those strange desert months in the Sudan. Omar had never complimented her on being the perfect hostess to Arabic men with oil interests or others from the Arab world whom he'd wooed and won and sometimes robbed.

Omar would hate for her to mourn him this way.

It was her way, and each cry for him was also for her father, that almost unbearable loss when she was fourteen.

Down on her knees, angry at herself and at Omar, for the times she had thought unjustly, *You have killed me, Omar. Who am I now?* She sank into the rug. The numbing tide of the music took her, and she swayed. Her body knew one movement, her upper body forward and back, forth and away. Singing. Moaning.

Joanna slipped back into the room and sat on her heels beside her daughter. Dru loved the touch of her hand, the feel of each line. Joanna had slipped easily from the Velvet Underground to the Haverford ways. Now her daughter mourned with dance, and her mother remembered another, more difficult, loss. She hoped Dru would not have to grieve with the intensity she had when Turk's boat failed to return, after the waiting, the waiting of a fisherman's wife. But there were too many similarities.

The worst kind. *Oh, my darling Dru.*

Oh, sweet Turk. I never meant it.

Keri slipped to the floor with them.

Then one Haverford cousin in Calvin Klein stockings and Chanel.

The other in Armani.

They swayed back and forth and Dru saw Omar's eyes and wept for the time they'd shared a bed. Too long ago. Months and seasons since they'd embarked on the plan for a baby. *Why didn't I say no? Why didn't I insist on something different, Omar?*

SERGIO OPENED THE DOOR, then pulled it wider. He smiled gently as Ben stepped in out of the biting wind. Sergio was whom he'd come to see, to ask a favor, to ask for clothing from a dead man's closet. Ben explained why, as a nephew, as someone so close to Omar, and Sergio said, "I will send something to your home later today. It should cause no distress. Rather the contrary. You're in 'Sconset?"

"Yes. Thanks." How well-mannered these people were. His tribe and their servants.

The dogs were loose and found Ben. He petted Ehder, whose brown eyes begged for his heart, while Femi caught his shoelaces like a puppy. Ben listened to the ceiling and knew he would not see her.

Better that way.

Standing, he spotted a blond man in the hallway, hands on the top of a door frame, a man too big and rough for this home. He was smiling at a pregnant woman, the only woman. The others must be upstairs, ringing those tambourines, beating the drums, sawing on a one-string box. Knowing Tristan by his scars, Ben felt new amazement that once they'd all been small.

Tristan saw him.

Under the singing and playing and clapping, the people downstairs parted. Roger, the fund manager, squeezed Ben's shoulder as Ben walked past, intent on Dru's twin. On Tristan, bound to him as she was.

The pregnant woman pressed her back to the vast hearth, leaving the men to meet.

Tristan cocked a sideways smile. He tried a fragment of

Bedouin greeting, shrugged and used profanity instead. His specialty back then. Something different and intentional now.

Ben wished him well.

They listened to the sounds from above.

Tristan was the tallest Haverford in memory and did not offer his hand.

Understandable. "What was your catch?"

"Thirty-four thousand pounds." Tristan worked his mouth, thoughtful. "We leave again tomorrow. Last trip of the season. Then we'll fish for lobster down here." Georges Bank.

"Out of Gloucester?"

"Oh, yeah. I'm heading back real soon. After I kiss my mother, my sister and my little girl goodbye."

"You still own a boat here?"

"Still paying for it."

Upstairs, the instruments stopped, and a door opened.

Ben nodded and left, feeling Tristan's eyes on his back.

Outside, he crossed the stretch of brick that had turned so slick in the rain last Wednesday night, or maybe the dogs had sighted something and tried to run, or maybe Omar had tripped. His bodyguard had said, *He went flying.* Hit a concrete step.

Tennis shoes pounded the walk, running. Long strides. A hand whirled him around. Discolored, glaring scars. Turquoise irises and sea-black pupils. "Do you love her? Are you in love?"

Time crept by.

If not for the car and the cameras, Tristan would have killed him. A certainty. Instead, a clicking and whirring caught the swordfish captain breathing hard and the tall, dark journalist distant and removed. Protecting his sources and his story. Unafraid.

The next day, the caretaker of the cemetery found a heavy stone at the head of Omar Hall's grave and another at the foot.

An Armani suit that had belonged to the deceased lay over the grave, upon the earth, that someone less fortunate might take it.

He had been buried as a Bedouin at last.

TROOPING DOWN the spiral stairs, wooden stairs, one of *the* Haverfords, Anne in Chanel, asked Dru, "Have you seen the Blades? Didn't you deliver their babies?"

Natural curiosity. Skye had died, and her widower, David Blade, had remarried. Dru had attended the births of his daughters. At sea. A sea the shade of green in the amniotic fluid that had spilled from Rika's bag of waters, had poured out as her head was born. "Yes." Rage—or something like it—flushing her. She wouldn't discuss Rika Blade's birth.

Why did I agree to help Oceania? What kind of midwife am I to agree to a birth I don't want to do?

"I guess deaths in this family always make me think of her. Skye."

Too warm in the stairwell. Should turn down the heat. All the bodies.

"Didn't you go to Africa with Skye? And stay with Ben and his father?" The name slipped in so casually, with no extra emphasis. Though everyone knew. About her and Ben. "Something happened. No one would ever say. How did Tristan get those scars?"

"He chose them. He should tell you. In the desert, things always happen. Many things happened." And changed the course of Dru's life, every choice she made with a man. "I miss Skye." But her sick warmth intensified, and she pressed Anne's hand and went away, hurried through the house and out to the garden to hide between the blue spruce and the pine, to crouch there in her heels, with her head in her hands, until Ehder, the blue brindle dog, came to kiss her, to sit nobly, knowing Omar was dead.

LATER THAT DAY, Tristan returned to Gloucester—and to sea.

Oceania and the paparazzi stayed.

Dru and Oceania ate dinner in the room where she'd listened to Omar philosophize through hundreds of perfectly prepared meals, where she'd helped entertain his guests. Afterward, Dru showed Oceania to her room. She brought a photograph, a writing tablet and pen. Oceania touched the nubby bedspread, old-fashioned and simple and fine. The room was open and white, like the others. Spare.

As Dru sat on the bed, too, Femi followed her in and sniffed at Oceania's sweatpants and the huge sweater covering her belly. Oceania petted the sand-colored dog and bent for a kiss. Dru met her eyes. "Tell me if you want her to leave."

The pregnant woman shook her head of dreadlocks, burnished by the sun.

"I want to ask you some things." Dru wrote her first question. *For the Baby: What are your plans?*

Oceania's script was small, upright, meticulous. *I will keep my baby.*

Do you have a place to go?

Yes. I can get there. No worries.

The rustling exchange of paper.

Wouldn't you prefer to have your baby in the hospital? Don't worry about the expense. They will cover you.

Oceania stared. She shook her head violently. Scrawled *You said you would do it. Here!*

Dru's throat dried up. Almost four hundred births as primary attendant. Then…Omar. The Blades' babies at sea and another birth, the birth from which she'd fled. Holding back the fullness in her throat. What she'd left behind. Maybe for the better. She wrote, *I am a certified nurse-midwife with an MS in Nurse-Midwifery.* Hand shaking, she added, *I saw you at Gloucester Marine Railways with this man.* And showed the photo.

Oceania was slow to take it. Short nails on those brown hands, on the fingers that gripped the pen. Hesitation. *Who is he?* Their hands touched, warm, as she thrust the pen back to Dru.

Oceania would lie about this. Dru saw it, felt it.

She wrote, *My father.*

Oceania's lips opened, then closed. She wrote, and the dog's ears twitched at the sound of pen on paper. *Not the same person. Like, but not same. Tom Adams takes cod from Bedford, Nova Scotia. I'm from there. He's family. I'm going back.*

The bottom of the sheet.

The end of Dru's questions.

Was it her imagination that Oceania had lied?

As Ehder, the blue dog, came in and sniffed the two women, Dru studied the photo. Wrote one last comment in a spot of white. *I miss him.* She ripped out the page and turned it over, furious now. *His boat sank on Georges Bank, they think. In 1983. I was 14. I loved him. T. loved him. He taught us to maintain the boat. We helped with the catch. I want him back.* She was wild, wanting Omar, too. Wanting someone else even more, despite everything the wanting made her feel. Those months that she'd traveled, searching for the right father for Omar's child, were friendless months. Finally, she'd made one friend.

She wanted that friend now, more than she wanted her dead husband, whose wishes had confused her. Who had wished her to make love with another man, who had hit upon *that* method for them, for her and Omar, to have a child.

Oceania contemplated a tiny watercolor on the wall, a fisherman hauling in a net of squirming fish, no long lines or drift nets. With her tablet and photo, Dru stepped around to meet her eyes. "Good night."

Outside the door, she trembled, nearly certain.

The man with Oceania had been her father.

THE CARETAKER CALLED before eight o'clock the next morning. Sergio told her gently about the grave, and she nodded, hugging herself, and retreated to her bedroom. Knowing Sergio must have given him the suit.

He was on island.

She stared from her windows, hoping not to see him.

Hating herself for hoping she would.

DANIEL MAYHEW, Keziah's father, had handled most of Omar's domestic legal affairs for twenty years. He was the executor of the will, and he phoned Dru in the morning two days after the funeral. "Would it be possible for you to come down to my office at, say, eleven?"

She blinked at her gray reflection in the gilded bedroom mirror. "You can't come here?" Never, never, had they gone to Daniel's office. Reasons for the change occurred to her. None made sense. Even if Omar had given everything he owned to charity, except for a box of tissues for her, why should…? There was no need for a dramatic reading of the will. Did people even do that anymore? Executors simply notified the beneficiaries. And Omar's will was in a trust. No probate, no courts, no publicity.

"If another time would be better…" Daniel cleared his throat.

The police chief, who had liked Omar, had finally dispersed the paparazzi, escorting them off-island. Nantucket was quiet, its aim to still the passing of time. Its cobblestone streets and gaslight street lamps clung to a bygone civility. Paparazzi were unwelcome.

Still, Mitch should drive her. It was one thing she'd loved about being married to Omar. That she was always guarded. In some way. Even when she'd thought no one was there. *Can't think about it, can't. Only think about Oceania and her baby. Not just get them the things they need. Must follow her when she leaves, can hire someone to do it, in case that man really is...*

"I'll be there." Her voice dragged, and she heard in it not only the grief of a widow but the assurance of an heiress.

THE OFFICE WAS on Main Street, with a bicycle locked to a gaslight-style street lamp outside. As Mitch pulled the Mercedes to the curb, Dru rubbed Ehder's silky fur and kissed his face. Femi next.

When Mitch came around to get her door, she took the dogs' leads, braced their bodies to keep them from leaping out first.

Her driver smiled. "Want me to walk them?"

She'd planned to take them inside, a response to being asked to come to the office. But it really was rude. And presumptuous. What had happened to her? "Thank you." Fingers wrapped around each dog's collar, Dru stepped out, then let them follow. "Ehder, sit." Lifting her hand, signalling him. "Sit. Femi." She worked the dogs, ignoring her watch, before handing the leads to Mitch.

Ornate iron railings flanked the steps of the law office. She wore low heels and a dark gray suit designed for her. The silk lining slid against her thighs, smooth as the light makeup on her skin. Soon she'd return home and wear the face she wanted. At home, she'd make sure Oceania and the baby had everything they needed for the birth and afterward. Nice things. She would care for the mother, then lie in bed and gaze into her soul at what she'd done and decide how bad it was.

The door chime tinkled as she entered.

The receptionist had already reached Daniel's walnut door. She knocked discreetly before opening it. "Mrs. Hall is here."

He's with someone.

Her stomach jumped. *What now?*

Daniel guided her inside and closed the door after her. And

there they were. Three. Tabloids would give tens of thousands
for this picture, as they had for photos of Dru Haverford Hall
in Gloucester, leaning toward, submitting to, so obviously
wanting this man.

Her husband's nephew and her own cousin.

His presence could only be some retribution beyond her
ken. Her heart began the stages of breaking. Exactly what she
deserved. "Hi, Ben."

CHAPTER TWO

From 1978 to 1981, my father and I lived in the Sudan, between the 'Atbara and Gash rivers, with a group of Rashaida, nomadic Bedouins whose ancestors had crossed the Red Sea from Arabia in the nineteenth century. With our guests, our cousins, we set out in our Land Cruiser to rejoin them. The vehicle had no mirrors and no left rear window. Desert sand, which is dust, had collected several inches thick in parts of the back. The wind and rain came in and moulded a small desert. Skye had brought her own mirror—two—but she didn't like the sand or wind or wearing long pants and long sleeves in the heat. "What do you mean this isn't hot? Was that a joke?" As the sun fell on the primitive track leading southwest from Kassala, I saw the dust rise, as it does in the desert, back-lit by sun, like steam swirling off a hot pool. Minutes passed before we met the other vehicle, a faded green Land Rover, and stopped to converse with the Americans inside, one of whom took out an Egyptian-made assault rifle and aimed it at my father.

"A fall cannot occur without potential energy."

—Ben, recollections of an early fall

Gloucester, Massachusetts
One week earlier
October 16

SOMETIMES, WHEN SHE was waiting—for food or visa stamps or bureaucracy at border crossings—Dru counted days. She had left her husband in Nantucket to fly to New York, then Paris, and on to Bamako, Mali, 218 days earlier. Between that day and this, she and Omar had spent thirteen days and eight nights together.

She had decided to tell someone.

Everything.

Tristan. She could only tell her twin. She couldn't tell Keziah. Keziah would have an opinion about what Dru had agreed to do for Omar, for both of them. Tristan might have an opinion, too, but it would be like hers, as though they owned the same head.

In their language, he might say, *Surfside,* which meant the apartment where they'd lived with their mother after the Tobias Haverford House was sold; Surfside meant better than a tent and worse than a boat. Here in Gloucester, Dru would jump on his back like a kid. Here, no one knew the person under the faded blue, almost gray, sweatshirt hood, behind gas station sunglasses, her brother's cast-off chinos cinched at her waist with a canvas belt.

But the *Sarah Lynnda* wasn't in port, nor her captain. Not for another week.

Dru would wait. Life had resigned her to watching the sea, knowing that fishing killed more men than any other job. A solemn fatalism prevailed.

Still, she loved Gloucester, the locals, the dingy Inner Harbor. She watched chain and gears haul a boat, an elderly dragger, up the railway and down through the brick archways to a subterranean pit. A cup of coffee warmed her hand, steamed in the air. A couple came from the docks. No. A man and his grown daughter, a white woman with dreadlocks. Pregnant and carrying in front, the baby already dropped.

Dru refused these thoughts, chose others. What would it be like never to comb her hair? She imagined charity auctions, benefit balls, state dinners.... Yes, yes. Her reverie broke.

The man. She studied his face, the fall of his gray hair. His cowlick. Just a ghost, a doppelgänger.

But Dru walked closer, could not help it. Because of the cowlick. His hair riding up just that way on the right side of his forehead, his bangs drooping on the other side. She had to know that it was an illusion.

Not.

Not.

He hugged the young woman, who turned and flashed him a peace sign. They hurried off in opposite directions. He went toward the docks. Dru lost sight of him behind a truck.

She searched frantically. *Was it him? Did I really see him?*

But the man was gone.

She landed in the present, in the facts of her life that remained the same even under a bleak sky, beside a bar with a barn-red exterior. The fact that she must go home sometime. What to tell Omar. What to say to Omar. What to feel toward Omar. What to ask Omar. Dru pushed back her hood. The plan was over. She had scrapped it. It was no more.

No longer would she wander the world searching for the Appropriate Man. She'd made up that name for him. She couldn't call him the perfect man or the right man. Omar was those. She'd wanted Omar's baby. *That's all I have to tell him. Again.*

When her father's boat was lost, she'd learned the nature of expectations. A baby was not a right. Period.

She held her hand to her forehead. Did she value her marriage to a man who'd suggested she have sexual intercourse with someone else in order to conceive a child? It was because of that bicycle accident in Utah, that terrible fall. At first, she'd accepted Omar's plan, knowing she should feel gratitude. She'd planned her quest. She'd gone. First to a place where she'd meet no one but the others on her guided tour. Seeking the notoriously inaccessible. Tumbuktu.

On the Niger riverboat, packed by class with desperate humans, Dru—desperate in her own way—had admitted that she hadn't come to find a man but for other reasons. She'd come in search of the Tuareg. She believed Nudar had been one of those nomads. And while her group camped among the Tuaregs of the Niger, a woman went into labor. Dru knew no Tamashek, but enough French to say more than *sage femme.* Yet Rika's birth at sea had returned. With anger. Why must Raisha, the Tuareg mother, have no option but childbirth in a skin tent? Dru touched the cowrie-shell fertility pendant that hung beneath her shirt. The *marabout* had said, *You must see that you're afraid.* No, Dru wasn't afraid to practice midwifery. But her reasons for giving it up—the paparazzi, such rude intrusiveness, the lack of privacy in the life of Dru Haverford Hall—would be incomprehensible to the *marabout.* Dru hadn't dared say, *My family fascinates Americans because we appear unlucky. And I fascinate them because my husband is richer than all the rich men in West Africa put together.* She couldn't hope to make a woman who'd never traveled further than Bamako understand. She hadn't stopped practicing because of meconium in Rika's bag of waters. Despite a master's in nurse-midwifery and 400 births, her own family's notoriety and Omar's wealth were enough to keep Dru from midwifery.

From Timbuktu, she'd rushed home to find Omar absent. He couldn't get away from Curaçao, must fly directly to Hong Kong.

Dru had left again, taking the dogs. To meet a series of men, a long line of men, and she'd ended up fiddling with her earrings or her hair or trying not to yawn. Then Key West and that bar... The carpenter she'd thought was cute reeked of Cuervo and they had nothing in common, and he kept talking about her body and how he liked her hips, how she wasn't "a stick" and he liked a woman with some meat on her. Meat.

She'd also worried that he was unintelligent, then hated herself for her prejudice. But she was selecting a father for her and Omar's child!

Back to Nantucket—Omar for one awkward night, when she'd decided she knew what a condom felt like to a man because some invisible barrier had covered her senses, numbing her utterly. *If you love me,* she'd asked, *how can you let me sleep with another man?*

With reluctance. Because I love you.

He'd left in the morning on business. She'd said goodbye to the dogs and flown to Europe. A month in Paris, two in Scandinavia, sightseeing. Emotions absent. Back to Africa. Cairo and Aswan.

Morocco was ghastly, with all the Europeans in Arab dress. One man, a software CEO, had worn jeans and a canvas shirt, his hair in a ponytail. It was so close to completion, almost settled, and she *couldn't.* Couldn't begin to tell him the plan, couldn't go to bed with him. He wasn't her husband. That was the problem.

She didn't want to do it.

She would tell Omar so. She was set to meet him in Nantucket soon—to *stay*—but first she needed this. To see Tristan. Have a beer and—

"Hi."

She spun, the gears of the railway looming over her, high above. The cup fell, coffee running down the concrete.

"Sorry," he said, folding the cup away in his pocket.

Him.

She had seen this man two months ago, at the camel market in Daraw, talking to a Rashaida sheikh. In Arabic. For Dru, in her circumstances, he'd been impossible to ignore. As now.

His hair was black, his build athletic. He wore a navy shell, thicker than a windbreaker. Brown eyes, almost black.

Nerves tingling, she backed away. Warm. Alert.

He stabbed his hands into his pockets. "I'm Ben Hall, your cousin."

The Sudan stormed her senses, blasting memories.

"Omar asked me to look after you these past few months."

Sea-cold drowned the Sahara heat. A passing fisherman glanced at them, and she didn't see. *Look after her*... He'd been *following* her? To watch her try to pick up a sperm donor?

And on the Niger...

No, it was impossible. Dru tossed her head back. "So where have you been?"

Whiskers coming through on his lean cheeks. "With you since New York, Paris, Bamako..." He closed his lips on Timbuktu. "We've been to Cape Hatteras and Key West and Greenwich—"

She held up her hand, stopping the recitation. Forget the problems of a woman traveling alone in Muslim countries. Greenwich had been a mistake, much too close to home. In her recklessness, she'd approached a lone and handsome man in the bar at the yacht club and said, *I'm horny. I want to get laid.* His mouth had tilted up on one side while he checked her out. Then he'd smiled tautly and edged away.

She'd realized she'd wanted him to, had said so with every word to the contrary.

Omar had provided a witness to her adventures, the one thing he'd promised not to do! She'd told him she couldn't bear to have a bodyguard. Not for this.

She'd married him because she would have a bodyguard.

She'd married him for many reasons. And loved him because he was safe. And kept her safe.

Dru wasn't going to ask Ben all he'd seen. "Well, your job is over, *cousin*."

"You don't remember me."

"I do. How could anyone forget?" She shifted deliberately from the allusion to their past and what had happened in the Sudan. Everything that had happened. "My husband calls you 'our young sheikh.'"

His mouth slanted.

Of course, that was an inherited title, wasn't it?

"Maybe he thinks your father *was* a sheikh." Flippant. Robert Hall was as unforgettable as the Sudan. And dead less than two years. "I'm sorry for your loss. Truly. And goodbye."

He fell in step beside her. Faded jeans and running shoes. "I'll stick close. Part of the job description."

"I'll bet talking to me wasn't. It never is." He was tall. Looking out for her. Maybe what bothered her was his face.

This unforgiving gray light had nothing to forgive in him.

A hot flush went through her, a stupid pheromone reaction. She was scared. *Scared.*

The Sudan. The boy he'd been sometimes appeared in her dreams, although never in her nightmares of abduction.

And never as a man.

Comfort came because he was beside her. Comfort. But heat spread at the juncture of her legs. Flushing. Riding through her.

It was too stupid and too impossible. *Forget it, Dru,* she muttered, even as she calculated how distantly they were related, the same consanguinity of Keziah, too far to mention. He was handsome. He resembled Omar slightly—dark eyes, oak skin, black hair. But the jaw was different, the long rugged lines of his face, and the aloofness that could turn wholly present in a moment with the sorcery of an interviewer, a seeker of truth. *He's sexy. Why did Omar send someone so sexy?*

Why had Omar sent Ben?

Brown eyes fixed on her, while wind whipped her hair in

front of her and one cool drop, wetness, hit her wrist. Then another. Rain.

She turned, but his hand caught her arm, bringing her around. The warmth through her sweatshirt made her shiver. Pulling away, she saw that his chin was hard, his eyes piercing. He kissed her mouth.

Dru put her hands up and shoved.

Her palms had barely connected with his chest when she flew backward. He caught her. Other than that, he hadn't moved at all.

"Don't," she said. She was glad of her shoes, trail shoes for running the dogs on gravel, because she ran through the moisture and the rain and the smell of fish, good and bad, and the smell of this centuries-old port. She ran, wondering if Omar had told Ben to try this as a last resort. Omar, who had *avoided* meetings with her, the days—and nights—they'd promised to spend together. *He wouldn't. He wouldn't.* Wouldn't avoid her. Wouldn't want her to choose Ben, his own nephew.

She ran behind buildings and found an alley and hurdled its fish scales and grease, sprinting until she reached the docks again. Alone, unseen, she wandered until dark, searching for the gray-haired man with the beak nose and her blue eyes and Tristan's hollow cheeks and the cowlick on the right side. The man she believed, in the wetness rising from the sea, was her father. Her father, who had somehow never died.

EARLY IN HER MARRIAGE, Dru had fallen in love with anonymity. She liked to travel, to be on the move. She found a way to be unknown and close to the memories she loved, to her twin's existence, to her father's grave. To the ocean. In port cities, she bought boats with Omar's money and registered them to her loved ones. Keziah's *Sunshine Daydream* hailed from Portland, Maine. Her mother's *Hot Babe* was berthed in Key West. Tristan's trawler, *Cup of Gold,* in Gloucester. And so on. The boats floated but did not always run. They were low on conveniences. Floating hovels. They were refuge. Her hostels and hotels.

When darkness came, she returned to the thirty-foot trawler. Somewhere, Ben Hall, journalist and trained observer, must be watching. But not for a story. She knew better, knew the quality of her family's ties. Still—*I don't want to be followed.* Why hadn't she ordered him to stop?

Because he was Omar's employee.

Below deck in the trawler *Cup of Gold,* she cooked the simplest of meals, ate and wished for a phone. She'd have to walk to the pay phone to call Omar. 53 telephone conversations. 311 calls.

She washed dishes.

Yes, she must walk, in the dark, to call her husband. 312.

She worked up to it as she dressed. A thick sweater, Nantucket wool. A wool cap that had been her father's, moth holes mended with her own hands. Her wet trail shoes, in case she had to run. Water licked the boat. Dru hugged herself and slipped out of the cabin into the wet cold and the silver-lit night. Security lights. Snow air.

"It occurred to me a few times that I should give you some pointers."

Dru banged her shoulder on the door frame. She locked the cabin door behind her. She liked him no better as a shadow. "Do *you* need some pointers? Let's see, in Arabic, it's *'Ma'assalama.'* In Tamashek, it's *'Harsad.'* In English, we say *goodbye.*"

He shifted on the aft seat. "Let me start over."

"You could leave. That would be a start. Of *the end.*"

"I had an idea that if you were set on this plan Omar told me about, I could—"

"Procure? Is that the word you're looking for?" What was it about harbors that made everything echo?

He cleared his throat. "Help. Was the word."

In the milk-black light, misty and heavy, Dru raked his jaw with her eyes. *I want my husband. I want to have Omar's baby, and it's impossible, and maybe he's become indifferent to me because of this, our infertility. I'm not going to discuss it with Ben Hall.* She must get to a phone and hear Omar's voice, his love for her. She must go home. Maybe before the *Sarah Lynnda* docked with thousands of pounds of swordfish in her hold.

Dru bundled her heavy sweater about her.

"Want to share a bottle of wine?"

Beside him in a paper bag. Big enough for glasses, too. The sea rolled beneath them, lifting the boats and the dock, everything singing. "Why?"

"Because, through the medium of conversation, you may find me irresistible."

Wood and floatation bending and straining, stays pinging masts. A fish jumped nearby, invisible.

"I find my husband irresistible. And you are one of his employees." She had never spoken to anyone this way. Family, no less. "Go away. Leave me alone."

"You know, twenty years ago, in a Rashaida camp, besides failing to conceal your—"

"Shut up. We were children. And, yes, I had a crush on you."

"Betrothed is the word. Ignoring our interesting child marriage, of course."

"What marriage?" She snorted. "And the engagement was conditional at best. The bride price you offered was paltry. An *intentional insult*." But her eyes steamed. Children bickering in the aftermath of trauma. Their innocence blocking out what they'd seen and heard. She closed her eyes.

"When Haamda told our fortunes before—"

She cut him off. "Who? I don't remember." He was courteous not to take her bride-price remark further, not to follow it up with an allusion to Omar's wealth. Especially tonight when Dru wore her watch—but not her rings. She would put them on when she returned from the phone. "For your information, I won't be looking for any more men or meeting them. Except my brother, if he comes in soon."

She listened to the harbor.

He watched her. "That leaves me."

Him? She moved closer, so he could hear her, and sat on a wet aluminum chest. "No. My husband has hired you, perhaps as a last resort. He probably finds you trustworthy, sufficiently intelligent and adequately attractive. Also, you live a reckless life in dangerous locations and are likely to die prematurely, not that anyone wishes it. You resemble him faintly, even with no blood relationship, and we'll probably never see much of you. The fact that you're family is another plus." She paused, not looking at him. "Our family has a genetic predisposition for dissembling. Even, I imagine, the journalists. Especially them."

Dru met his gaze. Poets recorded these echoes of the eyes.

"If you'll give me your keys and direct me to a corkscrew, I'll open the wine. Don't make me drink it alone."

She stretched out a leg to dig in the pockets of her jeans. The hand that took the keys from hers was a strong, lean shadow. His movement past was athletic darkness, muscle unseen.

Dru shivered. No thoughts. Nothing to think about. Just some wine after dinner with a man who obviously wasn't much of a drinker, living as he did in North Africa and the Middle East, sometimes crossing down to Mali or Niger for a story. As much a nomad as his father, Robert Hall.

He brought the bottle and glasses to the deck. "It's warmer below."

"And cleaner up here."

It was a merlot, poured by those strong, lean hands. Smooth, olive brown, she saw. The wine was good.

She didn't thank him.

"Omar," he said, "never suggested that I should make love with you."

Her toes were cold, and she wiggled them in her wool socks and running shoes. Omar seldom used that expression, found other ways to speak of intimacy. She missed Omar deliberately, missed his intelligence. She remembered their first year together, how he'd begun to explain finance to her, explained it in philosophical terms all his own. The tutelage had never ceased. He understood the sciences—and human nature. His were the genes she wanted to reproduce.

But no chance. His fall had stolen the chance of their conceiving together. It had happened on their honeymoon, while bicycling in Utah's canyonlands on their honeymoon, both of them impressed by how fit he was at sixty-one. They hadn't known that the fall had rendered him sterile, although they'd wondered. And discovered this year.

Omar's line had ended.

She said, "Don't you think that men perceive children as the means to continue their line, while women are more involved in being pregnant and giving birth and nursing and having and raising a child?"

"In love, you mean?"

Lightly deflecting the slur on his gender.

He drifted from her briefly. "And, given your plan, how could Omar be thinking of his line?"

She studied him, sensing an undercurrent. He stared over the stern and the dock at the water, and she studied his profile. A nose that reminded her of his first cousin, Keziah. Black hair. Lean face. Was it his chin that made her think of Omar? He'd gotten a great spill of dark beauty from their mutual ancestor, Nudar, and the Cape Verde sailor her daughter had married.

He's handsome. He's very handsome.

Anger curled inside her, stalking her, and pounced. It ran with the wine in her veins. The missed rendezvous with Omar. His near-insistence that she keep looking. The anger shredded her hesitation and doubt, and she turned off her internal calculator, lost the numbers of days since she'd left Nantucket and the other tabulated days with their uncertain meanings. Her line, a matrilineal line. Nudar's line. Ben Hall was part of that.

"Recommend yourself to me." No more surreptitiously studying strange men or offering herself in a way meant to bring rejection. On the deck of a defunct trawler, in an old sweater and torn chinos, she became Cleopatra, Mata Hari, Scheherazade, Isis, every powerful woman and goddess of myth and legend and history. She owned her power to seduce, to invite a proposition, to reject it if she chose. To accept what was worthy.

She asked, "Why do you want to do this?"

Ben straightened a little, suddenly farther away. He brought his glass to his lips. Drank half. Held the glass. "I would enjoy it. I think you would, too."

She winced, felt the expression on her face, the drawing back of her shoulders. "That's the best you can do?"

He refilled her glass, and she heard the wine fall in. "I've known Omar my whole life," he said. "In some ways—" unsteady "—I'm in his debt. And you want a baby." He paused. Stopped. Murmured, "Hard to talk about." A brief silence. "In February, I was in the Aïr Mountains with a Tuareg family I know. The boys are teenagers. They go into the mines and come out covered with uranium dust."

"Instead of indigo." She drank wine, and the rich velvet in her mouth and throat nourished the legend inside her, invoking her as a tribal queen who would choose the finest of the young men to continue her line. He'd be ritually sacrificed at the end of the year, and she could choose another... Her fancy drifted away, back to the Tuareg who wore uranium dust instead of indigo.

Ben might not have heard her comment, or maybe he thought it too obvious to mention. The Tuareg were the blue men of the desert, the nomads of the southern Sahara, whose wealth was their robes. No water for soaking huge garments, so they pounded the indigo dye into the cloth until it shimmered, rich purple-blue, and their garments stained their skin as well. Some of them were light as the Berbers. Some black. The women danced the *guedra;* some called it a trance dance, others a love dance.

She and Keziah had wondered if Nudar could have been one of them, living in Algeria back then, captured by another tribe, sold in Morocco....

"I'd lived there for a year, working," he said. Quiet. "Two men employed by Omar came to find me. But the government doesn't like westerners near the mines. I received a message from Agadez, the nearest town. Omar's men wanted to know could I meet them? I hesitated. Might not be allowed to return. But what Omar wanted had to be important. I went. Met his men at their camp. 'Omar asks you to please come to him.' I came to Nantucket, and Omar told me about your plan—"

"His plan."

"Your mutual plan. He asked me to look out for you."

She heard the unspoken. This silliness had taken him from where he preferred to be, from an injustice and a tragedy that must be observed and told and, if possible, stopped. The teenage boys should be building their herds—but the Tuareg herds she'd seen were scanty, a few goats. She said, "What qualifies you? To look after me?"

Even in the dark, his embarrassment was there. In silence.

She read his mind, his memory. No. He had been just a boy then, in the Sudan. Surely he didn't imagine he could have done anything to stop what had happened. Though...

She tried to lose interest and instead pictured him in the desert, not as a boy but a man. She drank more wine and saw him with a press pass, entering countries on journalist's visas, speaking with foreign soldiers, photographing a revolt. A smile, her mouth misbehaving. "You still haven't recommended yourself to me."

"In my spare time, when I'm not interviewing courteous but dangerous men or taking notes on the screams of prisoners undergoing torture, I perform the duties of leading my family of three women and twenty-nine children and teenagers, some of whom have married each other and given me grandchildren. The tents of my family are working laboratories. While I'm away from home, carrying salt across the Sahara in camel caravans, my wives and daughters remain behind in their tents, sewing patches for the hole in the ozone layer. As we cross the desert, pausing only to pray and eat, my sons and I study the problem of cold fusion. I own nineteen camels, six tents and four Humvees. Finally, from living a life of devotion, I have discovered how to make a woman have an orgasm during every sexual encounter."

"I'm sorry he brought you here for this. It was trivial." Her father popped into her mind. She'd seen him earlier. Been sure of it. The incident that afternoon seemed far away.

"Babies are never trivial."

"So I'd better get pregnant and have one, considering that you went to all this trouble?"

"You misunderstand me."

"Where does sleeping with another man's wife fit into your piety and devotion?"

His teeth scraped his bottom lip. He reached for his wineglass and lifted it. "To your keen insight."

"A heretic?" she murmured.

He gazed at the water, where it faded to black and vanished.

Dru dropped the topic. She loathed being asked about her religious beliefs—or discussing them. But she knew the world in which he moved. Faith was assumed in dress and actions, sometimes ordained by law. She asked another question for the second time, a different way. "What's in this for you?"

"You really don't remember our marriage in the Sudan. With the Rashaida."

"What are you talking about? No, I don't remember." She rolled her eyes. "And there's plenty I do remember. Do I have to ask again?"

What was in it for him.

"Fulfillment of desire."

"For a one-night stand." She didn't know how he'd gotten closer, their knees almost touching.

"For things you can't imagine." His black lashes hid his eyes.

She reached for the bottle, but he roused himself and poured. Sipping, she examined the label. A twenty-five dollar bottle of wine. "You want to sleep with Omar's wife. That must be it."

"I want you to have my baby."

Of all the lies, this was the greatest. "It wouldn't be. Let's get that out of the way. This is the end of your contact with me, Omar and the baby. This *is* a one-night stand. For all intents and purposes, I'm using birth control. Nothing will happen. Except sex."

"Is this your time?"

"Let me paint another picture. I am the queen of a matri-

archal society. You will briefly enjoy a position as my con-
sort.''

''Many positions.''

She rolled her eyes again. ''Then,'' she finished, ''you go.
Forever. You still haven't said what's in this for you.''

''I'm trying to help. Omar is a second father to me.'' He
paused, expressionless. The wine made her see Ben looking
for himself in her eyes. ''Omar wants a child,'' he said. ''He
wants you to have a child. I'm a sperm donor.''

''You took two hundred and eighteen days to volunteer.''
She hadn't meant to speak in numbers, had meant to erase
them.

He had to notice.

Black eyes like Omar's, like Nudar's. Horsetail lashes, long,
thick and black. He wasn't drunk and she was. His eyes spoke.
''Sometime I will tell you about those 218 days.''

Her shoulders trembled. The fabric of their pants touched.
She wondered who he was inside. She wanted badly to know.
And that was dangerous.

He'd abandoned his wine.

''What did you think?'' she asked. ''What did you think
when he told you his plan?''

His head swiveled. Saw her. ''That he has more faith in
twelve billion dollars than I would.'' Faith that money would
hold her.

''He has faith in our love.''

No comment.

So be it. If Omar wanted something… She couldn't guess.
But he *had* decided on this plan in love; she'd agreed for the
same reason.

''I would like,'' she said, ''to see inside your mind. I remember when you could hit an upright twig at thirty yards
with a slingshot. In the desert.''

''You remember a lot.'' He gazed at her for too long, as

though he understood things she didn't. "What do you think is in my mind?"

She didn't know. "Maybe…you're hardened. Maybe…you go to look at difficult things, as you've said, and you're silent and moved but you write what you feel. I read the piece in *Harper's*. It wasn't just journalism or essay-writing. Philosophy, too."

"And what's in *your* mind?"

She stared at the cabin, feeling the lock on her mouth, on the expression of her heart and her body. "It is the mind of Omar Hall's wife. Hedge funds and hedgerows—on Orange Street, that is."

"You're a gardener?"

"I don't want to talk about this." Her throat ached. She was freezing and didn't care. The wine was good. But it didn't let them communicate, didn't let her speak with his soul as she wanted. She would never criticize Omar. You couldn't know when you were seeing your loved ones for the last time.

Or when you would see them again. She remembered the face of the boy in the Sudan, the eyes in the tent.

He emptied the bottle into her glass. The boat rocked, sang with the others to the sigh of the dock. "You saw the birth of Raisha's child."

The Tuareg mother in Mali. She didn't ask him where he'd been, how he had followed them over the desert, across the Niger, along the river with the nomads, to Timbuktu. Or if he'd seen her flee the tent, drenched in sweat. For 204 days, she'd been in solitary confinement with the truth. Many truths.

"I want to know you." He paused. "I think we can be friends."

Her stomach hummed with heat, blood flushing her, seeping, pounding, while her skin reached for the hot quivering vibration. She smelled saltwater, fish, diesel and the scent of a man, carried on his garments. He moved closer on the aluminum locker. Closer.

"Tuareg is an Arabic name," he said. "The nobles call themselves variations of Imighagh, from their verb *iobarch,* which means to be free, to be pure, to be independent. All those things."

She breathed them in. All those things her counted days had come to be about. Tears gathered in her head and hid themselves, exerting pressure she ignored, except to think, *I must be a midwife. I can't be a midwife. I must be free. I'll never be free.* "Do you think Nudar was Tuareg?"

"I doubt it. I want to show you part of how they court. Ideally this would occur in your home, with your parents sleeping nearby. We mustn't wake them."

"Can we wake Omar?"

His nose neared hers. "It's this."

Her arms on his shoulders, his around her. He didn't kiss her, and she wanted it. His scent infused her, carried through the damp air. She breathed him; he breathed her. *No! No!* She wasn't a woman who did this, who would ever think of doing this. She would walk away from any man who made her consider doing this.

Because this was the moment of choosing whether or not to commit adultery, with her husband's blessing.

Backing out of the tent, then away from the desert sun, she drank more wine. Wiped her brow under her hat. The wool itched her skin.

He wanted to be friends. It was the only way this could work. More, and she'd be unhappy when she returned to Omar, dissatisfied with him. Less, and she could not trust. She spoke to a friend. "I'm not sure I want to do this. I'm not sure I can."

He took her empty glass from her. "Breakfast? I'll shop. And cook."

Why not? The trawler was private.

Dru tried to read her watch, from Cartier's, a wedding gift from Omar. Eight-thirty. "I need to phone Omar." Shaking. Shaking so hard. And not at the prospect of walking to the phone. "You're family. It might not be…what he wants."

He showed no reaction. They stood, still shadowed by the canopy. The skin at his throat was dark. Some black chest hairs, where Omar was hairless. "You might think," he said, "of what *you* want."

She released a cable to step down to the dock. But looked back first.

His eyes waited. He knew she might be afraid of the dark. Or, indelibly, of abduction. He would let nothing harm her. With a careless stroke of his gaze, he slayed her fear. His footsteps beside her on the dock were lazy, companionable, the angels of comfort. His warmth reached her through three hundred cubic inches of cold mist.

She could read the blueprint of a kind man.

Briefly, sweeping her hand over a wet and splintered railing, she wished he was cruel. Because she wanted to accept what he offered. And that was reckless.

She stumbled over chewing gum and cigarette butts. Her fears gathered and pressing on her, chanting in the key of doom that she should not. She should not. Dru walked through the chorus, losing his scent somewhere, until she saw the light above the telephone.

She dialed, followed the recorded prompts to enter her card number. Where was Ben? Even under the security lights, she couldn't find him. He must be near, would not have left her. Privacy. In the cold, under the skeletons and monsters of steel, under a dry-docked leviathan, Dru listened to the phone in Nantucket ring. *He won't be home. Again.*

Sergio answered. Then Omar was on the phone.

She felt half-warmth at the sound of his voice. And flatness, distance. Had part of her gone on leave from their marriage? She asked, "Do you really want me to do this?"

His soft laughter reminded her of nights of talk, Omar discussing the stars and the sight of snow on quahog shells and the antiquity of sharks and the intelligence of apes, then slipping past her to philosophy and quantum theory and the history of money and its future and the connections between all these things. "Aren't you really asking if I *don't* want you to do it?" His accent was all Massachusetts. Nantucket. Some people even called him an Islander.

Dru didn't. She was.

She said, "I've met Ben." Her heart pounded. Was Omar afraid, too? Did he know, had he known all along that she would find Ben attractive? Had he— "Did you ask him to be the donor? Did you plan it, Omar?"

"I asked Ben not to let you see him. But if you want him…"

"You know who I want."

"That is a gift in my life. In many cultures, love is considered a sickness, something to be avoided. Marrying for love is frowned upon, because love, particularly sexual love, is unstable, and marriage must endure. So, go forth, Dru, if you want to bear a child. If you develop feelings for the man with whom you conceive this child, even for…my nephew, Ben, they will go away when you return to me. The Chinese cure for lovesickness includes a steady regimen of sex with a person other than the desired object."

"I don't want to be lovesick. And he's a family member."

"It's nothing. Choose who you want."

Her fingers grew stiff, icy, around the receiver. "I guess this is how you create a fortune. Taking this kind of risk."

His voice roughened, a sign of life to her. "I'm sixty-six years old, and you want to make love with my handsome young nephew. This, Dru, is the gamble of my life."

She could tell him she loved him, promise to always love him and say good night. She should. She was cold. But if she let him go...would it ever be the same? "Is that why you're doing it? For the risk?"

"I want a baby. With you. And you have been a midwife and aren't now because of my circumstances, and I won't be responsible for your never bearing a child of your own."

Her sigh echoed under the railways. "You aren't *responsible*. We could adopt."

"I want to raise a child who is part of you, Dru."

"Are you sure you didn't ask him to do it? As a last resort, if no one else would have me?"

A moment. "The possibility that no one would want you has never crossed my mind. I'm going to Curaçao for a few days. I'll be hard to reach. If you need anything, please ask Sergio."

"I love you." She said it almost desperately.

"And I you. Good night, Dru."

Not *my love,* not *dearest.* He was telling her, *Go. Go do it.*

"Omar?"

"Yes."

"Our marriage is a pearl. I feel as though I'll mar it if I do this thing."

"A marriage shouldn't be so frail."

Really. He was guiltless as a conqueror. "Omar, *is* our marriage monogamous?"

"Finance is my mistress, Dru. Give me this gift. A child. And, Dru, it's good to enjoy it."

She hung up. Heard the water beyond the mist.

"What did he say?"

She jumped.

He leaned against a steel piling, needing a shave, his long lean face ending at that cleft chin.

Her cheeks hardened to thin sheets of ice. "Were you listening?"

"With limited success."

She strode past him, toward the docks. He followed, his footfalls silent. Without looking, she knew he was there and said, "You think nothing of sleeping with married women?"

"You would be my first. You're very traditional."

Was she? "I'm an Islander. I suppose you're not," she said. "Traditional."

No reply.

She walked. Heard her own breath. Never his. The moon appeared through clouds, a paler, more genuine sister of the security light. The dock creaked beneath her feet.

Such a frightening sound, behind and around her—her own breath.

At the trawler, he caught her forearm.

Warmth. Hard grip. Sliding to her hand.

Their fingers touched in darkness. He pulled her to him, close enough to smell, then her breasts against his chest. Omar was broad, with a different kind of power. She touched these new shoulders. Each hand fumbled, jerking slightly, removed from her will. She shouldn't touch him.

"Is it because you live in the desert?" She tilted back her head. "Have you not had a woman in so long?"

He watched her, reading her.

"Just tell me," she said. "Have you been traveling with some Oxford scholar or married the daughter of a chief?"

"No chief has offered me a daughter." He dropped his eyes, raised them. "As to the former—no."

"You're a virgin?"

The certainty of his hands denied it. He kissed her forehead. *Omar wants this. Wants me to do this. And Ben wants to help—for Omar.*

His lips pressed between her eyebrows and touched the

bridge of her nose. They nuzzled like animals, and she felt that stirring beneath his jeans. Strong and warm. His mouth touched hers, gently biting her lower lip.

For Omar?

Ben Hall didn't need to give his sperm to her and Omar. His wanting money was unlikely. Omar trusted him, and she'd never known a man so cautious with his trust.

Her body settled against that form under his jeans. Wanting. She should ovulate in a day, maybe two.

The deck was damp, the cabin door dewy. She unlocked it, opened it. She should say just the right thing, in just the right tone. But she wished she could tell him she was scared to death.

The sole bowed and bent beneath her weight. The utilitarian table, flipped up and out of the way. Nothing like a stateroom, just slim berths throughout and a wider berth forward of the galley. "That's it," she said, under a bare bulb.

The light made them naked, even in their clothes, everything so unreal, especially the stranger touching her lip.

"It doesn't have to be good," she said. "For me."

"Doesn't your orgasm increase the chance of conception?" Throwing aside his shell. Unbuttoning his plaid wool shirt. T-shirt underneath.

Her legs turned watery. She switched off the light. The boat was dark, except for the geometric patches of blue-gray from the dock lights and the portholes.

"It's unnecessary." Squeaking words. "I'm fertile; I'll ovulate soon. And I'm really not interested in your patented techniques learned on the women of Africa."

Ghostly blue and black dyed his face. The tilting of his lips was less than a smile. He nudged her toward the narrow berth. A bulkhead beside it had separated, a cheap panel peeling down like banana skin. All smelled damp and old. Only the mattress was new.

"You don't have any diseases, do you?"

A faint shake of his head. He watched her. "You like me?"

Dru swallowed. "Enough." She discarded her sweater. "I don't want you to make love to me. Just sex. I wish I had a turkey baster with me. Why *not* artificial insemination?"

The hard mattress brought her too close to him.

"I wish I knew," she said, "what's in it for you."

His lips tracked her jaw. His hand held her side, fingers spreading, guiding her down. "I can wait till you figure that out." His nose near hers.

"It's so appealing to be wanted as a one-night stand."

"This is not a one-night stand. You're coming back to the Sahara with me. My first three wives will be jealous and cruel to you, but you won't be spending much time with them, anyhow. You and I will make love all day."

His kiss warmed her lips, parting them. Their legs twined, the teeth of two combs fitting together. His skin swallowed her voice. "We weren't going to do it…like that." The words collided, falling on each other, never quite standing up, defeated by coursing blood, mating rites.

He said, "It's the only way I know."

Making love.

He was full of lies.

Dru searched her memory. Did Omar ever press his mouth to her as he spoke? Had they ever spoken this way? She was wild at his smell. At hard limbs. At a man her age. Her ears filled with shrieking winds, the sound of desire. It was evil, so cruel, to want anyone but her husband, the only man she'd ever known.

Evil to think, even for a second, *It's never been like this.*

Hot shivering.

Permission. Omar had given it.

She sat up, shaking rapidly, jerking in blurred time. Her body had not been hers. Almost. It was now. *Mine.* Dru de-

spised Omar, then imagined, then believed, she knew what he
wanted—for her to know this about herself, to come to the
point of refusing his Trojan horse. "Sorry. I can't." She
scrambled her vibrating, quivering body over Ben's and put
her feet on the floor. Yes. The sole. Standing. Swaying. The
hollow tinkling of water on the hull amplified. Unable to speak
for trembling. "I w-won't m-m-make l-l-l-love to anyone
b-b-but m-m-my husband."

He was half up. His powerful body eased out of the berth.
She followed his face, but he never rose. He dropped to the
warped and peeled linoleum, kneeling, stretching himself toward her on the sole like an unwashed man praying in the
desert, not for the end of a sandstorm or for nightfall or shade
or a drink of water or five times a day for God, but for goodness.

She had learned posture at the age of four and then how to
keep her weight low and her head high, how to put grace in
every gesture of her hands, every turn of her head. She had
learned the dances of the Berbers and their nomadic relations,
the Tuareg, of the Bedouins, of the Indians and Egyptians.
There were dances for women and dances for men, dances for
weddings, pregnancy and birth, sickness and death.

His dark head was bowed, and she recalled the advice of
the Chinese, their remedy for lovesickness. For Omar, she
must go home and dance the *guedra,* not the trance dance but
the love dance. And then make love with him.

She did not thank Ben Hall. She said, "You should go."

Slowly, he rose.

"I'm sorry this happened," she said.

He nodded, lips tight. Briefly, he spoke in Arabic. He called
her sister. He told her he loved her.

He told her goodbye as the Arabs do.

Which was to wish her peace.

THE KNOCKING INTERRUPTED her drowsing. She opened her eyes to light from a day she knew, without looking at the portholes beside her, was gray.

"Dru?"

The pants she'd worn the night before were heaped against the locker. She dragged them on and let her long T-shirt do as a top. Climbed from her berth and crossed the decrepit linoleum in her bare feet. To open the cabin door further and let him in.

She squinted at the object he held up.

And swallowed. "Where did you get that?"

"The hospital. The supermarket doesn't get their turkey basters for a few weeks." His cheeks darkened. "I told a nurse that it's...a home project."

If he'd blushed like that, no wonder the nurse had parted with the Tomcat catheter.

He murmured, "So...*Sabah il-kheyr.*" Good morning. "Let's make a baby."

CHAPTER THREE

Skye said she wasn't going anywhere at gunpoint. One of the men, who were mercenaries, yanked my father from our vehicle; my father clutched his arm and chest, crying out, moaning, eyes rolling back. "He's sick!" I said. They shrugged as he fell, threatening to shoot me when I tried to go to him. I opened my door anyhow, because of the things my father had taught me about the nature of men. The gunman yanked me back into the vehicle by the throat. While I choked and coughed and he started the car, another held a Makarov to Dru's head. But before we left, the third man turned the green Land Rover and drove over my father's body.

—Ben, recollections of a fall

Nantucket
One week later
October 23
The office of Daniel Mayhew, Attorney At Law

THE WORDS WERE THERE on the pertinent pages, and Daniel had given each of them a copy to read. After she'd entered the office and Ben had stood, she'd told Daniel that of course they knew each other. *Good to see you,* to Ben. She couldn't say his name again.

Now she studied black text on white paper, blurred in the photocopy machine, but not enough to misread "my natural son, the son of my loins, Ben Omar Hall.'' And the mention of ''other issue…or my wife, Dru-Nudar Haverford Hall, if pregnant at the time of my death…''

She felt Ben's presence as she felt the sun through the clustered window panes, paneling the maple floor and walnut furniture with light. His knees, in jeans, jutted into the slanting edge of one section, brightly lit. The rest of him was in shadow, beyond the edge of her vision unless she twisted her chair. It couldn't matter. Daniel would repeat nothing he saw.

Ben waited, eyes on the attorney.

She could pretend, too, pretend it was no surprise. Even though she wanted to demand, *Did you know? Did you know you were his son?*

Omar had known. Wasn't that bad enough?

''Tell me if I'm right, Daniel.'' Her courtesy was lost, smashed by surprise. ''I understand the provisions for Sergio and others. This is what I want clarified. I will receive, in any case, one hundred thousand dollars a year and the Orange Street House. But whatever is in the attic vault, which I never knew existed, and everything else that Omar didn't give away—we're talking about a lot—will go to…'' It took a long time, seconds, to decide what to call him. She broke her indecision with a sigh. ''…Ben, unless I'm pregnant right now. Since he—Omar—and I have had no child up to this point.''

''Yes.''

Her face must look like a strawberry. Daniel knew as well as everyone else, everyone who had seen the tabloids, about her and Ben. Ben would also receive the contents of a safe deposit box and some other things she'd never known her husband owned. *Did we need the cloak and dagger, Omar?* She held down some high terror that couldn't come from grief. ''How soon must pregnancy be determined?'' Her breath sounded coarse, unladylike, heaving like a horse. A tear hung in one eye. Not about money. Oh, maybe that, too. *Who cares what they think?*

She hated for Ben to see.

She took a handkerchief from her purse. It bore her monogram. Sometimes she'd used Omar's. Still did, at home. She wiped off her invalidated grief. *I want some answers.*

"Because of the size of the estate—" Daniel's eyes rested on her, apologizing "—as soon as an accurate result can be obtained."

"And if I'm pregnant, he and I split the estate?"

"Correct. And the unknown contents of the vault become yours."

The provisions were more complex than that. If she relinquished her rights. If he did. A web engineered to manipulate. Or so it seemed.

Beside her, Ben hadn't moved. Hands on the chair arms. Eyes on Daniel. His face frozen.

Had he known he was adopted—Omar's natural son? If he did…

Dru choked away her fears. Nothing real but this room. The will. "I suppose I'll need a test in a medical facility?"

"Promptly."

She could count. A test might be accurate seven days after conception. Nine to eleven, much better. But they couldn't have succeeded, even with Ben's tenacious effort and repeated donations. Her face heated again as she remembered things said, the emotions of an intimacy without touch, without invasion of each other's sexual privacy, yet throbbing and slippery and quiet with the hunger for friendship. She'd never been closer to a man—brother or lover.

And, all the time, he was Omar's son.

Who on earth was his mother?

Trouble silenced her curiosity. This new development would reach the papers. The world would watch to see…

If she was pregnant.

She said, "I relinquish my share in that portion of the trust."

Keziah's father chuckled sympathetically. "I would advise you strongly against that. But in any case, it's not that simple. If you're pregnant, then Ben—" his nephew, too, son of his wife's brother, one of her brothers "—will receive a smaller portion of the estate in any case."

Why had Omar done this to her? Confusion pressed in her skull. "Well, I might get a test." She shrugged. Pretending. Muddled. "It seems unlikely, though."

Nobody said aloud that she hadn't been in the same room with Omar for seven weeks before his death. The papers would say it for them.

Had Ben known?

Her molars ground against each other.

She smiled at Daniel and rose. "Well, I have other things going on today." Folding her copy of the document. Mitch would tag along while she shopped for things for Oceania. At home, they would write more notes. *Do you want to tell me about the baby's father? I want to help however I can.* Early that morning, Dru had begun looking into what a deaf mother would need. *A father for her child,* she'd thought with a half-sob, *like any other mom.*

A shadow behind her took away the window's light. "Uncle Dan, is there a room where Dru and I could visit?"

The attorney's mouth, Keziah's mouth, opened to get a word out. The word became a drawn-out sound. "Aaaaaahhh. Yes. Yes." Looking around. "Yes, that's possible. Ahhhh. Of course. You may use my office. I'll be in a meeting till one. But, ah, I must caution both of you, absolutely, to surrender no rights regarding this estate. You are both, ah, grieving. This is not the time for rash legal decision-making or, between the two of you, discussion of the estate."

Dru felt it was the perfect time. "Of course." She leaned forward and kissed Daniel's cheek. "Thank you for all your help and compassion. And your good advice."

Walking past her, Ben saw the attorney out and shut the door.

His scent spilled into her. His woolly sweater, a Harvard cardigan that might be from the fifties and must have been Robert Hall's, smelled of dry leaves. Dru wondered who had sewn the moth holes with such skill.

When he turned, his eyes were darker than the walnut paneling. She'd seen the sun shine through them and turn them golden and had reflected that Omar's were the same. She'd never suspected. Keziah had dark eyes, too, like Mary. Her mother. Ben's aunt.

His lips…no, so much about him was not like Omar.

"Explain." She hadn't intended to speak. *Don't stand so close!* Her breath quickened and Dru slowed it deliberately. Yet she trembled. "I'm glad I never slept with you. You're my *stepson.*"

"No." As angry as she was.

"You didn't know?"

"Sit down."

She moved woodenly. They chose each other's chairs.

Dru shivered in the sun. "My dogs are outside. With Mitch. I guess it's all right."

"We can go somewhere else."

No. Not now. "You didn't know."

"I was never told. I've known…my whole life. My father— took me to live among the Bedouin when I was a baby. My mother, Alma—" he fell quiet "—died in the desert, and a Bedouin woman nursed me. 'Ben' is Hebrew, but it means the same as 'Bin.' I am named Ben Omar, Son of Omar." He gave her a lineage in a dialect she did not know. "People in our family say I look like Omar. Other things." Flat. "When

I was nine years old, he gave me his father's dagger, brought over from Libya during the war.''

''You never spoke of it? Even with your fath—with your—''

''Father.'' Cold.

A picture flashed. Skin. The sensation of heat, of kissing, swallowing each other. Then, gone. Her stomach turned over. Her mouth filled with saliva, her breath altered. Love had briefly ridden over her vows. Though her husband, in pursuit of a child, had allowed even lovesickness. He'd surely never imagined the trawler, Ben's trips to the aft stateroom or the head to emerge holding that brown mug, a replica of a Nantucket lightship basket, the mug containing his sperm, nor Dru retiring alone to her berth, propping her hips up with pillows. Or the awkward, private, unforgettable tenderness between those times, when they were waiting, waiting till he felt ready again. He would cook her North African dishes and suddenly leave her to tend the stove while he took the cup away. Cup of gold. She wondered what made him come.

Five inseminations one day, three the next. She'd been fragile as eggshell, steaming with feeling, when she'd called home, keeping her marriage, and Sergio had told her Omar was dead.

''Alma was your natural mother?'' she asked. Had Omar slept with his brother's wife? *Why did you never tell me, Omar? Why did you never acknowledge your son?*

''She nursed me. I look nothing like her. It's possible, I've thought, that she and my father had a stillbirth immediately before they adopted me. But why was that a secret? Any of it? Incidentally—'' heat burned each word ''—adoption is anathema to the Bedouin. They can't conceive of it, the way you can't conceive of circumcising your daughters.''

As the Rashaida did. She didn't quibble about word choice with him, though the word, in the case of the Rashaida, was *infibulation.* Facts she'd picked up as an adult. She'd known nothing of it then.

Ben brought her back. "But he wasn't a Bedouin, except by birth. This is the greatest proof."

The greatest proof, Dru wondered, *that he didn't love you?* She could probe that wound no more. He couldn't know the identity of his natural mother. He had lived with that. Without searching records? He was a journalist.

Perhaps he hadn't wanted to know.

Dru swiveled her chair. Kept her voice down although the office was soundproof. "So you knew, and Omar knew." Her husband's name ached with this lie. *But he wanted a child of mine, wanted me to bear a child, in some deep love for me.* And she had wanted it, too. Such a pointless lie. Incomprehensible. "Neither of you saw fit to tell me." She released the top buttons of her suit jacket, then remembered she wore only a camisole beneath. And a Tuareg amulet. Perspiration chilled the silk between her shoulder blades.

A long time passed, a long time for both of them to spin their chairs and study shelves of law volumes, reading tragic stories in the ominous titles.

"Hungry?" he asked.

"No." She averted her face, controlling its tremble, the wetness of her eyes. Nothing to cry for. No Gloucester memories of Ben and no tears for Omar, who had encouraged this. Just anger. "You deceived me." Her mouth became an oracle of truth. "We weren't lovers, but you were willing. You gave me your sperm, and you never told me you were my husband's son." She rose. "Imagine when the world learns who I was with in those affectionate poses. Not my distant cousin, after all. You can do nothing to make me forgive you except disappear from the face of the earth. Was this a way of getting Omar's attention? Trying to seduce his wife? Or did the two of you plan it? I hate you! If Omar had lived, there would be a contest for who I hate the most. But he's dead, so it's you. Death ended my marriage, and you have ruined my memories.''

''He and I never talked about it, Dru. He asked me to look after you.''

Beside his chair, she paused. ''I'm so glad to hear you were acting alone. Each of you.''

He rose to stand between her and the doorway, bigger than her. Or Omar.

He spoke fast, urgently, so that she pictured him speaking for Tuareg refugees, begging a soldier for the life of a slave or a blind man, risking his life with his words. He said, ''These are the reasons I gave you my sperm, as you say. I resemble Omar Hall. I carry his genes. It was a gift to him. You told me you wanted Omar's child. This seemed close. It was also meant as a gift to you. I have no wife and didn't anticipate marrying. I was very close to you as a child. I find you beautiful and intelligent. I imagined the mingling of you and me. That was a gift to me. Those were my reasons.''

''There was never a moment when it bothered you that your father had abandoned you and three decades later married a woman younger than you?''

''Many moments.''

''You did this with no consideration of that taboo in nearly every culture?''

''You're not my mother and never were. Am I your son?''

No. No. Till this revelation. ''It's no better than Oedipus slaying his father and sleeping with his mother. In some ways, it's worse, because you and Omar knew. Did you never fear this moment?'' She pushed past him, careening into his side. Hard. Into muscle and warmth.

''What if you're pregnant?''

Her mind tilted, falling into the forbidden place, the hell place in which she'd yielded to a walk on the beach, trying to cool the sizzling wires of their project, trying to end a tension that had made her snap at him for putting a salt shaker where she couldn't find it. The touches on the beach, the frightening closeness for which she despised herself, were caught on film without their knowing. Although no one but the two of them heard their words. His. *How many camels must I pay for you?*

She had stridden away, had had to cling to the dock railing, nauseous, spinning, before she boarded the trawler again. Standing there beside her, his hands in his pockets, he'd said, *I'm sorry. I was flirting. I won't anymore. I get a little worked up...* A gesture toward the trawler. Toward the brown mug neither could see.

She could smell him now, touch him by a shift of her chest or her hips. "I don't want that for a child."

"What?"

"This is academic." Her voice was high. "But he or she won't be yours. Because if Unproven Baby exists, Said Baby will take no pleasure in the fact that Baby's mother made Baby via the turkey-baster method—or any other method—with husband's son. Something neither you nor Omar considered."

She zipped her purse, closing the will inside.

"Dru."

Counting his eyelashes would take her a day. She would never find another man so attractive. She would never believe again.

He asked, "Would you want the baby?"

Her heart gave a thud. Ben had been deserted by at least one parent. Even in their closest moments in Gloucester, his trust had been that of a wild animal.

Omar's eyes disturbed her now. She saw the differences in Ben's, the way they were still like Keziah's, his cousin's. She remembered all the good things she'd believed Ben to be. Were they changed by this?

It didn't matter. "Yes." She would want the baby. Precious baby. Not Omar's because—

"And me?" he said quietly. "How many camels?"

Not flirting now.

She twisted the door handle.

He held the door shut, above her head. "I'd never said the words aloud in my life—that he was my father. What if my suspicion was wrong, if I'd imagined it? I believed I would never see you again. He never acknowledged me till he died. And, truly, what we did seemed best for your wishes."

His shirt was made of fabric that looked handwoven. Her gaze fell into the weave, the refuge of the trivial.

"If there's a baby," he said, "we work on things together."

"Oh, the various permutations are clear." She raised her head. "If there's a baby, I receive half of what would have been yours. But as soon as you accept your inheritance, everyone will know you're Omar's son. They already believe you were my lover. And that is this child's future. If there is a child. Only if you sacrifice your interest in Omar's assets and let everything go to his charities, everything but whatever is in the vault I live with and have never seen and the safe-deposit box and a boat and whatever other artifacts he had tucked away and never told me about—only then can the fact he's your natural father be kept secret. But if I keep my interest, that means the baby was conceived before Omar died. And I wasn't with him, of course. So for the Unknown Baby not to know of the turkey baster days during my previous marriage, I should sacrifice my half by not being pregnant at the time of his death." She took a breath.

"And I, mine."

"That's up to you. But the answer to 'How many camels?' is all of your father's camels, yours and mine. Twelve billion dollars to Omar's charities. But I don't even like you. I don't think I could be physically intimate with you. As far as I can tell, you are completely without character. I would hate to marry another man like that. Goodbye." The impulse against which Daniel Mayhew had warned surfaced, and she seized it. "In any case, rest assured that the bulk of the inheritance is yours. I could not possibly have conceived a child before Omar's death."

He smiled a little, and she wanted to know why but didn't ask.

He offered his hand. "I'm sorry to meet you again under such sad circumstances. I'm Ben Hall, your cousin. We knew each other in Africa when we were children. At which time, we became betrothed."

Her mind flickered on the word "marriage," a marriage he'd mentioned that she couldn't remember at all. The thought was fleeting, and she dismissed it forever. She didn't touch his hand but turned the doorknob and fled, wondering if this was how abandonment felt.

SHE RETURNED HOME with a sweater and nightgown and some soft cotton nursing clothes for Oceania, and with blankets and little T-shirts and diapers for the baby.

She didn't want to think of the birth. It would take place in Oceania's room, where Dru had moved a beanbag chair and many large pillows, the kinds of props useful during labor. If only they had the immediate safety of the labor and delivery suite, as well. But the hospital was just a few minutes' drive away.

She trembled through the day, phoning Daniel's office for another appointment, telling him what she wanted, listening to the baby's heart, asking Oceania questions in nearly illegible handwriting.

Do you want to say who the father is?

Adam Peltier. I'll put it on the birth certificate.

He knows you're pregnant?

Don't know where he is.

Finally she asked, *How do deaf women take care of their babies?*

Very well.

Dru smiled. Scrawled, *What do you do? Are you a student?*

There was a long pause. Oceania's gaze flicked upward and to the left.

Dru was going to get a story, and she saw the man in Gloucester and wrote angrily, *Forget it.*

Oceania stole back the pen. *I work for Sedna.*

While Oceania continued writing, Dru's spine stretched higher. Sedna? They were ecopirates, environmental radicals, whose business was protecting the sea and who had named themselves for the Eskimo woman whose father had caused her to drown by cutting off her fingers that clung to the side of his boat. Sedna had sunk to the bottom and become the creatures of the sea, feeding the people what she felt they should have and no more.

The mission of the Sedna environmentalists was to decrease commercial fishing worldwide. Tristan couldn't possibly have known Oceania's background, or he would never have helped her. Dru couldn't quite share his point of view. Overfishing was stripping the ocean of animals, working its way down the food chain to take everything.

Distracted, she fell into the distant past. That fight the evening before her father's last trip. Blows among non-violent people. And accusations. His imprudence, his *absence*, her—

Oceania thrust the notebook toward Dru.

It's a volunteer position. I get room and board, so to speak. I'm a photographer and navigator. The flagship is equipped with aids. They were donated by the companies that make them.

Dru wished she knew ASL. She tried to foresee everything Oceania might want to get across during the birth and everything she and Keziah would need to tell her. Omar's absence, the rooms without him, began to seem normal. His deception had broken her mourning prematurely and swept it away. Yet fragments remained like glass shards waiting for her bare feet.

Daniel came over at five-thirty, as a courtesy because of her distress. In Omar's office, he said, "Are you sure? Understand that the will simply allows for pregnancy, with no—"

"I understand." Freedom hovered close, tantalizing. This house was hers—though she would sell it. Buy something smaller, perhaps in 'Sconset, near Keziah. No…not 'Sconset. Ehder pressed against her knees. He and Femi needed a yard. But the press would leave her alone now. Once she relinquished Omar's wealth, the media would lose interest.

She read the document Daniel had prepared, in which she declared that she was not pregnant…and would not contest the rights of other beneficiaries. Sergio came to witness it. His Greek eyes smiled at her afterward, with a certain sadness. She asked him to stay after the attorney left. To tell him she must put the house on the market. Even with her own money, gifts from Omar and earned in the stock market, the taxes would be too much. Besides, she wanted somewhere smaller— somewhere else. Without Mitch or Sergio…or memories.

My new life, the freedom whispered.

The older man, who had served Omar for thirty-five years, spoke first, which he had never done before. "If you will permit me… Mrs. Hall, your husband has provided generously for me. But if you have any use for an assistant, I would be happy to work for you, even temporarily, for the comfort of room and board. If you have no need of me, I will, when the estate is settled, return to my family in Greece."

Omar had given Sergio an annual income only slightly less than Dru's. He could do anything now, and his loyalty touched her. Ben's face froze in her mind. Sergio must know him, too.

He must have come here to see Omar.... And spoken to Sergio about the clothing for the grave.

"Your offer is so kind, Sergio. Thank you. Perhaps, till the house sells?"

The affection in his eyes was as a father for a daughter. "As long as you need me, Mrs. Hall."

The next day was another of speaking with servants, making plans. Although Omar had made her a generous allowance for the period until his estate was settled, Dru walked a tightrope between giving the servants fair notice and conserving her own resources.

Keziah came over to see Oceania, to help ease any of the mother's fears before the birth. Dru wished she'd help talk Oceania out of a home birth. But Keziah would never do that. Dru had told her about the meconium in the amniotic fluid at Rika's birth. Described trying to ease the breathing of a stressed baby two hundred miles from land, let alone the nearest hospital.

Keziah embraced Dru at the door, and they sat high up on the spiral stairwell to talk. "How is it?"

Keziah, she could trust. But she had to keep secrets, between her and Ben and the executor—Keziah's father. For the baby. *There is no baby.* She choked down her confessions, buried them. She said only that if she was not pregnant and there was no child, the bulk of Omar's wealth went elsewhere. That was how it would be. "And Keziah." She slumped against a white spindle. "I'm so glad."

Keziah's thick auburn hair struck her lightly. "Will you go back to New Bedford now? Or practice here with me?"

There were barely clients for one midwife on Nantucket, let alone two. Keziah supplemented her income with belly-dancing classes for pregnant women and by working as a doula, helping mothers during and after their births with labor support, breastfeeding help, help around the house—anything to ease the stress and increase the joy in having a new baby. But the Nantucket physicians were not appreciative of Keziah, at least in the role of home birth midwife.

Dru faced her friend, intent on giving reassurance. But her lips wouldn't move. If she resumed a practice it would be in conjunction with the hospital. For many reasons. Not just a single nerve-wracking birth at sea. "I would have a fight here," she said. "But I want to stay on-island. Close to my family. Thank you for your very sweet and, I know, impulsive offer."

"It stands," said Keziah.

They embraced.

Minutes later, the midwives listened to the baby's heart, another sound Oceania could not hear. Dru performed a vaginal exam on Oceania, feeling no fear, just thin steel inside herself, the core of memory. The baby's head was engaged, left occiput anterior. Size consistent with thirty-eight weeks.

Dru had put away her photos of Omar.

She set out pictures of her father. Everywhere Oceania would see.

MINUTES AFTER KEZIAH LEFT, Sergio handed Dru a fax. It was from the *Him,* the Blade Institute's research vessel, where Dru had attended the births of Cecily and Rika Blade. Jean and David had sent flowers for Omar's funeral. Now, Jean wrote:

Hi Dru:

I apologize for bringing this up right now. Did you get my last fax? I'm due December tenth. David and I had hoped to winter in Nantucket. We're looking at scallop harvest.

I know how soon this is, but is there any chance you could be induced (no pun intended) to attend the birth?

I've seen OB/GYNs in Nova Scotia and Newfoundland,
and everything looks good.

But she needs prenatal care now! Meconium in the amniotic
fluid—the color of Rika's water—indicated stress some time
before labor. And what had that stress been? With the kind of
work they did, David sometimes using submersibles at great
depth, anything was possible. Working as marine researchers
had some of the same risks as fishing. Nonetheless, the presence of meconium couldn't be accurately detected prenatally
by any non-invasive method.

Please fax back, my midwife. You saved Rika's life, and
I want you.

Love,
Jean

Sergio, still nearby, asked Dru if she would like him to reply.
She couldn't repeat the mistake she'd made in agreeing to
serve as Oceania's birth attendant. Between Keziah and the
proximity of the hospital, she had grown comfortable with the
prospect of Oceania's home birth. But only under similar conditions could she agree to Jean's. She made a note to drive
that day, to count the minutes from the Orange Street house
to the hospital. "I'll write her myself. Thank you, Sergio."
    And tell her, Dru decided, to sit in warm water twenty
minutes a day. That would increase the fluid volume—just in
case this baby released meconium, too.

Late that afternoon
October 24

"THAT'S ALL HE LEFT YOU?" Joanna Haverford had drawn her
pale hair into a braid. She looked closer to forty than fifty-
five, even in the bright light flooding through her front win-

dows, just two doors down from Dru's house. Whaling murals surrounded the walls, and Dru automatically played the childhood game she'd shared with Tristan, disappearing into the wall scene as a ship's captain hunting a great whale with the nature of Moby Dick. Unfortunately, now, she could imagine the blood, the gory decks. Now her whales always won. "I'm appalled," said her mother.

"It's complicated." Dru shrugged. "I really don't know what's going to happen to the estate." She couldn't tell her mother about Ben. No reason to get into it. Her bathroom cabinet was full of pregnancy test kits. She did not use them, deliberately avoided them, almost threw them away. *I'm not pregnant.* The chances with a Tomcat catheter and eight inseminations over two days just weren't that good.

"Where else did he leave his money? Was it a tax problem?"

"I have the house. You can imagine what that's worth."

"If you sell it!"

Tristan's daughter slipped through the opened double doors and flopped down on a couch with a scroll back. Keri held a stack of art sheets on her knee. One thing, Dru thought, that Tristan did right for his daughter. At sea he made pictures for her. Pen and ink, colored pencils, paint, sometimes engine grease. And she made pictures for him.

"Keri," said her grandmother, "Dru and I are having a talk. Could you please give us some privacy?"

"Everything will work out, Mom." Dru's voice was a whisper. "Come here, kiddo." On the couch. She and her mother invited Keri to sit between them, to look at Tristan's pictures for his daughter—the clean lines of an anchor—men hauling up fish. And her new batch for him, the talent passed on. A mermaid daughter and a merman father. Keri on the widow's walk of this house.

Tristan. Just come home.

When Keri's pictures had been admired, her rising was slow, one foot, then the other. "Dru, will you dance with me later?"

"Dru doesn't feel like dancing, honey. Her husband has died." As Keri left the room, Joanna added wryly, "I didn't dance for years after I lost Turk." Her face grew slack, eyes closed. Her expression betrayed things more complicated than sorrow.

Dru's heart pounded. Oceania. The man in Gloucester. But she couldn't tell her mother. Four other Nantucket men had died when that boat went down. Four dead, two with wives, one with babies. *He can't be alive.* He was the fifth.

And the fight—Tristan throwing himself at his father, almost snarling like an animal.

Joanna's *Tristan, darling, Daddy will never hurt me. It's all right, honey.*

Her twin's bald profanity, until her father had ordered him to his room. Out of the upstairs hall that had become like a stage set.

"Honey—" Joanna was southern, no islander, and indifferent to the fact "—do you want to say what all happened with Ben? Now, I'm only prying because of this business about the estate."

And from experience? Dru wondered bitterly. There were reasons, real reasons, her father might have wanted to disappear. "Omar and I loved each other." She'd meant to sound certain. In Gloucester, Ben had told her about Bedouin genealogy, that one had children, in part, to continue the line. Omar had stopped being a Bedouin in childhood, the death of his family so painful that he wouldn't speak of it. Yet he'd retained elements of a tradition as firmly held as Nantucket's own.

Easing back in her chair, Joanna waited, her posture like that of a model relaxing with a cigarette.

The tall portrait of Nudar reigned over the dark end of the room, over the piano.

"He hardly knew a mother's love," mused Joanna. "I haven't seen him for years. Good-looking scamp."

Ben. She meant Ben. "I'd rather not talk about it." Her voice was desiccated.

Joanna eyed her. "This estate business—it didn't have anything to do—"

She stopped.

Dru trembled. *With what?* Did Joanna know that Ben was Omar's son?

Dru didn't ask. She didn't want anyone else she loved to lie to her.

Joanna jumped. Stared. Shook her head. "What are you talking about? Does it have something to do with Ben?"

Was her mother acting? Dru whispered, "I'm so tired of people lying to me."

Joanna frowned.

Shaky with exhaustion, Dru stood, hugged and kissed her mother. "I need a nap. I'll see you soon."

"Darling?" Joanna peered up, stretched to touch her cheek to her daughter's. "You and Tristan are the most precious people in my life. Events always unfold as they're meant to." And she asked softly, "Is there anything I can do to make things better?"

Dru saw the trawler, heard Omar all but telling her to sleep with Ben. *How could he?* When she knew what kind of underwear and deodorant he preferred? When he woke her with a murmur from bad dreams? When they'd danced together with such pleasure at charity balls? When they'd held hands, watching the dogs run on the beach, dogs brought to America by Ben, his son?

"Oh, darling. Dru, whatever you do, when you walk out of this sadness, you must live."

Dru left in the lethargy of grief. She wandered back up the brick sidewalk unmolested. She dreaded meeting another face and wanted only sleep. Mourning the way things had once seemed, she became a sleepwalker. She dreamed nightmares and memories in her waking hours every day, except when she slept. That was peace.

Eight days after Omar's funeral, just after breakfast, Oceania found Dru in the garden with Ehder and Femi and signed that she was in labor.

OCEANIA'S EYES GLOWED as she and Dru climbed the staircase together. She seemed both excited and frightened, neither unusual. Calming words were on Dru's lips. Instead, at the stair landing, she turned toward Oceania. "Hospital? I'll be with you."

Oceania shook her head, frowning at the betrayal.

Dru touched her arm and met her eyes. She enunciated each word. "This is the hardest work any human ever does, and you'll do it. When you have, you'll know you can do anything."

From Oceania's bedroom, Dru phoned Keziah. She made the bed with plastic-wrapped sheets she'd sterilized in the oven. Oceania's contractions were still mild and several minutes apart, so Dru showed her belly dancing movements. She demonstrated bending her knees, lifting and lowering each hip, isolating movements. Step by step, she began teaching Oceania the Birth Dance, hearing the music in her own mind, then tapping the rhythm on the floor with a chair leg as Oceania began to dance. At first, Oceania laughed. Then her face grew still. She reached her head high, as though stretching to heavenly realms. When a contraction came, her eyes lit with the sensation.

Oceania had indicated that she was a fast typist, so Dru had brought in her laptop and set it to a large font for communication in labor. Her own hands were clumsy with the little sign language she'd learned.

When Keziah arrived, Oceania was four centimeters dilated. Oceania had just stood, which had become her pattern, for a contraction. She also sometimes chose to go in and squat on the toilet. As labor intensified, Keziah worked on acupressure points to ease pain, and Dru helped Oceania into more comfortable positions.

She did not progress, and Dru's limbs tensed. Like a curse, tension and impatience burst through her. Distracting herself, she grasped for any other thought. Even Omar. Making love to Omar, which had been dear to her because it meant so much to him.

So much that he encouraged you to do it with someone else?

The birth demanded her presence. Birth did not allow daydreaming, though it allowed coursing adrenaline, even in a midwife. What if they couldn't get to the hospital? What if there was a cord prolapse? What if…?

Beside her, Keziah sang to the woman who could not hear, and her utter lack of urgency enraged Dru.

Keziah, who must have spent hours this past week increasing her ASL vocabulary, signed, *Shower?* Oceania pulled herself to her feet, strode strongly toward the door, tearing off her nightgown. The bathroom didn't adjoin the room, not like the luxurious master suite. Dru and Keziah waited in the hall outside the bathroom, and Keziah slowly shook her head at Dru, then reached for her hands and forearms to massage them.

Dru pulled away, meeting brown eyes like Ben's. "I'm fine."

"Oh, right. Why don't you go in the studio and dance it off, whatever it is? Is this about Jean's birth?"

Dru tossed her braid back over her shoulder. "I'm just preparing for any emergency that could happen in this setting. I'm thinking ahead."

"You're making the mother tense, and it feels like fear. *Believe me.* Go dance."

There was hardly a time when they hadn't known each other. Eleven years ago, Keziah had given birth to her daughter while Dru looked on, until the shoulders were stuck, the midwife frozen. Then Dru had urged and helped Keziah to her hands and knees and pulled the newborn girl free, slimy, wet, perfect. They were both twenty.

Dru had changed from a major in Arabic to nursing two days later. Her vocation had called her.

Now, here they stood, with a woman in labor, her friend telling her that she was an impediment to the birth. Dru spoke curtly. "I'm sure you're right. Would you like to take over?" Her own inefficacy gathered up her dreams and flushed them into black muck. If she was afraid, it was that her days as a midwife were over.

"Is that what you want?" Keziah asked. "For me to manage the birth?"

Nothing could matter here but Oceania and her baby.

How odd to find herself in this puzzle when she had done all the right things at Rika's birth, as well or better than they would have been done in a hospital. Yes, things could go very wrong in a hospital. At a hospital, none of the nurses or doctors could give their entire energy, their whole energy, to the mother and baby, because they had others to serve, as well, and as they walked the halls they would find themselves thinking of what was in the freezer at home or which day they should have a broken headlight replaced or if they could get away for golf on Saturday.

Dru spoke from ancient memory, issuing her request to Keziah. "This problem I'm having, whatever it is, mustn't interfere with the birth. If it does, signal me, and I'll leave the room. For now, I'll prepare the herbs downstairs. I'll be your assistant. I want Oceania nourished in every way."

"You need to purge that fear, Dru. It's eating away inside you. I see it in your eyes."

"My husband just died. Maybe that's what you're seeing."

Oceania emerged from the bathroom, naked and ripe, thick white towels against her. She was beautiful, so obviously laboring, that her presence flooded both midwives with a sense of peace. Dru felt this, too, the sacred honor of being present.

In the bedroom, they practiced the birth dance again, with kettledrums Dru moved from her studio; Oceania could feel the beat through the floor. Her arms and hips flowed in a natural motion. She bent her knees deeply in the original dance of labor, of bringing forth. Until a contraction. Slow, stop. Clench.

Dru signed to her for a loose mouth, showed her own mouth. Dru herself had become completely present and remained there by the practice of tranquility, refusing to leave and visit places of fear.

Dancing. Slow, hypnotic, Keziah's singing from another century, another place, until Oceania made sounds with her lips and mouth. Her midwives encouraged her, knelt before her, signed her beauty and power. Hours passed. Oceania tried hands and knees, tried reclining in the beanbag chair. Dru never noticed the sweat on her own brow or under the sleeves of her sweatshirt. When Oceania reached eight centimeters, Dru covered the pine floor with more sterilized sheets, preparing for the birth.

She cried out, in strange screams, unlike any Dru had heard. Dru held her hand. Checked the baby's heart. Recorded everything.

Oceania left the bed abruptly and squatted over the sheet on the floor. Unguarded, Dru remembered Omar's sharp brown eyes and sharp features. Omar embracing her. *No, don't.*

Help this woman. She sat before her to make sure Oceania touched the baby's head.

Into Dru's ear came a harsh cry, inarticulate and primal. It came with defecating, projectile vomiting, a deluge of amniotic fluid and meconium and blood that showered Dru's chinos and sweatshirt and deflected up to hang in her long black hair. Keziah embraced the shuddering mother, supporting Oceania as Dru caught the head and shoulders born too fast, the baby there with his mother's scream.

A baby's head and body. Then, somewhere unique to her, Dru heard screams, such screams. A tent in the sand. Heat. A boy's dark eyes above his straight nose and the gag over his mouth. His dusty braids. And much later, Tristan's new marks, red, one infected, or maybe he'd gotten rheumatic fever some other way.

The newborn rested in Dru's arms. She'd suctioned him. *Oh, sweet baby.* Wrapping him in a sterile cotton baby blanket to hand to Oceania, who trembled as she took him. Who cried, her eyes reaching upward with joy in the precious gift she held.

"WHAT ARE YOU going to name him?" Keziah showed Oceania the home birth certificate, then signed to her. There would be other legal paperwork elsewhere.

Dru rocked the eight pound four-ounce boy, her breasts and womb aching. But she could take pleasure in Oceania's happiness.

Oceania turned to the computer, and Keziah read to Dru what she'd typed. "Dru, what did you say is the name of your father?"

"Turk." She kept from shaking, blacked out the night before he'd left for the last time. "Tristan Kirk Haverford." She eased onto the bed beside Oceania, ready to give her the baby after she'd typed the information into the computer.

Oceania wrote *Tristan Drew Mulcahey*. She turned and met Dru's eyes with unspoken emotion in hers and reached for her newborn.

Four days later
November 2

WE'RE GOING TO NOVA SCOTIA, Oceania wrote. *I have family there.*

Can you use my e-mail to contact them? Or shall I phone? Would you like me to buy the ticket?

Could you please make the reservation? And tell the airline people I'm deaf. Carrying Tristan Drew, as she called him, Oceania walked slowly to her knapsack of belongings, withdrew a woven wallet and a Visa card in her own name.

Dru reread the words on the computer screen. She wanted to write, *Please tell me. Why did you ask my father's name? Why did you really name your baby after Tristan and me?* But that was clear. They'd helped Oceania and her child.

And Oceania had written to her days ago: *I thought my work for Sedna was everything. I believe so much in saving the fisheries; my family was poor because of commercial fishing and subsequent restrictions in catch. They are taking everything—every last bit from the sea. But Tristan Drew is so precious. I never imagined.* And she wept as she wrote, then turned immediately to stare at her son, in love with him as no other human would ever be.

Now Dru dared herself to write, *Your friend from Nova Scotia. Has he gone back? Maybe he could go with you on the plane.*

No. He's gone. On a ship.

Dru pressed her lips together. As Oceania lay down on the bed to nurse, she heard footsteps on the stairs.

Sergio.

She met him halfway.

"You have a call," he said. "From Mr. Hall."

Ben.

Her body shuddering, warm, she hurried down to Omar's office.

Sitting in Omar's deep leather chair, she picked up the phone.

He wasted no time. "How are you?"

"I'm busy. Do you need something?"

"I need to know if you're pregnant."

She didn't consider his motives, didn't care what they were.

"I need your word," he added, "that you'll tell me if you are."

"As I recall—" her voice cracked as she stared at a sailing photo on the wall "—you're difficult to reach. In which North African country shall I find you?"

Quiet from him now. "You'll find me in 'Sconset. Anytime you like." Then, "I never meant to hurt you."

"You didn't," she replied. *I hurt myself.*

She hung up wishing she'd said something different, wishing there was room for something different between them.

November 10

THE WIND WHIPPED the beach below 'Sconset, grazing the tide-flattened sand. A nor'easter churned the granite sea. Two tall figures walked on the wet shore, hoods over their heads, while two leggy dogs raced ahead of them. Their athletic shoes left sharp imprints and crunched the broken shells. At Codfish Park, Dru had decided, they could walk on the beach in pri-

vacy. She'd just returned from the airport, from seeing Oceania and her baby off, knowing that airline staff would help them
all the way to Nova Scotia. Oceania had promised to write,
and Dru had sent her home with a laptop.

"Femi!" The dog was about to eat a dead shore bird but
stopped and looked back at Dru. Both dogs had excellent recall, Azawakhs more manageable than many other sighthounds
in that respect. "Femi, come!"

"I remember when Ben got them." Keziah shouted to be
heard. It was the first time she'd said her cousin's name.

Dru petted Femi, praising her. *Ben who?* No. Keziah deserved better, deserved more. Dru glanced toward her friend.

Black eyes stared out from pale angular features, the stark
lines of beauty, forever beauty. Keziah's hood topped a dark
gray wool cape, as stark and cheerless as the plain clothing of
those who had settled the island. As she stepped around a hill
of seaweed, a long lock of hair the hue of purpleheart escaped
her hood and flew free. "Okay." Keziah smiled. "You're not
curious. You know all about it."

Dru knew that Ben had brought the Azawakhs to the U.S.
for Omar to give her as a wedding gift. She was silent. She
and Keziah had grown up racing over the island on their bicycles, splitting up Dru's Radio Shack walkie-talkies. Following the summer people, just like Harriet the Spy and Beth
Ellen.

"You know, if you love Ben—"

"You've never mentioned him to me till now." Dru's out-
burst sounded like an accusation.

"You haven't always been around when he visited Nantucket. Before your wedding, he came to bring Ehder and
Femi, although he couldn't stay. We kept them for him—or
Omar—before the wedding. Nudar—" her daughter, the baby
girl Dru had maneuvered from Keziah's body with the help

of grace, named for the first Nudar ''—loved the puppies. Ben brought us Tuareg jewelry.''

Dru knew the bracelet. Envied Keziah.

''And of course, he's a neighbor. He has Uncle Robert's house, his dad's place.''

Yes. She knew that. In 'Sconset. The same house where Omar had grown up after the war.

''Keziah.'' As Femi raced after Ehder, Dru clutched her friend's arm. Heads closer than the wind. ''My hus—'' Stopping. Afraid to go on.

Keziah stopped, faced Dru. ''It's fine. Just let me be happy for you when the time comes.''

Dru breathed in, holding all her secrets.

As they walked, Keziah said, ''Will you try to get a place at the hospital?'' Abrupt shift of subject. ''You said you're staying on-island.''

Beach fences warped by the sand, the harbor covered in ice, all the seasons she would not miss. She would grow old here. Alone.

How many camels?

She didn't hate him now, today. Even if she believed him malicious, it always had to do with Omar, that he might have wanted revenge against Omar. And she could not blame him, with Omar going to such lengths to conceive a child. There must be a labyrinth inside Ben stocked with Minotaurs.

A place at the hospital?

''Yes,'' Dru answered. Like that. Entering into competition with her friend. But it wasn't competition! *I can help her gain acceptance at the hospital.*

Right. Dru had no relationship there herself. And these midwifery campaigns were wars, with battle after battle, change coming only after years and constant political turmoil. She'd seen other midwives go through it again and again, had kept in touch with them by e-mail and heard their blow-by-blow accounts. A CNM fired, a traditional midwife arrested, a physician who'd supported midwifery losing hospital privileges, having to relocate.

"You're always welcome in my practice." Stiff, straight Keziah, working so hard to support her daughter, sometimes waiting tables and cleaning the homes of summer people, whatever she had to do. Slowly marking off the clinical hours she needed to become a member of the American Herbalists' Guild. Offering to split her small income from midwifery.

"Thank you." Dru closed her eyes. "It goes without saying that the clients I want are not yours. I'd like to see a place for midwifery in the hospital here, integrating with your practice. I know this might hurt your business. But it might help. And it's a personal decision for me, to allow the possibility of midwife-attended births in Nantucket Hospital."

"I sincerely wish you luck," murmured Keziah. "The doctors would like to see me hanged as a witch." With sadness, resignation, in her voice, she remarked, "It's so bad here I've thought of going somewhere else. They hate home birth and hate traditional midwives. It might improve things, Dru, if they accepted you, if you can get that far with them. Have you heard back from Jean?"

Dru had told her about the fax, about the plan for the two of them to handle the birth together. The Blades paid well. *He inherited all of Skye's money.* Skye… The screaming at Oceania's birth returned to her. She hadn't told Keziah what had happened in the Sudan. Ever. Even twenty years ago, when she and Tristan had come home from Africa, months after Skye's return to California. Back then, Dru had said only that Tristan's scars, the initiation, were his choice. She'd said all the things she still said, the same story, two decades later.

"Dru?"

Keziah had asked about Jean. If she'd replied.

"Yes. It's all set. They're headed for Gloucester, then here." Her thoughts drifted.

The vault. She'd visited the attic. The vault mentioned in Omar's will was real. Expensive. The size of a refrigerator. What was in there?

Skeletons…

Dru checked her watch. "I promised to see my mother and Keri. I'm running up to Gloucester tomorrow." Messages for Tristan. He was returning to port prematurely. She needed to talk with him, to hug him, to tell herself he would not die at sea as her father had.

To tell him their father had not died at sea.

Keziah worried a hole in the left pocket of her cape. "He loves fishing more than he loves his daughter." Her disapproval reached for miles, like a lighthouse beam.

She hadn't always been like this. Dru remembered another Keziah, whose fiancé hadn't yet died before they could be married. A Gloucester man. Drowned off a gillnetter, in a squall. Dru had never met him. She'd been at school when Keziah met Halloran. One name. Irish illegal immigrant. Nudar's father. Keziah had tried to trace relatives in Ireland without success. He'd gone by the one name. *Full of blarney,* she'd murmured, sadness in her eyes.

Her eyes had changed in eleven years. "Can he do anything but fish?"

"It's his life. It was my father's." *My father, my father. I must tell Tristan.* During the days in Gloucester with Ben, she'd never seen her brother. Omar had died before the *Sarah Lynnda* docked. And at the funeral there was no time.

Keziah's brow furrowed. "Are you pregnant?"

Dru's chest filled. "No." She swallowed desert dryness. "No way."

A quick look.

Intuition from Keziah, who had shown up at the Haverfords'

shabby Orange Street house that night so long ago, the night the storm had picked up, stirring Georges Bank, and someone called the next morning to say they hadn't been able to contact her father's boat, the *Louise Andrena*. And her mother had abandoned makeup. Her hair spent the next months becoming gray, almost white, although she wasn't yet forty.

Keziah's intuition was often right.

A man by the picnic tables fingered a cardboard coffee cup and shifted to dig in a canvas bag, like a purse. Keziah had let Dru walk on the oceanside, less visible. He hurried to the sea. With a camera.

Dru dropped her sweatshirt hood, shook out her hair, faced the lens with her grief. Her dogs flanked her, prepared to spring at the stranger. "Keziah, I'm sorry. I'll call you later."

Their hands caught. Hands that had learned to trust in childhood, hands that had worked side by side at their first midwifery intensive in Boston. *And now I'm going to try to get into Nantucket Hospital.*

A camera chattered behind them. Feet on the sand. Dru snapped leads on her dogs. In the parking lot, she wished for security—for Mitch. Cold, damp wind washed her skin, waved her hair. His voice was louder, the flash brighter than the weather.

"Mrs. Hall. Mrs. Hall. Why weren't you with your husband here on Nantucket when he died?"

Flash.

Ehder growled and lunged.

"Mrs. Hall, is it true Omar was going to divorce you because you hadn't given him children?"

Dru unlocked the door of Tristan's '72 Mustang, her concession to invisibility, and slipped inside, butt first, hauling the Azawakhs after her.

"What were you doing with your cousin, Ben Hall, in Gloucester? Is it true you're now engaged?"

Letting the dogs bark and snarl, Dru locked the doors and lowered the visors. The photographer followed her from Codfish Park, and her hands shook on the steering wheel.

When Omar was alive, Dru had always been accompanied.

She'd enjoyed leaving without a bodyguard today, enjoyed her own courage, had counted on the privacy of this island, her home.

Never, never had she faced cameras and questions alone.

Alone.

She wanted to scream from the fear of living and dying with no one.

Femi's tongue licked her cheek and nose.

Dru laughed, pushing her gently to her seat with Ehder. "Sit. Good girl."

She longed to stop and take her purse from beneath her seat. Inside lay a tabloid magazine she'd stolen from the 'Sconset Market. So stupid. Why had she wanted it? The woman in the photos—clear photos, perfectly clear—didn't look like her. Shoulders and head back, dark sweater hiked above her waist, so much bare skin. But the man held her face. On the beach, in the cold. Men never touched her that way, not men like him. He could have been anyone. He wasn't quite six feet and was lean and muscled. His short hair made her think of World War II veterans, faded images of men in fatigues beside planes with nose art, maybe smoking cigarettes, the things they'd seen staring out from their eyes. You couldn't see the eyes of the man in the photo, only hollows around the sides of his mouth, a narrow face. Chin and jaw passed muster.

But no, that woman wasn't Dru Haverford Hall.

That woman was beautiful. She must be, the way he touched her.

She thought of this to distract herself from the eternal absence of Omar, the man she'd considered her best friend, from the forever void left by the man who'd made her laugh and shared her thoughts so completely that their leisure moments had taken patterns, conversations revolving from people to things to ideas and touching upon the spirit as it was expressed in nature and art— And never reaching that part of his past and his present. A son.

Keeping her thoughts on the tabloid, wondering who the woman in the photo was, how she held such a spell for the man, wondering what Omar had really wanted, what he'd imagined happening, she drove calmly, dry-eyed, numb. She would tear up the paper, destroy it. The evidence of her step off the high road of fidelity and tradition, turning from the gods who had shaped her. She braked at a stop sign. Checked for traffic. Watched the heavy woman on the bicycle, polyester pants, a wool hat.

Dru noticed each thing stirring outside but not where she herself was headed.

Absorbed in the enormity of the present, of no Omar, no Omar ever again, she steered by rote, heading toward Orange Street. Not to her mother's house, where Captain Haverford— all the captains Haverford—had lived.

To Omar's house and solitude.

THE FEDERAL-GREEK Revival was like a bare tree against the sky with no roses or delphinium blooming beside the porch, spilling against the white columns. Bleak in the daylight. The private drive on private property, with Sergio waiting. Only loyal Sergio, with the cordless phone in his hand, notifying the police of the paparazzi.

Dru thanked him as she passed.

He had the warm eyes of a man who liked women in a deep way, who loved his own mother. Seeing his face made her miss Omar. The real Omar? On the path, Sergio told her of two calls to be returned. One was from Daniel.

Off-lead, the dogs bounded upstairs ahead of her. She

crossed the clear floors, and hurried up the white spiral stair-well, with its narrow, white-washed wooden steps. The realtor believed it would bring five. Million.

At the top of the stairs, she felt Omar's absence.

Wanted him. Wanted him never to have lied—or put Ben on her trail.

She ignored her studio. Bare floors free of dust, the bed-room's bright planks spotless.

Her grief was too complicated for tears. The strangled feel-ings inside her always released themselves unexpectedly.

The master bedroom was simple. The sleigh bed with the cream bedding, the feather pillows, the windows with their filmy curtains looking out on the long, groomed, sunken gar-den and beyond that, sailboat masts, the water. Between the windows sat the inlaid Biedermeier chest, with a lightship basket on it. At one end of the room was an adjoining dressing room and bath; Femi rushed out, tail wagging and Ehder fol-lowed. Dru tossed down the package she'd brought in—the portfolio and a gypsy-style handbag. She tugged off her sweat-shirt, and one of the ties caught in her hair as the cotton cov-ered her face.

His voice came from near the entry to the dressing room.

"Salaam."

CHAPTER FOUR

They isolated us in separate tents. Despite our various lies, they accurately distinguished the twins. They separated them and separated the boys. Dru and I were gagged and bound in the same tent, a bought or stolen Bedouin tent. But we could hear. We could hear Skye beg, hear each "No." Sometimes, we heard Tristan, too. And that was always worse.

—Ben, recollections of a fall

Orange Street
Nantucket

DRU TORE the sweatshirt off, scraping her skin. She saw him in one glance, like a snapshot.

Dark hair grown longer than three weeks before; near the top, it stuck out at angles. Brown eyes and clear whites and golden-brown skin. He had shaved, but in his work pants and knobby, worn sweater he could have been taken for a Nantucket scalloper.

"If you'd rung the doorbell, Sergio would have let you in."

"Actually, he did. He's always liked me." Ben settled in the striped wing-backed chair near the window, and Ehder put his feet up on one shoulder. "Off." Dog kisses. Femi circled the chair, looking for a place to lie. A soiled gray hung over the sunken garden and the harbor. "How are you?"

"Let's try this again, my Bedouin friend."

"I'm not—"

"You go out *there*—" she pointed "—and announce your presence as a decent Rashaida—"

"—and certainly not Rashaida."

"Let's try *gentleman*. Get out of my space until you're invited to be here. Brat," she added and heard the dialect of *déjà vu*.

"You might never ask me back, which is more than I could bear. Sergio is an old man. After he and your lethal guard dogs—" one of whom had her head in his lap "—defended this impenetrable fortress, they'd all need to nap, and you'd have to nurse my wounds yourself."

Dru subdued a smile. Hadn't he broken the same rules before, in the Sudan? Oh, yes, a child running between the men and the women, indulged beyond belief because he was cute and smart and charming in the ways the Bedouin love. But to Dru, he'd dropped remarks about the girls that meant he should no longer enjoy the freedom of their tent.

They were vague, these memories, dreamlike.

There was no "child marriage" in them.

"How are you?" he said again.

A heartbeat.

Dru shrugged. When her father had died—*when we thought he'd died*—Dru had imagined nothing worse, except perhaps her mother's death. Now, she'd lost Omar, and he wasn't who she'd thought. Such a lie... Keeping it from her in the first place, never telling her he'd fathered a son, as though she was a child instead of a wife. Then...

Ben had done the same thing.

Well. Not exactly. She backed into a dresser, her arms clasped round her blue thermal undershirt. "Has Daniel told you the news? It's all yours." She wanted solitude and dreaded it. She must decide about Omar's clothes. Find someone else who could go through them; Keziah had offered.

She saw Ben and quenched thoughts of him, the fact that she *had* thought of him. So much. And, in private, intimately. Wondering why he'd wanted to know if she was pregnant.

Trying to forget the silent and separate tenderness in the trawler.

Trying to forget the wordless understanding between them. That humans are fragile, that each of them was. That she would thank his efforts and brush aside any failure. That he would treat her with the same gentleness.

He said, "I know you loved Omar. I'm sorry."

"Please, go." He must. She was bothered by his voice, the way his mouth moved. Bothered because she'd almost believed herself in love with him and half wished this awful thing. The angel she knew for the devil she didn't. But they were both devils now. She'd never known either.

And Omar was dead.

Ehder flopped on the floor at the foot of the bed.

Dru clasped the doorknob. "I'll show you out."

"Your husband's estate owes me money. I have receipts and a report."

Receipts. Report. About following her for seven months. Omar had hired him, his son. Had told her to... Her hand left the door. "Give them to me. I'll write you a check."

"Is there someone else you'd rather—"

"Very funny. Where are the records?"

He produced them, a manila packet. On the outside he'd totaled the months' work. She hardly heard the explanation of an expense account. The numbers didn't matter. She saw the bottom figure, returned to her purse for one of the checkbooks. Where had Omar planned to record this?

She pictured writing a check to Ben Hall for a sum in excess of sixty thousand dollars. Pictured someone seeing the check. The alternative was to send Sergio for cash. In that case, she'd have to wait. With Ben.

"Could you please light the fire?" she said. "It's laid." At the bed's edge, she balanced the ledger for the joint checking account on her thigh. Behind her a match struck.

Dru wrote his name for the first time, filled in the sum, added her signature.

She tore off the check, replaced the wallet in her purse and rose, collecting the manila envelope. In masculine handwriting, blue ink: *D. is at Sundown Condos, unit 4; I'm in unit 5. Returned from Fish Hook at...*

He straightened from the fireplace with its white border, its columns, the ship in a bottle on the mantel. She stood before him. The fire crackled. "Did Omar ask you to take notes on my activities?"

"No. Only where you were, to confirm that I was there, too."

Dru held out the check, keeping the envelope. "There you are."

He read it, folded it, put it away.

She plucked the fireplace tongs from the stand and stuck the fat envelope in their hold. As she thrust the envelope into the hearth, a receipt from a restaurant in Key West slipped partway out. The print was red, and the name began with an *A*. Dru laughed. One corner began to blacken till flames danced up.

They both watched.

She prodded, poked. Stepped back. Yes, going well.

Arm on the mantel, he stared into the bottle at the schooner. He walked the deck of the tiny sailing vessel.

"It's a model of a ship captained by one of your ancestors." She acknowledged his adoption in this way. "I don't need a receipt. The check will serve. So you can go." Her smile trembled through holes in the cloak of her confidence. The holes were what those receipts and notes represented. She would mend them against the wind of fear and nerves.

"Are you pregnant?"

"No." Quick. Remembering Keziah, the same question on the beach. The same answer.

"You've had a test."

"No, I haven't. It's immaterial now. No rush."

"Immaterial is not the word I'd use."

She pressed her hands to the edge of the bureau behind her. "What do you want? Do you have new plans to ruin my life?"

"There are test kits in your bathroom."

"You searched the bathroom?"

"It's the most telling room in the house. You wear sunscreen, Omar used Renova, somebody takes liquid vitamins—"

She reached for the intercom, thinking someone would get rid of him, and remembered there was no one but Sergio. She'd asked the others to leave, even the chef now that Oceania was gone. The intercom was unplugged.

Dru wheeled around. "If you were married to a woman thirty-five years younger than you, you might worry about your looks, too. You're not endearing yourself to me."

"I'll wait while you take a test."

She bent to plug in the intercom. "No."

As she straightened, he caught her arm.

She pulled it back. Tried to. The grip was firm but not painful. Walking, walking beside him, Ehder trailing along, tail wagging, practically an accomplice, while Femi watched from afar. "The test only works in the morning."

"Your memory fails you. I read the instructions. You *have* used these kits before." He paused. "Was it the bicycling accident?"

The dressing room's blackness and mirrors held the scent of Omar's suits.

"My husband wouldn't have died if I'd been with him instead of with you. His son. You both knew you're his son and didn't tell me. I never want to see you again. I find your touch repulsive.''

''I can live with your disgust.'' The floor of the bathroom was white pine, the walls white. A framed black-and-white photo on the wall showed a swordfishing boat in her berth in Gloucester. The *Sarah Lynnda*. Tristan stood on deck, his ponytail blowing like a flag, his scarification erased by distance. She longed for her brother. Tomorrow, she'd see him; she'd reserved a rental car in Hyannis.

Today, though—she'd never expected any of this.

Fluffy white towels, the finest in the world, hung on antique racks. An incongruous sunken tub of porcelain dropped into the floor beneath the window. Far from the door, the commode hid in its own private stall. Ben released her and shut the door. Leaned against it. ''I'll wait.''

She sat across from him, on the floor. ''Suit yourself.''

He eased to the floor, too, and draped his forearms over his knees. ''I apologize.'' Eyes on hers. ''There's no need for this. I'll go. Will you tell me when you know?''

She clasped her head near her hairline, nodded in numbness.

He spoke a Bedouin poem, spoke it as they would, in courtship. She was the one who came to him on a camel, her teeth like milk....

Gloucester crept in. Sand. The rocking trawler. The sodden and rank smells of the port.

Impossible to return to those feelings. That—innocence.

And she didn't know him, couldn't know a man who kept such a secret. As she'd never known Omar.

''What's on your mind, Dru?'' He spoke like her cousin, her playmate in the Sudan, who had, with her, made up stories and games to resolve their fears. Now he lulled her into trusting him as a friend, making her forget that his eyes were so black, a man's eyes in a man's face.

''Trust,'' she said.

His lips parted without giving words.

She longed for his thoughts, all of them. Did he have some agenda unknown to her? Did he find her attractive? When they spent time together in the trawler, had he liked her? Liked who she was inside?

"What kind of trust?" he asked.

"That you won't lie to me or keep secrets from me. I'm angry."

"Dru, I wasn't certain. How could I say to you what I imagined was true? I just wanted to help." He shook his head. "And after all those months—" another pause, more coming to grips "—I wanted you."

"Did you ever tell Omar so or ask him to remove you from your position?"

"Why should I? He'd offered you to whatever man you liked best."

She could have touched his anger.

"I'm sorry," he said. "I didn't protect you. Again."

Again? Why again? Was he talking about what had happened when they were children? The kidnapping in the Sudan? For a moment, she saw into two men's minds, Ben's and Tristan's. That episode had changed them both, changed them all. But to be boys, then, on the verge of manhood... Ben had accepted scars, too; she saw that now. Still open wounds. The wounds of inaction during tragedy.

Dru thought of Gloucester, of his valiant persistence in ejaculating into a ceramic mug shaped like a Nantucket lightship basket, with a closable top. They had laughed, Dru murmuring, "This is a basket case, all right." He'd groaned. The quiet laughter was gone, buried in misfortune. Why not take a pregnancy test now? It would be negative, and that would be the end of it.

And of her relationship with this journalist, who walked on

the edge of danger, always watching. Not, she decided, an accessible man.

Dru rose and opened the vanity. So many tests. So much hope, before they'd learned Omar was sterile. She removed a kit, peeled away the wrapper, popped off the cap. "I don't suppose this is past the expiration date." Casual voice, as though helping a mother at a prenatal appointment. Standing, he peered over her at the kit, and she raised her head. "You could give me more privacy."

"Just pretend we're at a bar and I'm your boyfriend and the line for the women's washroom is really long."

His sense of humor relaxed and scared her. She liked it. She slipped behind the stained-glass partition. The window beyond lit up a desert, waves and waves of sand.

Sitting. Checking her watch, she saw her rings. The diamond, the emeralds. Her wedding band. Pee for ten seconds on this portion of the tester, as she used to for Omar. Never while he waited. Too important, the need to succeed.

See where it got us?

The sink water went on.

Dru rolled her eyes.

Sometime, in the next minute, the significance of it occurred to her. He was here, wanting an answer. One answer or the other.

She emerged and set the tester on the sink edge and washed her hands. Two minutes to go. Ignoring the test strip, Dru toweled her hands. There would be one line on the strip. One line, and she would feel a strange quiver at seeing what she had so many times with Omar. And the deadness of disappointment, which had less to do with any man than with what she wanted.

Ben Hall's head was thrown back, hair pushed up against the door, Ehder lying at his feet.

One minute. One line. One line, and she could tell him to

leave. Her life would be hers. Her new and empty life. The hollowness of life without Omar.

She checked the indicator, the strong line and the weak line. A bungled I Ching reading. The weak top line indicates... Her stomach became light, queasy. She salivated heavily, involuntarily. Nauseous and dizzy.

He had moved. He looked, too. A non-breath. Falling back.

The second line darkened. A baby inside her. Not Omar's baby, but his son's. A baby who would grow, and she would grow, and she would labor, and she would give birth, and the child would be the child she'd made with Ben the week she should have been with Omar, holding his arm on his evening walk when he slipped on the bricks and fell and hit his head and died. But she wanted the baby.

She was happy. Joy burst through her, quiet and amazed. But Omar wasn't there to embrace her, to love her.

Dru vomited in the sink. No tears, just watering eyes, red-faced, throwing up again.

He grabbed one of the thick white washcloths and thrust it under the tap. Ehder rubbed her legs, almost knocking her over.

Dru snatched the washcloth. "Don't touch me. Just don't." Her head burned wildly. *Omar...* She missed him and hated him, but the hated one *wasn't* him.

Ben saw the grief take her. Run over her. That helpless hacking. Sobbing. Her agony echoed off the walls. Her cries, her bent-over figure, holding herself, moaning. She had loved Omar. No doubt. Ben knew grief, had seen many threads of its weave. This was grief.

"Is there anything I can do?"

She shook her head, the ends of her hair swatting the pregnancy indicator. The strip had changed again, slipping beyond correct. He dropped it in the trash and rinsed the sink.

Dru gasped, small breaths, half-whimpering sounds. She sat on the edge of the tub, the sunken tub, twirling her rings.

He joined her, putting his feet, his shoes in, as she had. Ehder came to sniff her head and lick her and finally lie beside her. Calmly, Ben saw moments from the past, from the Sudan. What she did not remember. He held it in his body, held it for her and would hold it until the light went on and she could see. He would be careful of this wound. And of her. He said, "I would like to marry you."

Dru shifted, thoughts muddled. Marry...for baby. If she didn't marry him, she would be a single mother. "I can manage. Keziah does." *And I have money.* She wondered what story she would tell of the baby's father and if Keziah's Nudar ever minded having a story father.

"This isn't a hard call, Dru."

Her eyes spelled disbelief. Thoughts swam, sucking at her. *What were we thinking? Any of us?* She exclaimed, "Of course, it's a hard call. My husband wanted to carry on his line, very deliberately—"

"No."

"He never asked when you planned to marry? If you wanted children?"

"Never."

Relief. The horror ran out, only to return in a different form. "How could you want to marry me, knowing what I did? And why should I marry you, knowing what *you* did? So we didn't commit adultery. Other things...happened." Some of them intangible, never acknowledged, like her knowing when he was aroused by her nearness, and her wanting that. Wanting to look at his body. "Why should either of us think the other would be faithful? Not to mention that you *lied* to me."

Ehder had climbed down into the bathtub. He gazed at her hopefully. "Okay. Move," she told Ben. "He's getting a bath."

Wagging tail, smacking them both.

"You bathe your own dogs?"

"When possible, I do everything for my dogs. Then they like me best. But Femi hates baths." Ben's presence was now a comfort. If he stayed, would death keep away?

Dru's hands shook as she removed her rings, then took them to her room to put away. Femi wanted out, and Dru let her go.

In the bathroom, she trembled through the bathing, the water soaking her and the floor. She quaked through their conversation about Azawakhs.

"There's a tea ceremony," he told her, "before you take one home. In fact, in Mali there are tea ceremonies for many things."

Dru's hair went uncombed, her clothes sandy and wrinkled.

After his bath, Ehder raced through the bedroom, pausing to shake, water from his short coat spraying the walls.

Dru lay down, gesturing to the striped chair for Ben. First, he lifted the crocheted afghan, covered her. "Tired?" he asked.

"No." She shivered warmly, frightened of how much she liked the tenderness. Omar had sometimes covered her, too. Her left hand felt light, although the white ring of skin on her third finger had almost merged with that around it.

Ben watched her. Her black hair parted down the center, arched eyebrows, schoolgirl face, hints of her dark ancestor. The most beautiful women in the world came from the desert. He saw the face of one he loved, one who would never have him. Timbuktu was an ocean and a desert away.

Dru came from this island.

She had been part of him for decades, something he'd kept locked away, for later. Until it was too late. When he brought the Azawakhs, her wedding gift, he couldn't face her. That was his chance, but how could he stand up to Omar? His father had wanted his bride. He'd returned to Africa. When Omar had summoned him to follow Dru, he'd entered the world of a man who comes too late. In such a world, the rules change. Falls are common.

She'd asked how he could trust her. She, who had navigated the sordid world into which her husband had sent her and displayed goodness, running from caresses Omar had urged her to accept.

"You'll be faithful," Ben said. "And so will I."

"There's a bigger problem." Only her head moved, to see him.

The will. The world knowing that he was her husband's son and believing they'd been lovers.

Ben took a folded piece of paper from his pocket and gave it to her.

Dru unfolded it. She'd signed something similar days before. *He can't have chosen this.* But he had. He had relinquished his inheritance. And no one would know he was Omar's son.

"You and I wait a month, get married somewhere inconspicuous, announce it, the baby's a little early, the gossip columnists whisper. So what?"

Dru propped herself up on one arm, one elbow. "Why? You're giving up a fortune." All his father's camels.

His spine fit to the back of the chair.

"You're a journalist," she said. "You travel. This is unnecessary. The baby—" she had trouble saying it "—will have male role models. Sergio." Her tongue and lips fell over each other. "My brother, Tristan."

He looked bored.

She waited for him to attack her twin. He didn't, so she said, "He's captain of a swordboat. It's his job. My family have always been fishermen. But he'll return to Nantucket when he's paid off his own boat." The same thought again:

If she'd returned to Nantucket earlier, she might have taken that walk with Omar. On the brick sidewalk, Dru would have held his arm. They would have been linked. He would never have fallen. "Do you hate him?" she asked. "Is that why you did this?" The piece of paper. Refusing every gift.

"No. I don't hate him."

"So you took what was in the safe deposit box and the other things." She wasn't sure what they were, these pieces of Omar's legacy.

"Oh, yes." He smiled, his look wistful, intensifying her curiosity.

She would never ask.

Marry him…the baby…single mother…marry Ben… What would Omar want her to do?

I don't care anymore!

But she remembered, very simply, very clearly.

Why, Omar? This is crazy. Why not a sperm bank?

I want a human being, a man who could look after you and the child if…

Then his saying yes, she should make love with Ben. Enjoy it. Her husband had manipulated her. And she'd still loved Omar before the will told her that he'd sent her to bed with his son. Now his memory made her distrust her whole world.

She examined the paper in her lap. This was no bride price for her, but a boon for charity. Most of all, it was a gift for their child, who must not be tainted by public name-calling and tragedy and his parents' folly. From here on out, they had to do their best.

Dru sat up, put her feet over the edge of the bed. Dreams came to her. Desire for something more than she'd ever had. The courage to reach for it. "When I receive a proposal of marriage," she said, "I will entertain the offer."

He laughed. "I've asked."

"Your gallantry was noted." But she remembered her sickness in the bathroom, vomiting up Omar. Her head still swam. She swallowed. "In North Africa, a widow cannot wear mehndi for four months."

Henna painted on her body. *And how could there be a wedding without mehndi?* Ben thought. In this family. "Who is your *hannaya?*" He used the Moroccan term for a specially trained artist, with ritualistic ability.

She didn't return his half-mocking smile. "Keziah and I used to work as mehndi artists for the summer people for money. Just out of high school. You can go now."

This time, he rose. "What are you doing tomorrow?"

"Seeing my brother."

"I'll drive you. I got a reservation for the ferry for tomorrow. We should be seen together."

Her chest constricted. "You reserved a place for a car? You must have had other plans."

He lifted his eyebrows, mocking her suspiciousness. "A date with you?"

Dru took a shallow breath. She'd like to be able to tell him she'd seen her father in Gloucester. She'd like to count on his help.

But she'd never mentioned it yet—whether from fear of being disbelieved...or believed.

Could she tell Ben?

It was just that her father, if he was alive... Was feigning one's own death committing a crime? She couldn't take the question further, because the easiest answer was to keep journalists far away. And never have to talk about the night before their father left. *We—Mom, Tristan and I—are the only ones who'll understand.* What it was like to live with that particular fisherman. To live without him.

But Ben was family; among the Haverford-Hall clan, this meant something. Even in a journalist.

"All right," she agreed. "You can drive."

Sergio came on the intercom, making her jump, bursting into their privacy. ''Mrs. Hall, there is a courier package from Mr. Mayhew's office. Your signature is needed.''

The document from Ben was in her hand.

She remembered the will.

She remembered the vault, that tall black thing in the attic.

The contents were hers.

CHAPTER FIVE

For more than a day, we were gagged. Then they let us eat and drink and speak. I believed my father was dead and believed I'd caused this by dreaming that my other father, my natural father, my real father, would come for me, take me to Nantucket. In my remorse, I prayed aloud in Arabic. Dru didn't cry, and her fears were for her brother. Only him. I thought the men would come for her next. I was twelve. I should stop them, but how? So far, they hadn't let us up or untied us for any reasons. They thought me dangerous. They were wrong. On the third day of our captivity, we heard, from outside, one of the men shout and a distinctive, hollow, whirring sound I'll never forget, because of the deafening gunfire that followed.

—Ben, recollections of a fall

"COME WITH ME," she told him.

The stairs to the attic were narrow. Omar had once said all the house's stairwells had been photographed for a coffee-table book. Had Dru been as pleased? Ben embroidered the ways she must have loved Omar. *She vomited when she learned she was carrying my child.* When she agreed to marry him, would she weep?

The attic had its own lock. She kept the key on her ring. The dogs rushed in past him and were sniffing the corners beneath the sloped ceiling when Ben saw the vault. Key and combination.

Dru read the numbers, worked the dial and turned the key. She didn't know how to move the latch, and he helped her, showing her the mechanism, while Femi sat and watched.

Dru scarcely noticed the latch, just his hands. She was having his baby.

The door to the vault opened. She'd opened it.

Cloth pushed out. Clothing.

"Oh, God." Dru stepped back. "Nudar's things. How did he get them?"

Ben began guessing. Nudar's possessions were passed from daughter to daughter, as the Tuareg passed theirs. They should have been...Mary's? Keziah's? He held Ehder as Dru bent to peer beneath the gowns. "There are more things on the floor of the vault," she said, "but these garments are fragile. Ehder, go lie down."

He didn't and she had to make him do it now that she'd given the command. She dragged him away from the vault, pushed him down. "Stay."

Ben searched for mechanisms to control temperature and humidity. "They've been safe in here." On their padded hangers. A bent nail protruded from an unfinished beam overhead. "Hang the clothes here," he said. "Hand them to me."

She did. She would give them away, return them, to Mary— or Keziah—but first she must see what her distant African ancestor had worn. "Oh, this one isn't hers. It's Josephine's." Nudar's daughter's. "I've seen the photos." Of her and her Cape Verde Portuguese husband. Next she passed him a long cotton gown with wide sleeves. Then silk drawstring pants. These were the pants in the oil painting of Nudar. The matching gown followed. A shimmering dark blue shawl. Dru lifted it to her face, smelling.

Ben caught the free end. "Indigo."

"She *must* have been Tuareg. Taken captive by one of their enemies."

He said nothing. Nudar was not his ancestor. He could not claim that heritage anymore.

She handed him another gown and another, yards of fabric to be draped. A Nantucket dress. What lace. "These were stolen from the family, I thought. Or lost. Around the time when Keziah's—and your—grandmother died. Before I was born. Ehder, lie down."

He did. His eyes comforted Ben from across the room. Ben recognized her moods and her grief and her interest now, her relief at something new to think about. Besides being pregnant. With his child.

Two white *haiks*—long overshirts—a tunic, a brocade skirt, a dark wool cloak. Gowns in silk, simple embroidered dresses that could have come all the way from Egypt.

On the floor of the vault was an antique jewelry chest and a large lightship basket and a sack. She opened the last first, sat with it in her lap. "Look. A counterweight for her veil. It looks Tuareg." And coin belts and rings.

"He could have bought garments and jewelry for her anywhere," Ben pointed out. "But, yes, she might have been Tuareg." The name of the people and the scent of indigo dye brought it to him, against his will.

Brought her to him.

Tanelher.

The day had dimmed outside. Dru said, "You've lived with the Tuareg, haven't you?"

"Yes." His eyes fell over the dresses. He remembered the woman he loved, the woman who had worn only blue, and sought deliberately to forget Dru, who would be his wife. He failed. Dru's goodness wrapped him in hairlike threads, binding him to her. Time to purge the love he wanted and make peace with the troth he had made and felt so young and saved for later. Later had come.

His father, his unfather, his uncle, had died. The dark spread around. And in the midst of darkness and death, the new was a tiny seed.

His dreamlike thoughts shifted to diapers and crying, then to the memory of a starving infant, skin tearing away, skin sores always the first sign of imminent starvation. Women nursing. Dru would feed this child they'd made from her body.

A baby.

''What are you thinking about, Ben?''

''Baby. I can't believe it.'' He shut his eyes. Opened them and saw indigo.

Dru clasped her abdomen. Smiled. Lit up like the single bright thing in the darkness. ''I'm happy.''

But she must have seen his eyes on the indigo. ''Tell me about the Tuareg.''

Her casual look saw into him. Already a wife sensing infidelity in her husband's heart.

Right, Ben.

He listened. The house hummed, like any house with utilities. Bicycles clicked and whirred past on the street. A man's voice reached them. But any sound of movement in the rooms below was faint, distant. An attic was a place for children and secrets. With his running shoe almost under her calf, he spoke. ''Because of my father's work and his inclination—his need to learn about Omar and have *me* learn about Omar, I grew up with the Bedouin in Libya. Briefly with a group related to Omar's tribe, who remembered his family. We lived in the midst of revolution, putting my father in some danger. I looked like a Bedouin child and believed I was. I learned the dialect of my Arab family before I knew English. The granddaughter of their sheikh became as a mother to me. I don't remember my own, Alma Hall, except faintly, like a sensation. She was the daughter of a missionary. I became, for all intents and purposes, Muslim. I could recite the Koran before I could read. I was loved.''

"Why did he care about Omar's background?"

"Why? I think this is why." He told her of the plane in the desert, the gunner, his grandfather, floating down. To bring home a Bedouin son and love him best. "Humans fall," he concluded. "In many ways."

Omar had fallen, too.

"I fell," she whispered.

"By wrestling with me on a narrow berth and leaving me and saying no? You're not suggesting that was easy."

"It should never have gone that far. From the first, I should have told him…."

Ben shook his head. The veil's counterweight had slipped halfway from her lap. He reached over and set it back, his body slowly stirring. From the heat of her.

She sat back on her hands. "Finish what you began."

He resisted, then yielded. He could make it emotionless and quick, give her no reason for doubt. "I was eight when we went home to Cambridge, where my father taught anthropology for two years, and I learned to be an American. Ten when we returned to Africa, this time to live with the Rashaida in the Sudan. Where I met you."

"Yes." The Sudan. She'd accepted the things that had occurred there. All she'd heard and seen had kept her from men so long, until she'd married one more than twice her age, thinking sex would be less frequent and more gentle. More tolerable than she imagined it to be.

Ben searched her face.

He'd mentioned the Sudan, so she brought up Skye—obliquely. "David—" Skye's widower "—has remarried. He and Jean are very happy. They have two babies." *I attended their births. And Jean is pregnant again.* Nantucket hospital…Keziah… ''And they have Chris,'' she added. The son of David and Skye. The last bit of Skye.

''She fell,'' Ben said. An echo.

Skye Haverford Blade had fallen, it was understood, from the bow of the ship that carried her name. Her husband's ship.

Dru glanced away. Skye's son, Chris, had told her the truth while she enjoyed their home, the new research vessel, a converted minesweeper, in one of the lazy days before Jean went into labor the first time. Dru had said, *I'm so sorry.* So sorry. That Skye had not really fallen. Yet had fallen so finally.

There had been only one person with whom Dru could share this secret. She had told her husband. She'd told Omar.

Ben said, ''After you left, we moved to the southern Sahara, and I met the Tuareg. We lived with a nomadic Tuareg family.''

Instinctively, Dru braced herself. *He has a secret, too. He loves someone.* Her fingers trembled on a coin belt. The attic's coolness was as still and stifling as heat. She said, ''What then?''

''This Tuareg family made me theirs. Their son, their brother. When my father returned to the United States, I asked to stay. He had allowed it before. But this time he kept me with him. Education.'' A shrug. ''We rejoined the same family when I was sixteen.'' Ben wanted to stop the story. It was irrelevant now. Plan B, the plan for Later, had happened. The jewel he'd carried, memories and fantasies of Dru Haverford, had become the here and now.

He wished he hadn't scratched the jewel.

He spoke with deliberate casualness, giving a report. ''My good friend Tanelher—like a sister—was betrothed to a nobleman of the tribe. We were invited to take part in their wedding.'' Quick now. ''My father and I lived with her family. She and I remained friends. Her husband, too. As a journalist, I was often their guest. Six years ago, while I was in Egypt, they attended a cultural festival...in Niger...where they live. Someone lobbed hand grenades into the crowd, because of what they call the Tuareg Problem. Nomads are always a problem for governments." His speech had become choppy. "My friend Tanelher and the son they'd called Ben were hit. He died a week later. She has no legs. I found her living in Timbuktu."

Dru sat. Waiting. There was nothing but him and the story he told.

"Her husband had died." He bit his lower lip. "Murdered by the government." There he stopped, at a place she knew wasn't the end.

But he said no more.

He followed me to Timbuktu, Dru thought. Did Tanelher still live there? Had he visited her? He would have been deserting his job, leaving her unprotected. And he'd almost certainly done it. Dru curbed her anger. "What did you do? When you found...her?"

"I could do nothing." It was time, he decided, to be silent. But more came out. "She rejected—offers."

"Of marriage?"

Quiet. Darkness in the attic.

"Among other things." He rose to switch on the overhead bulb. Returning, features murky, he said, "Look what you pried out of me. Now it's your turn."

"I'm not done prying. This woman is the love of your life." Her throat contracted as she said it.

"I hope not." He took his seat across from her again.

A kind reply. The kindest, for its credibility.

She replaced the long brass counterweight in its sack and twisted to set the sack behind her in the vault. The jewelry box was heavy, sixteen inches tall at least, with drawers. She shifted again, rose to her knees. Ben helped her bring it out onto the floor.

She opened a drawer. Coin necklaces, earrings, tarnished silver bracelets.

"Tuareg," he said, handling a heavy bracelet.

"A museum piece."

"That's up to you." He shrugged.

"There's a tradition. They go through Nudar's daughters. Really, these things are Keziah's."

He crouched beside her on his heels. "So how did Omar get them?"

She opened another drawer, liking neither the question nor the answers. Omar's having them made no sense.

The drawer contained woven bracelets from Africa. And valuable silver. A pair of pearl teardrop earrings, which the whaling captain must have bought for her. They were surely valuable.

Leaving the little chest out, she reached into the vault for its last piece, the lightship basket. The basket had been made since World War II. Sixties, Dru guessed, as Ben said, "Look familiar?"

Laughing, she saw the mug on the trawler. *It worked.*

She opened the lid. Lying atop blue metallic fabric, fabric that filled most of the basket and had stained its contents, sat two headdresses, drenched with coins. Dru removed one and, without thinking, put it on her head.

She heard his breath.

Saw his black eyes.

"Try the other one."

She did and watched his face as he eased back from her. Grace and its potency had always been hers. But not like this. Confused by Ben's darkened eyes, she set aside the jingling headdress, petted Ehder when he came to her. What else was in the basket? A manila envelope. Papers inside. She slid them out, a jumble of things, some loose photos. A handwritten note was clipped to a parchment document. The blue ink on yellowing paper read, "Joanna brought my son to the Halls in this basket. I swaddled him in the clothes Nudar wore from Africa."

Frightened, Dru read the heavy certificate beneath, breathing hard and noticing, too late, his breath warming her skin.

It declared the birth of Baby Boy Hall, in Gloucester, Massachusetts, on March 23, 1968, to Mary Hall and Omar Hall.

Dru's mother had carried Ben to his adoptive parents.

His hand warmed her shoulder. He had knelt forward to see better. Maybe he needed to steady himself. She shifted a sheet and found faded color photos of her mother in her Velvet Underground days with Mary Mayhew—Keziah's mother, Omar's sister. Ben's birth mother. Photos of Mary in a hospital room, holding a baby. Mary and her adopted brother, Omar, were Ben's natural parents. Dru touched the hand on her shoulder, and he stood.

"May I have those?"

She gave them to him. Letting him react privately, unobserved, she lifted the fragile blue fabric from the basket. A Tuareg robe. Voluminous. Hardly room for a baby in the lightship basket. *We made a baby with a lightship basket, with the mug.*

Ben's mother had given him away in one.

Ben watched the midnight waves unfurl, indigo garments of the Tuareg, Blue Men of the Desert.

Dru thought, *Blue woman. A blue woman.* And tried to imagine Tanelher's face.

She noticed Ben's each movement and every stillness. He was a man, taking this like a New Englander, not like the heroes of the tales of the Arabian nights, one of whom had, on hearing of the death of his father, fallen prostrate and been carried off by his enemies. But the dusty attic held sadness in the faint molecules of dust visible under the light.

Ben settled back in his former place, against the eight-by-eight post. The closed envelope lay beside him on the plank floor. "Was Omar the great love of your life?"

She expelled a breath. "I hope not."

"Who did you love before Omar?"

"No one. I loved my family, and I loved midwifery." The hospital. She needed to start a relationship with the hospital immediately, but how?

I could go to an OB/GYN about this pregnancy. Establish myself as conservative.

But was she? Working in New Bedford had left her exhilarated one day, murderous the next.

"You were a virgin?"

"That's none of your business."

"I'll bet you're going to say that a lot. 'No comment.' Come on, Dru, talk to me."

"Are *you* a virgin?"

His skin darkened some, his smile shy and appealing. The infuriating boy who'd won the heart of every Rashaida mother and daughter. And knew what to do with captured hearts.

She went on, insistent. "Tell me about your sex life. I'm dying to know. You said you can make a woman come every time. On how many hundreds did you try your technique?"

"I'm embarrassed. Let's drop it."

"Oh, no. Let's not." She crept to where he lay on the floor and stared deliberately at his canvas pants, watching him react to her.

Until reality, absence, wrote itself on every atom of her world.

Omar was dead.

What was she doing? How could her body feel this fire? She had never behaved this way toward a man in her life. Ben had just learned the identity of his birth mother, learned she was the woman he'd thought of as his aunt. He had to be wild inside, but it didn't show.

And Omar would never walk into this house again, never put on his pajamas and climb into their bed.

Touch burned. Ben's touch.

He pulled her near, his dark irises hiding everything but a man's need. She saw his body, and she mounted him, wanting to press against him. One knee on each side of him, she eased down to connect with his hardness, then laid her body against his chest. Against all of him. Thunder. His heart.

Or hers.

She smelled his skin at his neck. Saltwater. And his jaw. His hands stroked her back, her bottom through her jeans, and they kissed. She rubbed against him, her eyes flooding without reason. *I never want to stop. I never want him to stop holding me. Who is this Tanelher person who has marked his heart?*

But she squirmed restlessly. He held her head near his. "Always tell me," he said, "if you want something different or better."

She tasted something untouched in him and wanted it to belong only to her. She had never felt this way about a man, needing to be so close.

Kissing with their tongues.

She wanted to make love. This urgency was alien to her, had not been part of her lovemaking with Omar.

On their sides, against the wooden planks, they found more intimate touch. She put her hand over him, over the hard throbbing. He touched her, sure and gentle pressure where she craved his fingers. Wanted everything.

Until she saw his eyes, saw his eyelids drop, then lift to see her.

She backed away, sat up and clasped her knees. "Are you all right?"

He remained as he was. "I will be. Had enough?"

"No." She shook her head. She couldn't say to him, *I like you too much.* In his eyes, she'd seen the marks of violence

and mass death and individual, pitiable, long and wretche
death. But she'd also seen the fragility of a man. His hea
and soul and being, the essence of who he was at his best an
worst, now deserved her protection. Out at sea, you couldn'
protect a mother and newborn. How could she protect thi
complicated person anywhere?

She wanted him so much, but not now, in the attic. Forever

He could go somewhere and never come back! Like a fish
erman leaving port.

Quaking, she tried on a bracelet and took it off.

He sat up, to be close to her again.

They embraced. She said out loud, "I want you. So much."

He stroked her hair. Kissed her. Told her he belonged t
her and to their baby. Whispered these things.

She searched his face. "You keep it all inside, like it doesn'
even bother you. About Mary and Omar."

"It bothers me." Tense, so tense.

In his home in 'Sconset were photos of Alma Hall with hin
at her breast, most of his face shielded by her white blouse
"The Bedouin woman who nursed me in Libya after Alma'
death had a child younger than me; she was already breast
feeding when Alma died. Alma nursed me, too. The only
way—she must have had a stillbirth. They never told me."

Dru considered. A stillbirth made sense. Alma wouldn'
have relinquished a child for adoption herself, then adopte
Ben. No child could replace a stillborn child. But Alma ha
received a newborn for her arms, to put to her breast whil
she cried for the baby she lost. She'd surely fallen in love wit
the one she held.

But Dru pictured a somber child peering from the breas
into his mother's eyes of grief.

Finally she said, "You won't talk to Mary? Tell her?"

He blinked. "Would you?"

Speak to the mother who had given him away, yet looked on, from a distance, as he grew to manhood? "I don't know."

As he stared toward the dusty attic window panes, her gaze slid down his body, the folds of his worn canvas pants. Those nights in the trawler, when he slept a half-dozen yards away, she'd imagined things. Body hair and muscle. His erection. No barrier between them. No lightship basket mug or Tomcat catheter.

"What are *you* thinking?" He echoed and mocked her earlier question.

"Oh. Nothing." Almost absently, Dru fit the heaviest silver bracelet around her wrist. It looked and felt perfect and was Keziah's.

As she removed the cuff, he said, "Nothing?"

Not answering, she lifted a coin necklace from the box.

"Why did you stop? Just now."

"Stop what?" She worked the hasp on the necklace, never meeting his eyes or turning toward him.

He sat closer. "Stop making out." He picked out another Tuareg bracelet and handed it to her. "Instead of making love."

Was he always going to do this? No one had ever asked her these sorts of things. "Really, I have other things on my mind."

"That's what I'm asking about."

"I don't know what to expect from life anymore." That was more than she'd wanted to say, and she sealed her lips.

"What went through your head at the moment you decided to get off me?"

He was far too close, his voice making her skin warm, her nerves tingle.

She would never tell him she cared that he loved someone else. She turned her shoulders fluidly, decades of belly dancing commanding every move. "Physical attraction can be powerful. But it takes years to know someone.'' A spouse might have a child and never say. ''In fact, I don't think you ever can...really.''

Ben dropped his head, perhaps contemplating her words.

She started to remove a bracelet.

''Try on her gowns.''

All she heard was his silent agreement with what she'd said. For a flash, she knew him.

''I want to see them on you.''

Nudar's gowns? She must give them to Keziah.

Of course, Keziah would say, *Try them on for Ben.*

She needed to.

She needed it because he knew that her own husband had been willing to lend her to another man.

She needed him to meet the part of her that was Nudar.

Avoiding the indigo garments, Dru reached instead for a faded red gown. She would go behind the vault. She chose a headdress, as well, a coin necklace, bracelets. Behind the vault she dressed, as though for a ritual. She wished she had the red-brown henna paintings on her hands and feet. She came out, and he remained seated, eyes sliding over her. He said nothing.

Another glance at him. She'd aroused him.

He said, ''Dance for me.''

''This isn't a wedding.'' Mary had taught her these traditions. The only men Dru had danced for were Tristan and her father.

''Dru, even if you were Egyptian or Bedouin, you could dance for your kin. But no rules apply here. Nantucket's your home.'' He stood, walked to her till their feet were tangled. ''Never imprison yourself with unnecessary rules. Keep things simple.''

''Sometimes,'' she murmured, ''it's very clear you're not an Islander.''

His eyes flickered.

A dart hit her, the ricochet of ill-chosen words. "Neither," she said, "are the seagulls or the whales." Ben touched her hair, close to her cheek, brushing a coin on the headdress, cool against his hand. "I've never been a good protector, Dru. But I'll take care of you and our baby in all the ways I can. The best I can."

I've never been a good protector. She saw him twelve and helpless, bound and gagged in a hundred-degree tent. She heard his apology for failing to spot the photographer who'd photographed them in Gloucester. She wondered again if he'd left her unwatched in Timbuktu to visit Tanelher.

She said, "You took care of me in the Sudan." Twenty years ago. When they were bound in the same tent, when the gags were off, he'd comforted her with holy words in another language and poetry sung like a magician.

"Your brother saved the day. He'll pay for it the rest of his life. But we won't talk about that." He touched her head, the home of her thoughts. "I give you my best. And my devotion."

Her breath raked her throat. His hands on the sides of her head cherished her.

Then he stepped back and eased down against the post to the floor.

She saw no audience but family, waiting to admire and celebrate her arts. He had no instruments, but he was a participant.

All noise disappeared, because this was art, and each part of her collected to a single point of perfection.

She sang in Arabic, in 8/4 time,

*"Ah ya helu ya msallini
Ya-lli be-nar el-hagre kawini..."*

Her voice felt strong and rich, and her hips rose and fell with the rhythm, her body hot and fluid. He understood these words.

> *"Longing, I call to you.*
> *Worries, I tell you about them..."*

She awoke the snake coiled in her pelvis. Even as her feet sank earthward, she drew nourishment up from the earth, far below the attic floor. Ben caught the time and clapped and tapped the floor with her song. The beat vibrated through her, shaping each movement. Breath whirled in her rib cage as she became water, as each muscle moved in rapid isolation with her quick song. She knew the dance without thought. Her hands sculpted the cycles of life, and her hips kept the time of the earth, while her own voice lifted her to a place beyond, the place of the beloved. The beloved was holy. The beloved was her child. And his. The beloved was herself, some self she'd betrayed again and again, even in birth and midwifery. *No more.*

> *"Baheb wa hobbak.*
> *Birrouh bifdeek.*
> *Ya leyt yaleytak tirjaali..."*

I wish, I wish that you would come back to me. I wish. The last words fell from her lips, a mistake. The wrong song for the wrong man. Suddenly still, she waited for silence to replace the plea. It remained like a painting, permanent.

When she faced him, his eyes were on her. "Thank you."

"I wasn't singing about Omar." The worst thing to say. Her face heated.

"You dance beautifully."

He did not ask who'd taught her. He must know.

She looked at him, then bent to pick up the lightship basket. "It's a little small, but I'd like to put our baby inside. Just briefly. After all, he started that way." The words echoed like a faux pas spoken in a loud voice.

Ben got up and kissed her. Held her, making her want again. He teased her bottom lip and lingered in her eyes, his erection tormenting her even when they parted.

"I'd like," he said, "to make you dinner." He checked his watch, then bent to pet Femi. Crouching. Deep breaths. "Seven o'clock? In 'Sconset?"

"We're driving to Gloucester tomorrow," she reminded him, arms around herself.

"We'll have an early night."

Even through two layers of clothing, she glimpsed the muscles in his back. *It's all physical.* It had to be. Because... "What you and Omar did," she said, "lying to me, cut away a piece of my heart. My faith in all men."

He rose. His eyes could look so black. So like Keziah's. No wonder.

And he could be as cool.

"Believe that if you want," he said. "But if you do, you'll hurt people. Including yourself."

His grown-up wisdom stabbed her. "I'd like to see some remorse sometime, Ben."

"You should become more observant."

She drew back in the long gown, raising her head and the weight of the headdress. "I've observed that you're not remotely sorry for abusing my trust in you."

He bent to collect the envelope. "Under the circumstances, remorse would be as unseemly as regret."

He crossed the attic floor to the entrance. Watching in her musty finery, Dru swallowed, knowing all he hadn't said. She saw herself in Gloucester. Across the table from him in the trawler, eating an African meal he'd cooked. Huddling over cups of black tea on the deck, bodies buzzing at each other. His shyly handing her that mug, not quite meeting her eyes.

The attic door closed on her answer.

She held her abdomen. Baby.

His baby inside her. A baby she wanted. Wanted just this way. She wouldn't have it any different. She must tell him this, begin telling him—and others—now. She must tell the tale of her joy in this child.

ALONE IN THE BEDROOM she'd shared with Omar, Dru tried to go through things. Just a top drawer, to start. But she'd stuck a photograph of the two of them there. Omar smiling, handsome, his hair still black. She couldn't cry. Just put it away. Out of sight, out of mind. Suspended in grief and injury.

Do I call Keziah and tell her about the things in the vault? Dru wondered. *Or Mary?* Mary...

Where did you get them, Omar? And how do I give them back?

The first answer now seemed obvious. Somehow, he'd gotten them from Mary. But giving them back?

Adoption reunions were the sole domain of the mother and child. For them to decide. To understand. She must keep Ben's secret—forever if he wished.

She searched for a place for the lightship basket and chose the top of her closet. Someone must go through Omar's clothes... She was too warm, her thoughts one stage removed from the bedroom. She picked up the cordless. Keziah lived in 'Sconset in the home her father's family had owned. Mary lived in Nantucket, here in town, in her grandmother's house, the house where she'd grown up after Faith Hall's death.

"Nantucket Midwifery, Nudar speaking."

Dru smiled, hearing the voice of the first child whose birth she'd seen. "Hi, Nudar. What are you up to?"

"Reading." A lackadaisical sound. "Hey, Keri and I want to do mehndi this weekend. Want to come over?"

"Maybe." It was a North African custom that widows didn't wear henna for four months after the husband's death. In some places, they never wore it again, as though their lives were truly over—which they sometimes were. But Ben had told her those weren't *her* rules, that she should wear it whenever she liked.

"Are you going to work with Mom now?" Nudar's voice broke into her thoughts.

"Keri, may I have the phone?" Keziah asked in the background.

"Bye, Dru!"

Keziah came on. "Did you lose that creep?" The photographer on the beach.

Their walk that morning, the intrusion by the paparazzi, seemed a lifetime ago.

"Basically. Keziah, Omar left me something…that shouldn't be mine." Rules, rules… *Travel light, Dru. As he does.* But none of them—she or Ben or Tristan—would ever travel light. "He left me Nudar's possessions. Her Arab gowns and veils. Headdresses. Jewelry. The pearl earrings from the picture?"

Keziah said nothing.

She's Ben's half-sister, his half-sister…

Dru rushed. "I don't know where he got them, exactly. Anyhow, they're yours. Or your mom's? I thought I'd just give them to you, because they should be yours."

A moment. "Don't you want them?"

"I *want* them to pass from mother to daughter as Nudar directed. The gowns are fragile. Should maybe be in a museum. But this vault they were in seemed designed to preserve fabric. The jewelry's another issue. Want to come over?" Exhaustion poured through her. "And your mother?"

Ben's mother.

"I'll phone her."

Dru huddled on the end of her bed, Omar's and hers. She saw Ben as a boy, in the Sudan. He had been so at home, so immediately courteous when they arrived, accepting them as his personal guests. She had seen him kill a spitting cobra. He'd had no mother. What had he felt today?

Someone—Omar—should have told him before, not let him find out this way. Through the will. And the birth certificate and photos in the lightship basket in the vault.

But those were left to me.

To tell him?

"We'll be there soon," Keziah said, "or I'll call you back."

DRU LEAFED THROUGH the local phone book to find the hospital's phone number. Remembering New Bedford. She'd been an advocate for the women there, befriending all the doctors, even those she loathed, even deferring, girlish, asking, *Please can we let her wait just a little bit before you try the pit?* Pitocin. *I'll walk around with her, see if her labor really is going nowhere.*

Talking their language.

She could do that here.

But who would do it for her at Nantucket Hospital? She'd heard stories from Keziah, about all the usual interventions, either well-meant or for the convenience of a five-star physician who had to fly back to Hyannis or Boston. If a woman wasn't in control, she could wind up with an unnecessary cesarean. Would Ben understand her getting up and walking out in the middle of labor?

They'd hardly discussed midwifery.

She wanted two things. The first was a safe and natural birth for her child. The thought of someone giving her an epidural against her wishes, not allowing her up to go to the bathroom, not allowing food or water... *But that's the way it's done in hospitals.*

She'd fought at New Bedford. How can a woman labor without energy? The whole plan behind withholding food was to prepare for surgery, which wasn't the normal outcome of labor.

She'd lost the fight.

I can't have a baby that way.

But if she had a home birth, would they let her work in the hospital?

Can we cross over? Can't we work together?

Her place was in the hospital. She had a gift for working with doctors, for supplying them with alternatives to electronic fetal monitors, to epidurals, to episiotomies. She gave her women more time. And that was as valid as catching a baby at home. Maybe more so in some instances.

But she remembered the coercion of other nurses, of the doctors themselves. *You know what?* she'd heard them say. *If you're uncomfortable now, you're really going to be feeling it in an hour, and at some point we won't be able to do the epidural.*

Even the World Health Organization had turned their backs on epidurals.

She had to think, had to set aside the distant memories of deciding to marry Omar and leave New Bedford. Yet how could she? *You had to leave; you couldn't stand it another day.*

Just burnout. She was refreshed now. She phoned the hospital, asking for the administrator and saying that she was a CNM hoping to set up a practice on Nantucket in conjunction with the hospital. A secretary took a brief message.

In the meantime, she'd have to get to work. Update her résumé, draft protocols and create a formal proposal for introducing midwifery services at Nantucket Hospital.

Rubbing her neck, she phoned her mother. She resented the secret Joanna had declined to share—even though it was like the secret she herself held for Ben. In any case, Dru wanted her there, when Mary came for Nudar's clothes. Dru had always felt as though Mary was a second mother. Now she didn't know what she felt.

And how would it be for Keziah to learn what her mother had done?

With Omar.

She sat at a desk to work on her laptop, trying to keep the computer far from her body, until Joanna and Keri arrived, followed closely by Keziah and Mary and Nudar. It was almost five o'clock when they crowded into the attic, the dogs outside this time. Dru said, "So these are the gowns. We can hang them here." On the nail. Not mentioning Ben.

Not saying, *Oh, by the way, I'm having Ben's baby.*

Mary, hair darker than her daughter's, touched the indigo cloth. Dru watched her jaw slacken. She wore a combed cotton Nantucket sweater and slacks.

"Oh, cool. Look at the bracelet." Keri tried it on.

"Everything is *fragile,* girls," Joanna said.

Dru moved gowns, held them up, told Keziah and Mary they should decide what they wanted to do with them. She could have someone move the vault; they could protect everything that way. These things were theirs.

"Well, my dear," Mary pointed out, "Nudar only wanted them passed down to one of her daughters' daughters and so on. That doesn't need to happen. It doesn't matter—"

"Somehow Omar got them." A deep rose stained Mary's white cheeks. Joanna studied the floor. Unable to retract the words, Dru reached out to tug on Nudar's strawberry-blond herringbone braid. "Keziah's daughter had Nudar's name."

"You have her name, too." Keziah shifted the auburn wealth of her hair.

I must tell her I'm pregnant. That much.

But no, it was too soon. So many things could go wrong in the first few months.

The thought scared her.

I want this baby. I really want this baby.

Ben's baby.

She touched her abdomen, unable to help herself, the way she'd been unable to keep from pulling up her shirt, lifting away her bra, to see her breasts in her bedroom mirror. Her nipples had seemed larger, rosier, her breasts heavier....

Mary clutched the indigo. "Well, if you really want to give them up, Dru—we'll certainly protect them. I'd like to have these Tuareg garments."

The clothes she'd wrapped Ben in. Dru's body tightened. War broke out inside her, between the mother's rights and the child's. Hadn't those yards of cloth with indigo dye pounded into them been a gift to Ben? But Mary wanted them back. Dru thought, *Why don't you have a relationship with your son? That's more precious than a memento.*

Ben had said to choose her own rules. She was tied to no custom. Even Nudar's Tuareg tradition. "I want to keep those," Dru said softly. "The indigo." When everyone stared at her, surprised, she didn't say she was sorry.

But Joanna tilted her blond head and looked into her daughter's eyes, thinking, perhaps, of Omar's will. And their false conversation, hers and Dru's, in her living room, among the dying whales.

Dru couldn't speak to her now. Wouldn't ask for the truth. She knew now that her mother would not tell.

'Sconset

THE FRONT DOOR was painted pink long ago. The shingles had stayed gray. The porch where Faith Hall had slipped in the mud was replaced by a porch the width of the building, with a railing. All of it half-lost in the dark.

Dru had worn a hooded garment of Tristan's from Mexico, striped cotton, over an embroidered dress made of rayon patches and glittering with mirrors, a dress she'd bought abroad and never worn for Omar, who preferred her bright yellow Donna Karan suit, the suit she might give away because it was so full of memories. She'd bicycled unseen, her skirt gathered in one hand, the dogs running alongside her. As she brought the bike onto Ben's porch, leaned it beneath a window, he came out. *"Shalaam."*

"And peace to you," she answered.

Speaking to the dogs in Tuareg, he stood between her and the narrow dirt-and-grass road. Dru slipped into the house, its sea scent floating with sandalwood, and he let the Azawakhs in, then closed the door.

A Remington sat on a small rolltop in one corner, paper stacked neatly nearby, a laptop case beneath the desk. Above was a photo of Alma and Robert Hall and another of Ben and Robert. She studied the man with his white beard and unruly hair, big chest and long slim legs. His hair had been auburn in the Sudan twenty years before. She'd never seen him again. Ben's adoptive father.

Femi raced under the table, between chairs, galloped down the hall after Ehder.

"I like your home." He'd put candles on the checked cloth. Rustic table legs stuck down beneath. She read the titles on the walls of bookshelves. *The Illustrated Kama Sutra* leaned against a battered copy of the Koran. And all the tales from all those Arabian nights. Then the texts his father had written, tomes that were both immense and thin. *Bedouin Genealogy*. *Libya's Nomads*. There were others, some he had written, some by other authors. Then row upon row of ancient paperbacks.

"Dad's hobby." Ben pulled one out, with its cover art of a redhead with strangely purplish skin, in translucent harem pants and a fringed bolero bra that didn't close. A man played guitar in the foreground. Dru read, "Nine to five at the office wasn't for her...not when belly dancing could shimmy her into the big time." She burst out laughing. "These are great."

"Look at this one." He handed it to her and crouched to pet Ehder.

John Steinbeck. *Cup of Gold*. "'He sacked Panama for a woman's kiss.' Wow!" The cover showed a pirate dipping back a distressed maiden in a yellow dress. She seemed to be reaching for her forehead and had missed.

"He bought many of them new, before I was born. Later, when he was home, he'd cruise used bookstores. He preferred the theme of sheikhs and harems. The cover, he said, was everything."

While the dogs found places to lie, she set her day pack on the floor beside the bookcase. The pack was heavy with the hundred-year-old cloth rolled carefully inside.

"Swordfish okay?"

"Yes." She smiled. Tristan might have caught it.

In the small kitchen, Ben had cut vegetables, prepared the fish. Above and around the door frame on the ocean side of the house, from the right side to the left, someone had painted words in Arabic. Dru slowly translated. IN THE NAME OF ALLAH THE BENEFICENT THE MOST MERCIFUL PEACE BE UNTO YOU! A bumper sticker on the cheap sea-facing door read, in English, I BELIEVE IN LIFE BEFORE DEATH.

Dru grinned and found her eyes wet.

Ben touched the door frame. ''My father.''

''And that?'' Pointing to the sticker.

''Me.'' He smiled. He hadn't yet switched on the kitchen light. He lit the candles on the table, instead.

Dru held her abdomen lightly through her thin dress, then decided to take off Tristan's pullover.

She pushed her hair from her eyes. Found him staring.

''I have something for you,'' he said. ''Wait.'' And ducked into the narrow hallway.

Dru contemplated her day pack. Later. She didn't want to bring him any unhappiness.

He returned with a small, flat package wrapped in brown paper and tied with raffia. There was a card, a watercolor of a black-haired woman on a beach. She opened it.

> To my Gazelle with the Long Black Hair, Trained in the Arts of Dance and Midwifery. To 1001 years. With the deepest affection,
>
> Ben

It bubbled inside her, giddy, confusing her. She giggled.

''You're already disparaging my gift?''

''Not even your card. Thank you.'' There were two lights in her eyes, maybe reflection from the candles. ''Really.'' Feeling wetness on her lashes again, she pulled off the raffia ribbon.

''Dru.''

She tucked the raffia in a patch pocket of her dress.

As she did, he set aside what he'd planned to tell her. Caught her arm gently. ''You're wearing it.''

But it was her own silver bracelet. Not Nudar's. "No. This is mine. I have many things like this. Headdresses of coins. No," she repeated. "Keziah and Mary came over. I'll tell you about it later." Yes. Later.

"Later," he agreed. "Or never." An apologetic smile.

She was glad she hadn't opened her pack.

"What were you going to say?"

He nodded at the package. "It's...something of mine that I like. Now, it's yours."

She opened the paper, glimpsed a silver frame. The black-and-white photograph of two dusty children might have come out of an anthropology tome. A girl in a *mungab,* a virgin's veil—Dru remembered how heavy, how hot the black gown. A wiry boy in a white gown and defiant Bedouin braids. The two in the photograph were not like children playing dress-up. They were a study, sitting on a mat against a dark back-drop. A dagger lay in her lap.

Dru could not remember the place or the moment. She doubted she ever would. She held tight to the frame.

It was the only photograph she owned from the Sudan.

When she looked up, his eyes searched out the recesses of hers. They stood a foot apart. He'd put on jeans. Shaved. Black turtleneck.

"What you said is true," she whispered. "I guess we were betrothed." She knew this not from her memory of living with the Rashaida Bedouin—she couldn't even recall the moment of this photo—but from studying Arabic and Middle Eastern culture. The dagger in her lap was a symbol that he would protect her.

Though he didn't believe he could; he'd said so.

Ben found her slight, pert smile, a smile under strain and grief, very beautiful. He tried to remember Tanelher's smile, her teeth suffering as Dru's never would. Tanelher's poor body. The ache in him remained. Could he leave his own child for a woman in Timbuktu? He told himself he could. He could live in that remote town, so hard to reach, and pray to Allah and never drink wine and try to forget what had happened with Dru and even blame the corrupting influence of the country of his birth. He could live in that rhythm, under the siege of sand, stepping down from the sandy streets into his home, faithful to Tanelher, sharing her mourning for the child with his name.

Dru's eyes, some color he never saw in the desert, touched his gaze. "Thank you."

"You're welcome." He was glad she couldn't read his thoughts.

Which made him wonder how true they were.

And if they were false, why he embraced them, clung to the impossible when he could have fulfillment.

THEY ATE with the checkered cloth between them. He'd poured them both spring water. "I have coffee and tea," he told her.

"This is best for me. And the baby."

"No caffeine? You'll have to teach me about growing a baby."

Dru cleared her throat. "I think you've done well so far."

His eyes remembered the trawler, what had happened to them there. He lifted his glass. "Peace." He reached down the table to touch it to hers.

Dru drank. Set down her glass. The smell of the swordfish, the bowl of stir-fried vegetables, reached her nose.

He nodded at the food, encouraging her to eat. But she couldn't. "I'm sorry, Ben. About today."

Their eyes locked. "I'm not."

As she ate, however, he seemed to sort it out aloud.

"My birth father was Bedouin," he said, "and several generations ago, one of my ancestors was, maybe, Tuareg. The enemy of the Bedouin. Though Bedouins seldom intermarry.''

One married me. ''Why?'' she asked. Everything he'd said was a mirage.

''Because a relative will treat you more kindly. And won't take you away from your family. Many Bedouin groups arrange their tents so that the lines cross those of their kin.''

Dru remembered. The Rashaida had done this. ''So why are the Tuareg the enemy of the Bedouin?''

He cracked a smile. ''Imagine a large caravan, a few thousand animals, many families traveling together across the Sahara. From the sand appear masked men on camels who pull up alongside the caravan and ride beside a group. Silent and tall.''

''They're bandits.''

''They were. They would cut out a group and kill them and steal from them and eat their food. Then cut into the caravan somewhere else, the same way, living off them from one end of the desert to the other.''

His admiration annoyed her. ''Like parasites,'' she said.

''Yes. Centuries ago. Things have changed.''

''You returned to them as an adult because of your friends?''

''Because I'm a journalist and they've been herded into refugee camps, tens of thousands of them, between the borders of countries who won't admit them. Because they've been imprisoned and tortured and murdered. I write about such things.'' He'd angered her by telling her about Tanelher, knew it was a mistake, yet fed it. Pushing Dru away, pushing away the jewel that had always been part of his most private dreams.

The framed photograph lay near her on the table.

Childhood memories were always sketchy. But she should have remembered that one.

"What kind of journalism did you do while you were following me?" Dru asked.

"I was hired to follow you, so it would have been a breach of trust to focus elsewhere. When I wrote, I wrote about you."

"The notes I burned," she clarified.

Eyes suddenly on his food. "No. About following you. A diary."

Dru's carotid artery pulsed like a muscle contracting and expanding. "I want to see it."

"After dinner, I'll read you a page."

A page? "I want the book. I own it. You wrote it while you were working for my husband."

"Whose estate, except for the things you and I were specifically given, has gone to charity."

"It's mine." She drained most of her water.

He stood to refill her glass. "You're right. But I'll look after it for now. I have to write on all the blank pages."

He would take care of it, Dru vowed, only until it was in her hands. Why had Omar ever trusted a journalist?

The same reason I do. He's family. Still, the existence of such a diary, a written document, terrified her. It could be misplaced or stolen or found or published or seen by their child....

But what horrible thing had she done, after all, that he could have recorded?

Only what I did with him.

Sitting again, Ben remarked, "My grandmother was a midwife, you know."

Silverware scraped the ceramic plates. His grandmother was not his grandmother through Robert Hall but through Mary Hall. No—through Robert, his *father* who had loved him and cared for him. Adoption. Legal... Legal?

"I know she was," Dru answered unsteadily. "I think that's what inspired Keziah to have Nudar at home with a midwife.

was there.'' She hesitated. ''I've attended two births in five years. But I've kept up on my CEUs.'' Continuing education units. ''I called the hospital today. Trying to get an appointment with the administrator.'' She told him about her proposal for starting a nurse-midwifery program at the hospital.

Suddenly embarrassed—because of Keziah—Dru chose a piece of bread, fresh from the market in Nantucket, and buttered it. The meal was good for her and the baby. Fish and fresh greens—the spinach and kale. How different from tasting the food prepared by Omar's chefs....

I'll take care of you...my best. And my devotion.

''So... I guess we'll have our baby in the hospital?'' Wouldn't bother him. A lot could go wrong. He'd seen mothers and babies die. He'd also seen them live, again and again, and felt wonder.

''I don't know. I'd like to have Keziah.'' Impossible if she delivered in the hospital. ''But it's early to decide.'' Miscarriages happened. Stillbirth happened. Birth defects happened.

''Would your working in the hospital affect Keziah's practice?''

He was like a conscience, she thought. A man brave enough to be a conscience, with his writing, his articles.

''Probably. I'm not sure how. It *could* bring greater acceptance to her practice, even get her some physician back-up. I've told her my plan.'' Her throat rattled as she said, ''Jean Blade's daughter, Rika... I attended her birth on the Blades' ship. I'm telling you this as a spouse, Ben, in confidence.'' *Spouse. I called him my spouse.*

He nodded, eyes clear and true.

Leaving her food, she told him everything, about sitting in the head on the Blades' ship trying to clear the baby's breath. Thinking, *What if she'd aspirated meconium?* And so far from a hospital. Too far. ''She could have died. Because of where we were, the foolishness of it.'' She sighed in disgust. At herself.

Why was he looking at her like that?

She turned to her food, silently communicating with the baby inside her. *I love you, baby.* She said prayers without specific destination, prayers for her baby. *I want this baby so badly.*

''In Mali—'' he said ''—you went to a birth—and the woman at your house last month—''

Sweat on her upper lip, she told him about each birth.

''Are you afraid?''

''No. But I'd prefer to work in a hospital.'' The words sent shivers over her upper body, vibrating a signal. That she had lied.

Ben's gaze reflected her lie.

''Are you afraid of anything?'' she asked.

He laughed. ''Yes. Many things.''

''What happened—when we were kids—you never seemed afraid.''

''I thought my father was dead. Things couldn't get much worse. And I was fatalistic. I still am. *Inshallah.* Allah willing. As Allah wills. You say it enough, and it begins to mean everything.''

She lifted her knife and fork. ''That sure ought to take care of fear.''

He laughed again. ''Yeah, I've lain in my bed in a hotel that was being bombed, saying, *'Inshallah.'* Looking into the muzzle of a Vz.58, I say, *'Inshallah.'*''

''I wish I could say it,'' she replied soberly. ''And feel it. The best midwives do, in some way. They say, 'This thing, birth, is bigger than me.' Everything they do comes from there.''

Ben heard the tremor in her voice. She'd said Rika was born two years earlier. Had she ever told Omar how she felt? But he'd heard Omar dismiss her midwifery out of hand, barely acknowledging her education, her Master's degree. Ben said, "You talk as if you're different from those midwives. What do *you* believe?"

Her eyes watered.

Shit. I didn't mean to do that, Dru.

"I believe it, too."

She wept, and he took uneven breaths, watching from far away. Going closer didn't cross his mind.

Going outside did.

He thought of other things and put her anguish away from him. He asked, "Why did you give up Omar's money, Dru?"

She shrugged, wiping her eyes. "I didn't. He left me plenty."

In the dim candlelight, he looked directly at her. "Was it for the baby? So the press would never know I was Omar's son?"

"By anyone's standards I'm still rich. And this way—especially because you made the same decision—I'm free. I didn't do it for anyone but me."

Ben cut his swordfish steak in silence.

"What?" she asked. "Why? Why did you give up what he left you? Were you angry at him?"

"It would take some anger for me to turn my back on that kind of money."

Not an answer.

"Everyone likes to be free," he said. "I'm glad you and I both see it."

Dru tried to read his face, tried to understand him. Was there a double meaning in his words? "Free in marriage?" *Tanelher.* He would not go to Mali on assignment, he would not go to—

"I think we've covered that." He got up from the table, restless in his movements.

"You told me in Gloucester that you'd never marry. Why did you say that?" She would hate the answer, but she needed to know.

He stared at her until she realized she had nothing to fear. "You asked about the Sudan, about that experience. It changed me, too."

Dru didn't ask how, because the answers were locked inside her. She had spent nearly every minute of that kidnapping with him. Modesty stripped from both of them. They hadn't seen from the same pair of eyes or heard with the same ears. But they nearly had.

He walked to the table to pick up the framed photo he'd given her. "I think you're the only one I could marry. I've always thought that."

She shifted, jerking, and absently petted Ehder.

It wasn't Tanelher he could marry; it was her.

She said, *"Inshallah."*

"I WANT TO READ it myself." She must get that journal of his and never part with it.

He handed her the black-bound sketch book, open to a page.

"I can't read this. It's not in English," exclaimed Dru. She wanted to know what it said.

Before she burned it.

"That part's Tamashek. I'll read it to you. Come back in the sitting room."

The sitting room faced the black windows and the Atlantic, with the sea cold drifting through. Camel saddles and pillows edged a heavy oriental rug on which to sit. He lit oil lamps and arranged pillows against a camel saddle. "You comfortable?"

She nodded.

"One page. I wrote in the third person."

"Like a novel." Her brow lowered.

He opened the book. "'He watched them paint her skin on the street. For six hours, she sat, while the women in the dark veils let the henna drip through cones onto her hands and legs. Where would she be, in what city and country, when the henna wore off? People wear henna for weddings; the longer it lasts, the better one's chances of everlasting happiness. This was a dark application. She sweated, and flies buzzed around her as she sat on the stones, holding up the legs of her long white pants.

"He had already been to see Tanelher. She scooted on her hands through the dark mud-walled building, through the deep sand on the floor. He had brought gold this time.'"

Dru held her breath.

"'He—'" Ben shut the book.

"What? You can't stop there. Is this the time you made…offers?" *And how could you have made offers if what you said earlier tonight is true, that I'm the only one you could ever have married?* Not to mention that it was exactly as she'd thought—he'd left her unprotected.

Unprotected.

And had already admitted that doing so violated his agreement with Omar.

"I read you a page. That's what I promised. Let me get my bicycle, and I'll ride home with you and your dogs. I promised you an early night."

Because they were going to Gloucester.

Tomorrow. She'd planned to tell him that she was sure she'd seen her father. That she hoped to find him. Could she trust Ben now?

Ever?

She went to use the bathroom. Reaching it, she noticed an open doorway opposite, further up the hall. An accent lamp with a cracked Tiffany shade was turned on, and she stared in at the old four-poster and a dark writing desk. Photos were spread across the desk. Old photos, with white borders. Of the Sudan?

Femi joined her, reminding her somehow that she couldn't go into this room, probably his bedroom.

When she returned to the living room, she found the framed photo of the two of them on top of her day pack.

"What did you bring in there?" he asked.

"Something foolish." She met his eyes. "I gave all of Nudar's things to Keziah and Mary. Except the indigo garments that were in the lightship basket. They're yours."

His face lost some color.

"Mary wanted them," she said.

"You keep them safe for me."

At that moment, she didn't think of Mary Hall Mayhew, his mother. As she bent to tuck the photo in her pack, she thought again of Tanelher and wondered if she was the reason he didn't want to see blue.

CHAPTER SIX

Tristan came to free us. He had tried—and failed—to cover the bodies with sand. Skye wore clothes not her own, maybe belonging to the men, and she asked me, "Do you know this desert, little sheikh?" She got behind the wheel of my father's Land Cruiser, stolen by our kidnappers, and stayed there until I convinced her to move. A woman seen driving would be bad. Tristan had to drag Dru from the sight of the bodies, both his arms locked under hers. I had trouble persuading him or Skye to leave the weapons. I knew the way to the Rashaida's last camp, the camp they would keep for several weeks yet. They would greet us with Bedouin hospitality. It didn't matter. I was no longer afraid. I wanted only my father, who was dead, and whose murder Tristan, instead of I, had avenged.

—Ben, recollections of a fall

SHE WHEELED HER BIKE into the garden, and the outdoor lights switched on automatically. She could see the lamp's glow in Sergio's room, as well. Ben had left his three-speed outside the fence, against the house. She rested her bike against an iron table, not wanting to take it back to the shed. "Good night."

He studied the bright lights.

Under her wool gloves, her fingers were stiff. Her nose felt tight, membranes beginning to freeze.

"Want me to put your bike away somewhere?"

"I'm fine. Thank you for dinner and riding home with me. Good night." *Tanelher. He loves this Tanelher.* She reached for the back door, thinking she should get used to using her key. But Sergio had heard her and unlocked it.

"Good night, Dru."

She hugged herself, queasy.

He stepped toward her, edging her into the shadows.

Dru said, "You walked away from me in Timbuktu to give jewels to another woman." It came out wrong; the part about another woman wasn't supposed to be said. "I mean, you abandoned your job."

Shadows hid his face. "I'm sorry. I felt you were safe. In retrospect, it was inexcusable. Would you like your check back?"

She put her hand over her eyes, a desperate gesture in the dark.

He saw a woman struck.

"Dru. Please forgive me." He grasped her shoulders, which were strong and muscular yet seemed thin in his hands. Arms around her, head against hers, he could say, "I'm cruel when I'm scared. I'm sorry." Holding her.

"What are you afraid of?"

"You." He kissed her cheek and jaw, found her mouth.

Dru hugged him, around his shell and sweater.

The surge raced hot to her loins, pooling heat. Would it always feel this way to be kissed by him, with his unmapped desert spaces? Yearning acutely to know those places, to find an untapped well?

There had never been this kind of kissing with Omar.

His kisses had never excited her.

Other things had pleased her. His love of beauty. His cleanliness.

Not like this man who was saltwater and sand in Nantucket, who would be dust in the desert. He was unattainable adventure and wildness. He was the kind of man she'd known would never marry her.

The kind who never married at all.

His tongue caressed her, his arms settling her body closer to his.

She dared to touch his hair.

His eyes shot into hers. In Arabic he said, "Good night, gazelle," using again that word for a beautiful young woman. "I'll wait till you're inside."

When she had closed the back door behind her, before she left the solarium, she opened her pack to look again at the two of them, dusty urchins, his dagger in her lap. His grandfather's dagger. He looked wild, more Bedouin desert child than American. They were both sandy and beautiful.

And, Ben had said, betrothed. No. No, that wasn't it....

Dru took a message from her mother—*Don't forget to take Keri's art for Tristan.* To Gloucester. She said good-night to Sergio and went upstairs.

She'd changed the sheets in Oceania's room herself. It took only minutes to gather her toothbrush and toothpaste and a comfortable nightgown from the master suite. *I can't sleep in here again.* The room she'd shared with Omar.

In the spare room where Oceania had slept, she laid a midwifery text on the bedside table, then opened the stand on the photo's frame and set it on the table. She pulled it toward her again. Her fingers fumbled, and it fell, and she cried out before the glass broke. No sliver on the floor, everything contained in the frame. Tears filled her eyes. Using a *Mothering* magazine Oceania had left behind, she struck the glass out, then removed the back to get another piece. The frame was not new, she realized now, had held the photo for some time. The cardboard in the backing flew onto the floor and she clutched the photo and saw writing on the back, not in the hand of the card she'd received that evening. The script was similar, ma-

ture and masculine, but faded and more exact, neatly crowding
the back of the print. She squinted, holding the photo by its
edges to read.

The cohabitation forced on Ben and Dru by miscreants
was seen as ignominious by our Rashaida hosts. Almost-
marriageable adolescents had eaten from the same bowl.
This was the best remedy, under the circumstances. Here,
Ben chivalrously restores Dru's honor. Groom's dagger
in bride's lap symbolizes his protection of her and her
honor. Had to threaten him with return to Cambridge to
win his cooperation, but see the result!

The next morning
November 11

HE PICKED HER UP in a twenty-year-old brown Datsun with
faded paint and took her bags to load in the small trunk, then
helped her get Ehder and Femi in the backseat. She didn't
apologize for the volume of her luggage, a backpack and tapestry suitcase, plus the dogs' things, all dwarfing his scuffed
backpack and laptop case. Instead, as he slid behind the wheel,
she removed the photograph from the small manila envelope
in which she'd placed it and handed it to him by the edges,
upside-down.

He read it as people reread familiar things, the creases at
the sides of his mouth and at his eyes deepening. He handed
it back. "This just proves you've always been mine."

"It just proves you had to be forced at gunpoint—"

"Not at gunpoint." No humor now.

Chided, she retorted, "You get my drift."

"Arranged marriages sometimes work out very well."

She swore at him, and he drank from the paper coffee cup beside him, then switched on National Public Radio, murmuring, "The tape deck eats tapes. There's a thermos of herbal tea in the back."

"What is it?" Studying the writing on the photo, she knew she sounded shrewish, but it mattered. Not every herb was good for pregnancy.

"Celestial Seasonings Lemon Zinger."

"Thank you." She found the steel thermos. "Red raspberry is the best."

Drinking more coffee as he slowly negotiated the cobblestone streets, he said, "I'll remember."

As she waited in the car with Ben for the ferry to Hyannis, Ehder and Femi scrambled around each other in the backseat, barking at other dogs. Dru felt conspicuous. That morning, she'd decided against disguise of any kind. People needed to believe the baby had been conceived after Omar's death, however soon after.

The ferry arrived and Ben's car joined the others. The ferry bore only late-autumn Saturday morning traffic. Dru listened as the whistle blew the hour, thinking, *I'm lucky. I'm lucky to live here in this wonderful place, surrounded by my family. And Baby.* As she clasped her abdomen lightly, Ehder tucked his head around Dru's seat and kissed her neck.

Ben scratched the dog's head. "We know who you love," he told Ehder.

Fondling the dog's ears, her hand near Ben's, Dru said, "I wish I could go to Libya, to meet the people you lived with when you were young."

"It's not romantic. It's a developed country with cities and highways. Some of the Tuareg in the south are nomadic, but that's all. Anyhow, no one's getting tourist visas now."

Dru's window was on the starboard side of the ferry, no car to her right. Privacy. "When were you last there?"

"A few years ago. They were trying to promote tourism—before they stopped issuing tourist visas. I wrote a feature."

"For whom?"

"I worked for the Associated Press. You can see they gave me all the dangerous assignments. Because of my great courage. I had to quit to stay alive."

She ignored his levity. "I'm glad you're alive. You're a hotshot, aren't you?"

The ferry had begun to move, and he turned to look behind him at something. "So why are we going to Gloucester?"

A reporter's intuition? "To see Tristan." If only she could trust Ben. She wanted his help. "Have you been to Algeria?" she asked, instead.

"Not for several years, since they began saying that belly dancing is a prayer to Satan and that all journalists are non-believers who must die. Libya, Algeria—these must be suggestions for our honeymoon. Can I interest you in Afghanistan? The Sudan? Why didn't I marry a nice girl who wants to stay on-island? Isn't that how you Islanders say it?"

"We aren't married."

"I want that photo back. I've waited twenty years for my wedding night. Anyone would say that's given you adequate time to mature."

"I don't even remember what happened in that picture or why. That's how traumatized I was." Too late, she heard herself. But wasn't it fair response to Robert Hall's written record that he'd needed to *threaten* Ben? "And by the way, I have been legally married, so please stop pretending I never was." The words cut her, leaving her throat, the way she realized they'd hurt him, hearing them. He'd said fear made him cruel.

Me, too, she thought.

"What happened in that picture is obvious. Why is because we were almost sexually mature and spent time in a tent together when we were kidnapped. In the eyes of the Rashaida, you had brought dishonor on yourself and your family. My father wanted to smooth things over so we could stay and find Tristan.''

She nodded, understanding Arab ways and not wanting to talk about it anymore.

Femi and Ehder nosed against the top of the back windshield, leaving prints on the already-dusty glass.

Ben's fingers found the back of her neck. He massaged the muscles and tendons in a slow gentle rhythm, before he released her and turned her toward him. To hug.

She forgot this was the Steamship Authority ferry or that there might be others around. He was warm, smelling of coffee, pressing his face to her hair, swimming in it. ''You're beautiful. Though when I was twelve, it would have killed me if anyone knew I admired you physically.''

This, she thought, was how boys turned into men. In seconds and years. ''It hurt my feelings, the things you said about the bride price.'' Back then. His insults.

''You're wise enough now to know how twelve-year-olds show their deepest feelings.''

It didn't make sense. ''If we were forced to marry... I don't remember that, but I do remember those bride price conversations.''

''They happened later. The wedding was for show.''

''Oh.'' She peered at him. ''What was the bride price? In the wedding?''

''I can't remember. Probably a lie. Saying my father had sent your father money. We lived hand-to-mouth.''

The bride price was a lie.

What would her father have done had he received...? *Spent it.* She nearly laughed.

Then she told Ben.

About Oceania and the man she'd seen with her in Gloucester and all her written conversations with the pregnant woman who had named her child Tristan Drew. About a cowlick and the shape of the man's eyebrows and a bump on his nose and the way he had stood. Enfolded in the car on the water, she said, "I have to find out if that was my father, Ben." She raised her eyes. "You know what it means if it was."

Motion, over the waters of the harbor, away from shore.

"That other people died, and he's never faced their wives and children."

"Yes. And he abandoned his family, which is minor in comparison."

"Not quite minor. But take my word for it—here, have something—" Ben offered her a bag from the bakery. "Not you, Femi. *No—Ehder, sit.* You don't want to run after a father who doesn't want you."

The voice of experience.

He surprised her—that he didn't see a story in this. That he wasn't curious. The discovery washed over her, cleansed her. He was decent. He was a journalist, not a scandalmonger.

Seconds later, she wondered if she'd just fallen in love, at that moment, captured by his lack of interest in the sordid, which was like an Islander's.

Dru rolled down her window a few inches to let in the cold sea smell, to drag it into her. Ehder stuck his dark brindle muzzle out, to the noise of the engines and the wind and the water. "Maybe that's why I need to know about this man," she said. "To know he *isn't* my father. But the resemblance was too great. And if it's him, why doesn't he want me? Us? Any of us?" *Even Tristan and me.*

Ben collected stray crumbs into an empty bag, which he gave to Ehder and Femi to shred. Dru clearly didn't grasp the whole picture with this story.

"They shouldn't eat—" she began.

"It won't hurt them. What does Oceania do?"

"Well, she's going to stay with her sister in Nova Scotia

and take care of her baby. And do some computer— Oh.''
Dru stopped. It wasn't the first time the coincidence had oc-
curred to her, only the first time it had hit her with such force.
''She works for Sedna. The environmental group.''

He glanced at her.

''They're ecopirates. They're opposed to commercial fishing, in particular. They've scuttled commercial fishing vessels
in port and damaged others at sea.''

''Why?'' He could guess but behaved as though he had no
clue, assuming the role of journalist from habit.

''Overfishing.'' Dru said, ''He loved us. When he was
home, we were all over his boat.''

Ben knew ''when he was home'' wasn't often. And that
''we'' meant ''Tristan and I.''

Dru rolled up her window, closed out the damp.

He drank his coffee, noting her silence against the dogs'
chewing on paper in the backseat. Should he try to put it out
of her mind or tell her what he knew?

It was this. If her father was alive, someone would find out.
The story might involve only a handful of scallopers from
Nantucket and their families, but this was news—whereas who
she slept with was not. Not real news that real newspapers
covered. If Turk Haverford had walked out of the sea and
disappeared to involve himself with ecopirates, someone
would find out.

And unless Captain Haverford had suffered brain damage,
the angle would not be compassionate toward him or his family.

Ben found brain damage unlikely.

While the chance that Dru had seen her father seemed fair.

''Why's Tristan's boat in port? He just left, didn't he?''

''I haven't spoken with him yet.'' He was hard to reach.
And how would she have said who was with her? How would
she explain anything? He'd been told she was coming; that

was all. "I left a message at the marine store. The girl there said they had a problem with the boat's ice machine."

Pumped with Freon before the trip. The ice would cool the fish in the hold. Broken, the ice machine was cause to return to port prematurely. The fishermen wouldn't be paid. The captain wouldn't be paid. The ship's owner wouldn't have earned the cost of her few days at sea.

A thorough captain inspected and serviced his ice-maker before every trip. Tristan Haverford, given the kinds of vessels with which he'd been entrusted, the years he'd been fishing, would have.

He felt Dru watching him.

"I know you wouldn't write about any of this," she said. "You're family."

His dark eyes slid sideways. "If there is a story, you'll wish that I would. And that I'd been the first."

It scared her. He believed her and believed she'd really seen her father. But he was saying something else, something she didn't want to hear.

She chose not to hear.

Chose to squeeze it out.

Because it was huge and dark as thunderheads over the sea.

Gloucester

MOST OF THE world's ocean fishermen agreed that women on fishing boats were bad luck. Which hadn't stopped whaling captains from taking their wives to sea or women from becoming captains of fishing vessels, as Tristan's wife, Dorea Andrade, had. But Turk Haverford had allowed women on his boat, and his boat had sunk. And Dorea had died fishing haddock on a longliner out of Nantucket.

Dru wasn't welcome aboard the *Sarah Lynnda,* the swordboat Tristan captained for another man. Seeing her approach the ship's side with Ben and Ehder and Femi, Tristan lifted his black eyebrows in greeting and turned to answer a crew member's question. Dru thought no one could look so tall or handsome or more like a ship's captain than her brother with his jaunty blond ponytail and the scars on his face, lines running from beneath his eyelids to his jaw.

"Warm enough?" Ben asked her.

She had chosen a navy peacoat Joanna had given her, wore it over thick wool tights and a long fisherman knit sweater, and she'd used an oversized tapestry shoulder bag for a purse. "Yes." She held the dogs' leads tight as the sighthounds watched the gulls.

The *Sarah Lynnda* was a hundred feet long. She belonged in the category of vessels over 100 gross registered tons that groups from Greenpeace to the radical group Sedna blamed for destroying fisheries worldwide, and she was one of a fleet of sixteen boats owned by a billionaire from Portland.

As Tristan stepped down to the dock, his sea-colored eyes stared past her at her companion.

Ben nodded at the man he would have elected Most Likely to Commit Homicide at Sister's Husband's Wake. Tristan hugged Dru.

She held on, hard. Sometimes fishermen didn't come home. "You know Ben."

Tristan's gaze remained subtly murderous.

A breeze whipped strands of Dru's hair over her face, and she struggled to shove them back and hang on to the dogs. As Ben caught the leads, she withdrew from her twin.

Tristan straightened, growing like a tree.

Ben held to stillness, legs relaxed and steady on the dock. Wind orchestrated the constant ping-ping and clanging in the air. While the sea rocked the floats beneath them, Femi twisted several times around the blue brindle's lead.

Absently, Dru measured her twin's height against Ben's.

Tristan stood six foot three, Ben a respectable six feet. And Ben's form, lean and hard, and his face with his steep nose and lean cheeks, had become familiar.

Safe.

Where suddenly her brother's was not. Tristan's sometimes savage ways matched his scars, and he lived in her memory more than in her presence, so that she'd forgotten the exact effect of the three vertical scars gouged beneath each eye and of the teeth his childhood illness had grayed. Rheumatic fever... Dru saw into the past when the scars were wounds, open to strep, or maybe he'd had strep throat. A doctor had said more likely it was the unsanitary circumcision. But already, he'd become like this, and *this* was something she wouldn't define.

Finally, his shoulders eased, though his eyes never left Ben's.

It had never been like this with Omar. Just Tristan saying, *He's twice your age. More!* Never this. She removed the envelope containing Keri's art from her shoulder bag. "For you."

"Thanks." Tristan took it up on deck and slid it through an open window to the pilot house.

Dru waited until he returned. She said, "I think I saw Dad."

"You always think that."

Impatiently, he bent to examine something on the gunwale of the *Sarah Lynnda,* but he looked like someone reaching for a lover. She hated him for being a fisherman.

"We'll be here a week," he said. "There goes the last trip of the swordfish season. We're rigging for lobster now. Because of some asshole."

Dru scarcely heard. "I saw him with Oceania."

Tristan's glance included Ben in male dismissal of her imagination.

"He had that cowlick. Same nose. Eyes. I asked Oceania.

She said it was a man from Nova Scotia, but she took a long time saying it. She *knows* it's him.''

''Where is she?''

''She and the baby have gone to her family. Listen to what she named—''

''She's deaf!''

''So what?'' That was how much *he'd* communicated with Oceania. He hadn't even known she planned to keep her baby. ''If you spent some time ashore maybe you'd learn some things about the rest of the human race.'' She didn't say, *Including your daughter.* But she saw Keziah's flared nostrils, heard her mother's sighs. Any woman could hate his job. ''Deaf women can be good mothers, too.''

''I only wondered how she'd hear the baby crying. Relax. Was it a good birth?''

Her heart thawed. Tristan had always wanted her to practice midwifery. He'd held it against Omar that she hadn't, which wasn't fair. ''It was beautiful.'' No need to mention her tension, Keziah's bringing her into line. In a hospital, it would be better. It must be.

Ben was watching her. She noticed too late. Cleared her features. ''Will you visit us down at the trawler?'' she asked Tristan. The trawler where Ben had come in a mug like the lightship basket in which his mother had given him away. Where Dru had sent his sperm into herself with a catheter. Where they had become close.

Where they had become friends.

Tristan raised his eyebrows. ''You're planning to use my boat?''

His boat? It was, of course. One of those she'd bought while she was wealthy and put in other people's names to assure her anonymity when she stayed on them, took refuge in their cabins. Her eyes burned. Tristan's boat. Bought when she was filthy rich, rich enough to throw money at one thing or another with a husband who allowed it, the husband who had just died. Omar had all but disinherited her with that shocking and horrid will, blasting her with the news he had a son and with that son's identity. Now her brother…

She'd come to Gloucester wanting to bring away one souvenir.

That coffee mug resembling a lightship basket. Lightship baskets for precious babies… Making them. Holding them.

She and Ben had washed the mug in hot water and soap and put it away with the other cups. She had moved in shock as they cleaned the boat. White, like a zombie, as she dried the dishes Ben washed. Because her husband was dead.

Strange.

They'd cleaned up the boat before they left.

And Tristan had made a joke about whose boat it was—or thrown a barb at her and Ben, the tabloid lovers.

"Actually," Ben said, "we're going to mine."

Dru trembled. She'd forgotten. She'd forgotten that boat existed, although she'd guessed Ben must have slept on it the first night in Gloucester, when he'd followed her there. It was berthed in the next marina, and it must have been the boat mentioned in the will.

It was a boat with a history.

Omar had taken it out of circulation to spare the last owner pain.

Dru had never been aboard, never walked down to look at it.

It had belonged to marine explorer David Blade, whose youngest children she had helped bring into the world too far from help.

He had owned this ship before he bought his mine-sweeper.

Its name was the *Skye,* and Dru's cousin Skye had died after jumping from the ship's bow while it was underway. While her husband and three-year-old son looked on.

She felt all of it now. All she knew. She had been in the Sudan with Skye. Heard her screams, her pleas and begging, her sobbing, for hours. For hours.

She was pregnant, and she would sleep on the *Skye*. Instead of Tristan's boat. A boat of which Omar had said, "Yes, of course. Buy it," as he had said yes to so much.

She swung away, yanking the dogs' leads from Ben, and headed back up the dock.

No one called her or followed, and she was glad, because the tears streamed now, sticky and wet, tears for a time before Omar had suggested she conceive a baby with another man. For the time when she'd still believed he would kill another man who made love with her.

When she'd still believed in his love.

Long before she knew he'd succeeded so thoroughly in continuing his line. Or began to suspect that was what he'd always intended.

WHAT DRU HAD MISSED—Tristan's blaming his return with an empty hold on someone else—Ben had noticed. The story Dru had told him on the ferry was too present in his mind. Already, he had stepped out of himself and become an observer.

He'd observed Tristan's reactions to what Dru said. He'd observed Tristan. And the observer had tapped him on the shoulder and said, *You should have protected him.* Back then.

Skye was dead.

Next to her, Tristan had been damaged the most.

Now the observer said, "What brought you back in? Dru said there was a problem."

The wind had picked up. Tristan seemed not to feel it blast through the opening in his patched dark-green shell. He watched boats bob in their berths as he said, "What are you doing with her? First you sleep with her when she's married to…"

Ben listened. To Tristan's voice and the wind and distant voices on the *Sarah Lynnda.*

"You know, if you loved her and wanted to marry her, maybe I could forget you ever said you didn't. Or *didn't say that you did.*"

On Orange Street, after Omar's wake.

Tristan's gaze promised slow and interesting homicide. Eyes plucked out with fishhooks, feet removed with a fishing knife, body dangled from the stern of the *Sarah Lynnda,* head hung from the bow.

Ben moved away, hands in his pockets. Became the observer. He didn't have to wonder what had formed Tristan. He'd been there.

And he hadn't.

He kicked a crack in the dock. Lightly. Looked up. "I hope to be Dru's closest companion for the rest of her life."

The turquoise eyes, so much brighter than anything in the harbor, sharpened, then eased their focus. "Somebody broke the ice-maker. Sabotaged it."

Ben peered up the dock, searching for Dru. She'd found a bench, and the dogs had their feet up beside her, better friends than any human knew how to be. "What you said about the trawler made her cry. Percentage-wise, Omar didn't leave her much."

Tristan saw her, too, and immediately started up the dock. In long strides. He broke into a jog. Then a run.

Ben turned to the ship, gazing at it, memorizing it. Seeing already the story that would unfold. There was no such thing as coincidence. When a fisherman in overalls and a plaid wool jacket nodded at him, Ben introduced himself. Admired the boat. Talked fish as though he hadn't spent most of his life in the desert.

Because the rest he'd spent in Massachusetts.

The fisherman learned he was a journalist and asked him aboard, to look at the ice-maker.

SHE HADN'T SEEN HIM leave the dock, but Dru knew it was her brother before he sat down. The movement of air displaced by his body and his presence. The smell of fish. His canvas pants were grimy and the dogs loved them. His hands fell all over their coats, hugging them. He hadn't shaved and had dark whiskers the same shade as his eyebrows and eyelashes. This time, when she saw his scars, she thought, *Why did you do that? My poor half, what happened in the tent?* Though she had heard the cries.

All the cries.

And some were his.

"What's wrong?" he said. "Down. Get down," to Femi.

"You have to say 'Off.'"

While he did, she put her handkerchief away. Petted Ehder, made him lie down.

"So Omar shafted you."

"No. I'm rich. I've got the house and a hundred K a year. And some more, here and there, plus my own money. That's wealth."

"I was a jerk about the trawler." He petted Femi's head, stroking her sand-colored satin ears. "What's up, Dru?"

He meant with Ben.

Dru had planned for this moment, planned against the temptation to tell everything. For the baby's sake, she couldn't— shouldn't—tell him Omar's plan, which had revealed itself in so many dimensions, which might have been more innocent than it appeared. Yet had encouraged her to shed her honor.

She had agreed, and now it hurt.

"I'm having Ben's baby."

Tristan was motionless. She wished she could read his mind now. She tried and felt sorrow and rage, compassion and love for her. His arm stretched around her shoulders, hugging her. He rested his head on hers.

"We're getting married." She laughed, enjoyed the closeness for a moment, then produced the smaller manila envelope from her purse and handed it to him. "In fact, I guess we always have been."

Tristan's fair brow creased. Lips rubbing lightly together, he returned the photo, never reading the back. Had he been at the ceremony? Would he be able to tell her...? No. She knew that much. "Did you ever see me dressed like that?"

He leaned forward, elbows on his knees, admiring an ancient tugboat.

Dru carefully replaced the photo in the envelope and then in her bag. "I'm sorry for bringing it up."

He glanced up. "What?" Baffled.

"The Sudan."

He straightened. Shrugged.

Gone from her.

Dru clasped his hand, trying to bring him back. "You wanted to know about Ben."

A blank stare.

He searched the area, found the right dock, saw the *Sarah Lynnda.* Slowly relaxed. Held her hand between both of his.

She had to ask. Even when he was...not himself. "Tristan, do you remember all the time from the Sudan? Have you ever forgotten stuff?"

"I forget what we were talking about."

An evasion? Yes. On this subject, she never received anything else. "Ben. We were talking about Ben. My fiancé. I showed you that interesting photo."

"There have been a lot of interesting photos of you and Ben."

In the tabloids, he meant.

"But it's hard to see you having an extramarital affair, even with our childhood companion. So let me guess. Omar was unfaithful.''

''No.''

''You wanted a baby, and he couldn't give you one. Oh—that hit a nerve, didn't it?''

She felt him study her sadness.

''Was Omar the one who wanted a baby?''

''We both—I'm ashamed of agreeing, Tris. He didn't like sperm banks, said they were a bad risk, preferred that one of us—''

No comment.

No comment.

He allowed both Ehder's paws on his knees, stroked the dark ears. ''He sent you looking for a sperm donor?''

Particular sperm. She closed her eyes. Ben's birth was Ben's secret. The depth of Omar's treachery was something she didn't want Tristan to see or grasp.

Her twin hugged her clumsily. ''Do you want the baby?''

''I love the baby.''

I love Ben.

Tristan shifted, concern on his face. Arm loose around her, he stared out at the harbor. ''The trawler is yours, okay? You bought it. It's yours.'' His eyes were moving with the water as he spoke.

Dru broke from the circle of his hold. Faced him. ''I want you to make a plan with me. About looking for Dad.''

''Dad's gone, Dru.''

''Tristan, I've admitted when I've seen people who weren't really him, but this time it was.''

He sat forward on the bench, one hand on his knee, ready to return to the *Sarah Lynnda*.

He had taken their father's death even worse than Dru had. Because they'd struck each other. Fought. Tristan had never said how things were left after that strange and sudden violence.

But two years before his boat sank, the day she and Tristan had returned from Sudan, their father had picked up Tristan and carried him away like a smaller child, and Tristan, twelve, who swore he was now a man, had tightened his arms around Turk Haverford's neck and his legs around their father's waist.

That winter when their father's boat hadn't returned and their mother faced the shock of lapsed insurance, kids at school had said Turk lost the boat because he'd been too greedy for catch. Tristan had sent two of them to the hospital before he was suspended. The next time, he was expelled and had to go to a private school for half a year. They hadn't had the money, and home school had become delinquency. Nantucket did not appreciate graffiti. His teachers, who recognized artistic talent, had not appreciated Tristan's sometimes violent expression in the margins of his homework. Or instead of his homework. Dru credited Keziah with saving him, somehow, Keziah growing her herbs and vegetables and flowers, Keziah with her spinning and magic, with her Puritan posture and sharp tongue. Listening. Caring. Taking him out on her father's launch to gaze into the water. Pointing out that he'd never be a ship's captain without school.

They couldn't stand each other now.

Who liked to face a savior and remember a debt? Who liked to see the saved?

Tristan said, "You haven't told me one thing that makes me think our father is alive."

"He stood with his left shoulder below his right."

Tristan fit his back to the slats of the bench.

"His left eyebrow had a ripple right here." She showed where hers arched, more smoothly.

"Who did Oceania say he was?"

Dru dug in the tapestry bag. She handed him pieces of paper

she'd folded and tucked in her appointment book. "Our conversations on the subject. But she would sit and *stare*. And, Tristan, she works for Sedna."

"Sedna?" He snorted. "Dru, Dad may be alive for all I know. He might be pearl-diving in the Red Sea or soaking up the sun in Baja. But he's sure as hell not hanging out with a pregnant *deaf* woman who works for Sedna. He's a fisherman." He gave the papers back to her, and his thoughts branded her, his unspecific, hoarded rage. "And so am I. I have to work." He kissed her.

She embraced him. "Will you come for dinner tonight?"

"On the *Skye?* No, thank you."

So he knew which boat was Ben's.

Skye was a wound for all of them.

Especially Tristan. But maybe he wasn't thinking of the Sudan at all. They'd spent several holidays with Skye afterward, too.

"I've never been aboard," Dru admitted. "Have you seen her?"

"From the dock." He'd already sailed for distant seas, beyond these boats. He saw depths Dru didn't know, and she had seen Skye's eyes that way, and it worried her. Once, one of Tristan's crew had told her, *Your brother's a volatile man. It's a blessing he doesn't drink.*

"Please have dinner with us, Tristan. We'll go out. I want to be with you."

"I need to work. Rig." He rose, gone far from her.

Disappointed, she only nodded.

He said, "It's a boy."

Dru twisted her head sideways, squinting up at him. The gray sky was bright.

Grinning, leaving her unsure if he was teasing or had sensed something about the tiny creature in her womb, he covered her head with one big hand. "Take care." He began to walk away, then turned very suddenly, an athlete's spin. "I love you."

The back of her neck chilled at the look in his eyes. She wanted to ask if he was all right, to tell him she was always there, that she could help. But he strode away, sweeping his gaze around him. Femi tried to follow him. Dru pulled her back and petted her, then Ehder's silky fur. All three watched Tristan's retreating form.

The notes she'd exchanged with Oceania still fluttered in her hand, the way Tristan's hair blew behind him.

Their father was alive. Almost certainly. Why didn't Tristan care? Why wouldn't he believe or help her?

BEN TOLD DRU to take the dogs ahead to the *Skye's* slip while he brought their things from the car. They'd bought groceries in Salem, and he would carry those, too. *I'll make a few trips,* he'd shrugged. *Go ahead.*

But on the way to the slip, Dru saw heads turn to stare. Maybe at the dogs, maybe at her. *Don't recognize me.* She smiled casually, watched the behavior of the Azawakhs. Would these same people notice Ben, too, as he walked from the car to the yacht, carrying luggage and groceries? After telling Tristan they'd stay on the *Skye,* he'd come up with three or four other plans. He'd tried to persuade her to go to a hotel with him—or to accept Tristan's suggestion, that they should stay in the trawler.

Too late, Tristan.

It had become very important to stay on the *Skye.* Still, Dru glanced all around as she hurried down the dock.

She saw no one but a couple of yachtsmen engrossed in their own business and uninterested in hers.

Her eyes caught the letters on the stern.

Skye.

Exposed, she held the dogs' leads, the gray air batting her.

The baby was safe in her womb. The boat's dark atmosphere drew her forward. Morbid curiosity warred with compassion. She knew David and Chris; husband and son had both seen her…jump. From the bow, to be sucked into the screws.

No gangway in sight, no invitation to board this vessel.

From the dock, Dru reached up and lifted the mahogany railing. She stepped aboard ahead of the dogs and called them till they jumped up. She let them off-lead and ducked along the port side of the cabin, passing triple-paned cabin windows over stained glass. Fiberglass met teak at the aft deck. She entered an enclosed entry to the cabin, a diving alcove, Dru concluded, like that on the Blades' new ship. But these surfboard racks and dive lockers stood empty and dusty.

Once, Dru had asked, *Why did you buy that boat?* Omar had purchased it before she'd married him.

The Blades are family. Now they won't have to see it in some port or other and remember. A look in his eyes. Omar had known what it was like to want no reminders.

Family, he had said with need. His adopted family, stretching back to a captain named Haverford who had been Skye's ancestor as well as Dru's.

Dru unlocked the cabin door with the key Ben had removed from his key ring while she watched his fingers, finding them perfect, his hands muscular and lean and well-proportioned. She stepped down into the yacht. Sapphire carpeted its plush steps and the vacant, ghostly salon. Koa end tables, couch and chairs draped with sheets. Dru turned to peer down the aft companionway and saw her.

A watercolor. Skye, a tide pool sucking at her ankles. Dru's own eyes stared at her from the face of her cousin, and she cried. *"Skye!!!"* She sank onto the top step. Off-lead, Ehder had raced down the forward companionway and into the galley and crew's quarters, but he joined Femi, leaping toward her to lick her face.

She remembered.

No! No! God, Please!

The cries in the heat that parched your lungs, sometimes seared them. The screams, mingling with Tristan's different cries, the sounds of a long-ago Tristan, who hadn't yet become a fisherman or lost a wife or abandoned a daughter. Who hadn't yet scarred his face.

Skye used to say, *You are going to be so pretty, Dru. Look at you. You're a milkmaid. Want me to French braid your hair?*

Want to try my beer?

This is vodka and orange juice. It's called a screwdriver, and it's not fancy. Want a taste?

They'd spent many summers together, before and after the Sudan. Before and after the kidnapping there, the horror that, in future years, was never mentioned by Skye and her father. Of course, they'd all made a pact, back in Africa. Skye, Tristan, Ben and Dru. Right after it happened, while Ben drove the Land Cruiser...

Never mention it again.

One summer Dru and Tristan had gone to Montecito, California, Skye's home. *Okay, we're swimming to that point over there. I do it every day, whether I like it or not. In the winter, I wear a wetsuit. Sunscreen is a must. The sun is so hard on your skin.... Let's go shopping!...Dru, you have to have that purse—no, I'm getting it for you....*

The memories continued, even as she rose to find the aft head. There... *Did you ever look in this mirror, Skye?* Dru brushed her hair, freshened her lipstick. David's sister, Erika, had painted that picture out there, the watercolor. She'd painted one of Jean, too. The whole Haverford family, every last one, had always wondered what David had to do with Skye's death, how it had happened. Everything. *You should have told us, David.*

His son, Christian, had told her, instead.

She'd confided in Omar, and he'd said, "I don't really think so." Dru had let it go, but she should bring it up again—

Reality penetrated. She'd almost forgotten his death, had let it become wallpaper behind her. She had stayed away from him for all those months—*he stayed away from you, Dru!* Now she couldn't speak to him about suicide, about knowing Skye in her dark seasons, snapping and cruel and unwilling to leave whatever four walls she occupied. Or the chance remarks: *It's always good to know that if things get bad enough, you can kill yourself. It comforts me.*

Dru dropped her purse. Everything rolled out, and Ehder came running. She searched for her things, stumbled toward the aft staterooms, then forward. More doors, more options. One opened into the captain's quarters; it wasn't her boat, and she went no further. The other door led down. She sat stiffly in the galley.

If she was free—or courageous—she would walk to the beach to throw a Frisbee for her dogs, without caring who saw her.

It will get better. The media had already lost interest in her and Ben. But the papers had not forgotten Omar's death or the relief he'd given to many countries. Ben had bought *The New York Times* at a gas stop today. She hadn't looked at it.

Dru heard footsteps on the dock. Then voices. One was him, intonations she'd heard from no other.

Hungering for companionship, she hurried past Skye's portrait and up onto the aft deck as a man from New Jersey said, "Come on, Ben. If it isn't me, it's somebody else. Let's have a beer." Heavy-set, dark-haired, he nodded at her from the dock. His overcoat covered a button-down shirt, and he wore a driving cap with a snap brim and toted a shoulder bag. "Hi." He winked, with slanted eyes, finely drawn brows. "I'm

Cole.'' A fleshy hand thrust up toward the railing. A deep warm voice.

She lingered in the shadows before slipping along the cabin to the opening in the rail. Ben steadied her as she jumped to the dock. He had brought the groceries and her bags.

She shook Cole's hand. It was warm and heavy and not quite moist.

''It's a *pleasure,*'' he said.

Ben said, ''This is Cole Fletcher. Who are you with now, Cole?''

''Oh, I hop around. Had a feature in *The Globe* last week, covering this Sedna stuff. Ecopirates. Crippled a codfishing boat last week.''

Tristan was right. Her father wouldn't have anything to do with Sedna. And this man wasn't talking to her and Ben because of Sedna.

Cole beamed at her. ''Ben is very savvy not to introduce you. He knows what a charming guy I am. How are you, Mrs. Hall? Please let me offer my condolences. Your husband was a great man.''

''Yes.'' She gestured between Cole and Ben. ''You two must know each other. Enjoy your visit.'' She began to take a bag from Ben, but he shook his head, helped her board, instead.

''Bye, Cole,'' she heard him say as she slipped beneath the canopy.

''I have to write something, Ben.''

''Go ahead. It's not journalism.''

''Oh, words of wisdom from Journalism's Gift to North Africa? Or should I say, North Africa's Gift to Journalism?''

Dru paused out of sight, the cockpit and helm hiding her from the men on the dock. Damp harbor cold bit her cheeks.

''I was going to pass something on to you,'' Cole continued. ''But you'll find out soon enough.''

No answer from Ben. Something thudded onto the deck, one of her bags, she guessed.

"No, I'll tell you now, just because I'm curious. Did you always know you were the natural son of Omar Hall?"

Dru touched the door handle, emptied.

Then full. Not only with her baby, the sweet love inside her, but the precious infant Ben once was. A mother's wrath almost sent her to the port railing, to ask Cole if he could imagine what it was to be adopted, which didn't mean being chosen; it meant losing one's natural parents. Or being given away by them.

Ben rounded the corner of the diving alcove, into the dark shadow of the canopy.

"I'm sorry, Ben," Cole added. "I should have offered condolences to you, too."

Dru went below, leaving the door open. He followed. His cheeks were darkened with beard. As he closed the door, she said, *"Freedom."* That gift she'd dreamed of, they'd both dreamed of, over dinner the night before. The freedom to live as other people. The freedom to which she would never be entitled, for two strikes against her. She was born a Haverford, born into a family known for its bad luck, and she had married one of the wealthiest men in the world. She glanced at Skye's portrait, Skye languishing alone.

It had been just the same for Skye—and marine explorer David Blade, when he married her—though his family had its own acclaim.

Ben touched her hair, rubbed it against her scalp.

Her self-pity evaporated.

The dogs' tails slapped Ben, their bodies bumping his legs as he shed his jacket. He'd get his own bags from the car later. "The news about Omar—about me—it's out there now." He shrugged. "Sounds like one of Daniel's employees chose a ready-made retirement fund over the nine-to-five grind.'' He cast a glance at her, seeing how she took his fall.

I've never protected you yet.

And he couldn't protect her from what was coming, not this media frenzy but the story, the real story she'd come to Gloucester to find.

He wanted to smash glass.

As Ehder crouched nearby, regarding him anxiously, Dru tore a sheet off a couch and sank down. The sheet wadded beside her, spilling onto the carpet. ''I'm so sorry, Ben.''

For him. And noble in her acceptance of her own situation.

He would be noble in failure.

''It must hurt.''

What I know will hurt, Dru. It will hurt you. He didn't want to discuss anyone's parents, but later they'd have to.

''Daniel must be sick about it.'' She looked up, with eyes like those in the portrait, just the same iridescent shades of blue, like the inside of an abalone shell. ''It might be a little hard for our child to understand. Probably he—'' an echo of Tristan's prediction, boy ''—won't want to hear about it. And there's nothing unusual we have to tell, except that we fell in love—'' she stumbled, got up ''—so soon after my husband's funeral. I'm not sorry, Ben.'' The sobriety of her eyes again. ''I love this baby. I want this baby. *This* baby. I wouldn't have it any other way.''

The baby. Seeing the two lines on the pregnancy indicator, Ben had contemplated a valiant fight of sperm, the power of biology and attraction.

Until Dru threw up in the sink.

He heard her fineness, her abundant mother-love, and marveled. From far away.

''What would you like for dinner?'' he said.

''They're going to be all over us.'' Ignoring his question, she leaned forward, elbows on her knees, chin on her fists. ''You can't imagine how it is, Ben. With the press.'' She paused on the irony and left it. "I always needed security guards, sometimes several, and now I don't even have Mitch. They'll board this yacht. They'll camp on the dock."

Desperation in the media, in humans, wasn't new to him. But there had always been something at stake. It was different to enter an embassy after a bombing or be deafened by the cries of the grieving after a tragedy. Different still to follow a thread of suspicion...

He must protect her. This time he must. She was his betrothed, his bride, carrying his child, and he was all she had.

Failing—falling—wasn't an option.

In his coat pocket, folded pieces of paper...

She sat in the chair, madonna-like.

Just as he had that night in the trawler, when she was the wife of the man he'd believed—correctly—to be his birth father, he saw that her lips were beautiful, natural and perfect, her eyes mixed sea colors, pale turquoise and ice, with their own shadows, her eyebrows perfect. He saw the dirty child in the tent, bound and gagged. He saw her dressed like the Rashaida girls her age, her black hair covered. Besides his father's, she'd had the only blue eyes in camp.

In the trawler, he'd wanted her.

She'd never asked about the mental and physical process that had allowed him to produce sperm in a coffee mug. She was reserved. She'd blushed. Their touches had fractured him.

He hadn't understood his feelings, what was happening to him, and he didn't understand now. It was nothing like his longing and love for Tanelher.

Those two strange days of privacy had succeeded, and she said she was glad, even without Omar. Some women, he knew, wanted babies that much. At any cost. But that wasn't what she'd said. "You want this baby," he clarified. "In particular."

"Yes." Her hands spread over her still-unrounded belly.

Then she reached for Femi's long blond head. The Azawakh lay at Dru's feet, holding herself gracefully erect, like a princess, and Ben petted her, too. "Ben, I'm sure you wish Tanelher was having your baby instead. I'm honored that I'm the one."

He sat back, opening his mouth. It was like pulling into an intersection for a left turn when the light was yellow. Counting on the right thing to happen, the right words to come. An absent hand on Femi's back, he closed his mouth, unwilling to begin some lifelong process of lying to her.

She smiled, head tilted sideways in compassion. "Thanks for never lying to me again."

He rose in one motion, startling both dogs. "Since you can tell the difference between a story and a lie, thanks for never again suggesting I did." He plucked up the grocery bag and carried it into the galley.

Dru saw his back depart. Her eyes glistened. She was jealous, and a long time passed before she considered their exchange about lying.

He'd never been told he was Omar's son. He'd just believed he was. Ben was right. It wasn't a lie.

She walked slowly to the companionway, careful on the steps descending to the galley. "Where did you learn to cook?"

He turned. The refrigerator, the sink, the overhead lockers, enclosed them. "I'm angry. I'm angry that I didn't insist we go to the trawler. I'm angry that I let Cole see us. I promised to take care of you, and this is what you get. This ship should be scuttled. David should have scuttled it.

"It certainly is beautiful."

Hands behind him on the counter. Reserve behind his eyes.

She opened and shut the refrigerator indifferently. "I'm sorry I said you lied."

"I'm sorry you think I want anyone else to have my baby."

He'd thought the words would choke him. They didn't. They were true as flawless poetry. His body didn't move, but the blood inside him vibrated, rushed, his pulse quickening, his breaths shallow.

That hadn't been the hard part of what he had to say to Dru tonight. "I'd like to take you home," he said. "After dinner. You came to see Tristan, and you did." Silence. "But there are some things you should know, things we should discuss, before we leave."

She screwed up her face, puzzled, girl-like.

He swept past her and up into the salon. The pocket of his shell... He touched misery in the shape of a folded piece of paper. It had the sad, half-guilty and familiar feeling of journalism, of delving into darkness, looking death in the face, exploring the ruin of human beings.

In the galley, he handed her the folded page from a magazine. "A crew member on the *Sarah Lynnda* gave me this article on Sedna."

She saw the photograph of Sedna's newest ship, *The Dawn Treader,* ramming a two-hundred-foot Japanese fishing vessel. In the inset, two Sedna volunteers dyed seals to prevent an annual hunt. A woman's blond dreadlocks half-covered her face as she approached a dyed seal to photograph it.

"I saw her at your house after Omar's burial," Ben said. "I came in while you were upstairs. Talked to your brother. Is that Oceania?"

"Yes. Doing just what she told me."

"Have you heard of Captain Thomas Adams? Goes by Dolphin Tom?"

She shook her head. Then stilled. Looked up. "Tom Adams is the name— That's who she said the man was. But she said he was a fisherman. Cod."

Dru wished Keziah was there. Keziah knew all about Sedna. Greenpeace, Sea Shepherd, Earth First! Keziah belonged to every one, when she could scrape together the money. She was trying to get approval for a bio-dome greenhouse in 'Sconset, a community greenhouse. Concerned with the environment, oriented toward pristine health, she drank spring water and ate blue-green algae and winced over any food that wasn't organically grown. Meat never touched her lips—or those of her daughter, Nudar.

Because of Omar's interests, Dru had paid more attention to the global economy, to poverty and famine. Really, they were all connected.

She felt Ben's gaze and looked up. Into a face that wasn't always strictly handsome. She'd been near him enough to see him look homely, bones too prominent, something too primitive there. That attracted her, too. She studied the photo again, then skimmed the text.

Tom Adams? "Who's Dolphin Tom?"

Ben faced the counter. "Dinner will take some time. Let's have a snack." He cut carrots and broccoli and cheese, and Dru found the dogs' bowls and their food. While she fed them and filled water bowls, Ben opened Evian bottles for Dru and himself.

It settled into her, like sand finding the ocean floor after a disturbance in the sea. Tom Adams?

"Let's go upstairs."

To Skye's portrait. In the salon, Dru lay on the plush rug. *I'm not ready to hear this.* She stalled. "What did Omar say about that painting?"

"Nothing." He smoothed the magazine clipping on the carpet. "I'd never heard this till today. It's not the kind of thing I follow. But the man who founded Sedna, Dolphin Tom, is reclusive. He keeps to his ship and won't be photographed."

Dru had a piece of cheese near her lips. She didn't know what to do with it. She ate, resenting the moment till she could speak. "Where are they? Where do I find his ship, Ben?" *My mother. My brother. What will they do? What will any of us do?* "When can I see my father again?"

He didn't answer at once. "We would have to track them down."

What he'd said on the ferry came back to her. About looking for a father who didn't want anything to do with her. No wonder Tristan had walked away from her that afternoon, walked away from her idea that their father might be alive.

Because if he *was* alive, he had turned his back on Dru's mother, on Tristan, and on her.

But that wasn't the dark sickness lying within her—near her baby, her little baby. And it wasn't enough to have made Tristan walk away.

By hiding from the world under an assumed name, their father had avoided facing the wives and children of the men who had died on his boat.

And telling the story of what really happened that day at sea.

Did he feel a day of reckoning approaching? Or look in the mirror each morning and wonder if this would be it? His secret couldn't be kept. Cole Fletcher was writing stories on Sedna. And when he learned the truth—

"Dru."

She blinked.

Femi's sandy head was in Ben's lap, her eyes on his face, in love with him. "People disappear for a reason. You've thought for a long time that your father might be alive. Want to tell me why?"

No brown in his irises. Only black.

In tiny motions, she shook her head.

He moistened his lips, watching. "I'm going after this, Dru. It'll be best for everyone if I can break this story. You won't find a more sympathetic journalist on earth."

CHAPTER SEVEN

The mercenaries' vehicle had rolled over my father's
legs but in deep sand, dislocating a kneecap and nothing
worse. He found himself able to walk, and he limped
toward the Rashaida camp and spent a night alone in the
sand and didn't die. My ecstasy at his being alive made
me nearly indifferent to my companion's suffering.
When I saw Dru in Rashaida dress specific to her age,
I said I would like to marry her someday. She said, 'You
like Skye.' I answered, in Arabic, that Skye was not a
virgin.

—Ben, recollections of a fall

BEN STARTED to rise from the sole of the salon, to make dinner.

"How will you do it? How will you learn the story?" she
asked. "Are you going away?"

Something near his ribs constricted. His work was about
going away. He'd take his family anywhere he had to go, as
his father had. But never, knowingly, into danger.

Sedna wasn't dangerous. Physically harming other human
beings—even by, for instance, slowly sinking a boat with crew
aboard—opposed their tenets.

"I'm not going anywhere—" a stabbing catch in his throat
"—without you."

It was the look on her face then that made him head not for
the galley but for the deck. And the dock. To hold the railing

and try to ignore truth. When that failed, try to shake free from it as from a *jinn,* a demon.

But it was just truth.

He called the truth "Your Life Is Different Now."

It was an ambiguous name for pledging yourself to someone else. To have her for all the days. And for her to have you. That was what the Tuareg called *ténéré,* their word for wilderness. Their name for the Sahara.

His name for marriage.

Before his hands lifted from the splintered wood, he remembered she was pregnant and they were having a child. He dropped his wilderness metaphor in the harbor of the city where he was born and bound himself to the wet coast of his birth state and to a beautiful island where his family lived. He sweated in his clothes, fighting the *jinn,* the *jinn* that made him want to run. Not with her. Away from her.

He would be a good man, *Inshallah.*

"Inshallah, Inshallah, Inshallah…"

HE'D LEFT THE DOOR of the captain's quarters open while he organized notes for the story and transcribed his interview with Dru from an hour before. What she had first declined to tell, she'd offered in a change of heart. The tape recorder played beside him. He paused it periodically to catch up with his keyboard. "Tristan's basketball coach, Luke Hightower. Neither of us knew anything about it, but we heard her admit it that night. Their door—" *Pause.* Type. *Play.* "—Was open. We were supposed to be at the library, a research report. My mother said his name. She said, 'I didn't have sex with him, Turk. I had *emotions* with him.' Then she—" *Pause.* Type. *Play.* "—Gasped and seemed to run into something. My dad broke some curio, and my mother asked him to…" Her natural pause. Long. "Stop. Tristan went in, and it reminded—I thought of—"

One would. Tristan killing three grown men.

That wasn't all she'd told him tonight. She'd answered painful questions about her father's habits, about when his boat went down, about scalloping in general. She'd answered when he asked if she thought her mother had loved *him*. She'd answered yes.

"That was *why*," explained her voice without her body. "Tristan and I both knew that. My father was never home. He—I guess he handled money badly. I told you he'd let the insurance lapse. We found out later. She wanted to get his attention. It wasn't the best—"

Ben heard her filling the tea kettle in the galley and stopped the tape. His laptop's clock read 8:30. When she knocked on the open door, he said, "Come in," and saved again and quit his file. He shut down the machine, then flicked on a green-shaded lamp.

As the hard disk spun down, she climbed the steps in a black cotton dress, accented with Bedouin embroidery in red and gold. She was barefoot, although the ship was cool, and carried a tea tray. He stood to get it, and she rolled her eyes as he took it. "It's not that heavy."

But she almost tripped over Ehder, who had come up the stairs with her. Ben set the tray on the roll-top desk, which was bolted to the teak. Femi had lifted her head from her place under the desk but didn't rise. Ben held his chair for Dru. "Sit down."

Instead, she stood to pour his tea, adding sugar as she'd seen him do, then stood before him sweetly. "I trust in my cousin's honor that he will do all he has promised."

A smile pulled at his lips. "If it isn't my Bedouin bride, showing me her beautiful hair, no less."

She eased down to the teak sole, sitting back on her heels. From above her, he saw crescents of fair skin and a few freckles and the tips of lashes as thick and black as her hair. Her lips matched the red in her dress.

He crouched in front of her. "I'd hate for you to cover your hair."

Her eyes glittered at him in all their shades. Eyes like Skye's.

"By the way, your trust in your cousin's honor pleases me, but your trust in his memory—or maybe his powers of discernment—is misplaced. Which promise do you mean?"

Her chin was high, her eyes icy darts. Playful. Or passionate. "I know my cousin will name them for me."

He asked, "What's bothering you, Dru?" And immediately realized he'd said the wrong thing. The source of anger is fear. He sat beside her, the hairs on his arms rising. The reaction came powerfully. He couldn't sit beside her and not want to touch her. He looked into the ice eyes, tried to warm them. "I promised to take care of you. And devote myself to you. And to our baby." He searched his mind. "I promised, when I was twelve, to protect you." He knelt up to snatch his Cross pen, a gift from his father, from Robert Hall, off the desk. "I promised like this." He set the pen in her lap, on the handwoven cotton of her dress.

Dru saw his hand, a man's fingers, place a silver pen in her lap and felt a much heavier weight, a curved dagger given by a smaller hand. She swallowed. Robert Hall spoke to someone else in Arabic. A camera shutter clattered. The boy had Bedouin braids and beautiful black eyes, and she was getting married but, *It's not real. That's the truth, Dru. Still, you must tell no one that it's not real,* Robert Hall had said. *It's to avoid your having to go home without your brother.*

Who had run away.

Tristan's gone! Tristan's gone!

Dru asked the boy, "Are we done?"

She thought he nodded, and she began to stand, then stopped. To whisper, "Will you go look for Tristan with me?"

Ben's breath trembled. Her whisper belonged to someone who didn't know she was in the captain's quarters of an unloved yacht. But he knew what he'd done by placing the pen in her lap. She'd told him she couldn't remember the wedding ceremony in the Sudan when they were children.

Remembering could look like this.

Where had she gone? Where in time?

"Baby…" Ben caught her arms, noticing for the first time that her body was dear to him. The blue eyes that had been his comfort in the tent when the cries came from beyond were eyes he needed in his life.

Warm now. She was so warm. Lean back against the berth and hold her while her dogs came over to sniff her, to try to lick her. *Oh, little girl, I couldn't take care of you.*

"I want Tristan," she whispered.

A tear hit his cheek. A dog's tongue followed.

"To come back."

"Dru." He should take her to a hospital. He'd seen people like this before.

But not Dru.

His hands seemed bigger than the sides of her head. Easing the concerned Azawakhs aside, he turned her face to him. "Dru, look at me. Where are you, Dru?"

We're supposed to stay in the tent, the boy, her cousin, told her.

Was this when it would happen? Where were the women Skye said would hold her down?

"Don't touch me." She grabbed the dagger. Ready to use it on him.

He spoke Arabic faster than her; why wouldn't he speak English now?

She said, on purpose in English, "You're not supposed to

marry cousins, anyway. This isn't real. Don't do anything to me.''

What would I do to you? His look of disgust reassured her. *I'm not going to do anything to you. We're too young. But it is real. We're fourth cousins twice removed, and we're going to be married forever, whether you like it or not. I'll never let you divorce me. Even if we were actually cousins, the Bedouin marry their first cousins. They'd prefer if I married Keziah.*

''That's totally gross. I'm going to tell her you said that.'' He was being deliberately obnoxious, although his answer about their being too young had the ring of truth. But what if the women came? Skye said they would make him... Holding Ben's dagger, she started to stand. He took it back from her.

She went outside. Brightness. Dust. Animal smells and human waste, too.

She was married.

She was married to Ben Hall. It wasn't real. His father had promised they wouldn't even sleep near each other. She would still be with the women and children, while he would live with the men.

What Skye had said hadn't happened. No women to hold her down while Ben would...do that to her...and make blood to show everybody, everybody in the whole camp.

Ben hadn't even touched her.

She walked away from the tents, toward the desert, legs wobbling, nearly folding.

It didn't happen to her, what had happened to Skye.

Dru cried. She couldn't help crying, it was so awful.

It's so awful! Mom, I want to come home! I want Tristan to come back!

''I want Tristan. Tristan, come back.'' She sobbed, shuddering into warm arms, shaking in Robert Hall's arms. No. Men never touched her here or touched any of the women but the littlest girls. Fighting free of the body, the stranger, she saw him. Her mouth stretched wide, a rattlesnake strike, trying to scream. She didn't know him. *Who is he?*

A dog slurped his tongue over her eye. *Ehder. Femi.* She knew them.

And…

Dru. Dru. Baby, are you all right?

"Dru, it's Ben. Baby, it's Ben. It's okay. You're grown up now. You're thirty-one years old. You're on a boat. You see that? Look over there. I know, the windows are stained-glass. It's kind of weird. Do you know who I am?"

Yes. Not like she knew the dogs, though. *I'm pregnant. Little baby, are you still alive?*

"Dru, here. Shhh…"

"My baby."

"Your baby's fine. You're fine. Baby's fine." Ben touched her abdomen through her cotton dress. Its slight rounding seemed no sign of pregnancy. How could she feel so much for the fetus inside? It was probably an inch long at most. He held her against him and rocked her. "Your baby's fine."

Dru's mind churned. She was only a few weeks pregnant. Every moment mattered. *This moment.* The baby made everything clear. She knew Ben.

She remembered her husband had died.

As she wiped her eyes with her sleeve, Ben crouched beside her, helped her up slowly. "Will you lie down and let me cover you up? You and our baby?"

A thick comforter covered in blue plaid flannel fell over the edges of the bed, the berth. Ben drew it back to show a bed made with blue flannel sheets and a blue wool blanket. She sat at the foot of the bed, then crawled over the blanket to the pillow and lay down. Ben covered her, bringing the covers to her chin.

Then he knelt by the bed, the dogs beside him to watch over her.

The world settled.

Ben.

Her baby's father. Why was that so strange?

Some reason, far away.

Oh, he didn't love her.

He loved someone else.

"Do you know what happened just now?" he asked.

"Yes. And…a long time ago." She began to say it, to speak each moment. She told him word for word, except the Arabic. She threw it all out in a quick flat voice, emptying herself, even saying, "Skye told me you would take my blood." She said all the rest, too. Then uttered the final line of the story. "Omar was delighted I was a virgin."

Ben's jaw went rigid.

"Back then—even when I had to marry you—I was never afraid of you. Just of what other people could force us to do. You convinced me it wouldn't happen."

He hesitated. "It still does happen like that in some places. It's…what they did—when—where I was young. The blood is a sign of the honor of the woman's family. Sometimes, if there's no blood, her cousins or brothers kill her."

"God." Dru closed her eyes.

Her shaking had stopped. The focus had done it. He wanted to wipe her face, her tears. Words might be better. "Remember what I told you today? We would have had to leave the Rashaida?"

Without Tristan. Everything had happened so fast. Their arrival at the Rashaida camp—after that oath in the car. Skye's making Dru and Tristan and Ben swear not to tell about *her,* even though she would leave the women's tent each night to vomit, even though she had ceaseless diarrhea and trembling. She'd refused to cut short the trip, despite the unavailability of medical care. And Robert Hall had agreed that rape should not be mentioned among the Rashaida. Then Tristan had tossed out in front of several men that he'd shared a tent with Skye. Before the Rashaida could say that the girls had brought dishonor on themselves and their loved ones, regardless of the circumstances, Ben's father told his hosts that Skye and Tristan, who was so tall already, were married. But the Rashaida knew Ben wasn't and was, in his father's eyes, much too young.

Then Tristan left.

And Robert had told Dru, *You're going to marry Ben. Unless you want to go home.*

Without Tristan? Never.

The marriage had been nothing, sleeping apart, segregated by gender, because the Rashaida, too, agreed they were too young to be intimate, really too young to be married.

Ben knelt, resting his arms on the bed, plucking at her covers. "I never knew you were afraid. Actually, I—enjoyed—aspects of that situation."

"I couldn't remember. I'd forgotten so much till tonight. Months." But now she knew that he'd sometimes addressed her as his wife and had tried to order her around. He had been the person she knew best, her friend in a strange world, who had sometimes fixed her Arabic or told her she needed to do something differently. But most importantly, had come up with many scenarios of Tristan's adventures and return.

"Do you want to be touched?" Already looking under the comforter, he spoke casually, giving her room to refuse.

Dru nodded. Searched for warmth in the hollow space beneath the comforter. His hand. She closed her eyes. "You take good care of me." The words triggered recollection.

Seeing her forehead creased, the thought striking, he helped her out. "Before this happened tonight, I was trying to repeat my promises to you. I think you wanted me to do something. I'm pretty slow. I haven't guessed what you wanted."

She murmured, "Your journal."

Ben hit his forehead lightly, then stood.

Picking up his pen from the floor, he saw in his mind the photo of Sedna's flagship. He set the pen on his desk. Were all daggers so useless? He would find the story, *Inshallah,* and, despite what it did to Dru or anyone, would enjoy finding it, enjoy every second of horror and discovery.

But he couldn't protect Dru from her father's choices.

He had never once protected her.

From his pack, he removed the journal he'd begun reading to her the night before, at his home in 'Sconset. He joined her on the bed without asking, propping a pillow behind him. She rolled toward him, and he let his thigh touch hers, the comforter thick between them. Stirred, trying to quiet his own body, he opened the book. "'In the sand street, he watched men stare at her, in insult and admiration. With the mind of a man, he guessed at their thoughts, their desires for—'"

"That isn't where you left off last night." She sat partway, then all the way up. Away from him.

"I didn't promise to read it in order. It's hardly more than notes."

"You creep. You haven't changed in twenty years!"

"Give me a little more credit than that." He threw aside the journal to reach for her, and she was gone. Out of the bed, the dogs following her like a fan club.

Her gliding walk made her seem suspended from the ceiling, drawing his eyes to her straight back and smoothly held shoulders, her thick coal hair. She was carrying his child.

He said, "I love you."

They both heard it.

She stopped, stood unmoving.

"The one I hold in greatest esteem will hear nothing offensive to her ears if she stays."

Her back to him, facing a windowsill defaced with carving, with the word SKYE, Dru hugged herself. She heard again his rough, low voice with its accent of the world, a voice that had come to English second. She heard the dock and the water and I-love-you.

When she faced him, Ben was waiting, frozen on the bed. Only for an instant. He came to her. Still not touching her.

Dru noticed that most of all. *He can't possibly be afraid.*

"I didn't mean to make you uncomfortable," he said. "But you didn't see the men staring, all over Africa. Were you really looking for someone to—"

A quick shake of her head, just to cut him off. She'd been looking for herself. Dru.

At eleven, Ben thought, she'd listened to a woman being raped.

To…rapes.

As an adult, she'd married a man who would urge her to make love with someone else. *With me.* Here in Gloucester, he'd waited near the phone booth to hear what she said to Omar. What Omar said to her. His own emotions had been uncontrollable. Ben had moved through the chaos by focusing—on Dru. He had wanted her very badly. And very naturally. He'd had to put Omar out of his mind—as she'd had to put him out of hers. It had become easy.

"Your apology is accepted," she said, her voice wavering. "I was angry because I wanted to hear the scene you didn't finish reading." Her smile stretched like cellophane. "It's not important."

I held you, Dru. While you remembered a marriage ceremony in which we participated as bride and groom when we were children. Is that important? Did you hear what I said to you a minute ago?

Briefly, he hated all women.

"I'm also angry because I don't know you. I don't know what you feel toward Mary Hall. Or how much time you've spent with the person you've called aunt your whole life. And I wish you'd burn that.'' The journal.

He answered fast, spitting out answers. ''I've spent a total of maybe forty-eight hours in Mary's company. Twice that with Keziah. I feel the things adopted people feel. Other feelings I have? You're pregnant. We should be married. I wish I'd come for you when you were twenty-three, before he—''

''We fell in love.''

''Don't tell me about it.'' His forehead dark, brows lowered. She'd never said she loved *him*. ''And in my experience, people who want to burn words are nearly always afraid.''

The moment when he'd told her he loved her was gone, Dru saw, broken by this. She wanted it back but couldn't lift her voice above a whisper. ''Whenever you think it's appropriate, we can be married.''

If he reached for her, Ben knew, she would stiffen in his arms. There were no scorching looks like Tanelher's. Dru had a New Englander's reserve. But she was not the same woman who'd carried in a tea tray an hour before.

Unwillingly, he saw her in the arms of a sixty-six-year-old man.

His own father.

You told her to sleep with another man! You cast away her honor, that she saved for you!

Rage left him immobile, but Dru had been peering off, into nothing. ''Ben, I'm thinking about Sedna—and what you're going to do.''

Just like that, she was on another track.

Her eyes rose to meet his. ''We need to talk to Tristan. At least about Sedna. He'll know everything. I think we should go to the *Sarah Lynnda*. Tonight. He likes to work through the day. But he won't let me on the boat. I'm a woman.'' She slipped past him, sank down in his chair, Ehder at her feet.

''Good. You shouldn't go anywhere. Except to bed.''

"I'm fine. It's over."

Her quivering had grown fine, almost invisible. Yet remained.

"I worry about him," she said. He'd floated away that afternoon, in the midst of their conversation. The Sudan, of course. Hell. "I am worried. I need to talk to him again."

Tristan was a fisherman. Of course she worried.

"His psychological health isn't good."

This wasn't front-page news, either, as far as Ben was concerned. Nor did anyone have to search medical archives for the reason.

"At the moment, I wouldn't call you a picture of psychological stability. Dru, you weren't here. You spoke in the voice of an eleven-year-old."

"I know. It was real." Brushing past it. "I want to see Tristan."

An echo of what she'd said in her memory trance.

Maybe she *should* see her twin. Twenty years ago, they'd finished each other's sentences and spoken a language no one else understood. Their attachment was primal.

Feral.

When Ben and Tristan were covering the bodies of the kidnappers, the mercenaries, Tristan had said, *They wanted Dru next.*

Ben said, "Let's walk over there. Bundle up."

SHE WORE HER DRESS, long wool socks, and a pair of low black clogs, with her peacoat over the dress. A gray stocking cap over her ears. Ben wore his grandfather's flight jacket.

As he met Dru in the salon, one pocket sagged, clinking, tinkling with its treasure.

The dogs' leads were in the diving alcove, but Ehder stood beside her, wagging his tail, occasionally jumping up, while Femi raced around the cabin. *"Go lie down."* With some physical guidance, both dogs obeyed. "Ben, do you have that article on you? To show Tristan?"

"Don't need it. I'll talk to him." He'd get nothing useful from Tristan. It wasn't why they were going. They were going so Dru could see her twin, as she'd begged with tears on her face. This he could give her.

He surveyed the salon. One lamp burned. He'd shut the curtains earlier, over all but the stained glass windows, which were never covered. His fingers grasped metal in his pockets, felt the grooves of filigree.

Everything that had sounded fine in his mind earlier, while she dressed and while he opened his pack to search for the items now in his pocket, suddenly seemed crass, especially in the presence of two dogs eager for a walk. But Ehder had found one of the bones Ben had given them after dinner, and Femi darted after the other Azawakh, to wrest away the prize or share it.

Dru said, "Ready?"

"No." Eloquence had abandoned him, and she was too pretty and vulnerable, much too vulnerable, for a clumsy address. Maybe for any address at all.

"When you were eleven—" his voice was July in the Sahara "—a few months after the traumatic ceremony into which you were forced, I did say I'd like to marry you someday. I—" He wanted to thank her for being pregnant with their child, for loving that child so unconditionally. "I love you."

Dru memorized his lips and the pattern in which his beard grew. Her legs shivered; her heart pounded. A prickling warmth needled her face and scalp. She stretched, isolating muscles in natural motions that were dance, separating herself from his words.

The dogs shot the bone down into the galley and collided going after it.

Ben stood closer, touched her cheeks.

Want to kiss you... He wanted her.

Ténéré.

Love was a long wide desert, all right.

She was his well.

"I love you," he repeated. He would catch her if she fell into another fearful trance. Catch her whenever she fell or at least help her up. If he could do only that. He reached into the pocket of his jacket. "These were my grandmother's, a betrothal gift from my grandfather, a sheikh. I give them with love to you." He held them out to her, the silver ankle bangles with their intricate patterns, trimmed with bells. Dru took them, looked down to her ankles in her wool socks, then lifted her face.

He spoke in Arabic.

He spoke in the dialect of the Rashaida.

And of the Awlad 'Ali of Egypt.

And of the Harb of Saudi Arabia.

And of the Rwala.

And of his ancestors in Libya.

He spoke in every Arabic dialect he knew.

He said what he understood these people would say, and after he had asked her in so many ways to eat from his bowl and drink from his cup, he said, "Will you marry me?"

The bangles still in her hands, Dru touched his arms lightly, feeling only cloth at first. Then pressing to the warmth and strength. She envisioned Omar. Ben hadn't made the request so important to the Bedouin, had not asked her to give him many children, *Inshallah*. The agreement she'd made with Omar was why.

It was also behind her. Had to be.

Maybe the catharsis in the cabin, the memory of an earlier marriage, however invalid, had brought her here.

She saw the man across from her, and on the thought that she'd never love another, her eyes filled.

She'd believed that about Omar.

Afraid. I'm afraid. I'm not going to let it get me. This will be a long and fine partnership, Inshallah.

Allah willing.

The real meaning of the phrase came to her.

It didn't mean, *Please.*

It meant, *Let it be.*

It rested on her as peace and acceptance. Ben had asked her to marry him, and she must answer.

She pulled off her hat and unbuttoned her coat. Stepped out of her clogs. She sat to remove her socks and put on the bangles. When she stood, she sang—with no regard for anyone outside their tent, this boat. And no shyness before Ben. She sang a popular Arabic love song. The title meant ''Yes!'' Her hips lifted. They turned. Each gentle belly wave was a gesture of honor to him and his line.

Her forehead grew damp, the hair at her brow damp.

Yes, my marriage to Omar was real. Yes, we talked and loved and hugged. Yes, we ate together and discussed books and people we knew. Yes, I'll never know the rest.

Hips moving, saucy, agreeing.

Yes, Ben. Yes, Ben... I'm so scared of you, Ben.

She danced through the song, singing yes to his eyes, and her hands stilled.

Ben's tongue touched his bottom lip. He was flushed. She'd awakened him, and the sensations that had stirred her in the trawler during the days they'd tried to conceive flooded her body again.

To keep from looking at him, she eyed the bangles. ''Would it be too careless to wear these over my socks?''

He didn't answer, so she glanced up.

It was the first time she'd ever seen him smile that way, seen the corners of his mouth crease so deeply. Heard him laugh like that. ''I'm sure my grandmother wore them on the back of a camel, crossing the desert. You won't lose them or break them.''

He sat with her on the floor while she put on her socks. As he fastened on the bangles, she said, "It's graceless to mention it, I know, but I recall the Rashaida always sold or melted down a dead woman's jewelry." She recalled so much more now. "It was never considered suitable for a new bride."

"I thought about it." He shook his head. "Must be the New Englander in me. Can't let those heirlooms out of the family."

"It's the Islander," she said, picturing heirlooms she'd helped sell to keep the Tobias Haverford House. "It's the Islander in you. And I like it. Everything." Dru grinned. "Especially my bangles." She grasped her hat, tugged it toward her.

Immediately the Azawakhs dashed into the salon, racing up the stairs to bark at the cabin door.

"Cool it! *Soon.*"

Ben helped her button her coat. And brought her close. Close to his face and his smell.

Afraid again, afraid of loving so much, she thought *Inshallah.* Love truly was greater than her. His embrace was safe, eternally comforting now. When she'd fallen apart in the captain's quarters, his arms had held her together.

He said, "Time to make your dogs the happiest of creatures."

THE COLD AIR bathed her, awoke her, as Femi pulled her out to the center of the aft deck. No reporters waited on the dock.

They walked side by side, close, each with a dog, neither trying to make them heel but letting them stream ahead. In the night, the Azawakhs became elfin creatures, lithe, too graceful for reality. Dru felt the weight of the heavy bangles on her ankles and a floating sensation. Ben wanted to marry her!

He loved her.

And their baby.

Oh, baby, we're lucky.

With Ben, she scouted for press vultures. Not that anything could be done. In some acceptance of that, he gave her his free hand and she grabbed on. Heat surged into her stomach, and then phantoms confounded it, smothered the fire. Too close were the times she'd cuddled with Omar in the double recliner in the room she hadn't entered since his death, their small media room.

She couldn't remember how she'd first felt about conceiving a baby with another man. At some point, she'd decided she was giving Omar a gift, and he wanted her to see it as a gift from him, too. That logic failed her now.

Her mourning was peculiar. She couldn't help thinking that she didn't feel the right way, didn't feel what she was supposed to. But she had begun to remember death. The mist around the dock lights, the damp cold on her cheeks, the warm strength of Ben's hand—Omar wasn't part of these experiences. Wasn't privy to the glow of dock lights or the sound of the harbor or the sight of Ehder sniffing from post to post. Dead. That was dead.

Three drunken fishermen stumbled past, laughing, headed for another bar, shouting insults at one another, and Dru pulled Femi close with two hands, while Ben had Ehder next to him in a second.

Fishermen.

Surely Tristan would listen to them now.

As Ben nudged her toward the shadows, keeping them both out of the light, she asked, "Do people ever really get amnesia and develop whole new personalities?"

"It's infrequent."

"What about assuming new identities?"

"That happens."

Captain Thomas Adams. Dolphin Tom.

Turk Haverford had spoken of honor. Of taking care of his crew. And he had bought his daughter gifts he couldn't afford. Even when she was old enough to recognize fiction, he'd made up stories about where the presents had come from. The Prince of the Mermen. A sheikh of the Sinai Peninsula. A sultan of Morocco. She had a box of those treasures that she never wore, for fear of losing one, as she'd lost him. And girls' dresses she'd never let her mother give away. And books stored in a safe-deposit box. Omar had shaken his head at her, and she'd asked, *Well, what about your family's things? Why don't you have them out?*

Because the memories are too great. Of the war.

She and Ben had almost reached the dock where the *Sarah Lynnda* lay deep and heavy in the cold mist. "Omar kept his family's belongings in storage. He—" Dru stopped.

"I inherited those things. What were you going to say?"

"He was afraid of the power of the memories. But pain is part of the richness of being alive, and I think he missed good memories, too. That seems saddest of all." She told him about her gifts from her father, that she would begin to wear what pieces of jewelry she could.

At the *Sarah Lynnda's* dock, Ben asked, "What did he bring your brother?"

"Weapons. Antique weapons. My mother wasn't pleased. He brought her pearls. And other things. They would lock themselves in their room when he came home."

"That's good." And good, he thought, that Tristan had known weapons of any kind, when the time came to use an AK-47 on those who would have raped his sister. And would have, in the end, killed them all. "Is Tristan a wedding officiate, by any chance? Some captains are."

Omar had said, *Let's not do that, Dru....*

A dark shape peeled away from the wheelhouse. His hair down and blowing, ghostlike.

Dru heard again, saw again, Tristan's *I love you* of that afternoon, words that seemed, in retrospect, like a goodbye. Not that she could imagine him capable of suicide. She had seen him silent and solitary and heard him speak casually of death, but he was considered one of the best swordfish captains out of Gloucester. He was just…Tristan. With his scars and his way of seeing the world, which was from a longliner.

He came to the rail, and Femi barked.

Tristan said, "Shlogun, ye beast," a hello to a barking dog in the language he shared only with Dru and which she didn't even notice.

Femi quieted. Sat. Tilted her head while Ehder peered at flotsam in the harbor, a paper cup floating by in froth.

Ben nodded. "Dru missed you, so we came by. Busy?"

Tristan recited the temperature and barometric pressure.

Dru asked, "Hey, Tristan, can you still marry people?" He'd studied for his captain's license at a place that trained captains for cruise liners.

His teeth sparkled in the moonlight. No grayer than anyone else's. "I take my vow of celibacy tomorrow. Who's asking?"

Dru laughed, glad to hear him joking.

The glimmer of their eyes met in the night, over the water and the ship's rail, and she felt that wild love from his, something that had to do with purity, their ability to love each other without any version of the thing that had made Skye scream and beg and plead. It was forever clean and so much a part of her soul and blood that she was sure she would know the moment he died. Their parents had let them take part in a study in Boston just months before they went to the Sudan. They had scored like identical twins.

Tristan gripped the railing. "Getting married, Dru?"

Hand still in Ben's, she answered, "Ahsh-ta." One of their words.

Her twin swung under the railing and onto the dock. The

light fell in the dips and grooves of his scars. He offered his hand to Ben. "Congratulations."

"Thank you. Can you perform the ceremony?"

Tristan's eyes slanted upward in thought. He crouched to pet the dogs, to be kissed. Rising, he huddled in his sweatshirt and shell. "Yes." He pulled up the sweatshirt hood.

Ben wondered if he would always envy Tristan and always pity him and never fear him. He wrote in his head, notes that might find their way into a story about Turk Haverford. Sometime soon, he would step apart to scrawl blindly in one of the small spiral books he usually carried. *Rather than choosing, Tristan Haverford was chosen by destiny—to live as a man's man, lonelier than a priest, separate from the rest of us who share a pitcher with him in Conroy's Tavern and look and wish for the secret that sets him apart. But we would refuse it if it came. For we are men who love the warmth of the world and the tenderness of women more than the feeling of flesh under fist or the spit of salt spray or our own last moments lived again and again.*

And Ben saw the view from behind a military barricade while a photographer crawled forward, almost into the spray of bullets. But Ben only watched. He spoke into a microphone, recording the sounds and his voice. He wrote.

"What kind of ceremony?" asked Tristan.

Dru was glad someone had spoken. Where did her brother go, hands in his pockets, eyes on the ink of the water? Where did Ben go, studying Tristan, his gaze betraying a whir of thought? She said, "We haven't talked about it."

"I have some stuff," Tristan admitted. "Ceremonies you can change if you like. But you probably need to visit the courthouse. That would be Monday. We're sailing Wednesday."

Dru shot a glance at Ben. "Tuesday in Nantucket? Your house?"

He hesitated. *Mary,* she thought. His birth mother, who had bandaged five-year-old Dru's scraped knees, had never approached Ben, never tried to reunite with her relinquished son. With that thought, Dru cast away the wedding of her dreams, a wedding in the presence of all her loved ones, with singing and dancing and clapping and zaghareets, the ululating trills of the women, cries of celebration and admiration and triumph and of so many kinds of feelings. "Actually, why not do it here?"

Tristan said, "You loveboats work it out. It's bad for me to go to Nantucket."

Loveboats. Dru remembered. No such thing as lovebirds, Tristan had said, except among birds. Humans were loveboats, everybody loaded with...everything...out at sea alone. He'd said it of his own marriage. She'd believed him, until she married Omar. Then, she'd seen their life together as one boat.

And she'd agreed to set out alone in a tender, a dinghy....

Maybe Tristan was right, but the allusion annoyed her. A retort came to her out of childhood. She had borrowed *The Black Tents of Arabia* from Ben in the Sudan and never returned it but read it again and again, fascinated by the love story, dreaming of handsome Faris, imagining she was Tuemo, but Faris didn't die.... "He is a wild he-ostrich, and I am his she-ostrich."

"Good God," said Tristan.

Ben laughed out loud and hugged her.

Tristan laughed, too, a deep rare sound. "She wins. Lovebirds you are. Giants among lovebirds!"

Dru begged, "If I can't come aboard, let's go somewhere, Tris. Please."

"Dru-twin, I'm busy." He tugged on her stocking cap. "Wouldn't you rather be with your wild he-ostrich?"

The cold and the dark and Ben so close. "What are you so busy doing?" she asked.

"Stuff."

This was a twenty-five-year-old conversation. He'd always been secretive.

"Dru said your father gave you antique weapons."

"Want to see them?" Tristan said. "They're up here. But Dru should be escorted back to your boat. No women aboard. You understand."

Ben understood that Tristan had a daughter who lived with Joanna Haverford. That he had been married to an Islander who fished, and she had died. That Skye had fallen from a boat. "I'll look another time. Thanks." Ben helped Ehder untangle himself. It gave him a moment's respite. A chance to stand a little apart. "Dru's convinced she saw your father."

Tristan gave Dru an irritated shake of his head. "Enough already."

"I think she did." As the tall captain stood motionless, Ben said, "I've confirmed from a photograph that Oceania has worked for Sedna. Sedna was founded in 1985 by Thomas Adams, a former dragger captain of Halifax, Nova Scotia. Dolphin Tom, as he calls himself, is camera-shy. Has been known to hide his face, even from supporters. Goes after illegal boats and never gets arrested. No one wants to take his picture. His flagship is the *Dawn Treader*. Another is *Tomorrow's Dear*."

"I'm sorry." Tristan said. "For the boats."

The dock creaked as Dru sat down. The dogs came to her. *Dolphin Tom, Dawn Treader*… "Dolphin begins with D, like my name, Tom begins with—"

"Drop it, Dru. I don't want to hear it. Wouldn't that be a wonderful discovery? That he sabotaged my ship. Right."

Ben's arms hung loose at his sides. "I'm going to hunt down Sedna anyhow. See what they're about."

"Oh, thanks. They need a mouthpiece. Who speaks for the fishermen? Taking fish from the sea is a life."

Ben was silent. Briefly. "You can."

Tristan exhaled in a gust. "Write this. This country manages its fisheries, and commercial fishermen follow the rules. Sedna should go bother the Japanese. Let the government manage Georges Bank and Grand Banks. Get out of here and leave us alone."

Tristan had moved back into the shadows, and he stepped aboard the boat. Without looking back, he said, "Good night, lovers. Good night." The light caught strands of his bright hair before he faded, a black shape disappearing below.

Dru and Ben coaxed the dogs back up the dock, away from the *Sarah Lynnda*. Dru said, "When we were kids, I used to search his room. Whenever he said that thing, that he was busy with 'stuff.'"

More interested in fisheries management and Tristan's re-action to Sedna, Ben asked, "What did you find?"

Showing Tristan-twin's bedroom to anyone, even with words, seemed worse than her snooping. "He's lovable," she answered, recalling the drawings of whaling scenes and pirate battles. And notebook upon notebook fattened with photos cut from magazines, *National Geographic* and *Newsweek* and oth-ers, glued to lined pages. Later, the dark posters. That print of a hanged man. And dripping red-blood paint on the wall in the apartment in Surfside, to the landlord's wrath.

Suddenly, easily, her bare feet sprinted over grass and sod. *Tristan! Tristan!*

His blond hair flew around his tear-streaked face as he smashed the baseball bat against the back fence.

Her mother caught her shoulders from behind and Dru smelled Joanna's hand lotion. *Let him be. We'll patch up the fence.*

Why does he do it?

He misses your father.

"Dru?"

She came out of it abruptly, like the other time, but found

she could shift her mind and walk back into the past. Couldn't resist kneeling in the grass and dirt with Tristan, driving Tonka trucks in the flower bed, taking out some pansies, leveling the ground for the new weapons facility they were building.

"Dru?" In the shadows, Ben turned her toward him. "Where are you?"

She shook her head. "This memory thing. I just had another. It's like a movie, and I can step into it, and it feels exactly as it did then, when we were kids. I can play with Tristan again."

The set of his jaw and eyes as he nodded said he knew of this phenomenon, perhaps because he had lived in refugee camps and war zones. He smiled a little. "Is it fun?"

"This time." She laid aside the incident of the baseball bat and the fence.

He nudged her onward. "How would you feel about talking to a psychiatrist? That was bad, in the Sudan. Do you remember the bodies?"

"Yes." She avoided the vision. Not good for the baby. "I feel okay. I kind of like…" She returned to Tristan at will. She could smell childhood in Nantucket, the lawn and the flowers and the harbor and shells.

"Stay here with me." In the present. "Better for you. Here we are on the romantic Gloucester waterfront on a freezing November evening."

Her cold face cracking in a smile, Dru walked between the waterfront buildings and Ben, the harbor on his far side. The dogs sniffed each corner, each trashcan, Ehder marking half of what he found. Ben guided Dru to the shadows, watched every human form.

No more shocks tonight, *Inshallah*.

He said, "You put your bags in one of the aft staterooms?"

"The smaller one. It's fine." She'd found linen and made up the lower bunk herself. The upper bunk crossed the other way, perpendicular, and the doors of a low elevator from the salon opened beneath it. It was a wheelchair elevator, tiny, for when David's sister had been disabled. The doors of the aft staterooms, head and companionway were wide.

Ben's hand clasped her far shoulder. He fit her against his side as they walked. "I'd like to come back and be your cabinmate. Would that bother you?"

She shook her head; her hair, then cheek, brushed the leather of his grandfather's flight jacket. He hadn't invited her to his bed but had offered to share a separate berth in her cabin. She appreciated both.

But later, as she dressed for bed in the white cotton nightgown she'd brought, she felt vulnerable. The lace at the low neck of the gown was like net, embroidered with white satin. It buttoned down the front, but was old and unironed, and the fabric didn't really meet. Something she'd only worn when Omar was away, the first reason for her decision to pack it.

The second was that she would sleep alone.

Now she'd made up the top bunk for Ben in her stateroom. She brushed her teeth and ignored her hair. When she emerged, he was talking to the dogs, turning out lights. In the galley. In the salon.

She flicked off the stateroom's light and climbed between the sheets of her berth. It would be easy to sleep, even with him there. She felt alternate moments of lightness and disconnection, returning to the Sudan in her mind. Yet it was freeing to have remembered it all.

Her love swept to the baby, to the miniature creature working so hard each day, transforming within her. Eyes closed, she smiled. *Hi, baby. I love you, little baby.*

"Hi."

She opened her eyes.

He'd switched off the last lights, and the dogs were with him, circling the carpet, looking for the perfect spot.

His shadowy body, his naked arms and shoulders, sweat-pants sliding from his hips, stood over her before he sat on the edge of her mattress, close and warm. Better for being part of her worst memories—and some of the best.

Lying down with her, hugging her, his head next to hers on the pillow, he said. "Wake me if you need me, Dru."

So safe. He was so big.

"You, too."

"Oh, you wouldn't get any sleep." He kissed her quickly and rolled away and prepared to climb up to his bunk.

"Are we getting married on Tuesday?"

"Works for me." He turned.

In one picture, one moment, Ben saw Tanelher, walking on her hands, white teeth glowing, telling him there was someone else for him. He'd thought, *I left Dru unguarded for this,* and the thought had shocked him. Even though he'd known she'd be safe, with her tour guides and companions nearby and the mehndi sure to take hours. Tanelher had told him, *Ben, I don't have the feelings you do and that you want me to have.*

She'd spoken in Tamashek. Afterward, like a convalescent scarcely able to move, he'd watched mehndi artists paint the white feet and ankles of his secret princess, his destiny, stolen from him by his father and his own apathy.

Kneeling suddenly, he pressed his face to her heart, against the soft heat of her breasts. He kissed her through her cotton gown.

She was a princess.

She was Scheherazade and Yasmin.

Inshallah, she was his.

"I've been married to you," he said, "since I was twelve."

Dru touched his face. His hair. *Then why Tanelher?* she wondered. Her new memories were a strange treasure trove, where she might find a poisonous spider among the shell beads and abandoned toys. Tanelher wasn't there. Tanelher, a Tuareg woman who could have married Ben but had refused him.

She must not have loved him.

But why would he spend more than a decade infatuated with someone who didn't care about him? Ben could have...well, any woman he wanted.

Except Tanelher.

It shone at her from the junk of her memory box. A boy telling her he wanted coffee, that she was his wife and should make it. Telling her all the ways every other girl was prettier. Then, once, when they were alone tending the goats, calling her "Gazelle."

Dru held and caressed his head, clutched the muscles of his back.

He'd chosen devotion to Tanelher, the unattainable. Tanelher, who would never love him back.

As another would.

I've been married to you since I was twelve.

She pressed her cheek to his warm head and when he looked up, to see her, knew how far they had fallen into love. No surfacing.

She took her head in his hands, but then, he was in charge, his shape above her both familiar and unearthly. His skin, his flesh, the most coveted of all sensations. Kissing her. As she so wanted.

Wanted because of the way he loved her.

Enough to spend years loving someone else, someone who would never love him back. Enough to find some way to wait.

For time to dance to yes.

For her to dance her yes.

CHAPTER EIGHT

Afterward, every person in camp remembered hearing the engine start. But the Rashaida had trucks, too. Everyone, including my father on his cot, recovering from his injuries, imagined one adult or another was leaving on an errand for the camp. Later, seeing the vehicle gone, each person explained the absence to himself. There had been one witness to the departure, and the Rashaida boy was simply impressed that the blond non-believer was allowed to come and go and drive off whenever he pleased. My father hobbled with a walking stick to see the tracks. He let me come with him, and the sheikh and his eldest son joined us. Tristan had driven to the road and turned east, toward Ethiopia. He had a five-hour head start.

—Ben, recollections of a fall

Tuesday
November 14
6:45 a.m., EDT

SHE WAS TO BE MARRIED that day, and her family had come.

In particular, Joanna, her own mother, and Mary, Ben's birth mother. They came prepared to continue the pretense, and Dru played, too. She now had her own part in the drama of what was not.

She huddled, with a towel half-covering her, in the trawler

Cup of Gold, in the same berth in which her child had been conceived. She sat on the mattress, facing her best woman friend, and did not tell her she was pregnant and did not tell her mother or Mary Hall or either of the little girls, all crowded around, everyone but Joanna on the bed. They had come to Gloucester on short notice, even Mary's husband, Dru's attorney Daniel Mayhew, who was discussing some kind of business with Ben. They had spent the night in nearby hotels, and the women had come to Dru before it was light, to prepare her for the wedding, many hours away.

The mehndi recipe contained water, black tea, henna powder that had been sifted four times through muslin, lime juice and eucalyptus oil. The proportions were a family secret. Keziah had brought dozens of plastic applicators up from Nantucket, although her mother and Tristan's daughter, Keri, preferred using funnels made from plastic shopping bags.

No one had mentioned to Dru the now well-publicized fact that Ben was Omar's son. They were quiet, setting down designs of leaves, elegantly layered scallops, tiny flowers. Mary, silver threading her shoulder-length dark hair, was almost meditative as she painted Dru's back. As the henna fell cool on Dru's skin, Mary asked, "Girls, do you think this is going to be dark enough?"

Was she expressing her hopes that Ben would have a long and happy marriage? Ben was her son. He was Keziah's half brother. These facts tossed and banged inside Dru. Secret. Ben's secret.

"Dru, darling, you'll have a good eleven hours at least," Mary told her, "to let this set. When it dries, we'll put on the lemon-sugar water, and we'll flake off the paste last thing before you dress tonight."

There had been no mehndi at her first marriage. Omar would have taken no pleasure in seeing those designs on her skin. And Ben would... Hours away. Ben, who had slept near enough for her to hear his breathing the past two nights. Who had spent his days at the library and on the waterfront, tracking down her father. The *Dawn Treader* was at sea; she'd sailed out of Gloucester.

Joanna, casual in black slacks and turtleneck, her fair hair drawn back with a barrette, perched on the trawler's only portable stool, at the foot of the berth. Each girl, squeezing into her own place on the mattress, adorned one of Dru's hands, one doing a back, one doing a palm; then they'd switch so each hand would match.

"Your feet look so pretty, Dru." Nudar tipped her head back to see Joanna's face. "Are her feet going to freeze?"

"Of course not," Joanna replied. "She'll wear shoes on the way over."

Ben had reserved a room above Conway's Tavern, the largest he could find. It was furnished sparely, with a cot for a bed. From his house in 'Sconset, using a spare key, Keziah and the girls had brought big pillows, the camel saddles, and a rug.

"Ahoy?" A woman's voice yelled from the cabin door.

Dru jumped. "Sorry—" to the artists "—Jean! And Cecily! Look at you!"

Keziah put down her applicator to bow, hands flat together. "Hail, beautiful mother. And who is that little sweet pea? Oh, yummy!"

Jean Blade's waist-length gold-streaked curls cascaded down around her oversized sweatshirt and long skirt worn with hiking boots. Her belly, in these final weeks of her pregnancy, rounded out in front of her. Beside her was a small white-haired toddler in purple overalls and a pink parka. The little girl carried a stuffed owl.

Dru gathered her towel about her to scoot off the bed.

"Careful of the henna!" Mary and Joanna exclaimed in chorus.

On her feet, she kissed Jean and rested a hand on her abdomen. Feeling movement, Dru smiled into her eyes. She crouched beside Cecily. "Hello, sweetheart, I'm Dru."

Cecily finally dimpled, showing baby teeth.

Dru's mind shifted, a graceful physical sensation, as though something in the front of her head were turning or switching over to another mode.

Yaa, Matar. Guum yah, Matar. Dru lifted the sleepy, black-haired toddler into her own child arms, felt the soft curls against her neck. A baby at her breast, Matar's mother smiled at her, approving. Three-year-old Matar was Dru's favorite among the Rashaida children, and Dru loved to pick her up and…

She blinked. Saw Cecily. Heard the voices in the cabin. Knew she must be present, yet felt the other world drawing her. Heart racing, she wanted to say, *Stop, everyone. This is important. Let me remember.*

Instead, she picked up Cecily and hugged Jean, her towel slipping entirely. As Mary helped her, Dru asked, "Can I get you something to drink, Jean? How did you find us?"

Mary's arm restrained her. "We'll wait on Jean. You're the bride, and you're covered with mehndi and without a stitch but that towel. Be still, daughter of Nudar."

The others laughed, and Dru made introductions. *I have to tell Jean I'm pregnant. She knows how badly I wanted a baby.*

The lightship basket mug was wrapped safely in garments and plastic bags for transport home.

That badly.

Cecily tugged her hair, and Dru's mind slid onto the other course. The girls' special day. They would receive presents. Dru couldn't go to the tent erected far away, out of sight. Matar's mother carried her daughter. *You should wait for the right time,* said one of the other women.

This is better, the mother had replied.

Right time for what? The women and girls walked on without a backward glance, leaving her with the few women and small children who remained by the hearth. That was their place. The hearth for the women. The bed for the men....

Her eyes watched Jean set down two bulging canvas totes, saying, "—planned to see Daniel in Nantucket because of Omar's legacy. He was generous to the Blade Institute. Didn't expect to run into him here. We were photographing a boat unloading her catch when we saw Daniel and Ben out with your dogs. You knew we were coming to Gloucester?"

Jean's slanting sea eyes had become sharp. Pregnant women were particularly intuitive. Dru had to keep these strange—strangely sad—memories at bay. "Yes. I thought you'd be here later in the week. I'm so glad you're here now. Where are Rika and Chris?"

"With David. I'll bring her back soon. Chris is being a research assistant, for which he makes an exorbitant wage." She laughed, clearly proud of her twelve-year-old stepson. Skye's son. "You should hear Rika talk. Ben's nice, Dru."

So natural, ignoring that Omar, Ben's father, her first husband, had died so recently.

Early that morning, Dru had arisen alone in the trawler with Ehder and Femi. She hadn't wanted Ben to see her before the wedding and had convinced him to let her stay in the trawler without him. And in that hour when it was just her and the dogs, while she fed them and made her morning protein shake and an omelette, she had vowed she would never feel shame about this marriage or her pregnancy. The innocence of the child within her gave her that right. And that duty.

Soon, Keziah and the others had arrived, and Joanna had taken the dogs to Ben. To see Ben for herself? Dru had wondered. Or to meet him again? Her mother must have gazed into his eyes with that strict, protective look.

Cecily wanted to be put down.

As she let her slide to the sole to wander away, Dru's limbs became small and slender. Reaching for another child, doll-like in her new dress. But Matar didn't want to be picked up now. Cried. Wouldn't say what was wrong. Another girl, Fatimah, walking stiffly, the life cut away from her eyes, took Matar outside, to go to the bathroom....

"I can't stay." Jean hurried forward to embrace Dru. "I just came to drop off these bags. Will one of you—" her glance embraced the adult women, all but the bride "—look at them later? They're from the groom."

Nudar slipped off the bed to tickle Cecily under the knee. "She's so cute."

Dru saw from the corner of her eye, heard their voices. Trying to be present, she embraced Jean. They needed to do a prenatal immediately.

She asked her to come back later, and Jean said, "Three?"

"Good."

The memory returned, the dream that was more.

They stood in the dust, and Matar wouldn't squat, wouldn't pee, then had to, and cried while Dru stared. What was wrong with her vagina? Were those thorns? No wonder she cried when she peed through that tiny straw. Was this what happened to the girls who'd gone away?

Speaking to Matar in the Rashaida dialect. *May Dru pick you up?*

Lying on a mat with Matar during the toddler's nap. Telling Matar's mother, who had two babies, *She's hot. She has a fever.*

And the secretions. Green and rank.

Swelling abdomen.

The midwife summoned. Herbs.

Days.

Each day.

Matar hot every day. Moaning.

Almost forgot Tristan. There was no twin.

Catching her hurrying to the tent with a bowl of camel milk, Ben said, *Where have you been? You never come outside.*

Dru couldn't tell him what they'd done to the girls. Did he think that was normal? He might; he'd lived there a long time. *Matar's sick.*

Listless body. Brown eyes searching Dru's face. Head snuggling close to Dru's growing adolescent breasts.

Asking Robert, *Can we take her to Khartoum?*

Yes. Yes.

She heard the voices outside, the quick discussion, helped Matar's mother wrap the toddler, offer more water. Matar's mother tried to give her the breast, and Dru saw Matar's head fall back, like a rag doll's.

Her mother wailed.

Dru sat stunned, sat until her own girl's hand could touch the smaller hand and learn that Matar's skin had become the temperature of the air.

"Dru… Dru-Nudar. Artemis is calling you." Familiar voice, beautiful voice of her friend, Keziah of the herbs and spirits.

On the berth. She lay on the berth in— Getting married. Eyes full. Cheeks wet, very wet. Keziah faced her, and Dru looped her arms around her friend's neck. The girls stood worried beside the mattress.

Dru pulled in deep breaths. *Oh, baby, I'm sorry. You are so strong, my little warrior, to be with your mother in this.* She sat up, shivering. Full of secrets.

But this she could tell.

Must, must, so urgent…

"In the Sudan, a little girl I took care of—" The grief immersed her like a tidal wave. She cried, hard. She cried for the children she and Ben and Tristan and Skye had been. She cried for the subtle emptiness of her marriage to Omar, the barriers neither of them could break, his childhood and hers. She cried for baby Matar, whom she had loved so much that she'd forgotten her existence. "She was infibulated when she was three, and she died...." And that had haunted her when she'd seen green meconium, when infant Rika, Jean's youngest child, was born.

"In-what?" asked Nudar.

"Tell you some other time," murmured Keziah. "It's gross. Hey, girls, I think we've got to round up another lemon or two. Get your coats." She kissed Dru, whispering, "Leave you some woman space."

"I love you," Dru answered.

Keziah's eyes were sad as she waited outside the wall of secrets, important things that lay between them. A wall higher than she knew. Out of loyalty to Tristan, Dru could never tell her. His sounds had come from the tent, and afterward, he had killed three men. She, Skye, Dru and Tristan had all seen a war zone, seen what an AK-47 could do to heads and stomachs, seen how far flesh could spray. Tristan had done that.

She could never tell Keziah. It was his story to tell.

The other was Ben's.

Keziah and the girls left and quiet descended.

It was just her and Joanna and Mary. The women resumed painting her skin, and Dru meditated. Rika's birth had brought those feelings of the Sudan, of watching over Matar, seeing her die without help close enough, without anyone to help. *I'm a midwife. I'm going to be fine now.*

She was going to be fine.

Silence and cool trickling on her skin.

Mary and Joanna adorning her with henna.

Ben's secret.

No. No, it wasn't.

She had inherited the lightship basket and its contents.

Her breath rushed sealike in her ears. "Mom, I'm angry."

A pause. Her mother had been working on her feet, adding the last scallops to Keziah's work.

Mary was behind her, and when she stopped painting Dru eased to the corner of the berth, careful of the henna.

The women's eyes were solemn. Wretched. Mary asked, "Does Ben know?"

"Yes." She didn't want to talk about Ben, the grown Ben. "From Omar, I inherited the lightship basket, Ben's original birth certificate, some photos. We saw them at the same time."

"I must talk with him." Mary closed her eyes, arms around her knees, rocking herself.

I want to know what happened! But was that story only for Ben?

"It must have been a great shock for you—" Mary placed a hand on Dru's leg "—and for him...to learn he was Omar's son."

She wouldn't discuss Ben's feelings. Even if she knew them. "Ben and I are having a child."

Joanna's eyes went wide. She caught Dru's arm, spilling out, "Darling..." Some things more important than confession. Meeting Dru's gaze. "And how do you feel?"

"Happy. I want—" hands on her stomach "—everything to go right."

"Every mother worries, darling. You know that." Joanna clasped her head to kiss her. "I'm sorry I couldn't tell you about Ben. Some secrets are not ours to tell. And I know you understand that. You understand it very well."

The Sudan. Other people's secrets.

This was the same for her mother.

Dru swallowed. "I love you."

"I love you so much, Dru. You're the daughter I would have all over again."

Mary's mascara ran. "God, I'm sorry. Dru, honey, you're here. I'm going to tell you. I'll speak to Ben myself before you see him again. And Daniel and Keziah will have to know.'' Her sigh wavered, broke. ''I'll tell them. But let's work as I talk.''

Dru missed the group around her, Keri painting one hand and Nudar the other, but they would finish up later. There was sacredness in her mother and her future mother-in-law painting henna on her before her wedding. She was afraid, though. Mary was going to tell her about Omar.

He's dead, she thought, horrified and frightened as though she'd just learned it, the grief knocking her so that she disbelieved she could be marrying another man.

Her blood roared.

Mary said, ''As you may know, my mother died when I was two, and my grandmother took me to live with her.''

The mother who died had been Robert Hall's mother and Omar's adoptive mother, as well, and her falling to her death had affected each one differently and fundamentally made and shaped the life of the man who was son to all three.

Ben.

''Grandmother didn't care for my father, didn't have much to do with him. I really never knew either of my parents. I met my brothers as an adult. It was critical to me. Robert, as you know, spent most of his time abroad. But Omar worked from New York and Boston, investing and studying the market, and eventually he launched his first fund, as you know, Dru. And sweetheart, it kills me to be telling you this. I know your marriage to him was real and precious. He told me once that you were the only thing that really mattered.''

Dru's mouth cracked open, her eyes squinting, facial muscles tight. The first cry. *He loved me. Oh, God, you loved me, Omar. You really loved me. You weren't just using me. You were giving me a baby.*

She couldn't tell them, but she would tell Ben, for both of them and the child. She wept.

Joanna stroked her hair. "Oh, darling, it's so hard. Here's a handkerchief. Don't use that towel.

The small details of the designs tickled Dru, tightening her skin as the henna dried.

Mary tied Dru's hair in a knot, stabbed a hair stick through it, and resumed her art. "I'd been away to school, almost finished at Parsons and had a job lined up with a designer in New York. He liked my Egyptian-style dresses, perfect for the time, he thought. It was nineteen sixty-seven, May, and I came down to Boston to meet friends from Nantucket. I'd gotten a horde of tickets from someone in New York to see the Velvet Underground at the Boston Tea Party. He was rich, couldn't use them, gave them to me thinking I could invite friends from Nantucket. So I sent all but one to a high school friend—did you meet Bonnie back then, Joanna?"

"Not then."

"Well, she gathered a group, and you know Bonnie—"

"Bonnie Hales?" asked Dru. One of the women who had lost a husband when Dru's father's boat, the *Louise Andrena*, went down.

"Yes, she just remarried a year or two ago, you know— Keziah was excited because he's an obstetrician. But he works in Boston, writes textbooks or something. Never mind. Bonnie was a Coffin back then. Anyhow, she could never mix people well. But of course, it must have been hard to find eleven takers for the Velvet Underground. In Nantucket, you see, it was more like nineteen *fifty*-seven."

"Eighteen fifty-seven," murmured Joanna ruefully, Joanna—the Andy Warhol find whom Turk Haverford had brought home. She was the first hurdle, her Southern accent the second.

"Omar came. And Turk, of course. We were invited to a party afterward—"

"Where I met your dad, Dru." Joanna finished the work on Dru's feet, leaving the more difficult details for Keziah.

Dru grew suddenly still. *Dad. She doesn't know.* And the guilt Joanna must have felt before he left, about the high school coach. Could he have stayed away because of that? *She only wanted to get your attention, Dad. We needed you.*

But he was a fisherman.

"Omar and I split off," Mary explained. "He had a car, a beautiful convertible. We drove and drove. Some of this is too painful to discuss. He was my brother but he wasn't. And he was older and attractive. He had no qualms about me. Bedouins marry their first cousins, anyway, and he and I weren't even related by blood and hadn't known each other. He told me stories about his father and Robert."

Dru swallowed. No one could tell stories as well as Omar. Those he chose to tell.

"We spent the weekend together. After my graduation, we began spending every weekend together in New York, where I lived. New York is not Nantucket. My perspective became skewed. It seemed acceptable to be lovers."

Dru wanted to ask, *Do you love him?*

She remembered sitting at Codfish Park at sunset with Omar in private conversation.

He'd asked gently, and with some vulnerability, *I'm much older than you. Do you think you could be intimate with me?*

I've never had a lover at all. Looking at him. *Yes.*

Gone. He was gone.

"Dru, we don't have to talk about this, love," Mary said. "I made the foolish assumption that you were marrying Ben because your grief had spent itself, not in spite of the fact."

"Grief never spends itself," Joanna snapped at her best friend.

"I want to hear." Dru waited for the feel of wet henna paste on her back.

"Quickly, then. In the summer, I realized I was pregnant. Insensitive as it seems to you, I immediately knew I could not keep the baby. Omar wanted to marry me."

Dru let this slide through her, loving the words, for her and for Ben.

"But I knew we'd be outcasts on Nantucket. He was willing to live in New York, but it didn't matter. It would affect our family terribly. My grandmother was alive, and I thought it would kill her. But in the end, she helped." She paused, though she continued applying henna to Dru's back. "Omar was furious. He fought with me. He behaved as though the child in my womb was his personal property, and he could not be swayed from this position. He said he would keep the baby himself, raise the child himself. That was horrifying to me, for reasons I can't explain. I threatened to abort, said I would do it alone, no one would be able to stop me, and at that point he changed."

Dru gritted her teeth, eyes on Joanna's.

Her mother said, "Difficult decisions confuse people, Dru."

Ben, already alienated, would drift further from the human race, like a boat pulled loose from its moorings. When he heard this.

Mary continued her story. "He demanded I pay him for the theft of his line. If I did not, he would tell the truth to everyone on Nantucket Island."

Dru felt a dull understanding—and near admiration—for Omar's blackmail.

"He demanded my inheritance from my mother—Nudar's belongings. I gave them. He also demanded that adoptive parents be found on the island of Nantucket. Spring came, and I went to Gloucester, where the child was to be born. Joanna would be there. You'd married Turk in December, wasn't it?"

"Yes."

"They had decided to adopt the baby. Alma Hall, Robert's

wife, was pregnant, too. My grandmother was to be her mid-wife. Most women went to the hospital then, but Robert was eccentric and Alma his willing accomplice in every venture.

"Their child was stillborn. Joanna and Turk made the im-mediate decision that my baby should be offered to them. My son was born. You took him away, Joanna, strong friend. The Halls buried their child at sea and never legally recorded the birth. There's a memorial in the grass above the beach, beside the house, a small marble plaque with a cross engraved and no name."

Joanna sat back against a locker.

Mary said again, "I'm sorry, Dru."

THE OTHERS RETURNED. The girls sang as Keziah and Mary painted, and Dru's mother danced, her belly-dancing always holding a hint of the cabaret.

She was only fifty-four, still lovely.

Mom, Dru thought, *you never married anyone else.*

She reviewed her conversations with Ben, his evening re-ports on his findings. Going in search of a phone jack so he could explore the Internet, and phones to call contacts. He had not yet found a photograph, but she knew utterly that this reclusive environmentalist must be her father.

Tristan hadn't wanted to hear. How would her mother feel?

Dru was terrified to tell Joanna.

She was afraid to tell her mother that the husband Joanna had mourned so deeply and bitterly, who had almost certainly been her truest love, was not dead but alive. Was well and free.

And more deeply untrue than she had ever been.

Rocky Nest

MARY HAD SUGGESTED they come here to walk.

He'd shrugged, leaving David and David's son, Chris.

Skye's son, growing into her chin and cheekbones, her arrogant grace. Chris was twelve and assisting David in every way, working hard to earn money.

For what? Ben had asked.

I'm not sure. I have some collections. Coins—ancient coins. Asian weapons.

When Mary had said, "I need to talk to you, Ben," the Blades had probably thought it was about the wedding.

The tightness in his chest knew it wasn't.

At a picnic table, coffee and tea in front of them in throwaway cups, she told her story. And when she came to the reasons she couldn't keep him and wouldn't let Omar raise him, he saw that these weren't the real reasons.

"You didn't want a tie to Omar," he said. "Like that."
Like me.

"He was strong. He liked to make the rules. I didn't think he'd be good for either of us. I don't see that he was good for Dru."

He wanted me.

Another thing, that in some deep place, Ben had always known. From the time he was small, whenever he'd come to Omar, he'd been embraced. Always given the finest gifts. *My father's dagger. It was his badge. It showed who his father was and his father's father. It's for you, Ben.*

So much affection.

Ben imagined this was the problem with Dru's marriage to Omar. That her husband had always loved someone else better, some unnamed person.

He wasn't sorry for it at all.

He missed Omar. And treasured what he'd left. *Dru.*

"What are you thinking?" asked Mary. "Will you ever forgive me?"

"I forgive you." Indifferent. Easy to forgive where he'd already given up.

"I haven't told Daniel or Keziah. I wanted to tell you first. But I will tell them. And I'll try to be a mother to you."

It was on the tip of his tongue to say that he'd had mothers, two of them, one a Bedouin never even involved with his father. He felt the mark of manhood in his own tolerance. He stood and came around the table. She rose, too, and in the cool gray breeze, they embraced.

She did not weep, as he'd known she wouldn't.

"Thank you for giving me to such fine people." He begged that she would say it was so she could see him, glimpse him, watch over him.

Her eyes reached up and searched his. "I've done nothing you should thank me for. But lend my womb for your life."

They parted ways near her car.

He walked alone to the *Skye* and kicked in every stained glass window on the ship.

Evening

THE WOMEN'S RETURN woke her and she sat up on the berth, remembering. The trawler swayed gently with the tide or the wake of the boat in the harbor. She was going to be married.

Her mother peered in. "You're awake. Hello, sweetheart."

Joanna wore a flowing red dress, one Dru remembered her father bringing. A special-occasion dress. Keziah's was a black-and-gold trimmed gown of burgundy velvet; it matched lights the same color in her hair.

"Mom has the kids," Keziah murmured, looking vaguely gray. "You know, you might be the only pregnant bride in the world who did a prenatal exam on her wedding day. How are you, sleepy midwife?"

"Good." Remembering the prenatal exam with Jean, her

renewed confidence in her knowledge, that she so thoroughly understood the practice and science of midwifery, Dru lifted her face to kiss Keziah and search the eyes of her beautiful friend, eyes like Ben's. Had Mary told her?

Tight-lipped, Keziah hugged her again. "We need to finish enhancing your beauty for Ben." A sigh. "Ben Omar Hall."

Yes, Mary had told her. Joanna had wandered far aft in the boat, and Dru asked, "Is there anything I can do?"

"I can't sort it out here. In Nantucket, I'll have a chance to meditate, to come to grips with it. I bear no one ill will, least of all my brother. I always wanted one, you know." Her mouth twisted, a lop-sided grin. "Like you have."

The henna paste tugged at Dru's skin, begging to be flaked away.

Keziah told her, "Jean should be here any minute. She said she was going to leave the babies with David and Chris."

Jean had brought Rika, her youngest daughter, with her that afternoon. Dru had spent two hours taking Jean's history, performing a complete prenatal. Then Jean had returned to David, her husband. *Skye's husband.*

Keziah and Joanna worked together, gently flaking off the paste, and covered Dru with olive oil. As she wrapped up in a sheet, the cabin door opened.

"Hi! Sorry I'm late." Jean's boots pressed down the warped linoleum. "Your brother walked me over." She glanced from Dru to Joanna and back. "My curiosity has overcome my manners. I know a lot of people now, kids especially, are into scarification. Is that what he did?"

Keziah's eyes turned inward, in a withdrawal that had its roots in New England privacy or Haverford tradition. This was not a Nantucket question, and Keziah, for all her embracing of faraway peoples, witchcraft and the ancient art of midwifery, could not answer even this pregnant woman with anything but silence. Joanna was a Southerner. Her hands trembled as she searched for something on the floor. Her body jerked when she turned.

Facing Jean, Dru tried to keep the New England from her own voice. "He voluntarily underwent a rite of passage with an African tribe whose name we don't know. He was eleven." Dru felt the black emptiness where Skye had been.

Skye, who might always be for Jean, in some way, a rival. The first wife. Jean had told her once, *When I first met you I didn't like you, because you were part of her family and you have those eyes. I thought David was going to react to you somehow.*

She made herself tell Jean more about Tristan. "Such marks are considered signs of beauty and courage, because of the pain involved in acquiring them. When they occur on the body, they're found arousing by lovers."

"Right," snapped Keziah.

"I'm sure Dorea found Tristan perfect." Joanna spun each word in Southern flavors, deifying the name of Tristan's drowned wife, Keri's mother, and endorsing Tristan's scars—which she'd spent years discussing with eager plastic surgeons.

Unaffected, Keziah added, "Scarification also tells a tribe's patrilineal group. Historically, it protected children from kidnapping during war or being taken as slaves. And it made it possible to locate a child who'd been abducted."

"That's fascinating." Jean's serious interest was the essence of courtesy. "How sad to have to worry about that. Your child being taken as a slave."

"And the marks were said to alter a child who was sent by the gods or the ancestors—" Dru swallowed "—so that they wouldn't reclaim him. That's how I think of Tristan's scars." *Because he grew up to be a fisherman, damn it. How could you do that, Tristan? How could you let us wear out the floors*

*and carpets beside our windows, always watching the harbor?
And then choose a home port so far away?*

Hesitantly, Jean moved forward, toward Dru. "Your
brother's very handsome, very kind. What do we need to do
here?"

Fluid and quick, hiding some choking sound, Keziah darted
out of sight in the galley. She returned with a cube-shaped
box and a larger light-weight package, both wrapped in bright
purple, pink and orange tissue. "For the bride, with love from
the groom!"

"You'll need this first, Dru," said Joanna. Nudar's red
gown, silk, trimmed with cowrie shells and silver coins.

Keziah told her, "We voted that this gown is a gift to you."

"Mary's idea." Joanna pushed her own hair back from her
face. "She said to tell you that it's your gift from Nudar, for
continuing her traditions so beautifully."

Mary... *Ben.* Where was he? Dru knew his strength and
could picture him walking with his mother, hands in his pockets, possibly buying her a cup of coffee. *Are you all right?
Was she loving to you?*

Nudar's gown lifted the dark fog from the night, bringing
a sweet glow and scent. A gown of Nudar's for her wedding.

"And this goes with it." Keziah thrust a small, tissue-
wrapped package into her hand.

Bridal underwear in red. She drew it on, over the exquisite
body art. The rich brown covered her feet and the bottoms of
her legs, her back, narrowing down to the base of her spine,
and the backs and palms of her hands. Now, this translucent
red underwear.

"Mm." She giggled. Between the refrigerator and the table,
she lifted her hips and arms in the Loop of Infinity, followed
with a shimmy.

Keziah answered with a zaghareet, and the sound trilled and
echoed out into the harbor.

Jean laughed, and Keziah and Dru instinctively crowded near her.

"The dress! The dress!"

The packages glittered on the table top, with an envelope in a masculine handwriting she'd seen before, in his journal, other places.

The silk of Nudar's gown glided down against her skin, voluminous.

More trills and cries.

Grinning, Dru reached for the card.

Jean pretended to peer over her shoulder. "Your betrothed is so cute, by the way. I've seen his pictures in magazines before, when he was a contributor, and thought *'What a babe.'*"

Jean's relaxation, the way she made things seem normal, touched Dru for the second or third time that day. Because nothing about this was normal. She opened the card, staying in her world of spun silk.

The watercolor painting on the card showed a man and woman in turn-of-the-century—nineteenth century—hats at the railing of a ship. She opened it to the printed message *Forever starts today.*

And Ben's message, in that hard, strong handwriting.

These were my grandmother's bridal gift from her husband, brought to Tripoli on a camel by her son after her death and then by plane to America, to Nantucket Island. They were given to me, and I give them to you. They are your wedding gift. They are not your bride-price. Your bride-price is me. I am yours today, irrevocably, to keep under all and any circumstances, till death do us part.

Ben

As she tucked the card back in the envelope, Jean pointed to the larger soft-shaped package. "That one first. When Ben entrusted these to me this morning, that's what he said. And in fact he told me what it was," she went on. Her eyes sparkled. "And I told everyone else. Though they already knew."

Dru opened the tissue and almost immediately touched the handwoven cotton. She opened it, unfolded all the fabric, as voluminous as her wedding dress. The pieces took her breath. A black headscarf and headpiece, all heavy, rich, jingling with coins. Dru had taken off her bangles when she showered that morning. She turned and rushed to her locker to get them and put them on.

"Wow!" Keziah bent to peer close.

Joanna smiled, eyes quiet. "Did Ben give you those?"

"Saturday night. They were a gift to his grandmother from the sheikh." Dru felt what she'd just said. From Omar's father to Omar's mother. The parents Omar had seen die in the desert. She closed her eyes. *Dear Omar.*

"Try the veil. You don't *have* to wear it," Keziah said.

They helped her fit it on. Snug, it smelled of earth.

"How did they kiss at the wedding?" Jean wondered.

"I'm sure they didn't. You're beautiful, Dru," her mother told her. "But are you suffocating, darling? Ben was explicit—"

"Totally," Jean added.

"—that you mustn't feel obliged to wear it."

"And it doesn't identify *your* tribe, anyhow," Keziah pointed out. "You're the daughter of Turk Haverford, granddaughter of John Haverford—"

Dru took up the headpiece, set it on, and let Keziah fasten it in place with her hair. *Daughter of—* This would be her second wedding that her father had missed.

The scarf. Her head heavy now, weighted under coins.

Her face felt protected, her hair protected, too, as she sat to unwrap and open the box. To lift out the silver. Bedouin necklaces. Rings with silver balls. And bracelets, one with cones sticking out from it and chains that dangled tiny coins. Every piece chimed, tinkled. The finger jewelry must have come from Arabia, from the Gulf. She held a necklace against her skin, then glanced into the box again and noticed the hand-woven cloth in which they'd been wrapped, on which they lay. It was soiled.

With the fine gold-brown dust of the Libyan Sahara.

The desert dust called sand.

FISHERMEN RAISED their mugs as the women surrounded Dru, guiding her up the wooden stairs to the rooms above the tavern. Dru had never felt so well-hidden from the public as in this veil and head-scarf. Only her family's presence could reveal her to the media, and they had covered their hair as well, with their wraps and hats. In the darkened stairwell, Keziah said, "Everyone should be here, but I can already guess who'll be late."

Joanna sucked in her cheeks at the slight to Tristan, and Dru hurried along the hall, to the room with the door opened and soft light escaping. Candlelight and lantern-light and familiar voices—Keri, Nudar, Daniel Mayhew.

Jean slipped by and looked in, then entered. Joanna kissed her daughter's eyes. "Let's go in, too."

Dru was the last to enter. As she walked inside, somebody played some notes on a *rababah*.

Her family was not attempting to replicate Nudar's traditions so much as express their own. For that was all it was, removed from the piety and all-encompassing power of desert culture, of so many cultures existing together. This was something her ancestor had brought to them in the person of a wife in whom he showed great pride.

Fine rugs, deep silky pillows in purples and reds, warmed the floor. The camel saddles from the house in 'Sconset, clustered comfortably against two walls. Faces all turned to her in the dim, flickering light.

Jean was hugging her husband, tall David Blade with baby Rika against his shoulder. And David's and Skye's son, Chris, his hair still light, taller now and still skinny, holding his little sister Cecily's hand. Daniel and Mary Mayhew, Mary unsmiling, the skin over her cheeks grown thin and drawn. Daniel's expression thoughtful, warm, gentle. Keziah, Joanna, the girls in Egyptian gowns and headdresses.

And the men in the corner, near the standing candelabra. Dru really didn't want to look. Or be looked at. So she focused on the blond figure in his suit, long hair neatly bound, holding a folded sheet of paper.

It's real. She swallowed, seeking the familiar and finding a Bedouin wearing a belt and a dagger. She knew the sheath, had seen it in a photograph, the single existing photograph of one Bedouin orphan in Tripoli during the war, an American soldier's hands on his shoulders. She remembered it more clearly, now, on another boy's belt. She would know the dagger, too.

When he laid it in her lap again.

Ben smiled, his face too beautiful for anything but a mix of peoples blended over time.

Familiar, after all.

Friendlier than anyone here.

Closer to her than anyone had ever been.

He met her, brought her to where Tristan stood, then shifted beside her, shielding the exposed part of her face, her eyes, from the others. Intimate already.

"Thank you. For your card." She smiled behind her veil, then realized he couldn't see. She wanted to take his hand, comfort him. Because of Mary. "Everything okay?"

"You're beautiful. I was going to ask if *you're* okay."

Because of their first wedding.

"Yes."

He clasped her hands and looked at Tristan.

She never noticed the others, where music or sound came from. Just the candlelight and Ben. And Tristan. She heard Tristan without looking.

"Family and friends, peace. And welcome to the wedding of Dru-Nudar and Ben Omar."

Ben felt the dagger against him. Remembered the giver. And remembered the pen. Dru's eyes shimmered, lagoons. He floated inside them. *I'm getting married.*

And in love.

Not with...

The dark home in Timbuktu was on the fourteenth street from the mosque. Dru's face held him, a perfect narrow oval. Her lips reached into him, pressed the walls of his heart. He wanted to be alone with her. *Make love...*

Silence. All around him. Ben jerked his eyes from Dru.

Tristan was waiting.

Dru's face warmed. The veil hid it, but it couldn't hide her eyes, and she mustn't look at Ben, mustn't see his eyes, simmering coals.

"Dru-Nudar—" Her brother's voice began. These words were like a blood oath, but not the same words she'd said to Omar, words she hadn't chosen at that time because, back then, she was strong with babies and pregnant women but not with men. "Dru-Nudar, do you take this man to be your lawfully and truly wedded husband, to have and to hold from this day forward, forsaking all others, till death do you part?"

"I do."

"Ben Omar, do you take this woman to be your lawfully and truly wedded wife..."

How we picked those words, Dru reflected. How carefully. Neither would ever offer the other to anyone else.

Ben said, "I do," and came to her, his arms covering her shoulders. So much taller than she and stronger than her bones and flesh, so that even here she could let tears fall against his shoulder.

Close by, Tristan said, "Intermission?"

"No."

They answered in the same breath, although her reply was a gasp.

Tristan told the others, "You may have noticed that this ceremony encompasses aspects of many cultures. The bride crying during the ceremony is characteristic of weddings in many parts of the world."

Dru giggled against the damp cloth, the warmth of Ben's body. While Ben dried her eyes with a handkerchief from his robes, she said, "We're ready, Tristan."

Her family laughed.

They spoke their vows. Holding Ben's hands, standing close to him while the others gathered around, Dru repeated the words Ben, the writer, had helped her tease out. Then listened to his words.

Tristan said, "If the bride and groom would please take advantage of the beautiful rug brought all the way from Nantucket Island by ferry and automobile."

He gestured to the rug.

Dru eased down upon it, close to Ben, and saw his dagger as he sat. Without thinking, she reached across and slipped the dagger from its sheath, startled that it gleamed so sharp and deadly. She laid it in her lap. Taking back her first, maybe her truest, marriage.

"My sister," Tristan said, "has just demanded Ben's protection and that he treat her with honor."

Ben spoke to her in Arabic, telling her that her honor was his and his, hers. He would kill any man who tried to soil it.

Dru saw his face and thought she knew his thoughts.

Omar was already dead.

Seated, they exchanged rings, hammered-silver bands bought in Gloucester, while Tristan explained that Bedouins do not traditionally exchange wedding rings.

A tambourine, a reed flute...

Dru picked up the dagger, and he took it from her, kissing her forehead. Her eyes locked on his. He sheathed the dagger without looking, his lips slightly parted, his eyes black. Like twenty years ago. His desire now was an ache inside her. She yearned to be alone with him, wherever they were going.

He helped her to her feet.

Her mother embraced her, kissing her through her veil. "Darling. I want you to be so happy."

Tristan engulfed her in a bear-hug. "I'm not going to kiss you in that get-up. My wives are forbidden to veil themselves."

"Lucky them." Smiling broadly, so that it might be a compliment, Keziah embraced Dru. "You know, among the Tuareg, the *men* veil themselves. I think that's an idea with merit."

Dru's knees buckled, and hard muscle caught her.

Keziah almost gasped. "I'm sorry."

Tristan said, "For what?" and took a mug of water from Daniel, Keziah's father. "Thanks." He walked away to greet the woman who owned the tavern. The food came up from below, swordfish on borrowed tables with dark cloths over them. They sat on pillows and a few chairs, spread out around the room, and Dru kept close to Ben.

He asked, "What does she have against him?"

"She didn't realize what she was saying. Anyhow, Tristan isn't self-conscious about his face. You know that as well as I do. And women have always loved him."

"Women who love men who scare them."

Dru glanced at his face against his checkered head-wrap.

His hand, on her shoulder, stroked around her head scarf, toying with her earrings, brushing her neck. "It's fun to dress the way you like," he said, "and it would not be fun to be forbidden to touch you like this in public, on pain of torture, mutilation or death. By the way, this was the only occasion when the women of my grandfather's tribe veiled themselves. To get married." While she slipped bites of swordfish and scallops beneath her veil, he hunted for a way to kiss her. His lips found her neck.

Dru had finished her plate when Keziah joined them, crouching beside her. "Dru, do you have enough energy left for dancing? You look like a tired pregnant woman."

And Keziah looked like a woman who'd just learned a difficult secret about her mother.

"I can dance." Dru touched Ben as she rose, still drawn toward him. Walking away.

"This way." To the bathroom shared with the room next door, which Ben had also reserved. The girls ran after them. "Wait for us!"

In the small, rough bathroom, a fisherman's bathroom smelling stale and damp as the sea, Keziah said, "What are you up for?"

"Just the *guedra. Now* I'm starting to figure out what pregnancy is like. I'm already exhausted."

As Keziah laughed, Keri said, "My dad did a good job, didn't he, Dru?"

"The best. You have a wonderful dad." Dru kissed her niece's head. Swordfishing was almost over. But Tristan would stay with the *Sarah Lynnda,* fishing offshore for lobster from Georges Bank.

"I gave him pictures, and he had some for me. I made him a picture of you and him when you were little."

Dru embraced her again. Keri's choice of subject for her art was odd. But sweet. Dru gave it no more thought. She was going to dance.

They removed her veil and headdress, and Keziah brushed sandalwood into her hair.

"First this." Keziah opened a woven bag behind her. "Thank you for permission to search your house for your dresses and *haiks.*"

Dru saw the indigo. *No. No.*

But why should she be frightened? She finally understood Ben's attachment to Tanelher. *He loves me.*

She let Keziah and the girls help her out of the other gown. They fastened the single piece of cloth with hollow pins and adorned it with a Tuareg cross. Her bangles rested cool on her ankles, her Bedouin jewelry elsewhere, the henna dressing her hands and feet—and back, where only Ben would see. Tonight.

"Now close your eyes."

Dru closed them. Glasses tinkled in the other room. She felt something placed on her head, slipping down to just above her ears, covering part of her forehead. And something gently striking her face and hair.

Keziah steered her. "Look."

Dru opened her eyes. She saw a beautiful Tuareg in an ornate headdress with cowrie shells and horsehair braids dangling from it, cowrie shells at the ends of those. Keziah began braiding Dru's hair to sections of horsehair. "It's so beautiful, Keziah! And you made it."

"I didn't know why I was making it at the time." A tight

New England secrecy to her voice. "But it was made for you."

It was the traditional headdress for the *guedra,* the Tuareg blessing dance, the trance dance. Probably Ben had never even seen Tanelher dance the *guedra.* Not all women did it. She caught Keziah's eyes, a flash of stress her friend swiftly hid.

"Keri, Nudar," Dru said. "Will you prepare everyone? For the chant?"

When they were gone, Dru embraced her friend. "Keziah, it must be so hard. I love you. Please, always talk to me."

"The way you do with me?" Humor stole any resentment from her voice. They both had secrets. "My mother isn't who I thought she was. But it really is a gift to have a brother. I hope… It would be nice if he wanted to be one. Be an uncle to Nudar."

Dru considered. "I think that will happen. You live just a couple of houses away. I can't wait for that, Keziah."

When Keziah finished weaving Dru's hair into the braids, she studied her. "You are so beautiful."

No one was beautiful beside Keziah.

Dru saw her skin in the mirror, the golden seeming pale. She closed her eyes. *These clothes swaddled Ben when he was a baby. Dear little baby, given away in a lightship basket.*

As she wrapped her arms about herself, Keziah said, "We'll chant the wedding chant when you come out, and then we'll start the *guedra* chant."

But Dru simply walked out.

TRISTAN SAT in a corner with the cauldron drum. Dru felt, rather than saw, him there. It was years since he'd drummed or played any instruments when they danced. Since before he'd married Dorea Andrade, a tomboy fisherman herself who'd said matter-of-factly, *I don't dance.* Dru had liked her, had envied her courage and independence.

The drum pulled her in. It became the heartbeat she and Tristan had heard together in Joanna's womb, and he was playing it now. This love trance would make her one with a new partner in the larger womb of life. It would celebrate the heartbeat her child heard, her own, that bond.

Thoughts slowed, she imagined birth, unafraid of labor. Her mother had given birth to her in a taxi cab on the way to the hospital, Tristan on a gurney going in. Joanna had refused to stay even long enough for a doctor to get a scalpel on Tristan's boyhood. She hadn't let anyone take them from her or from each other, had gone home promptly with Daniel Mayhew and Mary, who'd been pregnant with Keziah.

The chanting had begun. It ran through Dru's veins like thick syrup, tree sap. She saw candlelight blurs, the colorful costumes of the women around her. Ben's *kaffiyah*. Ben's eyes, pulsing the drum.

The drum.

The drum.

And she did not know when she began to dance.

HE LISTENED to the chant, both familiar and different from the three *guedras* he had witnessed in Africa, one in Algeria, one in Morocco, the last in Mali. The women who had danced were tribal in their movements. Earthy.

So was Dru. But Dru was wind. And sand.

He clapped and sang the words to the chant, pronouncing each word more clearly and truly than anyone in the room. His eyes locked on her, tracking her dance. Tanelher, married already, had said, *They say it can attract a lover from miles away.*

Ben had said, *Want to run away with me?*

You will get in trouble if you say that in front of my husband. The kind of trouble where he kills you.

Dru's ankles were slim, the bangles loose on her. The henna

on her palms seduced his eyes. Feeling his penis stiffening under his robes, he pulled up his knees. His gaze followed her, back and forth, watched her sway on her knees as he clapped, seeing a picture clearly in his mind. A girl's eyes above a Rashaida virgin's veil. Crying. *Tristan's going to die.*

Then I will be your brother.

It had not comforted her.

The dream, clear as a movie clip, vanished, replaced by others, many he didn't want. Ben hugged himself, not knowing he had stopped clapping.

He found eternity in her face, and something whispered to beware, this was a deeper love. He didn't believe it, because the most beautiful women of the world were of the desert. But her hard beats, her vital movements, continued to stir him. She danced from her ancestors, all of them, and he was aroused.

The trance continued in candlelight, the chanting and playing. Her fingers gracefully outstretched, she swayed into his mind, through him, and he curled in on himself, feeling it and trying to hide the hot vibration of his body. Then, opening, stretching out on the pillows.

Take me, Dru.

His brain dazed, he drifted to Morocco and saw her walking on the stone beside the balustrades with a long silk scarf in pinkish red tied over her hair. She turned to face the sea. He throbbed.

He ached through her gentle motions. This wasn't supposed to happen, nothing so strong.

There was clapping, and he saw her eyes, half-slits, coming out of her own trance, her private communication with the spirit. They rested on him, opened a little further.

He dragged himself up, to take her hands. The Blades were packing up their bags and their children. Dru said, "I should say good-night."

Slipping from him.

Keziah waylaid her—walked along with her. "I apologize for what I said to Tristan. I wasn't alluding to—"

His scars. "He knows that."

"I think I have mother issues."

About Keri.

Dru's lips brushed her friend's cheek. "Not to worry. But—" *He's a fisherman.* Then, stunned, anew, *My father's not dead.* "You never know when you'll see someone again."

Keziah's dark eyes grew too wide in her white face. Belatedly, Dru remembered Halloran, that lover of Keziah's from New Bedford, Nudar's father, the fiancé who'd died at sea. She and Tristan had that in common. The way they'd lost their lovers.

Jean and David joined them, a child asleep on each of David's shoulders and Chris beside Jean. "We'll see you when you're back in Nantucket."

"Soon," Dru replied. No formal honeymoon. She and Ben had agreed that other things came first. Finding her father. Her contacting Nantucket Hospital again. Sergio had told her, on the phone, that the administrator had called and said they weren't interested in having a CNM there.

Dru kissed Jean on the cheek while Ben said something about *really* disliking veils. And as the Blade family departed, saying good-night to the other guests, he murmured, "At the moment, I wouldn't mind losing the clothes, either."

CHAPTER NINE

My father reached Joanna and Turk Haverford by telephone and told them Tristan had run away. But it didn't look as though they could obtain visas for the Sudan because the civil war was stirring again. Dru, they said, must come home. Everyone knew Dru would run away, too, before she'd leave the country without her twin. My father, her guardian for the trip, stood in lines in Khartoum to renew her visa. But Skye left, to return to school, to face It, she said. "Tristan is my knight!" she told me. He had been a warrior for all of us. The women casts fortunes. They said Tristan would return as the lion cub who has grown a mane, and the land would be his own. My father told the twins' parents that Tristan would be back within a year. And, at the end of the month, he convinced Dru that we must move with the Rashaida.

—Ben, recollections of a fall

DRU FELL ASLEEP against two big purple-and-red pillows while talking to Joanna and Keziah and the girls. Mary and Daniel Mayhew had already left to return to their hotel, and Tristan told Ben, "We'll get all of this out of here tomorrow. I'd better see if your dogs have torn up my boat. Miss Mayhew is taking them while you're on your honeymoon?"

Keziah. "Yes. Thank you. For everything." Ben handed him an envelope.

Smiling, his brother-in-law took it. They leaned against the wall, watching the women and girls. Tristan said, "So, this obsession of Dru's." He didn't say what, didn't give Ben a chance to ask. "She's always been like that. Thinking she sees him." Fingering the envelope, he said, "I hope you're not the kind of journalist who digs up dirt on your family."

Ben was quiet. "There's a difference between dirt and news." He had asked David Blade about Sedna. The group focused on Northeastern Atlantic fisheries, and David had seen their ships often. The complaint was overfishing. That problem, David said, was ubiquitous and grave. He had never met Tom Adams. Ben turned to Tristan, whose boat consistently unloaded more than all but one or two other swordfish boats in Gloucester—and went out with more than 12,000 pounds in sea animals aboard as bait. "What do you mean, anyhow?"

Tristan's head fell back, the three scars on the nearest side of his face dark grooves, where strips had been dug from his fine skin, curving over his delicate bones. Without these marks, he would look like a movie star. With them… Ben had grown accustomed to them, as he had the raised bumps on the foreheads of the Shilluk or all the other tribal scars he had seen in his life. Sometimes he envied Tristan for the courage they represented.

But never for what had provoked that courage.

Tristan didn't answer.

The story was forming itself. In taverns and on fishing boats, Ben had shown the photo of Turk Haverford that Dru had brought to Gloucester. And he'd talked to David at length, never saying anything about Skye in the Sudan, slowly realizing no one ever had, including her. He wrote every night. Next stop was Nantucket, to read seventeen-year-old newspapers.

It gripped him, held him, this unfolding mystery.

He said good-night to Tristan, and the women moved from

Dru as he came near. Her indigo gown shimmered in the candlelight, and her skin glowed softly golden. One hand, adorned with henna, clutched indigo fabric. The *haik* had risen to show more than just her feet and ankles—all the ornate designs in rich dark brown. He murmured, ''Thank you,'' to Joanna and Keziah.

For the third time that evening, he met Mary's eyes. His smile faded.

Dru stirred, awakening as he lifted her. Nudar darted ahead to open the door, tossing back her blond hair.

''Thank you.''

Dru blinked. Met his eyes.

A fisherman dragged himself up the stairs to his room. ''Hey, man. Party.''

The tavern was secure. They had eluded the press completely. He unlocked the door of their room and carried her into the dark, then closed out the light behind them.

Her eyes had shut again. She didn't see the black tent, the tent he'd brought home five years before from a dangerous trip to the Sudan, had been unable to refuse for many reasons. He remembered how, waiting at the airport with this oversized article, he'd fought tears of frustration, exhaustion. He'd brought the dogs for her wedding to Omar; what was he supposed to do with this?

This.

It was small for a Bedouin tent, stood seven feet tall, with its wooden poles shipped from Egypt. He'd lined it with a rug and sheets and pillows, all smelling of sandalwood. On the sheet, she stirred again. Opening her eyes, a glitter in the dark. Closing them.

Ben turned away to light a small lantern. He set the protected flame on a table, locked the door, then moved into the tent and lay beside her, comfortable in the Bedouin *kaffiyah*, the same he'd often worn in the desert. He could smell her, faintly. And he could smell indigo, see it on his own clothes and his hands.

She was not Tanelher.

No, she was his life. From the time he was twelve. From when he'd seen the muzzle of a semi-automatic pistol against her head and begun sorting through scenarios to make sure she remained alive, *Inshallah*.

They'd been married twice with his grandfather's dagger as his promise.

He hadn't promised to protect her life.

But her honor.

He wanted her. She smelled of sandalwood, and it was impossible to lie beside her and not desire her intensely. Black hair, eyebrows, eyelashes, pupils, white skin and teeth, red lips and cheeks, round and long and fine and small in every way she should be. And his.

His nomad's soul recognized her; she was the black tent that meant comfort and pride for the man whose wife spun the wool and wove it and provided hospitality for the stranger, the guest. No matter which of him saw the tent, he was welcome.

This had waited in his heart.

Quietly, she came awake. She began freeing her hair from her headdress. Watching, Ben wanted to help, hurry to release her, as though some Bedouin part of him hated, *loathed,* her Tuareg costume. And the dance that had possessed him.

His penis was full, and when he'd set aside the headdress of dangling shells and braids, he guided her back beside him, rubbing his clothes indigo blue.

Her eyes half-closed. "I wanted...to dance more...for you."

"I want to make love with you." And please her, *Inshallah. Inshallah.*

Her eyes blinked open. Wider. Focusing. Dru had been half-asleep, but now she was present. This familiar face and lips and— She touched the checkered cloth, unbound it from him.

He nuzzled her. Removing the Tuareg cross.

Kissing.

Honor, he thought, holding her head. *I will protect your honor now.*

Kissing with their tongues.

Dru remembered tastes of this.

Reality was more, mingled with eternity.

They removed the volumes of cloth. She rolled away to set aside yards of indigo, and Ben saw her back in the candlelight, the henna painting, and grabbed her, kissed her, touched her, tasted her on his tongue. Unfastened her bra. *I want you... Wanted you so long.* Yes, he would kill anyone else who touched her this way. He drew on her nipple, licking her, his hand finding her lower belly and lower, stroking her. Almost uncontrollable. His mind losing the fight to do things as he knew they should be done.

Dru wanted the warmth of covers, and he stretched them over her, enshrouding them both. He wanted her to cry out loudly enough to wake the building. Or just the graveyards in him.

Her response to his touch was enough. She did toss and make the private sounds of love that were neither whimpers nor cries, neither moans nor screams, but all these things in a woman's breath, in her teeth against him, begging by biting so lightly, holding on.

"Ben." She said his name and wanted him to say hers the same way, wanted him to tell her he loved her *now,* now while he eased into her, something new, accompanied by his head against hers. She gasped, her heart pounding its message. *I love you.* She was... Spinning... Warm... "Don't..." What?

A cry through the tent. From her. Against him, so near,

holding so tight to his hips, his back, his lean chest and muscular shoulders looming over her. *More...*

His quaking embrace, the aftershocks of love. One after another, until he lay still, head tucked sweetly into hers, the two of them cast together in one mold. Dru recognized perfection and knew the rarity of this—when what was perfect for one was perfect for the other, too.

"I'm in love with you," he whispered. "I'm so in love with you."

Dru clutched him tight. Harder. "My love." *I'm his wife. I'm really his wife.* On her wedding night with Omar, this bliss had been missing.

Ben rearranged the covers but left the lantern burning.

When he returned to bed, he shifted toward her, fit her against his side. Men were physiologically incapable of being alert after sex, Dru knew. He would go to sleep now. Possibly doze and then want more.

She gazed at the wood beams in the tent roof.

"It's yours."

"What is?" She looked. "The tent?"

"Matar's mother wove it for you with the wool you spun. She said you spun all of it. That's why it's small. She'd remembered you saying that children had playhouses in America and explaining playhouses, and she thought your children might like to play in your tent."

Dru turned to face him. "How is she?"

He touched her hair. "I saw her five years ago. They'd moved to Kassala and were making tent cloth." He left out other things. Many.

"How kind. I hope there's some way I can reach her, thank her."

"Your heart will do it."

"You've had the tent all this time?"

The fact brought more than a twinge. "Yes."

Dru changed the subject. "Ben, why haven't we seen your reporter friend, Cole Fletcher?"

"Your husband is capable of great dishonor when it comes to protecting his wife."

"You lied to him."

"I promised him an exclusive on our wedding on Nantucket this weekend and arranged for the use of the church, which I have canceled. And then you went and veiled yourself in public. Dru, you're very beautiful. You're so beautiful—" his breath stopped "—and sensitive—I want to tell you something." Things for which there were no right words. Secrets for the tent. A tent secret. At the tent for his soul, her tent, there would be hospitality, courtesy and welcome.

Facing him, she touched his lips with hers. He tasted of love. The universe spun into place and settled. Ben was an extension of herself. This was the person she'd married as a child, who'd visited her in her dreams, whispering of things she couldn't remember.

"I'm..." He pressed his warm face to hers. "Always tell me. What to do better."

"It was perfect." Hugging.

"I've been living in Arab countries. With some of the same...memories as you. I've...been with western women. I—" No words, already dark words spoken. "Form me into yours. I just want to please you."

She began to understand and held him close, kissing his face, his head, tasting his loneliness and the place in his heart not for Tanelher but for her.

Ben heard her whispers, telling him what she was feeling. How hard she'd come. "I love you so much," she murmured, almost inaudible. "You're so sexy. I'd get excited just standing near you in the trawler. I used to look at..."

Briefly, for less than a second, he saw Tanelher, like a photograph. Her inky head scarf and voluminous *haik,* her robe of a single piece of cloth. It was years since he'd pictured her walking in the sand. Now he only saw her on the dirt floor and single rug, moving with her hands. Her baby dead.

He kissed Dru's body, touched her abdomen, could hardly believe there was a baby inside. He kissed her mouth, couldn't help it, was sucked into her scent, mingled with the sandalwood. Stirrings, already. She swam toward him, a woman wanting him so much.

So close. Making love to her.

When he was joined to her, Ben's eyes watered. He pressed his damp lashes and wet skin to her hair. Tears, which he must dry. Fogged by emotion, he felt her stroking his hair.

"Ben?"

He slipped away from her, enough to bring her to his chest and drag his arm across his eyes.

She sat up. Touching him.

He tried to smile.

"Everything all right?" she asked.

He saw Mary Hall on the bench at Rocky Nest. Just her picture. No words. Nothing to do with this emotion. "I'm fine. Get your hairbrush, and let me brush your hair."

Dru did as he asked. She rose naked in front of him, blazoned with mehndi that would fade over the next weeks.

Her brush was elegant, the handle ebony. Omar must have given it to her. Ben did not resent it. Omar had not rejected him. She dropped hair elastics beside him. "I want Bedouin plaits."

He smiled and brushed her hair. It fell past her shoulder blades. He kissed her spine and shoulder blades, tasting henna and lemon. Dividing her hair. Married women, of his father's—of Omar's tribe, of his ancestor's tribe—wore six plaits in back at the neck and a triple plait on each side. It was a Sinai custom but not unknown in Libya.

"Nantucket tomorrow?" he said.

"Yes. I need to press the hospital administrator again. I'll just mention, 'Okay, that's fine if you don't want me. I'd just as soon do home births with Keziah.' And Ben—in some ways I would." She told him about New Bedford, her sense, in the end, that despite her beliefs, she was helping doctors perform interventions with which she disagreed.

She sighed.

"There's something about Keziah's practice you don't like," he guessed.

"We have different styles. This is just between you and—"

"Dru?"

She looked at him.

Intensity of connection, of something very deep and primal, shot between their eyes. He felt it—that he, not Tristan, was her twin. That Dru was made for him and he for her, even to be together in the Sudan in a nightmare.

"Never tell me that again. Everything you say to me stays with me." He turned her away, holding her hair, finishing a plait. He had a small boy's memory of women braiding each other's hair, of his Bedouin mother's plaiting his, too—only his, because he was already circumcised. An eight-year-old Ben was a boy with Bedouin braids. There were pictures of him in his father's books. Pictures of all of them.

She said, "Do you still love Tanelher?"

"I never would have mentioned her name if you hadn't thrown up when you learned you were carrying my child." He continued braiding.

Was that true? she wondered.

His hands brushed the back of her neck, gathering more hair. She turned against the force of a held braid and kissed his mouth. His lids dropped, his dark eyes on her lips.

"I love this baby so much. I'm so glad it's yours, Ben."

He turned her around again.

She said, "You never answered my question."

''Want me to tell you all the kinds of love?''

''Yes.''

''I can't. The way wolves in a pack love and human mothers love their babies and dolphins love and men love philosophy and music and art and war. A man can love a people and their dignity in their struggles. He can love a sister. He can love a friend. He can love the only female with whom he has shared truly intimate conversation. He can love his god and his religion. He can love a woman so much that he believes he's in one of Scheherazade's stories, and he gets the girl. He can believe Allah made this woman for him, Allah ordained this from the time he was born, it was Allah's will that her mother once carried him in her arms—or even a lightship basket—to the home of the people who really loved him, when his own mother did not. He can love so that he thinks other people can see light rising from his skin. He can love so that he believes now he is the man he was meant to be. He can love so that all he thinks about is being inside her, because she makes him better than he was.''

Dru held herself.

His arms looped round her shoulders. His body surrounded her tightly. Hugging, enfolding her. ''I love you,'' he said, his lips on her jaw, ''like that. I've loved you since I was twelve. There's such a thing as being scared of feelings. I'm still scared. But at least I've found you.'' In Arabic, the only language with the right words, he told her about the tent. The black tent for his soul. The truth seared. Pain in his body, the ache of wanting. Like a fever, with sex steaming off him. Touching her hair, which he hadn't finished braiding. Breathing his pleas. Knowing his child was inside her and wanting to pray five times a day because of it.

She stretched out before him in love and trust. On her prone body, he traced the henna lines with his finger and his mouth, making love to her till she moaned. He wanted that sound. He tried things he thought might bring that sound from her. She like closeness, liked them to be as close as possible, the very closest. New sounds. Small beating hums and hymns and kitten song. A whimper. A yearn. A beg. The hollows beneath her arms and the dips on the sides of her breasts. He learned her, just the first letters of the alphabet, the first note of the song. When she came, his eyes watered as they had before. And he came inside her, saying, "I love you. I love you so much." Rubbing his face against her back. This must be like paying out fishing line and realizing you'd dropped an anchor instead and couldn't bring it up.

"Mm. I need to move, sweetheart," she whispered.

No one else in his memory had ever called him that.

They lay side by side, and Dru saw his eyes and kissed them, not wanting to ask again why they were damp.

Finally, he rose. "I want to read you something." She watched muscles in his legs, watched every part of him, until he disappeared around the side of the tent. "I want to read you the page you wanted to hear. Then you can have this, if you like, and know how I began to learn I wanted you."

She looked at the page as he sat beside her.

"I'll refresh your memory." He translated as he read about seeing the mehndi artists painting Dru with henna in Timbuktu. About his visit to Tanelher and bringing her gold. "'He had brought her necklaces and bracelets from the Sinai. She wouldn't accept them at first. He said, from instinct, that he might not see her again. And that her wearing the jewelry would make him happy.'"

"'She accepted the things. He drank the tea she had made. While they drank, she told him she had never felt for him what he felt for her. The Tuareg proverb about tea promised he would find the first glass bitter, like death; the second gentle, like life; the third sweet, like love. For him, the reverse occurred. His had never been a love returned, and when he said his thanks and goodbye, he knew he would not be back, that he must never worry about his Tuareg friend of so many years, his good friend with no legs, for she had urged him to go.

"'He walked—'" his voice trembled "'—back through the alleys, between the mud houses until he could see the mehndi artists and the woman he had been asked to protect. Her face was more a girl's than a woman's. It reminded him of another girl's, the girl he'd been forced to marry when he was a child and had, in odd ways, considered his wife. He moved close enough to see the patterns emerging on her feet and hands. He tried to understand the kind of man who would give her to another. He remembered when they were children and he had not protected her but was bound beside her, as helpless as she was. She'd grown up pretty, into another woman he could never have.'" He stopped, dropped the book and picked up her hairbrush. "Stay where you are. This side."

"You do have me."

"I know. I was supposed to protect your honor. My error was letting you marry Omar. That was my fall." The sound he made was sad or mocking. "In the Sudan, I was only as helpless as Tristan, who, by sheer will, tore a gun from a grown man's arm and killed him and two others." He saw the blue eyes of the gagged little girl, her unbrushed black hair. He said, "To be without a tribe is to have no past that matters. Honor is part of the present and the future. When it's gone, a wanderer can move on and no one will know of his dishonor."

Dru heard him speaking of himself.

He finished one section of the triple plait. She eyed his notebook. Saw again that his love for Tanelher had been escape. She smelled the passion she'd shared with Ben. It perfumed the tent. The curved sheath of his dagger lay on his clothes, a promise to protect her, some promise he'd felt when protection was all but impossible—except for Tristan. Proof to Ben of his own inadequacy.

She saw in full the weight he carried, how heavy the dagger.

She heard the stuttering machine gun and saw her brother's face as it was tonight and as it had been so long ago, and the flies in the tent and his fever. And the ghastliness she was not allowed to tend but for which Robert Hall had taken him to a blacksmith healer. Ben, just twelve, had explained, *Don't worry, Dru. The blacksmiths were there when Allah made fire. When flesh is cut, it happens with weapons they've forged, so they know how to heal cuts. They'll take care of him. But don't tell the Rashaida. Some of them go to the blacksmiths, too, but they don't want anyone to know.* Most clearly she remembered Tristan's catching his reflection in the oval upstairs mirror each morning before school. He'd always paused and looked, and peace came to his eyes. His scars were beautiful to her.

Ben wished he had killed, as Tristan had.

Or perhaps he didn't, and wished that he at least wished it. Dru had been in the tent with him. He'd resigned himself and all of them to death with a peaceful acceptance that was its own brand of courage or faith. "From what perspective do you condemn yourself?" she asked.

"As a Bedouin. That was the code of my childhood. I'd imagined doing what Tristan did. But I knew I'd be killed. This is called cowardice."

"Or wisdom."

"Tristan and I were equally sure of their intentions. There are university classes on the subject, Dru. Let's not debate it. I was a year older and a head shorter than Tristan. I believed my father had died." He was quiet, finishing her last triple plait, winding her hair around the base of each braid. He checked her head from various angles. Her hair was like that of a married Bedouin woman. He kissed her cheek, then arranged their bed while she slipped into the tiny adjoining bathroom.

When the light was out, Dru curled close to him, accepting his chest against her back, letting him surround her. This journalist who had hunted stories in every country in North Africa, who had worked in war zones as an American at the mercy of hostile governments and considered himself a coward because of something that had happened when he was twelve.

Cowardice had never even occurred to her, in childhood or later. *I imagined we would be rescued.* Because, despite the screams, she still hadn't believed in a world where people were not rescued.

But Ben had believed they would die.

So had Tristan. Because he hadn't hesitated to kill to save the lives of those he loved. Most certainly, to save her life.

She asked Ben, "If that happened again, would you do things differently?"

He covered her, with himself. "Yes." Into her hair. "*Inshallah.*"

CHAPTER TEN

Dru's parents obtained visas. They came and then left again. They'd planned to take her home with them, and she hid, quite effectively, in the back of a Rashaida vehicle beneath blankets. After a conversation with her father, she was allowed, again, to remain. She was learning the Rashaida dialect and dressed as a married woman now, though her parents didn't know the difference and no one told them. She had let someone cut her bangs and hair like the Rashaida, which angered me. I liked her black braids. It rained that year. Those months passed, and Ramadan came. That month, we never looked for Tristan or the vehicle at all. My father and Dru and I fasted with our hosts. And prayed. Each day, Dru and I hid together and discussed how Tristan would return. Inshallah.

—Ben, recollections of a fall

November 16
'Sconset

THEY SLEPT in his grandparents' four-poster bed, massive and narrow. Ben had brought Skye's portrait home and hung it in a spare room, what had been Omar's childhood room. He and Dru slept in his room, the master bedroom, hardly bigger than the others, but the most private. The dogs liked to wander between their room and the sitting room.

Sergio had made arrangements to return to Greece. Dru had taken what she wanted from the Orange Street house and left the rest to others.

The cottage in 'Sconset felt like hers from the first. Each morning, she took the dogs out and let them run on the beach, then returned home with them to stand by the railing facing the sea, thinking. If only she could see Georges Bank, could see her brother's boat. Often, Ben brought her oatmeal to follow her blender protein shake. He rubbed her back and peered curiously at her stomach, looking for changes. Femi frequently sat alert, watching, knowing things they didn't.

They were outside Thursday morning, Dru bundled in sweats and a heavy sweater, when the phone rang. He got it, grabbing a cordless just inside the door, no doubt hoping it was David Blade. David had planned to go out to Georges Bank for three or four days. Jean and the girls would stay in the harbor on the *Him*.

Ben wanted to go on the chance the Sedna vessel was there, in any case to watch David's work. He had already found the families of the sailors who'd died when the *Louise Andrena* was lost. Only one still lived on Nantucket. Bonnie Hales, now Bonnie Daumal. Ben had interviewed no one, only explored what had become of the women. Two were sisters and lived in Attleboro with their children. The teenage son of Turk Haverford's first mate had been arrested for drug possession; the boy's female cousin was pregnant at fifteen. The fifth wife had moved to Boulder, Colorado. She and her second husband owned a pagan bookstore.

Ben hadn't volunteered any of this to Dru. She'd read his computer screen over his shoulder until he'd turned to draw her into his lap.

That was last night.

She left the biting cold, the wet, and called Ehder and Femi to come inside.

Ben was still on the phone, laughing. "I loved those chess games. I didn't care if I lost. Which was good, because I never did anything *but* lose." The caller's answer made him laugh again. "I don't remember that. Okay, she just came in." He handed her the cordless. "Dr. Pierre Daumal."

She squinted. Daumal was the name of Bonnie Hales's new husband, but he wasn't practicing here. How did Ben know him? *And* the Nantucket Hospital administrator had simply said he didn't have time to sit down with her. They just weren't interested.

"Hello, this is Dru Hall."

"Mrs. Hall, this is Pierre Daumal. We haven't met." His French accent remained strong, although Keziah said Dr. Daumal had lived in the U.S. for twenty years, teaching in Boston. *No use to us,* she'd added with a sigh. He said, "Please forgive my forwardness in calling you at home, but my wife is an old acquaintance of your mother's. And I had the pleasure of knowing your husband when he was a boy. He and his father were twice my neighbors in Cambridge."

"Oh, how wonderful!"

"Ben would often come over to play chess and listen to me discuss my ideas of which primal stimuli trigger certain physiological reactions in labor and birth. Though he was more interested in learning about the Situationists. He read Dada writings, then wrote his own. He memorized more easily than anyone I've ever met. We were good friends." Dr. Daumal paused. "It was a continual treat to introduce him to American culture. We saw *Star Wars*—in nineteen seventy-seven, this was. And when they came back from Mali, we saw *Return of the Jedi* and *The Right Stuff* and—oh, it will come to me. And swimming. Every day. We all went."

"How wonderful for Ben to speak with you again."

"I'm the fortunate one. Every man goes through life lonely for another male who speaks his language. Now that we're both on Nantucket, I hope Ben and I will spend some evenings together. No doubt, after you've been married a little longer.'' A smile in his voice.

Dru said, ''How is Bonnie?'' *Dad, how could you? How could you? These women, these children.* Bonnie was still childless. ''I hope she's well.''

''She is lovely. She wants to be involved in this project, too, that I'm about to mention to you.''

Probably a birth paper or something. Academics.

''I understand that you inquired at the hospital about a nurse-midwifery program. I, too, hoped to see such a thing, but the facility is small, and they like their maternity program as it is. For the past two years, Bonnie and I have been working on an alternative, for which we've found substantial financial support in Nantucket. We plan to open a birth center in Monomoy. We'll offer waterbirth and would like to have a midwife. If you're interested, I would like you to visit our new facility, so you can see how you like it.''

''Yes.'' She grinned wildly. ''Please. Just tell me when.''

Off the phone, it took her only seconds to relay her excitement to Ben. ''And it may even be good for Keziah. If he's liberal—''

Ben burst out laughing.

She ignored him. ''Maybe he'll provide back-up for Keziah. Some women will always want to give birth in their homes. Nothing we do will change that. This is *perfect*.''

Ben smiled, clearly somewhere else, with Professor Daumal of Cambridge. '''There is no such thing as chance,''' he quoted. '''A door may happen to fall shut, but this is not by chance. It is a conscious experience of the door, the door, the door, the door.' Kurt Schwitters. Dada genius.''

Dru studied him. ''It's so odd to hear you talking about something besides North Africa or the Sahara.''

He gave her a tolerant look. ''You'll get over that.''

She hugged his neck, and he kissed her, growing more interested in taking off her sweater.

They were caressing each other as honeymooners in their home when the phone rang again.

Ben took the call, still holding her, not letting her get away. At first. "So—right now. One hour? I'll be there."

Georges Bank. He must be going with David.

Disconnecting, he turned to Dru. "He found a boat. Packing won't take a minute. Let's— Let's make love," he said, breath shaky.

The dogs followed them to the bedroom.

On the hard mattress, beneath his flannel sheets and the thick blue comforter, she held the heat, resented anything that could take him away, even for a few days. His lips on her jaw, his words barely reached Dru's ears. Describing things he hadn't done before. "Did you like Omar to...?"

She couldn't speak above a whisper. "This one's new for me, too."

He held her face as he kissed her. Hugged her.

Then, more.

So intimate.

Things she'd never been sure she wanted till they happened with him. She was safe here. Love was safe with the one whose ears had heard what hers had, who knew what it was to be bound and helpless and afraid. She exposed herself to him, let him guide her. This only man she could really love made love to her with his mouth, discovering how with her, exciting her, until she cried out. And pleaded in a whisper, "Ben, let me..."

Hugging. "Was that okay?"

"Yes. Yes."

She loved him with the same intimacy, then fell upon him. One with him, flushed and excited as he was, learning the strength of his arms, Dru understood how much she hated for men to go to sea. In her waves of pleasure, in his deep tremors, she heard his voice crying out, saying her name.

All her cautions—to remind David that Jean was pregnant, that Ben should remember she was, too—sounded trite. The weather was fine. But he would be gone, gone so long. "What if Sedna's not even there?"

"They will be. They sent out a press release. I received a fax this morning."

"You didn't tell me."

"Hardly had a chance."

She studied his eyes. "Are you telling me everything?"

He shook his head.

Her heart pounded. "Are you going aboard to interview them?"

"Don't get your hopes up. David arranged it, using his clout, the Blade Institute." He shrugged. "Probably won't happen."

She tried to dismiss it, too. The possibility that he'd be face-to-face with her father. "You have the photos." *Right?*

"Yes." The most recent protected in plastic for the trip.

His skin heated her. She pressed close to him, preparing for what already seemed like more than a few days. And felt new pain for her mother, who had lost her lover to the ocean.

Who might find him now—and wish she never had.

"Promise me one thing," Dru said. "Promise you won't fall in love with the sea."

"I promise. I can't swim."

Dru grabbed him, half strangling him. "Liar."

November 18
Georges Bank

THERE WAS NO DANGER of his falling in love with the sea. The fifty-foot boat tossed in the waves, and it was almost twenty-four hours before Ben's stomach began to settle.

In the small cabin, Skye's son, Chris, told him, "I hardly ever throw up anymore. But I used to."

None of this was surprising. Chris had spent more time on ships than land. Every morning, the twelve-year-old practiced the art of tae kwon do with his parents. On rocking boats.

"That's what I'm telling myself," Ben answered, sipping some ginger ale. "I used to throw up." He studied Chris's face. Consensus said he looked like David, with David's sandy hair. Ben saw Skye in his high cheekbones and his mouth and chin.

Chris, with his own glass of orange juice, read his stare. "You knew my mother."

"A little." Biting his lips against what Skye had suffered, recalling instead her courage afterward. "I liked her. Very much."

The boat rocked, the engine deafening near them, with David at the helm.

"Hardly anyone says that. Like they mean it. She was an alcoholic and took drugs," Chris reported matter-of-factly.

Ben had no answer. None he could give Skye's young son. Or anyone. Skye's secret. *All right, we're making a pact. No one here tells. It's mine. This is mine.*

David didn't even know. Or he would have asked about it. Surely.

"My dad said you might talk to me about her."

"Sure." Ben's single word was slow. Holding down the past but choosing from it, he said, "She was beautiful inside and out. She was funny. In the desert—she was just fifteen then—she didn't like the heat. But a lot of the things she said were very funny. Kind of sarcastic. She saw our car and said, 'I beg your pardon?' Then I opened her door, and she told me I was a sheikh and she would come back and marry me someday. Good thing she didn't."

"Or I wouldn't be here. So, like—" Chris shifted tone "—I've heard Anne, my mom's cousin, talking. What's this bad thing that happened? No one really says what it is."

Ben sensed a third presence and remembered that this family of martial artists could move like air.

He'd never heard the cabin door.

David found a seat beside the scarred chart table. Chris had inherited his brown eyes. But David's could remind a man that this fifth-degree black belt knew how to kill.

And how to get what he wanted. "Chris, I need you topside." A jerk of his head, unspoken commands because the two knew each other and boats so well.

Chris rose fast and left the cabin, slamming the door behind him.

David said, "What was he talking about?"

The question.

Skye, you should have been able to tell your husband. I'll never know why you couldn't.

And yet…he did.

"Skye, Dru and Tristan came to the Sudan, the summer she was fifteen. On the way to the Bedouin camp where my father was working, we were kidnapped. Skye was brutally raped. We escaped—" The need to keep secrets. It held him. As his eyes held fast to David's. "She was very brave. Self-possessed."

David was white, his body vibrating elusively, almost invisibly. But not quite.

"We went to the Rashaida—the Bedouin—camp. There was no hospital nearby. She spent the rest of her vacation at the camp and then went home."

"Tell me everything, Ben. I need to know everything."

No, you don't. He told him more.

"What about Tristan?"

"What about him?" Ben found himself back in bed with Dru, in the safe place, where no one could do to him whatever had been done to Tristan.

"They didn't touch him?"

"It doesn't seem relevant. I didn't see anything."

"The three of you—four of you—kept this secret."

"Skye asked us to. We pledged, because she'd been hurt so badly. My father knew, of course."

"He didn't take her to the hospital."

"She wouldn't go. It was hours away. She was terrified of being on the road again and being in the hands of doctors."

David said, "She killed herself. She jumped off the bow."

Ben jerked back against the seat cushion. Closed his eyes and hid his own face.

"Chris told Dru. I'm surprised she didn't tell you."

"Then you don't know Dru."

David lifted his eyebrows, admitting the mistake.

The cabin door. "Dad! There's a lobster boat out here bringing up her traps. And the Sedna boat is following her, demanding she release the lobsters. They've shot red goop at her—the pie filling stuff—with a cannon."

This was a typical Sedna stunt, annoying to fishermen, non-violent and good for publicity. Hoping the interview was at hand, Ben grabbed his pack, keeping camera and tape recorder zipped in his shell. While David corrected his heading, Ben watched a boat flying the orca-and-Earth flag of Sedna head at an angle to the starboard side of...the *Sarah Lynnda.* They'd spotted the lobster boat—she was a lobster boat now— early that morning, her blue steel hull and white topsides easy to spot with the line of red at the water and the red trim above. Ben had talked to Tristan on the radio, made plans to accompany him back to Gloucester to photograph them banding the lobsters.

He'd never expected this.

Discouraged by the distance necessary for safety, Ben joined David and Chris in the cockpit. "Any contact with Sedna on the radio?"

David nodded. "The interview was refused." Sharp eyes. "Very odd. Tom Adams was supposedly eager and agreeable yesterday."

"Was he on the radio?"

"No. I'm not sure he's on the ship."

"What was said?" Ben knew. He knew what had been withheld before and spoken this time. "Did you give him my credentials?"

"Briefly. Your name should have been enough. You're in some outdoor magazines. Other important magazines."

Ben studied the radio, listened to contact between the *Sarah Lynnda* and the *Dawn Treader*. "But you told him my name earlier."

David looked over his shoulder at Ben. Faced the bow. The sea ahead. "No."

He was left to take photographs. From the rail of the boat David had rented. Ben focused the telephoto lens on his Canon, a cheap SLR he'd twice had to buy back from soldiers and border agents after handing them blank rolls instead of the exposed film they wanted.

He adjusted to the boat's tossing, moved down the rail for a better angle. David was coming in at the stern of the *Sarah Lynnda*. What was Sedna doing? Tristan was legal. If Sedna damaged the craft, the law would show them no leniency. And from what he'd learned, Sedna never broke the law.

He shot some photos of the *Dawn Treader* as she changed course. She was twice the size of Tristan's boat and iron-clad. She used a loudspeaker as she eased into position, starboard and past the lobster boat. Turning. "SARAH LYNNDA, RELEASE YOUR CATCH... WILL RAM YOUR VESSEL."

What?

Turk Haverford couldn't be on board. Who would do this to his own son?

But who would...

He spoke to the tape recorder around his neck. "What kind of man would do this work? Choosing so fiercely what he believes and clinging to it. Scuttling fishing vessels. Risking freedom for the cod population. For the sea.

"What kind of man?" He swallowed. "Only a man who loves the sea best." He almost whispered his thoughts, almost left them unspoken. "Better than anything—or anyone."

A few feet away, Chris silently observed him.

Ben kept talking. "I have never been so close, at sea, to a ship the size of the *Dawn Treader*." The shutter. Winding. "The lobster boat looks like a toy. The *Dawn Treader* has ceased firing pie filling and promised..."

For the first time, he really wondered if he'd taken the wrong tack entirely to assume that Tom Adams was Turk Haverford.

Am I wrong?

He studied the vessels through the glasses, his perspective now from the stern of the *Sarah Lynnda*. The *Dawn Treader* repeated its warning. Minutes passed before she moved, deliberate and huge and powerful. Ben lifted his camera. Through its lens he watched the nose of the Sedna boat. The whir of his camera met these other sounds. An endless low dull ringing and crumpling. He saw steel bend, give, form a new and awkward shape. A wound. The *Dawn Treader* veered away, and David headed sharply east, the rented boat leaping far to the starboard side of the *Sarah Lynnda* and well clear of the *Dawn Treader*.

Sarah Lynnda limped.

Ben went to the cockpit, where David was on the radio. A

voice crackled back. "*Tiger Lily,* this is *Sarah Lynnda.* The Coast Guard has been notified. Over."

Tristan.

"He's legal, isn't he?" Ben asked.

"I wondered that, too. Sedna goes after the law-breakers no government has the inclination to catch. Bo Holloway, who owns that boat—the *Sarah Lynnda*—runs a pretty clean operation. On the other hand, there's a lot of cheating in lobster fishing. For instance, dipping females in chlorine bleach to get the eggs off so they look legal. Obviously, depletes the population."

"*Tiger Lily,* they just repeated their command to release my catch. We're taking on water in a starboard bulkhead. Bound for Gloucester. Over."

Beyond the filmy cockpit windows, the fishing vessel lugged awkwardly through the water. David eyed Ben thoughtfully, then suddenly hunted for Chris and grabbed him in a hug. Told him he loved him. Kept his arm around his shoulders as he said, "*Sarah Lynnda,* we can come around your starboard side and inspect the damage. Over."

"*Tiger Lily,* thank you. Over."

David gave the helm to Chris, beside him at every minute with advice. The big Sedna ship was slowing. Ben watched them begin to pick up lobster traps Tristan's crew had baited again. He photographed a college-age boy with a beard. A bald man with glasses. Down on a platform, releasing lobsters. He counted all the crew he could see, which was eight.

David explained the quirks of *Tiger Lily's* engines to his son. They had left the *Dawn Treader* behind them and slowed to cross well aft of the *Sarah Lynnda.*

Ben found a new seat in the cockpit. He'd photograph the damage when they reached the *Sarah Lynnda.* It bothered him in a way stories rarely did. He said, "I read somewhere that lobsters can live one hundred and forty-five years and can travel a hundred miles.''

Pressing his back to the console, David shook his head. ''Dad?''

A thorough look at their position. ''You're fine.''

David's relationship with Chris made Ben want a son the way carrying Cecily or Rika or kidding with Nudar and Keri made him want daughters.

Keri.

That was her father in that ship. Ben knew how Dorea Andrade had died. Falling, a hook stabbing her chest so that she hung on it like a Sioux sun dancer, but beneath the sea, while the seventy-five foot boat dragged her. Keri was three. The family said that Dorea, always a fisherman, had missed the sea, that she'd become thin and almost withered until she returned to fishing. A fish out of water, Keziah had said once ruefully.

Ben had promised to return to Gloucester on the *Sarah Lynnda.* He reminded David of this, and David nodded, but didn't take up the radio. Instead he said, ''Qualities of lobsters aside, they're overfished. There isn't a fishery in these waters that isn't. What's more, the depletion of one species alters the marine ecosystem. A lot of the fish taken are bycatch, tossed back, dead or dying. Longliners—'' he nodded to the *Sarah Lynnda* ''—will make you sick.''

Ben had heard and read the same. The UN's Food and Agriculture Organization estimated that marine catches could rise by nine million metric tonnes with changes in worldwide fishing practice, especially if juvenile fish were allowed to live longer before being caught.

David said, ''On some level, I don't have much problem with Sedna. And I've given personal money and equipment to Sea Shepherd, Paul Watson's group.''

The first and greatest of the ecopirates. Glad to be photographed and arrested. Glad for the chance to tell people the seas were in peril.

Unlike Tom Adams.

David, Ben suspected, would have plenty of trouble with a man who wouldn't face the families of his dead crew members.

Almost everyone would.

"Chris, just hold your course."

David and Ben left the cockpit to inspect the damage to the other boat. But first Ben glanced toward the southeast. The Sedna ship was hardly moving, still collecting lobster traps and waiting for the Coast Guard, waiting to be arrested. Was Dru's father on that ship?

He snapped photos of the damage to the hull, seeing, he thought, where the sea was leaking in.

Tristan came to the rail. Yelled, "What do you see?"

David yelled back while Ben photographed them, recording the conversation, as well.

Afterward, David spoke to Jerry, Tristan's first mate, on the radio. He said they'd put a tender down for Ben. David and Chris were headed for Nantucket. They'd let Dru know, before they reached the harbor, that Ben had gone to Gloucester.

The fishing boat lay ahead and to port less than fifty yards, and one of Tristan's crew lowered a tender into the tossing waves. Wearing his pack, Ben embraced David and Chris. "Have a safe trip home." He kissed them both, which was a habit of the desert. *"Inshallah."*

As Chris hurried back to the helm, David said, "Thank you for your loyalty. To Skye."

"I loved her. We all did."

The tender's motor whined close, running over Ben's words.

David spoke his own tongue, the language of his martial

art, and the phrase he chose was the silence of a low, straigh
bow.

Monomoy, Nantucket Island
November 20

SHE DROVE BEN'S CAR to the Daumals' birth clinic. She'
asked the estate manager to sell her cars that had come wit
Omar's estate, a Mercedes convertible and a Humvee she'
never really driven. Yesterday, she'd seen the car she wante
and she'd already asked the owner about it, but she wante
Ben to see it. Keziah, who had been with her, along with th
girls, had said, *What makes you think he knows anything abou
cars?*

Dru had blushed. Finally said, *He's my husband. I can't bu
a car without him, all right?*

She wanted him *home.*

The clinic was gray clapboard, set close to the road ye
made to look weathered and authentic, unlike a new building
The largest cottage, with dormers above, was surrounded b
four smaller one-story cottages, each with its own shell pat
to the main building. Good-sized trees had been transplante
for shade, and a sign whose logo showed a mother's arm
cradling a baby, umbilical cord fading into the water. Th
name was painted in clear script, pink-and-black on white.

Nantucket Maternity Services
Holistic Prenatal Care • Natural Childbirth • Waterbirth
Pierre Daumal, M.D., OB/GYN

Yesterday, at the beach, Keziah had said, *I saw that buildin
going up. I thought it was going to be another real estat
office, or something else we don't need.* As she spoke, she'
glanced away, her thick straight hair billowing in the wind.

Keziah had become pregnant with Nudar at nineteen, during her second year at the American College of Naturopathic Medicine in Salem, one of the country's oldest accredited colleges of naturopathy. She'd planned to get her undergraduate degree before becoming a nurse-midwife. Some weekend, Keziah must have gone to Gloucester—or Halloran had come to Salem. He'd drowned in March. Keziah had finished out the year, but it was her last.

She and her baby had lived for a time with a midwife in Salem, then come home to Nantucket. Doctors there didn't like her two years studying naturopathy, might have liked her better if she hadn't gone to school at all.

With her graduate degree, Dru had chosen New Bedford, enjoying the work—and keeping her distance from Keziah's. Years had passed before she'd really believed her friend was well-trained.

Somewhere in her own education, Dru decided, something had happened to her. It was a kind of arrogance related to medical facilities, to having them close at hand.

Well, she would see if Dr. Daumal liked her.

As she walked up the shell path to the front door, a car pulled up behind her. Glancing back, she expected to see Bonnie Hales. Bonnie Daumal. Instead, a dark-haired woman in her late thirties emerged from a silver minivan. She was pregnant, maybe sixteen weeks or so, Dru thought, and held the door for her.

"Oh, thank you, dear." Gave her a second glance. "Oh, hi, there," she added, as though they'd seen each other around.

Dru followed her in.

A white-haired man with a long nose strode in from the back room. "Oh, good, hello, Dru. Dru, this is Michelle. Michelle, Dru is our midwife, and she'll be doing your initial workup. Michelle just moved from Hyannis, and she wants a clinic birth."

So this was what he meant by getting together to talk, seeing how she liked the clinic.

She liked it.

She liked him, with his kind eyes and gentle manner.

She said, "Michelle, let me put down my things and wash up, and I'll be right with you."

As she walked back into the clinic, past the vacant reception counter, she heard Michelle say, "Isn't that Dru Haverford Hall?"

"Oh, yes, yes. She's a good midwife. I know her professors at Georgetown."

Dru grinned. A door to the left led into a brand-new kitchen made as comfortable as any home. She found the coat closet with a Harriette Hartigan poster on it reading, *Birth is as safe as life gets.*

As she washed at the sink, trying to contain the pleasure in her veins and also aching for Keziah, hoping she could help her friend, Dr. Daumal strode past. *"E.T.!"* he said. *"And Tootsie."*

Dru laughed, imagining him at the theater with Robert Hall and a young Ben. "Good ones," she agreed.

Night.

HE HAD PHOTOGRAPHED the men running the bilge pumps, lobster cars filled with banded lobsters, their claws bound with rubber bands to keep them from killing and eating each other. He'd sniffed the air for the smell of bleach. No trace. Relieved, he'd searched out new angles from which he could capture the exterior damage. Before the collision, Tristan had spoken to someone young and male on the radio.

Ben had asked, *No one else?*

His brother-in-law had sighed. "Give it up, Ben. I knew him. All right?"

The boat was sticky with pie filling. Two days of it clinging to shoes, catching clothes, while he interviewed each crew member and Tristan, who was surprisingly patient—and unable to see Sedna's point of view.

I'm within the law. They're assholes.

Ben liked night on the deck. The cold, the misty air, only the running lights and the nonstop sounds of the engines and the pumps. The hollow shifting of water in the lobster cars. A fascination with these captives. Urges he would never act upon—to free them. In the galley, he could write in his notebook at night by the light of his head lamp and disturb no one. Transcribe sentences from his hand-held tape recorder. Time to do that now. Pulling his wool hat down further, bringing his jacket up over his chin, he strode along the port rail, glancing ahead toward the portholes of the crew's and captain's quarters. In the last, just behind and beneath the wheelhouse, the faintest light glowed. Ben slowed in silence, close to the cabin. Tristan's cabin.

Impulsively he climbed the metal steps and knocked at the cabin door.

A moment. Shuffling.

Involuntarily, Ben saw again the bodies in the sand. Smelled the rich reek of death—and vomit. Tristan had thrown up while trying to bury the men.

He hadn't known, back then, that everyone falls. But he'd seen in the way of a child that Tristan must have shattered into many pieces, yet held together like a shattered window or vase. A delicate object like that might never fall apart, but if it did, the fragments were many and small, impossible to mend. Better never to fall.

Tristan answered the door in a long undershirt and canvas pants bleached almost white but stained, now, from fishing. He lifted his eyebrows. "Can I help you?"

Ben felt a click of new awareness, of something different. He made it go away. "Hope I'm not bothering you."

Tristan shook his head, pulled the door wider, eyeing Ben carefully, as though hoping to learn something from him.

Ben went in. Drawings, some Keri's, some not, covered the walls. One illustrated *seppuku*. On the desk, bolted to the floor, lay more artwork. And a photograph. He'd last seen that picture on the day Dru had shared their first meal at his house. Sorting through pictures of the Sudan. This photo showed Tristan and Skye, leaning against the Land Cruiser. Tristan with no scars.

Skye with no scars.

The cabin door swung shut.

"There is no such thing as chance. A door may happen to fall shut, but this is not by chance...."

The picture had been in his house. The art pieces were signed by Keri. Keri had been in his house, to get things for the wedding.

Tristan leaned beside the door. Stepping aside to show him the picture, Ben wondered whether to protect Keri. "Where did this come from?"

Tristan wandered over. Stared down. "Don't know." He searched Ben's face again.

Ben decided to talk about it. Helped himself to Tristan's berth. "I told David."

Silence.

Tristan said, "I need to be honest with someone."

Ben's neck hair rose.

"I don't know who I am. And I don't know who you are."

"Are you speaking metaphorically?"

"That, too."

There is no such thing as chance....

This was the fall. And it wasn't chance, that he was here when Tristan had fallen. Tristan needed someone to sweep up the bits, to collect each one and return it to him, for the mosaic of his life.

He needed someone who would recognize the pieces.

Ben stood. ''You know who you are?''

Tristan pressed his lips together. They parted, and his mouth was wider and more sensuous than Dru's; he had a certain kind of Scandinavian face, lean and delicate. With scars.

He hadn't shaved.

He hadn't bathed.

''No.''

''I'm Ben. I know who you are. And I'll help you. I'll stick with you. I'll answer all your questions. I think you had a shock today.'' Tristan was fine after the collision. But reactions could be delayed. ''Things should get better.''

Tristan nodded like a trusting child.

The cabin smelled of mold, dirty socks, bait.

He felt the past. Every time he'd told anyone what had happened in the tent, he'd lied, because he knew. Tristan had told him one part. He'd heard the rest through the desert air. He and Dru both had. They knew. And no one had told Robert Hall, as though it didn't matter.

Ben took the captain's chair. The photo lay there. The photo...

Tristan sat down on the sole, leaning back against the door.

''Do you know that you're captain of this ship?''

Restless eyes.

Jerry, the first mate, would have to bring the ship in.

Ben planned. Alert Jerry. Get Tristan from Gloucester to Nantucket. He hoped there was a good psychiatrist. If not, he'd find one elsewhere.

As Tristan reached for a travel guide, something he must have been reading earlier, Ben remembered about things that fell and shattered. You could get all the pieces back. With patience, you could put them together again.

But the cracks of the broken would always show.

CHAPTER ELEVEN

He returned on the day of his birth, on foot, in Arab-style clothes protecting him from sunburn, eyes older than my father's. He spoke English as though it was a foreign tongue and he had to hunt for the words. My father, always the anthropologist, asked to know his language and where he had won his scars. Tristan answered briefly in a tongue no one present recognized. The Rashaida men showed their feelings in scowls and distress and talk of vengeance, all as baffled as we were by the thought of anyone subjecting himself to traditional scarification as Tristan said he'd done. Dru was the first to come from the women's tent, running. She stopped five feet from her brother, then hurled herself at him. She was the one who touched the unhealed wounds, framed in red, and said he had a fever. There were other wounds, too, wounds she would never see. He had chosen circumcision, as well.

—Ben, recollections of a fall

Nantucket Maternity Services
November 21

DR. DAUMAL HURRIED through plans he hadn't had time for the day before. He'd needed to rush her and her client out so that window blinds could be installed. *Come tomorrow at eight!* he'd called. *We'll talk.*

They talked in the clinic kitchen over tea and oatmeal with blueberries. Bonnie Daumal was there. Dru remembered her husband's memorial service, the services for all the men who'd died. Bonnie was lovely toward her, feeling only that Dru had lost her father, that they'd shared a tragedy. How would that change were the truth about her father to be revealed?

It will be. It must be.

"Your client Jean," said Pierre. "Jean may come here for prenatals. I will see her as her physician and, of course, you may attend her at home. I do ask that you please run your practice from this facility. You will have your office here and of course do home births as you wish. I like home birth. But we must be friendly with the hospital. The politics will be very sticky while we're building our clientele. There is already animosity, but I have my privileges." He drew in a breath, like a triumphant warrior.

"Have you met Keziah Mayhew?" Dru asked. It was relevant, not just trying to put in a good word for her friend.

"Nantucket Midwifery. I haven't met her. Have you?"

"Oh, they're good friends. I told you." Bonnie rolled her eyes.

Dru blushed. This was bad. She mustn't do anything to risk her position.

She sensed the baby in her womb, had the thought that if she wasn't generous, wasn't loyal to her friend, she had nothing.

Pierre lifted his furry white eyebrows. "And is she a good midwife?"

"She handles half a dozen to a dozen births a year. Mothers return to her. She and I attended a home birth recently, and—" She'd walked into a mire. She would walk out of it, as she could at a birth. "I had trouble with some trauma I experienced as a child visiting the Sudan and memories of a recent birth, far from a hospital, with a potential disaster on my hands.''

"Tell me."

She did.

He nodded at each new revelation, then told her and demonstrated, using a seat cushion, another means for easing a baby's respiratory distress. "But your way is very good. It would be my first choice."

She told him about Keziah at Oceania's birth.

The phone rang, and Bonnie left the room to answer it.

"I must meet her," he said. "She will want physician backup, and I will say no, so that someday I might say yes."

Dru understood. He wanted to be solid in the community and develop a solid relationship with the hospital and let his practice grow until there would be outcry if he left. Part of the idea behind the little cottages close to the house, she'd learned, was for mothers from off-island to come and stay for several days as their time grew near.

"Dru? Phone."

November 22, 6:00 p.m.

JEAN HAD BEEN her last client of the day, David with her.

Afterward, they lingered, and David described for Dru the Coast Guard's arrival, their arrest and immediate release of the captain of the *Dawn Treader,* everything he'd seen. Newspapers reported the arrest and release of Tom Adams. The owner of the *Sarah Lynnda* did not wish to press charges. He had sabotage insurance.

David spoke to the twin of Tristan, not to the daughter of Turk Haverford. No one but she and Ben knew of her suspicions. And she was lost between the chance that the man who'd used his family's initials on his vessels might need their love and the fact that he'd acted and continued to act with gross dishonor. Now she was certain it was him. What Ben had described as Tristan's "memory loss and mental health problems" was proof enough. She'd said so on the phone, said Tristan would never break down if his boat had been rammed by anyone else. Ben had said that Tristan had never seen Tom Adams or heard his voice. The photograph must have triggered his amnesia.

Dru. He'd said what neither of them had ever spoken aloud. *Your brother was raped.*

The heavy sensations had swallowed her.

Truth.

She murmured some thanks to David for telling her the story and showed them out to the shell walk, where their rental car waited. Chris and Keziah's daughter, Nudar, were watching the babies.

Keri was with Joanna, home on Orange Street, waiting.

Pierre emerged from the back of the clinic. "Dr. Silko will be here soon."

The psychiatrist, Alex Silko. People said he was good. "This is so kind of you."

"Not at all. There's a group meeting at his office tonight, and he thought fewer faces might be better for Tristan."

Dru smiled. "Dr. Silko would never do this if not for you."

A car turned in outside. Then another.

Voices, her brother's only a murmur, with one-word answers.

Pierre opened the door and let in the blond, mustached psychiatrist, Tristan, and Ben.

Neither Tristan nor Ben had shaved, and Ben didn't leave his spot by the door to try to embrace her.

She stepped toward Tristan and his look held her back.

He did not know her.

She said, "My brother, I'm Dru." She found herself speaking too slowly, as though he was stupid.

He nodded once—a jerking motion. "Hi." The clean-cut, sandy-haired physician watched everything. Waiting for Tristan's eyes.

"I'm Dr. Silko. And you are…"

Following Pierre's lead, Dru murmured, "Excuse me," and started away, pausing only to glance back at Ben.

"Tristan Haverford," her twin said.

He seems so normal.

"My friend Pierre has a very comfortable sitting room in here. Shall we sit down? We can talk a bit. Then how would you feel about going to the hospital?"

Tristan rubbed his head, seemed distracted by the feel of his own long hair. "I don't want to be locked up."

"Nantucket has no lock-up facility. This is a voluntary unit. You can leave anytime you want. The most important thing right now is to make absolutely sure you didn't hit your head during the collision with the other boat. Do you remember that?"

"No. But Ben told me."

"I'd like to look at your eyes with this flashlight. Good. Just look right here."

Cooperative compliance.

As the psychiatrist put away his light, Ben touched Tristan's arm. "I haven't spoken with my wife yet. Dru, where will you be?"

"First door on the left."

"That's where I'll meet you."

Dr. Silko was nodding. Dru stared at her brother, his tall straight strength shed like a skin. Because he'd misplaced his identity and history and was so lost.

I want him back, Inshallah. Bring him back.

But she'd trained and worked in hospitals, doing a nursing rotation on a psych floor. And she'd sat bound in a goat's hair tent in the desert and heard... *Oh, Tristan.* The twin she'd seen a week earlier was gone forever; he would never be back.

He was down, and when he stood up again—*when, Inshallah*—he would be a different man.

December 6

BEN PICKED UP the phone before dawn. "Hall residence." They were expecting to hear from Jean, that she'd started labor.

Dru was already sitting, prepared to go, listening.

"Hello, Joanna."

"Is Dru there?" her mother asked. "He really wants you, but I'm sure Dr. Silko doesn't want to encourage that dependence. I know Alex socially. His wife has explained to me how he works."

"What's happening? Tristan's...home again?" He kept himself from saying "out."

The bed creaked. Dog tags jingled.

"He doesn't like it in the hospital. But this is so bad for Keri, having him here."

A click. Dru had left the bedroom and picked up another line.

"Mom, I'm sure it's not," she put in. "He's not violent, is he? If he is, he has to go the mainland."

"He's restless."

"Didn't they give him something?" asked Ben.

"He's an adult, so I know nothing. Everything's a secret. I can't watch him full-time. He resents it. I'm his mother, and he may not know me but he recognizes mothering."

Dru couldn't watch her brother full-time, either, although she would have if she didn't have a job. And Ben was working on a book proposal about lobsters and two features tangential to the Sedna story.

"I'd like to talk to him." Ben was mild. While Tristan's condition exhausted everyone else around him. Including Dru. "Is he there?"

Dru put down the phone, respecting this relationship of trust between her husband and her brother. Ben, who swore he couldn't protect anyone, had protected Tristan and his crew. He was her brother's protector.

She returned to the bedroom as Ben said, "Right."

She began to strip off one of his T-shirts and dress to take the dogs out.

On the phone, Tristan said, "You know, I've lost my memory. I don't recognize anything. From before. But I can function just fine."

"What do you call that?" Ben asked.

"Amnesia." He laughed.

"The diagnosis?"

"Dissociation? Dissociative disorder? Fugue? He's not in a hurry to say." Tristan's breath whistled through the phone. "Anyhow, I still haven't found a job. Still here on Brick-Sidewalk Street with Joanna and Keri. Keri's great."

Ben heard the door shut. Had Dru gone out? The two of them had discussed this. She'd said he was free to offer. Neither of them liked it. "You can move in here."

Voices in the front room. "...So I'm like, 'We have had *no* prenatals. I don't know your history.'"

Keziah.

"Finally, I agree to look at her, and she's had a cesarean. A stranger—in labor—trying a VBAC—in my house. I just drove her to the hospital where, great blessings, I was seen by no one who hates me and would make up lies about it!"

"Does she live on-island?" Water going into the teakettle.

In the receiver, Tristan said, "I don't know. I'll think of something. Maybe a boat."

No one had told Tristan that he owned a scalloper, was

paying it off, that he could sleep on that boat. Ben didn't tell him, either.

He said, "Why don't you stay here? I'll come get you."

"No, I'll come over. Just to hang out. I have a car. I've been driving."

Ben squeezed his eyes shut. "Okay."

He hung up and the phone rang again. He grabbed it. "Ben."

"Ben, it's Jean. Is Dru there?"

THE BIRTHING TUBS at Pierre's clinic were partially sunken, a design of his own to facilitate the process for both mother and attendant. In a bathing suit, Dru sat in the tub with Jean and David while Pierre assisted, usually from out of the water. Chris had come, too; the girls were with a sitter Jean had met at the park.

Jean moaned, mouth loose, David caressing her, calling her love names in one of those Asian languages he knew. This was Dru's third birth with the Blades, but she'd never seen them so loving, David so intense.

Once Jean whispered, "I think it's today."

"The baby might be born today," he agreed, "or tomorrow."

"Oh, God." She laughed and moaned at once, with a contraction.

This is the most beautiful birth. Dru listened to the baby's heart, checked Jean's dilation.

Eight centimeters. And so relaxed. The water and Pierre's waterlike nature nearby—and Jean and David were divers. Their baby would slide into gentle warmth, an environment most like that she'd just left. Hormones and a low metabolic rate would help to inhibit breathing before the baby reached the surface, where warmed towels awaited her.

The room was deep in steam, and Dru hardly remembered

the midwife who'd been afraid in the head of a ship at sea, miles from land. She was an older midwife now. She had gone down and stood up a different woman.

As the time came for Jean to push, Pierre knelt near the edge of the tub, instruments and supplies ready. Dru supported Jean's perineum.

Jean sang to her baby as a whale mother, a seal mother, a dolphin mother, the language of the sea. She sang her baby out, and this luminescent water spirit lifted her small arms and face, and Dru felt that it wasn't her hands but the newborn's own power that brought her to the surface.

Jean caught her in her arms and held her, face out of the water. Gazing. Enraptured. "David, we have to ask Chris."

Dru remembered what had happened on December sixth, St. Nicholas Day, nine years ago.

"I know what he'll say." David smiled. "He'll ask when he can hold her."

Pierre slipped out of the room to summon their son, so that after his stepmother he was the first to hold baby Skye.

2:09 p.m.

HER SPIRITS SOARED on the way home from the clinic. The Blades would stay in one of the cottages overnight, and she would return in the morning to check little Skye.

Tristan's Mustang sat at the edge of the snow-sprinkled gravel outside her house. *Our house.* How fast she'd grown to love this cottage of Ben's.

I want our birth like that.

It wouldn't be, she knew. It would be theirs. Unique.

She hurried inside and smelled split-pea soup and heard voices from the ocean side of the house. The dogs met Dru, and she hugged them, then made her way to the sitting room.

Keziah was still there—or had returned. She lounged by the windows with Tristan and Keri and Nudar.

"He's writing," said Keziah.

"Oh." Dru burst out, "I'm so high!"

"How did she do?" Keziah's black eyes sparkled. Dru hadn't expected it. Her friend had bowed out of Jean's birth shortly after Dru began working at the clinic, clearly to avoid putting Dru in an uncomfortable position.

Tristan sprawled against a camel saddle, his eyes missing thirty-one years. For Keziah, Dru briefly detailed the birth, the whale song, the name.

"That's generous," murmured Keziah. "Bless her."

Nobody named their children from generosity. It was love. And she could never tell Keziah why. "They love her. I did."

Tristan hadn't so much as blinked at the name or the story. He said, "I like dolphins. And whales."

This was Keziah's cue to say, *Then why don't you stop killing them?* Which he was doing, she said, by depleting fisheries. But Keziah removed a key—her house key—from her MY-OTHER-CAR-IS-A-BROOM key-ring and took it to Tristan. She knelt on the rug by him. "Do you have a place to put this?" Like a mother. "Don't park too close to the roses, because my neighbor is an intolerant human being."

"A hundred a month," he said. "Me and Keri."

"Hooray!" Nudar and Keri exchanged high fives.

Dru walked away, surprised that it seemed like a good thing.

In the bedroom, she shut the door, and Ben closed his laptop, almost as though hiding something.

Scarcely noticing, she told him about the birth and the baby's name. They hugged on the bed, and both wanted to make love. She got up to lock the door, gesturing toward the sitting room. "I can't believe it."

"Believe it."

"They hate each other."

''Negative. Dru, come here.''

It wasn't for lovemaking but for love. In Ben's way. With the truth.

He opened his computer and hit a key. An alarm said he'd been disconnected. But the picture remained, with a story about Sedna. *Sedna founder Tom Adams is a former fisherman fighting for the species he used to harvest.*

Ben looked at her, waiting.

She felt more shock than she'd anticipated. Because she'd believed it for so long.

No.

She believed it now.

''That's my father.''

THE OTHERS HAD cleared out of the house when Dru and Ben left for her mother's. They took the dogs, letting them into her yard on Orange Street.

Joanna came onto the back patio. ''Where's Tristan?''

Dru gave her an abbreviated version.

Ben had his laptop in a backpack. He frowned. He'd told Dru they should do this; she'd agreed quickly. But Joanna was going to find it difficult....

''Keri is not moving out of this house!''

''He's her father,'' Dru answered mildly.

''He's mentally ill. He needs a parent looking after him.''

''Keziah will look after everyone,'' Dru promised. Maybe Tristan needed to be in a situation with Keri in which Keri would have to turn to him instead of Joanna. Which meant he would have to look after her. Keziah wouldn't let him get away with ignoring his daughter or handing the responsibility of raising her to someone else.

That responsibility was always more than he could handle.

''Keziah does not eat meat. She's thin as a rail, and so is Nudar.''

"Joanna." Ben shifted his pack. "We came here to talk about something else. Unpleasant."

She noticed his pack. Her eyes narrowed.

"Let's go inside," she said.

BEN OPENED THE LAPTOP on the dining room table, hit the key to awaken it, and set it in front of Joanna. She squinted at it.

Read.

Sighed.

Sat back in her chair.

Ben pointed out the names of the boats in the text.

Dru held her mother's silky hair, hair like Tristan's. "I'm sorry, Mom. I wasn't going to tell you. Dr. Silko didn't seem to think the collision triggered Tristan's memory loss. But with what happened…I'm just not sure what to do."

"Well, I am." She shut the computer. "I'm angry. I'm ashamed. And I'm sick for Bonnie and Lorraine and Jette and Helena and…" She named every family member who had been left without husband or father when her own husband's boat went down. "This makes me feel dirty by association."

Like I felt when I read Omar's will…

"But I have no reason to feel dirty. And Dru, this is not your mission. It's mine. I will speak to those families and show them this—if Ben will tell me how. Because they're the people who have a right to know, to track him down and have their questions answered. But I won't expose him in any other way, Dru. Because of my child. I would kill for my child. That man has hurt Tristan already. I don't want Tristan ever to see his face or hear his voice again." She turned to Ben. "But you said they never spoke on the radio. This is because of the Sudan, isn't it?"

"Oh, I would guess."

Joanna regarded him for a long moment. "You're a fine man, Ben."

He looked up at Dru, who stroked his hair. He murmured, "Thanks." Then added, "For her."

CHAPTER TWELVE

I don't remember their departure, except the feeling in
my chest. These were my American cousins, part of a
family it seemed I was never to know. Of the three I'd
met, Skye was the most accessible, Tristan the least. He
had attained states unknown to most others. His eyes
never let anyone forget it. He was arrogant as a warrior.
His sister adored him, trailed after him in a way that
shocked the Rashaida even as they praised her devotion
to her kin. Most days, I would have given anything to
be him. The traditions of the peoples with whom I'd
lived sometimes disturbed me. I did not yet long for a
man's relationship with a woman. But Dru's adoration
I would have liked.

—Ben, recollections of a fall

JOANNA DID NOT GO to see the families of the men who'd died
on her husband's boat. She met the *Dawn Treader* in New
Bedford and spoke to her husband. When she returned, Dru
rushed to the Orange Street House, alone. She carried her
mother's bag upstairs for her. "What did he say? What happened?"

Joanna turned slowly, not to look at Dru but at the mirror.
Her own long braid. As though she considered cutting it. She
faced her daughter again. "Honey, he's just not the man I
married. You need to think of him well, so call him a vision-
ary. His vision is safety for the creatures of the sea, and he

loves hermit crabs and krill more than any human on earth. Except, I like to think, you and your brother. Because symbols of you are all around him. But keep him as a memory, Dru. He's best that way.''

Two months later, in February, Tom Adams exposed his history to the press, resigned from Sedna and stepped out of the light.

Days afterward, watching a movie at Keziah's, Tristan grew white and confused, asked how he had gotten there. Strode out without jacket or hat. Ran, then walked, heading from 'Sconset to Nantucket. He was picked up in Surfside, violent and psychotic. In the hospital, he began breaking everything he could lay his hands on and was sedated and transported to Boston.

Ben and Dru went with Keziah to visit the locked ward, all of them claiming rights as family. Keziah called herself his ''domestic partner.''

Tristan didn't want to see anyone. He trembled.

He had nearly hanged himself by tying together rubber gloves left in his room. He had also attempted to bash his own head in.

As they left the unit, Keziah said, ''Dru, your mom's watching the kids. I'm going to stay up here.''

Dru started to say they'd all spend the night.

''Sure. We'll take over with the kids if Joanna's had enough,'' Ben answered. ''Stay as long as you need to.''

Riding back to Hyannis in their rental, Dru said, ''She's not his *lover*.''

Ben touched her abdomen.

She said, ''I'm not going to tell Mom.''

''That's an unfinished sentence.''

''That he tried to kill himself. You know, Keziah has no clue. She knows nothing about the Sudan. She doesn't know what happened to him.''

"Then they have something to talk about. And I know what really bugs you."

"What?"

"That Tristan might love someone more than he loves you."

Dru slid her eyes sideways.

Then felt her stomach leap, felt her child move for the first time.

Their child.

She grabbed his hand.

July 4

THIS WAS NOT the right day. It was not the right day, because Pierre and Bonnie had gone to Boston for a wedding and because Keziah wasn't here. She and her household, these days a fairly quiet household, had gone camping in the Appalachians.

There was one midwife on Nantucket Island, and it was Dru.

I'm not in labor. These are just unusually strong, inexplicably rhythmic cramps.

It was ten, and Ben had gone to town to photograph egg tosses and three-legged races in the park.

She didn't even know Nantucket's obstetricians, besides Pierre. She'd met one of them at a party she and Ben had attended to help hospital/birth-center rapport. She remembered thinking that at least he wouldn't be catching her baby.

Dru paced, stepping out onto the oceanside deck in the sunshine, followed by Femi. Femi's tail thumped the deck. She scooted her seat.

"It's true," Dru told her. "You're right."

She called her mother and got the machine. No message.

What other woman would she want with her?

A year ago, she could have answered the question easily. But she'd hardly seen Keziah's mother since the wedding.

Ben loathes her.

She could not have Mary here without asking Ben. *I should go to the park. Look for him.* But which park?

Another contraction.

Really nothing. *No. That was something. And I'm a prima, which means it feels worse than it is.*

I don't want to monitor my own labor. I want to have my baby.

She couldn't just *sit.* She decided to walk on the beach, remembered the tourists, and rejected the idea. She walked on the road, instead, without the dogs. Alone, laboring. A car came up behind her, and she moved aside. It did not pass.

He said, "Are you in labor?"

She ran, awkwardly heavy, around the front of the car to get in.

Ben hugged her. "Something told me to go home."

"Ben, Keziah's not here, and Pierre's in Boston. I don't want to do this alone, and I don't want to go to the hospital. I thought of calling your mother—she's been to births, at least—but I thought I could just labor at home and go to the hospital at the last minute."

"In a taxi?"

She started to laugh. "There. That's a contraction." Moving her belly, lips loose. Control slipping to the place where she must exist and ride, surrender to labor. "Ah. You know, women complain, and…this is nothing but…I can see it's going to be uncomfortable. At least the head's engaged. Baby's in a good position."

He watched her stop, gone to another realm.

When she returned, he said, "Your every wish is my command. If you want Mary Hall, you may have her."

"I'll call her." Between contractions.

Ben was grateful for that wish.

The woman coming for the birth of this child was not his mother, and he was not her son.

MARY AND JOANNA arrived together in the same car and came through the door talking, never knocking. Ben heard them from the bedroom, where he was kissing Dru, touching her breasts, feeling her restlessness between contractions. She was relaxed, for a woman who seemed to disappear into some silent thrall every minute or two.

Earlier, she'd had him baking their sheets in the oven to sterilize them, performing half a dozen other tasks to prepare for the birth.

Her water had broken, splattering Femi.

Things had become intense right then.

Now she had some rhythm, a meditation. She breathed.

Mary said, "Well, we timed it at ten minutes."

To the hospital, she must mean.

"The traffic, though!"

They looked in the bedroom, neither reacting at all to a man being a lover to his laboring wife.

Dru blinked. "Hi, Mom. Hi, Mary."

"Hi, darling."

"Dru."

They came near, cooed over her during the next contraction, went to wash their hands.

"Ben, check me."

He knew this was a look, don't touch.

He touched anyhow. Their baby's head. "You can touch her-his—head, Dru. Give me your hand."

"Do you have the sheets? The head—"

"I remember everything."

"Not even, *'Inshallah'?*"

"Always that."

The sound she made then reminded him of lovemaking and of something else forgotten.

He was giving her more pillows when the women returned.

Joanna held a soft cloth, one of those he'd set out beside the sink. She'd moistened it with the tea mixture Dru had prepared. Ben reached for it. The women sat on either side of Dru. She watched only Ben, hardly with him. Concentrating, instead. Pushing. Pushing. The sudden sting of tissue as her perineum loosened again. She breathed gently, waiting.

"We're fine."

Her lover. She pushed, and his hands brought the baby up, managing the head.

Is the baby all right?

"Boy." Ben's eyes were soft.

Her hands were familiar with slippery bodies. She sat up more, women's arms holding her, and carefully turned him, wrapping him in a blanket thrust into her hands. Such a tiny face. All Ben. The mouth moving so many ways. "He's beautiful." *I love you so much.*

Ben crawled over Dru's leg and up the bed to see his son. Joanna gave him the place beside Dru.

The baby's dark eyes blinked open. Ben couldn't breathe. Just bite his lip.

"Ben, you looked at me just like that," Mary said. "I love you very much, son."

He nodded, his head against Dru's. He really didn't need to hear anything else.

*   *   *   *   *

*Watch for Tristan's story—and Keziah's—
in Margot Early's next Superromance,*
THE STORY FATHER,
coming in 2001.

HARLEQUIN®
SUPERROMANCE®

*Pregnant and alone—
these stories follow women
from the heartache of
betrayal to finding true love
and starting a family.*

THE FOURTH CHILD by **C.J. Carmichael**.
When Claire's marriage is in trouble, she tries to
save it—although she's not sure she can forgive her
husband's betrayal.
On sale May 2000.

AND BABY MAKES SIX by **Linda Markowiak**.
Jenny suddenly finds herself jobless and pregnant by
a man who doesn't want their child.
On sale June 2000.

MOM'S THE WORD by **Roz Denny Fox**.
After her feckless husband steals her inheritance and
leaves town with another woman, Hayley discovers she's
pregnant.
On sale July 2000.

Available wherever Harlequin books are sold.

HARLEQUIN®
Makes any time special ™

If you enjoyed what you just read,
then we've got an offer you can't resist!

Take 2 bestselling love stories FREE!

Plus get a FREE surprise gift!

HARLEQUIN®
Makes any time special™

HARLEQUIN® AMERICAN ROMANCE®

WANTS TO SEND YOU HOME FOR THE HOLIDAYS!

AmericanAirlines®

LOOK FOR CONTEST DETAILS COMING NEXT MONTH IN ALL HARLEQUIN AMERICAN ROMANCE® SERIES BOOKS!

OR ONLINE AT
www.eHarlequin.com/hormefortheholidays

For complete rules and entry form send a
self-addressed stamped envelope (residents of
Washington or Vermont may omit return postage)
to "Harlequin Home for the Holidays Contest
9119 Rules" (in the U.S.) P.O. Box 9069, Buffalo,
NY 14269-9069, (in Canada) P.O. Box 637,
Fort Erie, ON, Canada L2A 5X3.

HARHFTH1